THE Choice

Nora Roberts & J. D. Robb

Remember When

J. D. Robb

THE
Choice

NORA ROBERTS

ST. MARTIN'S PRESS
NEW YORK

First published in the United States by St. Martin's Press, an imprint of St. Martin's Publishing Group

THE CHOICE. Copyright © 2022 by Nora Roberts. All rights reserved. Printed in the United States of America. For information, address St. Martin's Publishing Group, 120 Broadway, New York, NY 10271.

www.stmartins.com

Interior photographs: clouds © Max play/Shutterstock.com; mountains © Harry Beugelink/Shutterstock.com; river © Atstock Productions/Shutterstock.com; dragon © afrinedesign/Shutterstock.com

Endpapers: texture © Luria/Shutterstock.com; pattern © ATeam/ Shutterstock.com; mound © beast01/Shutterstock.com; Dolmen © Gareth McCormack/Alamy; mountains © daniillphotos/Shutterstock.com; sky © brickrena/Shutterstock.com; dragons © Valentyna Chukhleybova/Shutterstock.com

The Library of Congress Cataloging-in-Publication Data is available upon request.

ISBN 978-1-250-27272-0 (hardcover)
ISBN 978-1-250-27273-7 (ebook)

Our books may be purchased in bulk for promotional, educational, or business use. Please contact your local bookseller or the Macmillan Corporate and Premium Sales Department at 1-800-221-7945, extension 5442, or by email at MacmillanSpecialMarkets@macmillan.com.

First Edition: 2022

10 9 8 7 6 5 4 3 2 1

For Griffin,
our magickal child

PART I
LOSS

Give sorrow words; the grief that does not speak
Whispers the o'er-fraught heart and bids it break.

–William Shakespeare

Earth felt the wound, and Nature from her seat
Sighing through all her works gave signs of woe,
That all was lost.

–John Milton

PROLOGUE

Throughout the span of time, the worlds of man often believe themselves singular. Those who believe and accept they aren't alone in the vastness tend to consider themselves superior to those who share the vastness.

They are wrong, of course, as the worlds of man are neither singular nor superior. They simply are.

In the worlds upon worlds that spin, some proclaim for peace even as they beat the drums of war. That they beat the drums with an insatiable greed for power over others, for land, for resources and riches in the name of their favored deity rarely strikes as wrong, or even ironic.

It simply is.

In some worlds, war is the deity, and the worship of it bloody and fierce.

There are worlds where great cities rise from golden sands, others where palaces glitter under the depths of deep blue seas. And those that struggle to life from hardly more than a spark in the dark.

Whether the denizens of a world climb the high mountains or swim the oceans, whether they live in great cities or huddle over a fire in a forest, whether they beat the drums or rock the cradle, all share one common goal.

To be.

In one such world, in the long ago, Man and Fey and gods existed. In this world grew cities and palaces, lakes and forests. Mountains rose high; oceans ran deep. For a time out of time, magicks shined under sun and under moon.

Wars came as wars will. In some, greed prospered. And in some, the thirst for power could never be slaked, even with the blood of the conquered hot in its throat. One dark god, crazed with power, drank deep of man and Fey and more, and was cast out of the world.

But this was not an ending.

As the wheel of time turned, as it must, snakes of suspicion and fear slithered into the harmony of man and gods and Fey. For some, progress at all and any cost replaced the bond between magicks and man, and the worship of the more took over the reverence once given to the gods.

And so there came a time of choice, to step away from the magicks or to preserve them, to abandon the old gods or respect them. Making this choice, the Fey broke away from the worlds of man and the suspicions and fears that burned them at stakes, hunted them in forests, condemned them to the axe.

So Talamh, a world from a world, was born.

Those wise enough, with vision enough, created portals for passage between worlds, as by law of Talamh, all and any had the choice to stay or go. There, in a land of green hills, high mountains, deep forests and seas, magicks thrived, and under the leader—chosen and choosing—peace held.

But this was not an ending.

The dark god plotted in his dark world and gathered his army of the demons and the damned. With time, with blood, he harnessed enough power to pass through the portal and into Talamh. There he courted a young witch, one chosen and choosing as taoiseach, and blinded her with love and lies. She gave him a son, and in secret, while the mother lay in enchanted sleep, he drank power from the babe, night after night.

But a mother's love holds great magick, so she woke from this forced sleep. And awakening, led an army against the god to cast him back and seal the portal. When it was done, she deemed herself unworthy to lead as taoiseach, so cast the sword back into Lough na Fírinne and gave the staff to the one who lifted the sword from the water.

So once again, peace held, and in the peace of the green hills and deep forests of Talamh, her son grew. One day, with pride and sorrow, she watched him lift the sword from the lake and take his place as taoiseach.

Under him, peace held; justice was served with wisdom and compassion. The crops grew and magicks thrived.

Fate deemed he would meet and love a woman, a child of man. Through his choice and hers, he brought her through the portal to his world, and there, out of love and joy, they made a child, a daughter.

The magicks in her beamed bright, and for three years she knew only love.

But the dark god's thirst was not slaked, and his rage only grew. Once again, he amassed his powers through blood sacrifices and dark magicks, aided by a witch who turned from the bright to the dark.

He stole the child, imprisoned her in a glass cage beneath the waters near the portal. While her father, her grandmother, while all the warriors of Talamh rode or flew on wing or dragon to save her, she who had only known love knew fear.

And that fear in one so bright bloomed into a rage as wild as the god's. So her power bloomed with it and struck out at the god who was her own blood, her own kin.

She broke her cage even as the Fey attacked the god and his forces. Once again, the god was cast out and left beneath the ruins of his black castle.

Her mother, human in her fear and with a fear that turned to bias and a bias that tainted love, demanded to take the child to the world of man, to have the child's memory of magicks and Talamh and all who dwelled there erased.

Out of love for the child, and for the mother, the father granted this and took them through the portal, lived with them in the world of man, returning to Talamh for love, for duty as often as he could.

But though the love for the child never dimmed for the father, the love between the child of man and the child of Fey couldn't survive, and his efforts to live in both worlds carved pieces from his heart.

Yet again the god threatened Talamh, and the worlds beyond it. And once again the Fey, led by the taoiseach, defended. The Fey drove him back, but with his dark magicks, with his black sword, the god killed the son he'd made.

So another time for mourning, and another time of choosing.

A young boy, mourning the taoiseach as he had mourned his own father, lifted the sword from the lake, took up the staff.

While the boy grew into a man, one who sat in the Chair of Justice in the Capital or helped his brother and sister with their farm in the valley, while he flew over Talamh on his dragon and trained for the battle all knew would come, the daughter lived in the world of man.

There, with her mother's fear and resentment, she was taught to step back and never forward, to look down rather than up, to fold her hands instead of reach. She lived a quiet life that brought little joy, and there knew nothing of magicks. Her bright came from a friend who was a brother in all but blood and in a man who stood as a mother of her heart.

She dreamed, sometimes of more and different, but too often her dreams came blurred and dark. And in her heart lived a sorrow for the father she believed had left her.

One day a door opened for her. She made a choice, this woman who'd been taught so rigidly not to risk, not to step forward, not to reach. She traveled across the ocean to Ireland in hopes of finding her father and finding herself. In her travels she found a love for the place, for the green and the mists and the hills.

In a cottage by a bay, she explored those dreams of more, and reached out for those even as she reached in to find herself. One day, she came upon a tree deep in the forest that seemed to grow from a stand of rock. She climbed onto the long, thick branches.

And stepped out of the world she knew and into the world of her birth.

Her magicks stirred awake, as did her memories, aided by the grandmother who loved and had longed for her, by the faerie who'd been her friend in childhood, and by the boy—now a man—who had lifted the sword from the lake.

She learned of her father's death, and mourned him. Of her grandmother's sacrifice, and loved her. She discovered her powers and the joy in them. And though she feared, she learned of her place in Talamh, the threat of the dark god who was her blood, so she trained to fight with magicks, with sword, with fist.

As weeks turned to months, she, like her father, lived in two worlds. In the cottage she pursued her dreams; in Talamh, she honed her powers and trained for battle.

She allowed herself to love the one duty bound to Talamh, found the courage she wore as a symbol on her wrist. She embraced the wonders of the Fey, the winged faeries, the blurring speed of elves, the transformation of Weres, and more.

When evil came to Talamh, threatening it and all, she wielded fist and sword and magicks against it. She killed what came to destroy the light, faced down the darkest of magicks with that light.

So she became what she had been born to become.

But this was not an ending.

CHAPTER ONE

After what came to be known as the Battle of the Dark Portal, Breen stayed in the Capital for three weeks. The first days were as painful as any she'd known as she helped treat the wounded, helped bring in the dead from blood- and ash-soaked battlegrounds.

She held Morena as her oldest friend wept and wept and wept over the loss of her brother. She did her best to comfort Phelin's parents, his pregnant wife, his brother and his brother's family, his grandparents even as her own grief cut like a blade.

She'd only just remembered him, only just seen him again after so many years, and now he was lost, killed defending Talamh against the forces unleashed by her grandfather.

She stood with the family at the Leaving, clutching Morena's left hand while Harken held her right.

Her friend's grief rolled through her like a tidal wave as Phelin's ashes, and so many others, flew back over the sea to the urns held by loved ones.

She held Morena close before her friend and Harken flew back to the valley. And knowing their sorrow, watched Finola and Seamus, hands linked, spread their wings before following.

With Keegan busy with council meetings and patrols, she visited the grieving until she was so full of their sorrow, she wondered she didn't drown in tears.

After the first week, she pushed Marco to go back to Fey Cottage. Under his trim goatee, his jaw set. "I'm staying with my girl."

Since she'd expected that response, she'd prepared for it. While they stood on the bridge below the castle, watching her Irish water spaniel, Bollocks, swim and splash in the water, she hooked an arm with Marco's—her closest friend, she thought, one who had always, would always stand by her. And who'd proven it by leaping into another world with her.

"Your girl's fine."

"Not nearly. You're worn out, Breen, taking on so much."

"Everyone's taking on, Marco. You—"

"I helped, sure." He looked across to a field where people trained with sword and fist and bow. And remembered the blood and the bodies strewn over it.

He'd never forget.

"I helped," he repeated, "but you take on more than anybody, and you take it on here." He tapped his heart.

"Odran did this, all this, to get to me. Not my fault," she said before he could speak. "Not mine, not my father's, my mother's, Nan's. It's all his. But that doesn't change the fact so many are dead because Odran wants me, what I am, what I have. So if I can lessen a little of the pain even for a little while by taking it in, that's what I need to do."

He unhooked their arms and used both of his to draw her in. "And that's why I'm staying."

"That's why I'm asking you to go back." Lifting a hand, she stroked his cheek, looked into his warm, worried brown eyes. "I want to go back myself, but I feel I need to stay awhile longer. But that means I'm not there for Morena, for Finola and Seamus. They're family to me, Marco, and I'm not there for them."

"You were, and they know you're here now for Phelin's mom and dad, for his wife, his brother."

"That's a big part of why I need to stay. Go, be there for Morena and the rest for me, Marco. For the valley. We lost too many. Go back with Brian."

"First, Brian's leaving tomorrow at freaking dawn, and he's heading west on his dragon. No way in hell, girl, I'm flying on a damn dragon again in this lifetime."

He made her smile. "I could make you a calming potion."

"Hey, there's an idea!" His big brown eyes rolled. "I fly on a dragon but get high first. How about no?"

"How about you ride on a horse? Keegan's sending Brian and some troops west, and some will be on horseback. You like riding. Hell, you ride better than me, which sort of pisses me off. It would take a worry off, Marco. I swear to God that's the truth."

"Let me see that face." He cupped it, looked into her eyes, then sighed. "Damn it, it's the truth. I don't like leaving you."

"I know, so I know I'm asking you to do the hard. But I've got Keegan and my fierce dog."

Bollocks leaped onto the bridge, shook joyfully. Water flew; his eyes danced. But she remembered how he'd leaped into battle; she remembered the blood on his muzzle and the warrior gleam in those happy eyes.

"And," she added, "I just happen to be a pretty powerful witch."

"*Pretty powerful* doesn't cover it. I'll go, but you have to promise you'll send a message. Every day, Breen—that's deal-breaker time. Send, you know, a falcon or whatever."

"I went to Ninia Colconnan's shop yesterday and got you a scrying mirror."

"A what now?"

"It's a way to talk to you. Plus, it's pretty. Consider it a kind of Zoom call. I'll show you how it works." She pushed her hands through her mass of curling red hair. "This takes a load off, seriously. Plus, the practicalities. If Sally or Derrick try to get in touch, they can't reach us. They'll worry."

It was a good lever, she'd calculated, using Sally, the mom of the heart for both of them, to nudge Marco along.

"Yeah." He shoved his hands in his pockets. "Yeah, I've been thinking about that."

"So you can head that off, do a little FaceTime with Philadelphia when you get back. And"—she drilled a finger into his belly—"get the hell back to work, for me."

Crouching down, she ran her hands over Bollocks to dry him, had his purple-hued curls springing.

"What about you? I know you can't be writing much."

"A little." She gave Bollocks's doggy beard a gentle tug before she rose. "I haven't been able to work on Bollocks's next adventure, just can't write the happy right now. But I'm working some on the second draft of the adult novel. I've got more insight into battle scenes now."

"Ah, Breen."

She leaned against him. She could always lean against him.

"It's okay, Marco. We covered that already. We fought and killed evil things." She looked back at him, her gray eyes hard, her shoulders set. "When the time comes, I'll do it again. And again and again, until this is finished."

Then the hard softened, and she took his hands. "Come on, I'll help you pack and give you a lesson in scrying mirrors."

She stood in the dawn mists to watch him go. Her Marco, the born-and-bred urbanite, sat in the saddle as if he'd been born in one. The frisky mare danced under him, and she heard him laugh as he set off in a trot with the warriors, heading west.

Overhead, a trio of dragons, bright as jewels in the dawn light, flew over a gray November sky with their riders. A pair of faeries winged behind them.

Battle and blood would come again, spilled and waged by the fallen god Odran. Her grandfather.

But Marco would be safe, she thought, as safe as anyone could be in a land devoted to peace and threatened by a god determined to bring war.

And he, the best human being ever born, would be with the man he loved. For now, it was all she could hope for.

"He'll be more than fine." Beside her, Keegan watched those he'd sent west slide into the mists. "And you were right to push him to go."

"I know. And I know he'll bring comfort to the valley. It's important."

"Aye, it's important. You'd bring it as well. I want you here for . . . reasons, but I know you'd serve a purpose there, and find comfort yourself."

"I'm not ready for comfort." She studied him, this man, this witch, this warrior she'd come to love, to want, to need almost more than she could stand. Strong, and strongly built, his dark hair with its warrior braid disordered. And she saw both fatigue and anger in the deep, deep green of his eyes.

"Neither are you."

"I'm not, no, I'm bloody well not."

"And with Odran sealed up again, there's no one to fight right here, right now."

He gave her a long, cool look. "To wish for war is to wish for death. That's not our way."

"That's not what I'm saying, Keegan. You train for war because Talamh and all the worlds need protection and defense. You taught me that, the hard way, by knocking me on my ass countless painful times in training."

Shrugging, he glanced over to one of the training fields. "You're not as easy to knock down these days."

"You hold back. I hate to admit you always did. I'm never going to be a brilliant swordsman—woman—or a Robin Hood with a bow."

"Those are good stories. The Robin Hood stories. And no, you won't."

"You sure don't hold back there."

He smiled a little and wound one of her curls around his finger. "Why lie when the truth's right there? You're better than you were."

"Which isn't saying much."

"You're better than you were after you were better than you were. Your magicks are . . . formidable. They are, and will always be, your keenest weapon. And this?" He lifted her hand, turned her wrist to run a finger over her tattoo.

"*Misneach.* Courage, and yours is as keen as your magicks."

"Not always."

"Often enough. You sent Marco away, denied yourself his comfort for the comfort of others. That's courage. You'd go with him, but you stay because I need you to stay."

"For reasons."

"For reasons."

The young ones trooped into the training field, some on wing, some with elf speed, some still yawning the sleep away.

Not a school day, she realized, as Talamh stood strong for education. She glanced down at Bollocks and his pleading eyes.

"Go ahead."

He darted off, barking with joy.

"You don't ask what they are," Keegan noted. "The reasons."

"You feel I'm safer here, with you here. Shana tried to kill me, twice, and she's his now. She's Odran's now."

"All the portals are guarded. She can't come through. She can't harm you."

"She won't kill me."

His eyes narrowed. "You've foreseen?"

She shook her head. "I know I won't give her the satisfaction. Then there's Yseult. She's tried for me twice, not to kill—because unlike Shana, she's not, in Marco's terms, crazy as fuck—but to disable me enough to get me to Odran. The first time, she'd have succeeded if not for you. The second time, right back there."

She turned, pointed. "I dealt with her. But I let my emotions, my anger, my need to hurt and punish her rather than just end her get in the way. I won't make that mistake again."

"You've grown fierce, *mo bandia*."

Fierce? She didn't know about that. But resolute. She had become resolute.

"I believed myself ordinary—less than even that—for a very long time. I know what I am now, what I have, and I'll use it. You worrying about me takes your mind off what you need to do. You should stop."

Like her, Keegan watched the littles line up for training. Young, he thought, with a mixture of pride and regret. And, laying a hand on the hilt of his sword, remembered he'd been the same, done the same.

"Do you think the only reason I want you here is worry for you?"

"It's a factor, but I'm also useful here, and you know it."

"Aye, you are. You helped with healing wounded and brought comfort—bring it still with your visits to those in mourning. And you take too much there. It shows."

"Thank you very much. I'm going to start using glamours."

"You're beautiful."

The way he said it so casually, as if it simply was, brought her a ridiculous thrill.

"Even when you're tired," he continued, "and too pale and I see their grief all over you."

"You do the same. Yes, you're taoiseach, yes, it's duty, but it's more than that. You grieve, too, Keegan."

"Don't take that from me." He gripped her hand before she could lay it on his heart. "Even a shadow of it. I need it, just as I need the anger, as I need the cold blood. I know you helped with the dead, and I wouldn't have wished that for you."

"They're my people, too. I'm as much Talamhish as American. Probably more when it comes down to it."

"And still, I wouldn't have wished it. You sent Marco back, and I can't offer you, not now, the same kind of companionship here, in a place that's not home to you, like Ireland or the valley. I've hardly had time with you other than sex and sleep—and more sleep than sex, I'm sorry to be saying. This, here and now, is I think the longest we've spoken alone since after the battle."

"You're taoiseach, and you've had council meetings, Judgments. I know you've spoken to all the wounded, all those who lost someone. I know because they tell me. There are repairs and training and I can't even imagine what else. Do you think I expect you to spend time with me when you have so much else to do and think about?"

He looked at her in that way he had, so intense. Then looked away again, to the training fields and the village.

"No, you don't expect, and maybe that's why I wish I could give it to you. You're a mystery to me still, Breen Siobhan. And all I feel in me for you, another mystery. I don't always like it."

He made her smile again. "That's often abundantly clear."

"I need you here, for all the reasons you said yourself. All of those, aye, but I need you here for myself. I don't have to like that either, but . . . I'm explaining, as best I can."

It touched her, in the deep, that he'd bother to try.

"You're getting better at it. The explaining. You're never going to be brilliant at it, but I think, with practice, you could be competent enough."

A smile twitched at the corners of his mouth. "That's a bit of a poke, and well done."

"I thought so. I like being needed." She skimmed fingers down the warrior braid on the side of his head. "I went so long without being needed. Marco, yes, and Sally and Derrick. But that's different. So right now, the sleep and sex and whatever else we can fit in, it's enough."

"I haven't any more right now. Bloody council meeting."

"That's fine. I'm due in the training field soon. Bloody archery."

"I'm told you're not as pathetic as you were."

"Shut up. Go be the leader of the world."

He cupped his hands under her elbows, lifted her to her toes. Kissed her, and kissed her while the mists thinned away and the sun showered through.

"Keep Bollocks with you, would you? And someone—Kiara or Brigid or whoever you like—along if you go off to the village or visiting."

"Stop worrying."

"I'll worry less if you do those things."

"All right. Worry less. I'm going to get my bow and be less pathetic. I also think I'll have a better time than you will."

"No doubt of that. Keep the dog close," he repeated, then strode back over the bridge toward the castle, where the banner flew at half staff.

She stayed busy, day after day, training, helping with repairs—both magickally and practically—and spent as much time as she could with Phelin's family.

Her family, too, she thought as more and more memories of her first three years shimmered back. Flynn's big hands tossing her high in the air so she squealed, Sinead frosting cookies, running in the fields with Morena, with Seamus and Phelin always plotting an adventure.

She'd been as at home with them as she'd been on the farm where she'd been born.

But it was Flynn, warrior, council member, father, who finally snapped the tight rope she'd kept binding her own grieving.

She wanted the air, and she wanted the quiet. After giving herself two early-morning hours to work on her book—and hoping for another two in the evening—she took Bollocks out for a walk and a wander.

Just a little time, stolen time as she thought of it, to do nothing. Then she'd work with Rowan—council member and of the Wise—along with a few young witches on potions and charms. They'd continue to rebuild the supplies used during the aftermath of the battle.

Magicks weren't an abracadabra thing, but effort, skill, practice, and intent.

She'd fit in some gardening work to help replenish crops destroyed during the battle. She hoped to persuade Sinead and Noreen to work with her there, to get them out in the air and the sun for even an hour.

Field training after that, her least favorite part of any day. Sword work and hand-to-hand made up today's torture, and she already anticipated the bruises.

It amazed her how full her days here were, how one tumbled right into the next. Though she found the castle endlessly fascinating, the wild roll of the sea exhilarating, she missed her pretty cottage on the other side, missed the farm in Talamh's west, her friends there, her grandmother. And, she could admit privately, the self-satisfying routine she'd developed since she'd left Philadelphia so many months before.

But she was needed here, for now, and had come to understand that simply seeing her go about the daily tasks gave people in the Capital hope after so much loss.

She let Bollocks play in the water under the bridge, and through her bond with him knew that while it made him happy, he missed their bay, missed running the fields with Aisling's boys and playing with Mab, the Irish wolfhound that minded them.

When he scrambled out to shake, she dried him with a stroke of her hands. The November wind came brisk, smelled of the sea and the turned earth. She saw some busy in the gardens on the rising hills and fields, bringing winter crops back to life.

She'd worked with others of the Wise to heal the charred and bloody ground, and now saw the fruits of the work in the orange pumpkins and butter-yellow squash, the greens of kale and cabbage.

Flowers and herbs thrived again. She saw fresh thatch on the roofs of cottages, children playing in dooryards, people in the village browsing stalls and shops, smoke puffing from chimneys.

Life and light, she thought, were stubborn things. They must, and they would, bloom and shine against the dark. They would not be snuffed out like a candle, but flame on and on and on.

She had a part in that, and she'd do whatever she needed to do to keep that fire burning.

Bollocks pranced ahead, then under the dripping branches of a willow. She followed him through and found Flynn sitting on a stone bench with Bollocks's head on his knee.

She didn't have to see the man's grief when she felt it like an anchor on her heart.

Still, he smiled at her as he patted Bollocks's curly topknot. "Here's a joy of a dog."

"He really is."

"And soon to be far-famed in song and story. You can see much from this spot. The village and its bustle, the fields and the hills, the shadow of the mountains, all the while if you listen, there's the drumbeat of the sea behind you. Your nan had this bench placed here before I was born. Many's the time I sat here with your dad, thinking thoughts and finding the quiet.

"And there?"

He pointed, so she stepped closer.

"In that cottage there lived a girl I had a terrible yen for in my wild youth. Before Sinead, of course, for there's a woman who put a lock on my heart that can't be broken. But the yen was real enough while it lasted, and the memories of it harmless and sweet."

"Where is she now, the girl?"

"Married a farmer, she did, and they had three children—no, four,

I'm thinking. They're in the midlands, and travel here to barter and trade. Come sit awhile. I wanted the air for a bit of time."

She hesitated, but instinct told her he needed the company now as much as the air. And when he put a hand over hers after she sat beside him, she felt his heart and knew she was right.

"When your father and I were boys in the valley, I yearned for the Capital, this bustle. No farmer was I, not like Eian or my own da. Nor clever as my da with the building of things. There was music, of course. Ah, that was a thing that bonded me with Eian tight as a drumskin. And how I loved our times in the pubs, here and on the other side, playing. Me, Eian, Kavan, and Brian—brothers they were to me always. But I wanted the warrior's life, that's the truth of it. Raising a family with Sinead in the valley, that was precious, a time of joy, and peace as well. For a time."

He turned to look at her. "Your ma made him happy. You should know that."

"I do." For a time, Breen thought.

"But you, little red rabbit, you were the beat of his heart, the light of his soul. When Odran had you . . . A lesser man might have gone mad, and let that madness and fear rule him. Eian was no lesser man, so he locked up that heart, used his mind, his power, his strength. As you did, barely more than a babe. As you did," Flynn murmured.

"Your mother flew me home again, and Sinead rocked me and sang to me. I remember it all so clearly now, how they made me feel safe again after I'd been so afraid. When I first came back, Nan helped me see, in the fire, how my father fought that night, and how she fought. And . . . you, with your great wings and sword. You fought for me, for him, for Talamh."

"A terrible, brutal night it was, but I yearned to be a warrior, and so would have died for you, for him, for Talamh. A choice I made. But I lived. We lost Kavan that night."

"I know."

"A brother to me. Then Brian fell, and then Eian. Their deaths, my brothers', took pieces from me, as death should. But I lived, a warrior, a husband, a father—and grandfather as well—as the pieces death takes from you find a way to live without them. You honor their death by living and doing and standing."

"I know you do." She looked out, as he did. A rabbit, gray like her eyes, hopped its way over a field and to a row of cabbage to munch.

"I never lost someone close before. I thought my father had just left me behind."

"Never he would. Never."

"I know that now, and so I know you honor the death of ones you love by living and doing and standing."

"I sit on the council and do what I can to be wise and true there. I fight what comes against us. Now, Breen, now I hold my wife, the wife of my boy, his brother, his sister, my own ma and da. Those arms must be strong for them because those pieces are lost inside them.

"But my boy, my child who came into my hands on his first breath, is gone. And the child waiting to be born will never know his father. His wife will never again feel his arms around her. His mother will never hear his voice again or look on his face.

"Those pieces are gone, and I don't know how to live without them."

She had no words, so simply put her arms around him. She couldn't take his grief, no power could. But she let it come into her, the overwhelming pain of it, so at least it was shared.

"You're a warrior," she said at last. "A husband, a father, a grandfather. You'll stand. All the pieces death took from you, the light of the lost fills them. Phelin's light's in you and always will be."

Tears wanted to flow; she wouldn't let them.

"I can feel his light in you. And my father's." She drew back enough to lay a hand on his heart, and with her eyes on his, pushed what she felt into him. "It's so bright, even death can't dim it."

Flynn laid his head on her shoulder, sighed once. "He'd have been so proud of you."

"His light's in me, too."

Flynn lifted his head, stroked her hair. "I see him in you, and it's a comfort. You're a comfort to me." He pressed his lips to her forehead. "I thank whatever powers put me in this place at this time, and you with me. Little red rabbit," he murmured before he kissed her again, then left her alone under the willow.

And alone she wanted to shake under that shared grief, just crumple under the weight of it.

Not here, she thought, where someone might find her, see her. Stepping out, clear of the branches, she called her dragon.

Yes, yes, dear God, she needed air, and distance, and release.

When Lonrach landed, she climbed onto his gold-tipped red back. "Just wait," she told Bollocks before he could scramble up with her. "Just wait."

And sent Lonrach bulleting into the sky. High and fast so the air streamed over her, sent her hair, her cloak flying. The wind bit as they went higher, higher, through the clouds and the damp held inside them. When Talamh below her spread like a child's toy with the distance, she screamed.

Screamed, screamed out the rage so tightly bolted to the grief. She felt the air shake with it, heard thunder boom with it, lightning flash through it. And didn't care.

This was hers, and hers alone, for every drop of blood shed, for all the tears, all the loss. Dark and light, twin sides of her rage, clashed so the sky swirled and shook, the clouds broke and wept. Lifting her arms high, hands knotted into fists, she welcomed the storm.

"I will damn you!" She shouted it. "I swear by all the gods, for my father, for Phelin, and for all, I will bring you death."

She took Lonrach down and down, showing him where she needed to go, where she hadn't had the strength to go since that bloody day.

When he landed in the forest, with the trees whipping, the rain pounding, she leaped off to stand facing the Tree of Snakes. Her blood had opened this portal to bring a hell to Talamh; she, her grandmother, and Tarryn had closed it with theirs.

She drew power, more and more, lifted her face to the storm, merged with it. And stood, lit like fire, both in and outside herself.

"Hear me, Odran the Damned. Hear me and tremble. I am Breen Siobhan O'Ceallaigh. I am Daughter of the Fey, of man, of gods. I am the light and the dark, hope and despair, peace and destruction. I am the key, the bridge, the answer. And with all I am, I will end you. Your blood will boil in your veins, your flesh will burn, and all the worlds will hear your screams of fear and pain. Hear me, Odran, as the gods once cast you out, I will burn you to ashes that even hell won't take. And you will be as nothing. This is my vow. This is my destiny."

She stood, hands lifted, light swirling from them, and her eyes as dark and fierce as the storm.

"Breen. Step back from there."

Her head whipped around, and power with it. Keegan had to hold up both hands to block enough of it to stay standing.

"Step back," he repeated. "Would you risk opening it with your fury?"

"It will not open. But he hears me."

"So you've had your say, now step back." Because she stood too bloody close with power rolling off her, wave after wave, he strode up to her.

When he took her arm, the jolt all but rattled his bones, but he pulled her away.

Bollocks stood wet and whining as she stared with power and fury into Keegan's eyes.

"Do you think you can stop me?"

"If I must." He put himself between her and the portal and saw some of the temper dim into confusion. "You have to let it go now."

"What? Let what go?"

"You brought the storm, now let it go."

"Oh God." She pressed a hand to her face, shuddered. "I'm sorry. I'm sorry." Shaking, she lowered to the ground. "I'm so sorry."

The wind snapped off; the rain died. The power that quaked in the air faded away.

"You had no business coming here alone," he began, but she curled into a ball and began to weep.

With the rage emptied out, she only had tears.

Keegan lowered down as Bollocks ran over to cry softly against her.

"All right now." He stroked her hair, her back, her shoulders to warm and dry her. Then he wrapped around her, searched for words. But all he could think of was: "All right now."

"I'm sorry."

"So you've said. It's done and finished. Weep if you must until that's done and finished as well."

"I sat with Flynn, and he . . . I couldn't hold it anymore. I couldn't just lock it inside anymore. I needed to . . ."

"Scream at the gods."

When she lifted her head, he cocked his. "I expect they heard you all the way to the Far West."

"Oh, stupid, stupid." She covered her face with her hands. "I shouldn't have— I scared everyone when—"

"Scared? Woman, we're Talamhish, and not some weak-knees to fear when one of our own unleashes her power. And such as yours, such as it was, well now, there's some rejoicing for that. The storm, now, was a bit much, as people will be some time chasing down clothes that flew off the line and such."

"I'm—"

"Don't say it again, by the gods, it's tiring. You promised me you wouldn't come here alone."

"I didn't mean to." On another sob, she shook her head. "I mean, I didn't plan to. I think I went a little crazy for a minute."

"A bleeding hour at the least. It took a bit of time to find you, and would've been longer without this one here." He gave Bollocks a good rub. "He came and got me. I was about to hunt you up, before the heavens opened. I expect you're tired out now after all that energy and a few gallons of tears. We can leave in the morning instead of this afternoon."

"Leave? For where?"

"The valley." He stood, offered a hand to help her up.

"No. Keegan." She pushed up quickly. "I needed to purge or vent, or just—" She looked back at the portal. "I needed to let him know. But you can't just send me back because I had . . . an episode."

"An episode, is it? First time in my experience I've seen sheep fly."

"Oh my God."

"None the worse for it. And while it's true enough I'd send you back—and I'm taoiseach, so I could do just that. But I'm needed elsewhere, and I've given the Capital the time it's needed. For now. You'll go with me because I need it, and I know bloody well you do as well."

"Yes." She stepped into him, dropped her head on his shoulder. "Yes, I need it. Can we go now?"

"We can. After we clean up a bit, you can say your goodbyes and put together what you need to take with you. And I wouldn't mind it if you let Marco know through the mirror so he can make a meal. His meatballs would be a fine thing tonight."

"Okay." She breathed out. "Let me do a glamour so I don't look like I've been crying."

"No." He gripped her hand. "They heard your grief, let them see it. Let them see you. And let me say to you Odran hasn't a prayer in heaven or hell against the woman I saw standing there, burning like a thousand candles. Not a prayer.

"Now come along. The day's wasting."

CHAPTER TWO

She said her goodbyes and tucked messages from Morena's mother and Keegan's for their daughters in her bag. And as she sat on Lonrach's broad back with Bollocks, she thought of the wild flight to the Capital, of the urgency and fear that had sent her hurtling east.

Now she flew home, forever changed.

She knew what spread beneath her in the shadow of Lonrach's wings. She knew the green hills and fertile dales, the scent of thick forests, the majesty of mountain peaks. The villages, cottages, caves, and all who dwelled in them.

There, beneath the clouds, a horse and rider at the gallop, and a woman in a cloak with a basket on her arm. There a stag, regal as a king, poised at the edge of a wood, and there a woman on the banks of a stream, her line in the water and a swaddled babe on a blanket beside her.

There would be Trolls mining the deep caverns in the mountains, and children in the schoolroom bored with their lessons and dreaming of adventures. Farmers would check their winter crops and sharpen their plows; mothers would tuck the littles up for a nap.

And warriors would train and train and train, honing every skill to protect the hills and dales, the mountains and streams, and all who dwelled there.

She was part of that now, as even with the magicks, the shared blood, the knowledge, she hadn't been. Because now she'd fought and killed and bled for Talamh.

She looked over at Keegan, so alert, she thought, so intense. An impatient man who somehow held bottomless wells of patience. A hard man who was, in essence, made of kindness. A living, breathing contradiction.

It fit, didn't it, she decided, because he would fight and kill and bleed for the single most vital goal of his world.

Peace.

She edged Lonrach a little closer to Cróga so she could call out over the wind.

"What happens next?"

He glanced at her, but only briefly before he continued to scan the land, the air, the distant sea.

"You go back to training, in magicks, in combat, as before."

"No, I mean now."

"That is now, and tomorrow, and the day after. We have time, but can't waste it. Odran lost more than we did. He won't grieve as we have, as the demons and the dark he sent through to destroy us don't matter to him. But he lost power."

"He has to gather it again. It could be weeks, months, even years."

"Not years. Not this time."

"Because I'm here."

"So close, he'd think, to taking you and all you are. You, the key, the bridge, Daughter of man and Fey and gods hold all he covets. So close, he'd think, to taking all he wants and raining vengeance on all the worlds."

Keegan glanced over again. "But he's wrong. He's only farther away than he once was."

"Why?"

"Because of all you are. Now, do you want the valley or the cottage? I'll take you where you wish before I go south."

"You're going south?"

"I have duties I couldn't attend to while needed at the Capital. Mahon's handled the repairs there, and the razing of the Prayer House, the building of the memorial. I need to show the South the taoiseach remembers."

"Then I want to go to the South."

"You haven't been home for weeks now."

"Neither have you. No, I'm not taoiseach," she said before he could. "But you said to let them see my grief. Let them see me. Was that only for those in the Capital?"

He said nothing for a moment, only studied her. Then, with a nod, he veered south.

"The warm," he said conversationally, "will make a pleasant change."

"I won't mind that. But I don't mind the cold. I like seeing what it does to the trees. The green of the pines seems to get deeper with the colors that burst out in the oaks and chestnuts, the maples. The light changes, and nights go long. The deer build their winter coats. I never expected to see fall here, or the winter that's coming so fast. Not when I came to Ireland, or even when I first came through to Talamh."

She gestured to a pair of dragon riders plying the sky north.

"They're ours," he told her. "Patrolling."

"Ours. Odran doesn't have dragons," she realized.

"No. He can't turn them or enslave them as he can with some Fey. They're pure."

"If he turns their rider?"

"They won't turn, even for their rider. They'll mourn, and often die of grief if their rider turns to Odran. If their rider was enslaved, didn't choose, they wait."

As he rode, Keegan ran a hand over Cróga's smooth scales. "He'd destroy them all if he could because they'll never be his. There." He gestured. "The South, and its sea."

Distant yet, but she saw the bluest of blue water stretched into the forever, and the golden beaches that edged it.

Faeries on the wing, and sheep on the green, green hills that rose and rolled toward the sun, and thick forest that spread beyond the sand.

On a hill above the beaches and the sprawling village, she saw a large dolmen, white as chalk.

"Is that the memorial?"

He circled to study it from all sides.

And yes, he remembered.

"There stood, year by year, the Prayer House, granted to the Pious after so many of their faith—and this is the wrong word, for it's not faith that had them torture, persecute, and kill. But this was granted to them, in treaty, with their oath to devote themselves to good works. Toric and his kind used this gift, this forgiveness to betray all. For them, there will be no forgiveness, and the house that stood holding its evil is gone, the ground it stood on consecrated.

"The dolmen stands for the sacrifice of the fallen who gave their lives here to protect all."

"It's beautiful." And sad, she thought. Like grief held in stone. "It's all beautiful, the sea, the beaches, the village. What we saw in the fire on Samhain was hard and brutal and brave. I watched you fight, you and Mahon, Sedric, all the others. Now it's beautiful again."

"Talamh stands, because it must."

He guided Cróga to the hill, leaped down, then waited while Bollocks did the same before he held up a hand for Breen. She took it, and though her stomach dropped, dismounted to take the jump to the ground.

"We'll let them fly awhile and find a resting place. They'll come when they're needed."

"So will he. Go ahead," Breen told Bollocks as he danced in place.

He streaked down the hill, across the beach, and into the water. A young Mer spun out of the water with a laugh, then dived again to play with him.

"He always finds the fun." She turned to face the dolmen. "It's powerful, a powerful symbol. Reverent." She laid a hand on one of the legs that rose taller than two men. "And warm in the sun."

Then stepped back as Mahon flew to them. Keegan's right hand and brother-in-law folded his wings as he landed. "Welcome, and you timed it well. We only raised the capstone this morning."

"And well done," Keegan told him. "How go the repairs?"

"All but finished. Mallo and Rory had some unkind words when you stole Nila." He grinned, stroked his mahogany beard. "I won't be repeating them. But they worked wonders true enough, kept the work moving steadily. You can see for yourself, the village thrives again, and those who come for a holiday enjoy it as much as the dog down there."

As Breen had, Mahon laid a hand on the stone. "And this stands to remind them why they can."

"There's nothing left of Toric or his kind here," Breen said. "Here where the ground is fertile and green again and the dolmen rises in reverence and remembrance for the brave, for the innocent. And stand it will, for all time, as the Fey stand."

Caught in the magicks, in what stirred in her, she walked between the two legs to stand under the capstone.

"But when they look on this hill, when they walk on the green, there must be more than sorrow. There must be . . ."

She trailed off, held up a hand, shook her head.

"No, let it come," Keegan demanded. "What do you see?"

"First, I feel. Power, white and bright and strong, that lives in the stones, in the ground beneath them. I feel the air and the sun on my skin, so warm. When night comes, the twin moons rise up and over the great monument to the brave, the innocent, the lost. This is true faith and honor.

"There, trees, three that bloom in spring as hope blooms even as the air shakes their blossoms to cover the ground. They fruit in the summer, for this is bounty, and their leaves burst with color as the wheel turns to autumn, for this is the cycle. So as they fall, a dance in the air, the wheel turns and turns until they bloom again."

She stepped out, stepped over. "The pool, with water clear as glass, and any who drink feel at peace. And on the great stone, the fire eternal, and in its flames lives strength and purpose.

"So all who look upon this place, or walk on the green, know the four elements linked together and bound by magicks. All who come honor the brave and the innocent, and feel hope renewed as they know death isn't only an ending, as life and love and light renew."

She shivered once, then shoved her hands through her hair. "That was . . . a lot. I'm sorry, I don't want to—"

She broke off when Keegan simply held up a hand in a signal to stop. "We'll make it so. Mahon, we'll need faeries to work on the trees, fruit trees, and a mason to build the pool, witches to fill it. Send an elf up, if you would, with a copper cauldron. Once you have, go home to your wife and children. If I stop in the valley before you do, I'll have Aisling kicking my balls, and I'd as soon avoid it."

"Happy to oblige you. Will I see you there soon?"

"By morning if not sooner."

Mahon turned to Breen, kissed her cheek. "I don't see what you do, but I look forward to when I do."

After he flew off, Breen clasped her hands together. "Keegan, if I overstepped—"

"Did I say you did? I'm saying you've the right of it, so we'll put it right."

"But this is what you wanted, what you saw."

He studied the dolmen, the stark white stones. Aye, he thought, this he'd seen and no more.

"I saw through grief and anger. The stones stand, for I was right to have them raised here. But it's not enough, and there you've the right of it. Without hope, grief loses the strength to live on, and fight on, and hold.

"The faeries will bring the trees, and we'll have the pool, and you and I will make the fire eternal."

"I've never— I'm not sure I know how."

"You do, you will. It's your vision, after all. Even in the dark, there'll be light. We'll hold to that."

When the boy brought the caldron, big and bright so it gleamed in the sunlight, Keegan sent it into the air, higher and higher until it rested in the center of the capstone.

"Well done," he said to the boy. "You chose well."

"Mahon said big." The boy grinned. "May I watch, Taoiseach?"

"Of course." Then Keegan looked out and down. "Wait. Run down and tell all to watch. To watch while the taoiseach and the Daughter of the Fey light the fire eternal in this place of remembrance."

The boy let out a whoop and blurred away.

"Great. Now I'll have an audience."

"Breen Siobhan," Keegan said, impatience shimmering, "you worry yourself about the small. You came to be seen, and had the right of it. Now you will be. And those who witness this will not forget. Those who witness this will tell children yet to be born of it. And all who come here will remember we stood, taoiseach and Daughter of the Fey, for the brave, for the innocent, and for all. We stood, as they did, against the dark. And we brought the light."

"You're good at this," she murmured. "Sometimes I forget how good you are at this. Being taoiseach."

"It's only sense."

"No, it's leadership." She smiled as Bollocks, as if he knew, came running back up the hill. "Besides, if I screw this up, I'll blame you."

People gathered below. She saw them coming out of shops and cottages, pausing their work to look up. Couples and families who'd strolled the beach or splashed in the waves stood now, watching. Mers floated on the endless blue or slid sinuously onto rocks.

Men boosted young ones on their shoulders; women balanced babes on their hips. In her mind, Breen could hear them:

Watch now, watch. And remember.

"Take my hand," Keegan ordered. "Your nerves are wasted, Daughter of Eian O'Ceallaigh. Let it rise now, let it come. Say the words. The words are in you."

They were, of course they were. She felt the power pulse from him to her, from her to him. Merged, joined, doubled. And the words came.

"This power, old as breath, we call to honor life and death. A spark to flame, a flame to fire, to burn and blaze and so inspire. We owe a debt we will not forget."

"Here light," Keegan continued, "burn bright through day and night. Eternal to rise into the skies. No flood, no wind will dim the flame kindled here to honor their name."

And with the power blowing through her like a wind, she, like Keegan, lifted her free hand toward the cauldron and let it fly.

"Ignite," they said together, "burn bright, eternal light." It rose up, gold, pure, and strong, smokeless towers of flame. And its terrible beauty brought tears to her eyes.

"Shine forever for all to see," they said. "As we will, so mote it be."

On the beaches below, in the dooryards of cottages and the doorways of shops, cheers erupted.

"No tears now." Keegan took a firmer grip on her hand. "This is not a grieving, but an honoring. A moment of strength, not weeping. Turn now and show them who you are."

She struggled the tears back and did as he bid.

Keegan lifted his sword, and those below roared as the keen steel of Cosantoir gleamed like the fire behind them.

"For the brave and the innocent," he shouted. "For Talamh, and for all!"

"I don't know what to do now."

"Because it's already done." He sheathed his sword. "Call your dragon. It's time to go home."

They cheered still as she and Keegan flew over the beach and away. She looked back, back at the fire that had come from her.

No, she wouldn't forget.

She went to Marg first, and though the air held a chill, the bold blue door of the cottage stood open for her. Bollocks let out a joyful bark and raced inside.

When Breen followed, she found Marg in the kitchen, already getting the dog a treat. The fire crackled, the kettle steamed on the hob, and the scent of baking filled the air.

All her emotions rose up and tangled inside her. She thought: Home. And went into Marg's arms.

"There now." Marg held tight.

"I missed you. I'm so glad to see you."

"And I you. But there's more here." Marg drew back to study Breen's face. "You'll tell your nan now. Come and sit. We'll have some tea and ginger biscuits, and you'll tell me."

"I didn't realize, not all the way, until I got here. It's all been so much. That day—the fighting, the blood, Phelin, and all the rest. Sometimes it's all a blur, and others every moment is like cut crystal. And the after, all the after. I wonder, Nan, how people go on. But they do. They do, even knowing they'll have to go through it all again."

"Sit now and let me pamper you a bit." Marg heated the teapot with her hands. "When I lost my boy, when Eian fell, I wondered how I could go on. You were on the other side, with no memory of me, and my son, slain by his own father. How could I live? How could I walk or talk or eat or sleep? But I did."

Breen sat and watched as Marg put ginger cookies on a plate. She'd bundled her red hair up and wore trousers and a green sweater and boots that told Breen she'd been in the garden.

"You're so strong."

"I wasn't. I was broken, in my heart, in my spirit, and near to it in my mind. I cut my hair," she murmured, looking back. "Brutal short. In the night I'd wander out, into the forest, over to the bay, anywhere, aimless. Sedric didn't think I knew he'd followed me in cat form, in case I needed him. We never spoke of it. He grieved, too. Eian was a son to him. For a time I wouldn't, couldn't share my grief with him, refused to acknowledge that grief shared is grief lessened, for both of us, Eian's ma and da. I was selfish with my grief."

"Nan."

"I needed to be, for a time. I needed the selfish and the wandering. What's needed is needed," she said as she brought the teapot and cups to the table. "And patient, Sedric waited for me to turn to him, for me to let him turn to me. In time I did. So we walked, we talked, we ate, we slept. We lived."

"I'm glad you had each other."

"He's the love of my life, and the love beyond this life we have. Now, tell me."

Over tea and cookies, Breen talked of trying to offer comfort, helping to bring burned fields back to life, of sitting with Flynn and the storm that followed.

"I think . . . I wasn't prepared, not equipped for all of it. When I look back, my life was sheltered and simple. No, I wasn't happy, not really, but I got up in the morning and went to work, I came home, graded papers or worked on lesson plans. I had Marco, and Sally and Derrick, and I could, and did, just blend into the walls. Go unnoticed."

"And here you're not sheltered, and things aren't so simple. You're noticed and looked toward. Are you happy, *mo stór*?"

"Yes." Breen pressed her fingers to her eyes, then let her hands fall. "Yes, even with everything that's happened, could happen, I'm happier than I've been for so long. I have so much. You." Breen reached for Marg's hand. "I have you. And what's in me, and what's in me brings me such joy. But what I did in the Capital this morning—just this morning," she realized suddenly. "That was reckless. I let what was in me take over. I didn't control it."

"What's needed is needed," Marg repeated. "Was anyone harmed?"

"No. But—"

"Ah." Marg held up a finger. "Do you trust me?"

"Completely, in all things."

"Then trust this. What you have, what you are, couldn't and won't bring harm but to the dark, to what threatens others. I know this, as you're my blood. You're from my son."

"Part of me is from him, from Odran."

"As part of Eian was. He mistakes you, mistakes thinking he can use that part. It's that part, *mo stór*, that will end him. Is this a worry of yours, that you'll do harm?"

"It wasn't until this morning. It was like with Toric at the Judgment. Just overwhelming. The heat of it, the strength of it."

"It frightens you a bit."

"It does."

"It should. Power is a wild thing, and turned, consumes the one who wields it. But leashed too tight, it weakens and thins. We'll practice, and we'll work, but in the end, you have to find your own way."

Every knot inside her loosened.

"This is only one of the reasons I missed you. You keep me steady. And the valley. Just coming back to it calms me. The Capital is beautiful and so full of life, but . . ."

"It's not home."

"It's not home. I've seen the South now, and it's beautiful, lively, and tranquil all at once, but . . . Oh, I almost forgot. The monument."

"Sedric and I went to the South two days ago. Keegan sent a falcon to ask me to go, help with the raising of the dolmen, as he couldn't yet leave the Capital. It's a beautiful, stark reminder of what was lost and what was defeated."

"Yes." Now Breen pushed at her hair. "Maybe I made a mistake and it should have stayed beautiful and stark."

"What do you mean?"

"When we stood there—Keegan and I—I felt, I saw . . . something different. Something more."

"What more did you see?"

"I saw . . . Could I show you? In the fire?"

Rising, Breen went to the hearth, held out her hands, and waited for Marg to join her.

"I saw this."

Spring first, with the trees blooming pink and white, the little pool at the leg of the dolmen reflecting the stone and the light, and the fire rising gold. Then blossoms falling to carpet the ground and fruit budding out, growing, ripening, the leaves going red and gold before they fell and the branches stood bare and waiting.

And through all, the fire burned gold.

Marg pressed a hand to her mouth as tears glimmered.

"This you saw?"

"So clearly, Nan. Keegan and I made the fire before we left, and—"

Marg simply turned to her, embraced her. "This was vision born of love and compassion as much as power. This is your father in you, for I believe with all my heart he would have seen the same."

"You do?"

"I do. And bless Keegan for being wise enough to know it. He was wise to tear down that house of evil, and to put in its place the stones, the strong. Wiser still to hear you and add the light. What a day you've had."

"Feels like a week."

"So I'll walk you to the Welcoming Tree, and you'll go over to the cottage."

"I haven't seen Morena, or Finola or Seamus."

"Tomorrow's soon enough for that. Take your evening." Marg went back, took her cloak and Breen's from their hooks. "Sleep well and take your morning for your writing. We need what we need," she said as she put on her cloak.

Breen couldn't deny the need as she climbed the little stone steps to the tree and turned to wave to Marg. The farmhouse stood behind her, smoke trailing up from the chimneys in the fading light.

She loved it here, loved the feel of the air, the look of the land, but she had a need for what waited on the other side.

So she stepped onto and over those wide, curved branches, onto and over the smooth rock, and into Ireland.

Bollocks pranced again, his whip of a tail swinging like a metronome, untroubled by the thin, cold rain that fell from a leaden sky.

It didn't trouble her either as she lifted her face to it, then walked on. The air smelled of damp earth, dripping pine. Instead of his usual detour to splash through a stream, or racing back and forth, Bollocks headed straight down the path.

"Ready to go home, aren't you?" He looked up at her, topknot bouncing. "Or maybe it's because I am. Either way, we'll be there soon."

She let out a sigh, drew in another breath. "Can you smell it? Peat smoke, the bay, wet grass."

When they came out of the woods, she saw it, the peat smoke, the bay, the wet grass, her herbs and flowers. And the cottage, the thatched roof, the sturdy stone walls, the charming patio, the lights in the windows.

And like the first time she'd seen it, it simply filled her. All she'd ever wanted.

Bollocks didn't dash to the bay, but to the door. And barked.

Before she could get there herself, Marco—his beautiful braids tied back, a dish towel over one shoulder—pulled the door open. Music pumped out.

He laughed as Bollocks reared up on his back feet to dance. "You got you some moves. Dance on in here out of the wet. There's my Breen!"

"Marco." She'd have flown to him if she could, but settled for a short run and a jump into his arms.

He swung her around out of the rain to give her a noisy kiss.

"Keegan sent your stuff over a bit ago. I got meatballs simmering in red sauce 'cause your man has a fondness for it."

"He's not exactly my man."

"Please." He kissed her again. "I've been keeping an eye out for you. Brian'll be home in a while, and when he and Keegan get here, we'll have us a feast. But right now, I've got you all to myself."

He whipped off her cloak, tossed it onto its peg, then grabbed her again to circle. "I love this place. You'd be crazy not to. But it's just not the same without my girl in it."

"I've missed it, and you, and everything, everyone."

"Got your laptop set up for you so you can work when you get up before any civilized person does, and your blog posts are holding strong. We'll talk about all that stuff later. Let's feed this fine dog here, then sit ourselves down with a glass of wine."

"Oh yes. Let's."

She threw her arms around him and thought: Home. This was home.

How she could have two worlds mean home should've been a mystery. But she found it a gift.

CHAPTER THREE

She woke before dawn and found herself alone. For a moment, she lay in the quiet, in the glow of the flickering fire, just holding on to the moment of comfort between night and day.

In the night, Keegan had slept beside her, and Bollocks had curled in his bed. And in the evening that had stretched before it, they'd shared food, along with Marco and Brian, conversation that hadn't centered on war, battles, or preparations for them.

They'd had music, companionship, laughter.

And in the glow of the flickering fire, she and Keegan had turned to each other in want and need before sleep.

An interlude, she knew, and for her a hope of what could be.

But it could be only if they battled, prepared to fight, and won the war.

So she rose and pulled on her workout gear. She'd tune her body, then sit at her desk and tune her mind with work. Then once again, she'd cross over to Talamh to practice her magicks, to see Morena and all the others, to train with Keegan for the battles to come.

But before any of that, she thought: Coffee.

On the way downstairs, she heard the mutter of male voices, smelled bacon. Burned bacon.

She found Keegan and Brian in the kitchen, Bollocks busy chowing down on a bowl of kibble, and a scorched frying pan on the stove.

"Having some trouble?" she asked, and aimed straight for the coffee maker.

"This stove is . . ." Keegan scowled at it. "Complicated."

"We thought to take turns on breakfast." Brian stood, tall, muscular, blue eyes dancing. "As Keegan took the first round, we found the complications."

After getting a mug, Breen nodded at the pile of scrambled eggs, more brown than yellow from overcooking in a scorched pan.

"So I see. Well, I'd advise regular training and practice to improve pathetic efforts to passable."

"Ha." Keegan tossed bacon, heaped some eggs on a slice of toast. "It's fine," he claimed, and ate.

"Enjoy then."

She went to the door, and when she opened it, Bollocks streaked out. As he raced to the bay, she stepped into the morning chill and pale dawn light.

Mists spun, thin as gossamer, over the gray waters of the bay. They crept, wispy feet, over the damp green grass. She smelled the rosemary, the spice of the firewitch dianthus, the vanilla of heliotrope.

Berries, pretty red balls, shined on the holly, and a rosebush bloomed defiantly, the color of summer sun, in air that whispered of winter.

She stood, drinking her coffee, watching her dog splash and the whip of water tear at the mists as the sun pushed and pushed through the clouds.

Once, mornings meant rush and hurry. Coffee to go, wait for the bus to take her to a job she didn't want and felt ill-suited to hold.

She'd loved her little slice of Philadelphia, its color, its feel. But all the rest? Gray shadows, and she the grayest of all.

Now she had this, something she'd once felt unable to even dream of. She had work she loved, and she had purpose.

Even when that purpose overwhelmed, when it frightened, it belonged to her.

And so, at least for now, she thought as Keegan came out, did the man who stood beside her.

"I know you and Brian weren't talking about burning the bacon when I came down."

"It wasn't burned, just very crisp."

"Right. Either way, I'm glad we could take last night to talk of something other than Odran and war and all of it. But I know you have to go over plans and duties with your warriors, like Brian."

"And it's done," he said simply. "You'll work on your stories this morning, and I'll give Harken a hand at the farm for a bit before I tend to other things. The sun sets earlier now, so I'll want you in the training field an hour before it does."

"All right."

He glanced back as Brian came out.

"Have a fine day, Breen."

"The same to you, Brian."

"An hour before sunset," Keegan repeated. "Don't be late."

He started across the grass to the woods, then stopped, strode back to her.

She thought he looked just a little on the fierce side as he wrapped one arm around her, pulled her to him, and kissed her.

"Don't be late," he said again, and left her.

Breen just smiled into her coffee and watched the day bloom.

It felt good, ridiculously good to work up a sweat with her workout routine. And maybe, just maybe, she preened some examining the sharper cut of her triceps. She might not reach pro level with sword or bow but, by God, the unrelenting practice had some personal benefits.

And the shower after? Sheer heaven.

She dressed for the day, then armed with a Coke, settled in her office. After booting up her laptop, she took a breath, then glanced back at Bollocks, who'd settled himself on the bed.

"Your turn," she told him.

She'd barely touched on the next Bollocks story since the battle. Simply hadn't had the heart for it.

But now, home, the dog on the bed, the cottage all around her, she slid right in. And found the joy.

When she surfaced, she'd lost all track of time. Bollocks no longer curled on the bed, and the scent of something glorious reached her.

She went out, saw Marco had his own laptop set on the table where he worked. He stood at the stove, one he obviously didn't find complicated, adding some white wine to a big pot.

"What is that amazing smell?"

"Hey, girl! You were in deep. Bollocks just went out again. Did you get something to eat? I came down about nine, and you were solid in the zone. Looks like you stayed there."

"I did. I really did. I told you I could work on the adult novel at the Capital, but I just couldn't pull into Bollocks's next adventure."

She swung to the refrigerator for another Coke—a personal reward. "And today, bam! God, it was so much fun!" She did a little twirl. "Just pumping out like it all needed a switch to flip. I guess it did."

"Glad to hear that, even if it tells me you didn't eat. I'm going to make you a sandwich."

"I can make my own sandwich, but why can't I have whatever's in that pot? What's in that pot? It smells like I feel, which is fantastic."

"You can't have it, 'cause it needs to simmer here. You're going to do that woo thing and keep it like I want it after we go over. We're going over, right?"

"Yeah, sure, but— What time is it?" Her mouth dropped open when she saw the clock on the stove. "Crap, I should've shut down a half hour ago. I need to go!"

"We'll get there. Do the thing, and I'll put a sandwich together you can eat on the way."

"What am I doing the thing for?"

"I came on all French this morning," Marco said as he sliced bread. "So par-lay voo, I made a couple of baguettes, and got us chicken en cocotte going."

"What's chicken en cocotte?" She lifted the lid. Inside she saw plump pieces of chicken, delicately browned, hunks of potatoes, carrots, celery, onion.

The scent—she could only think: Orgasmic.

"God, it's . . . Is this even legal?"

"It is in France. I came across the recipe last week, and was going to make it for your homecoming, but Keegan had that request. So for tonight."

"You're a wonder, Marco."

"I'm all of that." He handed her a sandwich of ham and smoked Gouda on brown bread.

They got boots and jackets, Breen wound on a scarf, and they started out.

Bollocks rushed to them, ran a circle around them, then dashed to the woods.

With a cap cocked over his braids, Marco pulled out his phone. "Brought it along to take some pictures for the blog before we get over there where it won't work. You sure there's nothing you can do about that?"

"They chose magick, Marco."

"Yeah, yeah, and I get it. Still."

He paused to take a shot of the cottage, another of the bay, then as Bollocks sat at the edge of the woods, cocked his head, one of the dog.

"I'm going this weekend and getting us a Christmas tree."

"Christmas."

"It's coming right along. We're getting lights and ornaments, the works. We're going to do it up right."

"I would love that. Wrapping paper and bows—I have to get presents! Oh, and we've got a Christmas wedding to help plan."

"I didn't say anything last night, because it was time for celebrating some, but Morena's changed her mind back and wants to wait on the wedding until spring or maybe even summer."

"What? Why? Oh." He didn't have to answer. "Phelin. Losing her brother, it's so hard. I wish I'd had more time with her after, but she needed to come back to the valley, needed to be here, and with Finola and Seamus."

"Finola asked me to talk to her—to Morena about it." He stopped to take more pictures in the woods. "Said she'd tried, but our girl just hedged. Same with me. So maybe you could give it a try."

"I will. Still, if she's really not ready, needs more time, Harken understands. No one understands better. I'll get a feel when I see her."

When they came to the tree, he put the phone away. "I'll give you some space. Sometimes a girl just needs a girl, right?"

Together they stepped from one world to another.

The sun beamed bright and strong so the sky cupped the world in hard, bold blue. Fields shined green and gold behind their stone fences. With no interest in the newcomers, sheep in their wooly coats grazed.

She saw Harken and Morena in a cart behind one of his sturdy horses.

"They're bringing in peat from the moors," Breen realized. "What they've cut and dried, bringing it in to stockpile for the winter."

"Finola says Morena spends most mornings with them, doing chores and so on, then most afternoons here, working with Harken. Goes off now and then with that hawk of hers, but mostly . . ."

"Working." Breen nodded. "I was going to go straight to Nan's, but I'll spend some time with Morena first."

"How about I go tell Nan what's up? And that'll give you the space."

"Yeah, thanks."

They crossed the little field, climbed over the wall.

"Tell Nan I'll come when I can—or if I can. I want to see what Morena needs."

"You got it."

When they reached the road, he started down it, and Breen crossed over to the farm. Bollocks gave her a look, got a nod, then ran toward the cart, barking his greeting.

The bark had a trio of birds shooting up and away like blue arrows.

Morena spotted her, waved. Breen saw Harken give Morena a kiss, a nudge. Then she was off the cart, giving the happy Bollocks a rub before hurrying to meet Breen.

"Harken said you were back. I'd hoped to see you."

And when Morena wrapped her arms around her, Breen felt the joy, the relief, and the sorrow.

"I'm so glad to be back. The Capital, well, is the Capital, but the valley—"

"Is the valley," Morena finished. "And your timing's saved me from stacking peat. Do you want to come in, have some tea?"

"I've spent most of the day sitting, working. I'd love to walk if you're up for it."

"I wouldn't mind a stroll." She bent to rub Bollocks again. "And I bet this one would like a jump in the bay."

"It's warmer than I expected," Breen began as they started to walk.

"Good strong sun today, but Harken says the wind'll blow cold tomorrow." She tossed her sunshine braid behind her shoulder. "Now then, he might've said it to get me out there hauling peat."

"Where's Amish?"

"Oh, gone off hunting." After tipping back her cap, Morena looked to the sky, where her hawk so often circled overhead. "So, you were working on your stories today."

"The next one about Bollocks, and when I finished, Marco informed me we're getting our Christmas tree and decorations this weekend. My first Christmas in Ireland, and here. It'll be busy," Breen said easily. "Since Aisling's said the baby's coming around Yule rather than in February, she may have the baby by then, and there's your and Harken's wedding."

"I'm thinking we may wait on the wedding until spring, or summer maybe."

"Oh?"

"As you said, there's Yule, and a baby coming, and all so busy a time. I wanted spring at the first of it, so I'm thinking it feels . . . I can't ask my family to celebrate at such a time, Breen. How can I reach for that at such a time? Harken's fine with the waiting."

"He's good at it," Breen agreed. "And only wants you happy. That's love. He'd never push. But I'm going to."

"Ah, I wish you wouldn't."

"Only push for you to listen, and whatever you do, I'm with you. You're my oldest friend, and whatever you need, I'm with you. I'd forgotten you, for so long," Breen continued. "Then it all came back. I'd forgotten Phelin, forgotten your family. Then it all came back. When I saw them again, it all rushed back. Your family, and they were my family, too. They are my family."

Bollocks raced ahead toward the water as they stepped off the road and onto the beach.

"It meant the world you stayed after. That you spent time, every day, my mother said, with them. I wanted you here, I'll admit it, and still I was glad you stayed."

"We were all where we needed to be."

Morena closed her eyes, let the air wash over her face. "He was the best of us, was Phelin. I love my family, every one, but when I think on it, he was the best of us. Kind and funny and loyal. A trickster, aye, but never with harm. He loved his wife so, and could barely wait to be a father. Now he's gone. And I know he gave his life for Talamh, for us, for all. I honor that, I swear to you."

"I know you do. That doesn't make it hurt less."

"Will it ever, do you think? Hurt less?"

Taking her hand, Breen walked toward the water. "I thought my father had left me, that he didn't love me enough to stay. And that hurt, it cut so deep. Then, when I came here and learned he'd died, and how and why, it was another deep, deep hurt. Even as I came to understand the why, it hurt.

"Now, with some time, it hurts still, but in a different way. And when I remember him, and times with him, I can feel some joy with it. So will you, with Phelin. And I think with time, the joy eases most of the hurt."

"I've stood for friends and for neighbors at Leavings, but never before for one so close. Starting my life with Harken, asking my family to come and dance and share in that, it's selfish."

"Here's where I tell you you're wrong about that. Before I do, I'll say again, I'm with you whatever you want and need. But I did spend time with your family, so I know what it means to them, you and Harken starting that life. Your mother talked to me about it, and how she held on to that."

"A mother will, but—"

"And Noreen, and your brother. It would lift some of the sorrow, seeing life—this part of your life—begin. But most of all your father needs to see his daughter happy on her wedding day. Spring if you want it, or summer, or a year from now. Or on the solstice. It brings light, Morena, and they all need the light."

Tears welled and glimmered as Morena searched Breen's face. "Are you sure of this?"

"I wouldn't say it otherwise. If you're not ready for it, then you wait. But don't wait for them, and don't think you must or should."

"Nan's saying how she talks with my mother every day in the mirror, and they talk of the wedding, and the flowers and the dress, and . . . She says she won't tell Ma I'm putting it off, that's for me to do. She says it lifts Ma out of grief to talk of it, and she won't take that from her, so I must."

"And you haven't."

On a sigh, Morena swiped the tears from her eyes before they could fall.

"I haven't, no. I tell myself I'm going to. Every day, I'm going to, then I don't, as she's carrying on about all the fussy business of it."

"Because it lifts her out of grief."

With another sigh, Morena tipped her head to Breen's shoulder. "I don't want to wait. It's why I changed from spring to the solstice, because I don't want to wait."

"Then don't. Phelin's in the light. I know you believe that."

"I do believe it."

"So he'll be there, on your wedding day. I put off for so long taking what I wanted, trusting myself to take it, to reach. That's not you, Morena. You already have what you want. This is just promising to keep it, and respect it, and love."

"You're what I needed." Turning, Morena embraced her again. "You're just what I needed here and now."

"Then go tell Harken."

"I will. Then I'll go to Nan so we can talk to my mother about wedding business until my head's throbbing from it."

"Then after, you'd better come over to the cottage, have some wine, and tell me and Marco."

"Be sure I will. Thank you." She gave Breen one hard squeeze. "I swear you've lifted a stone off my heart. I'll come for the wine."

She started off at a run. From above Breen heard the hawk cry.

She watched it circle, then glide to Morena's arm.

With Bollocks, she walked down to Marg's cottage, where she found her grandmother deadheading roses in the front garden.

"Go on in," Marg told Bollocks, "and ask Sedric for a treat." As the dog took Marg at her word, she turned to Breen, nudged back the brim of the gardening hat. "Aren't he and Marco in there, as deep into baking apple pies you'd think they were after solving all the mysteries of the worlds."

"And you escaped to the garden."

"I did indeed. Why don't the two of us walk over and shut our-selves in the workshop for an hour or so?"

"I was hoping we could. I know I'm a little later than usual."

"How is our Morena?"

"The wedding's on."

"Now, there's happy news." Marg gave Breen's hand a squeeze as they walked to the stream and the little bridge over it. "She needed you to ease her mind on it, and so I said to Finola, who's been fretting over it. It's time for the happy and the hopeful. We mourn and honor our losses, every one, but if we don't turn to the happy and hopeful, we diminish their sacrifice, don't we?"

"Hope builds strength, and the promise Morena and Harken will make to each other, well, it's a promise to all, really. We go on."

"How much you've grown, *mo stór*, since you first came back to my door."

Breen looked at the workshop, snugged in the trees, banked by rivers of flowers.

"Show me more, Nan."

"You've outreached me in so many ways."

"But not all, not enough. Show me more."

With a nod, Marg held up a hand so the workshop door opened. "So I will."

They spent an hour in the workshop, and nearly that in the woods.

"You are the air, and the air is you. It holds you as you hold it. The breeze, the breath, the life it brings."

Marg crossed her hands over her heart as Breen stood inches over the ground, eyes closed, her own hands cupped as if to hold the air. "The earth releases you and waits for your return. Trust the air to hold you as the earth does."

She felt—not weightless. She felt her body, her skin, heard the beat of her heart. She felt quiet, quiet in her mind, and as if the air be-neath, above, around her invited her in.

And she held it, not just in her hands or her mind but in the whole of her.

"Holy shit!"

Marco's exclamation shattered the moment. Breen dropped back down with a thud, had to throw out her arms to keep her balance.

"Sorry, wow. Did I do that? Sorry." Marco stood, gaping still with a cloth-wrapped pie plate hugged against him, and Sedric smiling beside him.

"Girl, you were floating, like Doctor Strange."

"Levitation. If I can levitate an object, I can levitate myself. Apparently," she said, looking back at Marg. "I lost my focus and control."

"You did well, and that's more than enough."

"How'd it feel?" Marco demanded. "To float around like that?"

"Like I was part of something. No, of everything. And now? It feels like I had a couple shots of really good tequila. Apple pie. I can smell it, but more. It's like I can taste it. Everything's so sharp, so clear. The cat's in your eyes," she said to Sedric. "Why couldn't I see that before? He's in your eyes."

"We're one."

"Let it go now. Release the air as the earth released you. It's enough for this first time."

Breen nodded at Marg, then closed her eyes again, spread her hands, and let go.

"Maybe one shot of tequila now."

"A walk will clear the rest. Keegan will be waiting."

"Right, and the humiliation waiting with him will bring me back to earth. Thank you, Nan. Sedric, I wish we had more time to spend."

"We'll have more, and we all used that time well today." His eyes met Marg's over Breen's shoulder when Breen kissed his cheek.

"We'll be back tomorrow."

As they walked away with the dog in the lead, Sedric moved to Marg, put an arm around her. "You gave her a gift."

"No, she is the gift. I was prepared to help her, just give her a taste, but she didn't need me. Or needed me only as a guide, or a tether. She'll guide herself before it's done, and nothing and no one will tether her."

"But she'll still need you. Come, these young ones wear us out. Let's sit down by the fire with a whiskey."

She slid an arm around him in turn. "Aye, that's just the thing."

Marco peppered Breen with questions on the walk to the farm. How did she do it, how did it feel, could she do it again?

She didn't mind. She no longer rode on the air, but she definitely rode on the afterglow of power realized.

"I don't want to try it without Nan right there," she explained. "I'm not sure how well I'd control it on my own."

"Whoa, you mean you could just float off or something?"

"Well, now that you've put that in my head, maybe. Basically, I want more practice. On everything. Except all this," she said when she spotted Keegan setting up targets in the training field by the farm.

"You're getting better at the archery thing. I still suck at it."

"You're right. You suck at it more than I do. Look, there's Aisling and the boys."

"That girl doesn't have a baby bump. She's got a baby mountain."

"I'd advise against pointing that out."

"I look stupid to you?"

Bollocks ran ahead, leaping over the stone wall, then dancing circles around the big wolfhound before rolling into a tumbling wrestle with the little boys.

All Breen heard was joy as Aisling, one hand on the baby mountain, slowly walked toward them.

"*Fáilte! Míle fáilte!*" She embraced them both.

A little pale, Breen noted, and that was fatigue. But even the pallor had a glow, and that came from the light growing inside her.

"You look wonderful."

"Ah now, I'm big as two cows if one swallowed the other. And all the while, the one inside is hell-bent on kicking its way out again."

"You're shining," Marco told her, and lit up her smile.

"Nearing the time I'll hold this one in my arms instead of my womb, and that's a happy thought. And with it, you made my brother happy, Breen."

When Breen looked over to where Keegan set up for archery, Aisling shook her head. "Not that one. Harken. He's been singing at his work since Morena came back from talking with you. So we'll have a wedding and a birth all but on top of each other the way I'm seeing it. And both here at the farm."

"The wedding's here?"

"So she said, after going back and forth on that one. No doubt her nan's cottage is a thing of beauty, but we've more room here. And this will be their home, where they'll live their life together. So here it will be.

"And here's the singing groom now."

Breen heard him first, the voice she'd once heard in a dream, before Harken walked out of the barn. He sang in Talamhish, but she didn't need to know the words to translate the happiness.

As he saw them, changed directions to come their way, it struck Breen again how alike and yet how different the brothers were.

The same unruly dark hair, but a farmer's cap for Harken rather than a warrior's braid. A strong, leanly muscled body for both, but work gloves in Harken's pocket instead of a sword at his side.

Handsome faces both, of sharp angles and long planes, but Keegan's was often shadowed by a day or two's worth of beard where Harken went smooth shaven.

He walked straight to Breen, and to her laughing surprise, kissed her warmly on the mouth.

"I can now attest Morena's a very lucky woman."

"Ah, she's all that. I love my sisters," he continued. "This one here, of course. And Maura and Noreen, who are sisters to me, and you as you're a sister to Morena. But today, Breen Siobhan Kelly, you're my favorite sister of all."

Turning, he put an arm around her as Keegan walked their way. "She's my great favorite today, *mo dheartháir,* so mind you're not too hard on her or you'll deal with me."

"I'll risk it."

"As I've enough trouble keeping my two boys from bashing each other, I'm taking them in before they see their uncles acting the maggot. We're grateful for the peat, Harken. Mahon's busy stacking it behind the cottage. I'll save you a plate if you want it, and one for Morena as well, as I'm going to feed my hooligans soon."

"Thanks for that, but we're fine."

"Go, get off your feet," Keegan ordered her. "You're big as Harken's prize cow."

The fist she planted in his belly only made him grin.

"Come see me when you've the time," she said to Breen, and smiled sweetly at Marco. "And you of course. We'll take Bollocks to play with the boys for a bit, as he's always welcome. But not you," she added, and this time drilled a finger in Keegan's belly.

Calling to the boys, she walked off.

Keegan shouted after her, "If men had to go about the making of more of us, there'd be the fewer."

That made her laugh and send him a sparkling look back.

"Nice save," Marco observed.

"Well, she'll get off her feet, won't she? Come, get your bow. Harken'll work with Marco."

"Why don't you and Morena come over to the cottage and have dinner with us? And apple pie?"

Now Keegan sent a look over his shoulder at Marco. "That's bribery, brother."

"I wish I'd thought of it," Breen muttered, and picked up the bow.

CHAPTER FOUR

She slipped into routine like a pair of warm slippers. It wouldn't last, she knew that, but for now no dreams haunted her sleep, no threat lurked around every corner.

They'd come back. It would all come back. So she hugged the routine and all the bright spots close.

Could a spot shine brighter than helping her friend pick her wedding dress?

"I've three," Morena began. "My mother sent them by dragonback, because she wouldn't be denied. And the truth is, doesn't trust me not to wear whatever I can find in my own wardrobe. Which I wouldn't because I know very well it matters, and wouldn't I want to look a treat on such a day?"

"You're her only daughter," Breen pointed out. "I'm surprised she didn't send a dozen."

"Left to herself it would've been that, or one only, with her sure I'd be glad not to fuss with the matter myself."

"Take this"—Marco offered her a flute of champagne—"and get yourself into one. Need help?"

"No, I want you to see it all at once. And give me nothing but truth." She took a sip, a breath, then a second sip. "All right then, we're off."

She started toward the downstairs bedroom, where she'd put the choices. "Are you sure Keegan and Brian aren't coming back soon?"

"Keegan said near to midnight if at all," Breen called out. "It's just us."

"Is this fun or what?" Marco handed Breen a flute.

"The best."

And she wondered should the day ever come, what her own mother would do about a wedding. Would she even come? And would she want her mother there?

She didn't have an answer to either question.

"All right then, here comes the first. Only truth now."

She stepped out and made Breen sigh.

The gown was white, like fresh snow, with a full skirt falling in soft layers and a slim, snug bodice that sparkled like diamonds in the sun.

"It's stunning. You're stunning."

"Give it a twirl, girl." Marco circled his finger.

The bodice's sheer back dipped into a V, and the skirt simply floated, gossamer clouds.

"Your mom knows her wedding dresses. How do you feel in it?" Marco asked her.

"Well, you'd have to feel beautiful, wouldn't you then, unless you're a gobshite. So I do, feel beautiful, but like someone else."

Breen glanced at Marco, and both nodded.

"It's more the Capital than the valley," Breen said. "It's gorgeous, and you look gorgeous in it."

"The dress glows, girl, but you don't glow wearing it. It's not saying it's mine to you."

"So I can say no, and not be an ungrateful eejit? Breen?"

"Absolutely. I have to say it's one of the most beautiful wedding dresses I've ever seen, but . . . it's not your wedding dress."

"Thank the gods, as I swear I don't think Harken would know me in it."

"Let's see number two." Marco gestured her away. As she hurried back, Marco lifted his flute at Breen. She tapped hers against it.

"What if they're all wrong?" Breen said quietly.

"Then we get real busy finding one that's right."

"There's only a couple weeks now."

"Sweetie pie, in a world full of faeries and witches and all that, I think we can come up with the right dress. Like you do with Halloween costumes."

"But those were just illusions. This needs to be real."

"So does yours. You're standing up for her."

"I can't worry about mine until she has hers."

"All right now," Morena called out. "Here's the next."

Morena stepped out in soft, creamy velvet. The straight simple lines said regal.

Breen sighed again. "You look like a queen. A faerie queen. The way it's belted, sparkling there and at the hem, and the neckline shows off your shoulders."

"Got elegance all over it," Marco agreed.

"But?"

"It's not your dress," they said together.

"It's maddening." Morena walked over, poured more champagne in her flute. "If we could just say I'll have you and you'll have me and have a good party. Well, I said truth, so we'll try the last."

She went off again.

"Okay, we need a plan if the last one doesn't work." Breen paced. "I can talk to Nan about it, getting the right dressmaker, and getting a better idea what Morena really wants, because we haven't heard that out of her yet. We'll have to move fast, Marco, but we can do it."

"People are always getting married in Ireland, right? We can check out some bridal shops."

"That's a thought. That's a good thought. A day trip into Galway City maybe. There's got to be—"

"Here's the last she sent."

Breen turned. And covered the gasp with her hand.

"Oh" was all she could manage. "Oh."

It floated around her, pale, pale violet threaded with silver, skimming just above her ankles, a cloud of silk.

Marco knuckled at his eyes, then gave her the twirl signal.

As she turned, the skirt billowed and fell. Silver straps crossed her bare back where a bow sat at her waist with its long ribbons trailing.

"Cancel that day trip." Marco beamed at her. "That's your dress."

"You're perfect." Breen swiped at tears. "You're absolutely perfect. It's like your wings. It's yours. It's you. It's perfect."

"Are you sure? Because, oh, I love it so much. I didn't want to say because I know it's not so magnificent as the first, or elegant as the second. But I feel like a bride in it. I feel like me. I feel like Morena Mac an Ghaill being a bride."

"Because it's your wedding dress." Sighing, Breen swiped at more tears.

"Boots the same color," Marco decreed. "With some sparkle on them."

"Oh, aye! Oh, won't I look a picture? Marco, I need you to do my hair, please, say you will. I want a head full of braids, and just a wreath of flowers over it. Say you will."

"You—you want me to do your hair? On your wedding day! I have to sit down." He actually staggered. "I need more champagne but I have to sit down."

"That means he will?"

"It means he will," Breen confirmed. "More champagne!"

"I have to take this off before I spill something on it. Then I'll drink you both under the table."

December blew its cold breath so the trees shivered and the bay chopped. It spread a thin lacing of frost that crunched under boot-steps and had hooves ringing like bells on the hardened roads.

In Fey Cottage, Christmas ruled. Brian brought Marco a tree from the high country, and it stood sparkling with lights, dripping with ornaments. Breen bartered with Aisling and hung the four brightly woven stockings from the mantel.

When Keegan pointed out Christmas stockings were for the littles, Breen stated, firmly, everyone was a little at Christmas.

The air smelled of pine and Marco's relentless baking.

In Talamh, she found much the same: the twinkle of lights, the ladened trees, the hopefully hung stockings. And more with the faerie tradition of little silver bells strung on branches and posts, the Elfin addition of bundling nuts and berries as feasts and treats for wildlife.

After a time of sorrow, joy spread. Breen worked through it, writing, training, practicing magicks. She worked on gifts, to buy, to barter for in Talamh, to make in Marg's workshop.

So when the dreams came back, they came as a jolt, a strike of dark against the light.

She saw Yseult in a workshop of her own. Her dark red hair held streaks of gray, and she moved slowly, stiffly. Even in sleep, Breen felt a surge of satisfaction.

She had done that.

And even in sleep, she felt the stings of black magicks, heard the hiss of the two-headed sleep snake as the witch milked the viper, as the poison dripped, thick and gray as a slug, into a bowl.

Done, she placed the snake in a basket with a pair of quivering mice. It struck and struck while the mice screamed. Then it devoured.

"Rest now, my darling."

She crossed the room, one alight with a hundred candles, to cages stacked together. Breen saw young deer, rabbits, goats, lambs, and, to her horror, a child. A human child, she realized as Yseult pulled the little boy, no more than three, out.

He didn't cry or fight, but simply stared with blank eyes. Bespelled, she realized, her heart breaking. Then her heart stopping as Yseult picked up an athame.

She drew it across the boy's palm, a deep gash where scars from other cuts marred the young skin. The blood spilled into the bowl. Then she turned the child so his tears followed it.

As she might have with a jar of herbs, Yseult put the child back in the cage.

She chose a bird next, sliced it open to take out the heart. She added it to the bowl.

She gathered other ingredients: belladonna, black crystals, wolfsbane, three small teeth, sharp as razors.

When she lifted her arms, Breen heard her gasp in pain. She had to bend over, sheet pale, to catch her breath.

Her eyes went black as onyx as she straightened again.

"You'll pay and pay and pay, mongrel bitch."

Face stony now, she lifted her arms again.

"Gods of the dark and damned, hear me! Grant me, servant of Odran, your strength. Imbue me with your power, black and terrible.

This brew I make, her will to take. Daughter of the son of the god unholy I strike with the potion I make this night.

"Blood and tears from a human child, heart of a sparrow trapped in the wild, teeth from a demon pup to snap and bite, dark crystals ground to dim her light. Herbs to choke away her breath and take her to the edge of death. Milk from the snake with twin heads brings sleep, but with this spell the pain runs deep.

"Now fire burn, now smoke rise. Bubble and boil and swirl and stir. And with this turn, all light dies. This will be the end of her."

As she stood in the smoke that clouded the room, the gray in her hair began to fade. And the pain that had rippled over her face turned to power.

"For Odran's glory and in Odran's name this spell is done, and be damned to the daughter of the son. With her end we ride to victory. As we will, so mote it be."

Breathless now as the smoke thinned, Yseult braced a hand on her worktable. But in her eyes lived a terrible kind of joy.

"What a terrible stench!"

She whirled at the voice, threw up a hand. "Stay back, stay clear of the smoke."

Shana stood in a doorway, sleek and glowing in a gold gown. Her silvery blond hair fell in intricate curls, scooped back to highlight the fat rubies at her ears.

"I go where I please, witch. Mind your tone with me, or Odran will punish you. Again. You're weak, and barely any use."

Smiling, Shana toyed with one of her curls. "He'll torture you if I ask him to. You failed him. I did not."

She took another step in, and Yseult pushed at the air to hold her back. When fury erupted, Shana hissed like the snake.

"You dare."

"I dare to protect the child in you. Odran's child. The smoke is toxic, and while it may do you no harm, it may harm the child. He shares blood with Breen O'Ceallaigh."

Now Yseult smiled. "If you bring harm to the child, Odran will be displeased with you."

Shana shrugged but stepped back. "We can always make another. I've proven fertile, which is more than you."

"You silly creature. I gave him three, three he drained for power as he will what's in you. And with their power, and with their blood, he moved through the portal to make the child with Mairghread, and again through to take the Daughter. I have cleared the path for him, year by year."

"Only to fail him, year by year." Shana merely waved a hand, glittering with rings. "I will not, and will rule beside him after he turns Talamh to ash. But for now, I have a task for you. I don't wish to look fat and waddle about while Odran's son grows in me. You'll do a spell so I won't."

"It will be illusion only. Any more could harm the child."

"Then do that!" Shana snapped. "And be quick about it."

"Tomorrow then. Come to me tomorrow."

"Come to me. I'm Odran's consort. You're only his witch."

"As you wish."

The pleasant smile faded as Shana glided away. "I can find Odran a dozen of you, ungrateful child. I swear, the babe's first breath will be your last."

Once again, the room filled with smoke. And Breen woke.

In the firelight, Keegan sat beside her in bed. Bollocks, front paws on the bed, watched her.

"Tell me."

"Give me a minute."

"You weren't in distress or I'd have tried to wake you, or join you. It was a watching dream."

"Yeah, but I still need a minute. I know I can't forget how dark, how evil, how terrible, but maybe I did for a little while."

"Here." He held out his hand. An instant later he held a glass of water. "Drink some, take your minute."

"Thanks." She sat up, took the water. When she shivered, Keegan waved a hand toward the fire to boost it.

"I saw Yseult in what must be her workshop. She's not fully recovered, and I—I felt good about that. A year ago, I wouldn't have been capable of feeling good about someone—anyone—suffering. But I did."

"A year ago, you didn't know of such as Yseult."

"True." And the truth wiped away any small sense of guilt. "She's almost worse than Odran. She was born in the light, trained in the light, and made the deliberate choice to embrace, well, the dark. She was making a potion—a poison. For me."

"You're meaning for you, specifically?"

"Yes." She drank more water. "Very specifically. A year ago, no one plotted to kill me—or I sure as hell didn't know about it. So there's that, too."

"Did you see all she used to make it?"

"I think so. It was venom from one of those horrible snakes."

"Sleep snakes?"

"Yes. And, God, Keegan, she has cages. Young animals, babies really. And a child. A human child." She began to cry then, silent tears as she spoke. "He was two or three, and catatonic. She cut him, and I could see scars from where she'd done it before. His blood with the venom, then his tears. A sparrow, very young. She cut it open, took its heart."

After swiping away tears with the back of her hand, she listed the rest.

"What words did she use? Did you hear them?"

"I heard everything. It was like watching a play onstage, and I was front row center."

He rolled out of bed to get one of her notepads and a pen.

"You'll write it down, all the words, as you remember them."

"Why? It was black magick, and we'd never—"

"Don't be an eejit. For a blocking spell. We know what she's done, and we counter it."

"Oh, like an antidote."

"No, antidotes come after. We . . ." Filling the air with impatience, he searched for the word. "Immunity. Do you see? We conjure immunity to this poison."

"Okay, that's brilliant. And comforting." She began to write. "She didn't see me or sense me. I know that. Part of it may be she hasn't recovered, not all the way. She got stronger during the spell, but that faded after. She's in pain, and so angry and bitter. It's not just for Odran now. She wants to pay me back."

"You'll disappoint her there."

Breen glanced up and over, then smiled. "That's the plan. And it's not just me she . . ." She stopped and turned to him now. "Shana came in, right after Yseult finished the poison. Keegan, Shana's pregnant with Odran's child."

"I'm sorry for it."

"But not surprised," Breen realized. "Why aren't you?"

"Did you think Odran had Yseult bring Shana to him so she could scrub floors or stir up stews?"

"No, but I thought he took her in for her knowledge. Her father had been on the council, she slept with you. She knew—knows—things."

"Aye, he'd want all that, of course. Add she's young, beautiful, and surely ripe for the planting. She'll birth a demigod for him in time."

"And you know why. I don't have to tell you he drains his own children, babies, sacrifices them—murders them—for power. Yseult gave him three. You knew this."

"Not how many of Yseult's, but logically she'd have proven herself to him this way." Understanding sleep was done, he rose again to pull on pants. "I send spies to Odran's world from time to time, as your father did, as those who led before him did."

He shoved a hand through his hair before reaching for a shirt. "You think, why don't we find a way to save them, these innocents?"

"Babies, Keegan. There has to be a way. Beyond the fact he increases his power through them, weakens the portal seals with their blood, they're babies."

"The taoiseach before your father lost three warriors in a rescue such as this. Two, both wounded, brought three infants through the waterfall. They lived in our world less than an hour.

"He marks them at birth," Keegan told her, "so they can't survive the coming through. They die there, by his hand, or here by his mark. Still, Eian tried, in his day. We would counter the mark, unwind that curse before bringing a child through. He sent a witch to pose as a nursemaid, and as she began to unwind the curse, the babe died in her arms. She sits on the council, does Rowan, and still can't speak of that moment and her own sorrow."

It made her sick, in body and spirit, but she made herself get up. "He made a mistake with my father. He didn't mark his son, didn't see the need. And the longer he kept up the pretense of being husband and father, the better the chance he'd conceive another child with Nan—another vessel to drink."

"Aye, you see it clearly enough. He doesn't make the mistake again."

"Why didn't he mark me when he had me?"

Keegan tapped a finger on her temple. "Use your head, woman. You don't come from his seed."

"All right, bloodline isn't enough for this kind of infanticide. You can't save them, and I know that weighs on you."

"We think his death breaks the curse and removes the mark. But we can't know until we know."

"She didn't care. Shana." Breen picked up a band to tie back her hair. "I think, though Yseult gave up her babies willingly, she felt something. It cost her, if you know what I mean. She didn't hesitate to pay the price, but it cost her. Not Shana."

In the mirror, her eyes met Keegan's. "The pregnancy gives her status, and she's enjoying it. The child itself means nothing beyond that. She can, she said, always make another. Her concern was how she looks. She ordered Yseult to create an illusion so she doesn't look fat, as she put it."

"Well, that fits, snug as a round peg in a round hole."

"She bragged about killing Loren. I'm not telling you all this to slap at you for having a relationship with her before."

With a shake of his head, he laid a hand lightly, briefly, on Breen's shoulder.

"I cared for her. I won't deny the sex held the biggest part of that, but I cared for her, or what she showed me of her. I saw her flaws, and I thought clearly enough. There I was wrong, as they weren't so simple as flaws, but deep and wide breaks in her. I regret not seeing what should've been clear."

"I don't think it was clear, over and above how sex and beauty can cloud vision. Something snapped in her, so all those breaks inside, smoothed over by charm and beauty, killed who you'd cared for. If she'd convinced you to marry her—"

He let out a half laugh. "That, I can promise you, would never have happened. I cared, but only that."

Because it felt important, she turned to face him.

"She believed otherwise. I'm saying if she'd managed to pull in more power, she'd have abused it, and snapped. There was no way for you to win with her, Keegan."

He considered it as he strapped on his sword. "You've the right of it, and only prove women are a bloody mystery more than half the time." He stepped to her to cup her face and kiss her. "An early start to the day for both of us. I wonder if you'd use part of yours to cook up some breakfast, since I'm so poor at it."

"And men are bloody simple more than half the time."

"True enough. Give us food, sex, and a pint, and we're happy enough."

"If only that were true. But I can scramble you some eggs before I work out."

"I'd be grateful." He took the paper where she'd written the spell, tucked it in his pocket. "I'm thinking I'd be more grateful yet if you could see your way to making those pancakes like Marco does, with the blueberries in them."

She glanced up at him as they walked out of the bedroom. "You'd be pushing both our luck there, and trust me, you wouldn't be grateful at all unless you have a taste for doughy rubber."

"I'll take the eggs."

She made enough for Brian when he came down, and managed not to overcook the bacon before she took her coffee outside to watch Bollocks play in the bay under the fading stars.

The content of the dream left her unsettled, but the fact of it bolstered her. She'd watched, undetected, and had learned vital information. She could do the same again, prepare first, and watch, listen, learn.

Through Yseult, she decided. That was the weak link now.

Poison me, will you? Poison me so you can dump me at Odran's feet, helpless and beaten? Use the blood of a child to do it?

Weak, evil traitor to your kind, we'll see who pays who back.

As the night thinned, she heard the first notes of a lark. Her breath came in clouds as the frost broke under her feet. Even as she reached the door, Keegan and Brian came out.

"You made fast work of breakfast," she noted.

"It went down well."

"Since it was my turn," Brian said, "my thanks is doubled."

"Morena's family travels from the Capital today. My mother and Minga come with them."

"It'll be good to see them all."

Keegan looked toward the first break of dawn, nodded. "Aye. Keep the dog and Marco close today, until we've conjured the immunity."

"All right. I'll talk to Nan about it when I come over."

"I'm going to her now. No," he said before she could ask, "you've given us what's needed. Do what you do, then come. It may be Marg will want my mother's hand in it as well."

He bent down, kissed her. "Don't be late for training."

As they walked toward the woods, Bollocks, sending water everywhere, raced over to see them off.

"Guard her well today." Keegan gave him a brisk rub to dry him.

"I can stay," Brian said as they moved into the woods, "or send someone back."

"It'll only put her back up. She's not a foolish sort, so she'll be careful. But I'll be sending a falcon to my mother and asking her to come straightaway with a dragon rider. The sooner we counter this poison, the better."

"No one and nothing comes through the portals."

But Keegan only shook his head. "There are other portals in other worlds. If she means to find a way to get through, or send an assassin, she'll work the way. It may take time, but she'll work a way."

"But Breen said Yseult was weak."

"She did, and that the spell-casting made her stronger for that time. In her place, I'd use what I had in me to open a window. It takes power and strength to open a temporary portal, but I'd invest it there, and in one of the unguarded worlds. I'd send the poison with an assassin who could move from world to world to world."

"And still any assassin would have to get past our guards."

"He could try for her on this side. Marg has a strong protection spell around the cottage, but he could try. On ours? It's why a Were would be best. An owl coming through in the cloak of dark, a dog burrowing under the snow in the north.

"It's how I'd do it, or try."

When they reached the tree, Keegan swung onto a branch.

"Or the assassin's already in Talamh, and she only has to find the way to get the poison to him."

"Such as that living among us."

With Keegan, he stepped through and into Talamh.

"More than one of them in our world." Keegan looked out over the valley, the greens and golds waking under the soft dawn light. "And we'll make them sorry for it before we're done."

CHAPTER FIVE

Keegan went to Harken first, found him in the kitchen already in his outdoor gear as he poured a cup of tea that looked strong enough to toss Harken's prize cow half a league.

"Well now, in time for the morning milking."

"I'm not, sorry. I need to speak with Marg but wanted to see you about it first."

"There's trouble."

"There plans to be. Breen had a dream, a watching dream, of Yseult brewing up a potion and spell. She's not all healed as yet, Breen says."

"Dead would be better," Harken said, and drank some tea.

"On our father's honor, that day will come. Breen wrote it down, what she used in it, and the words she spoke."

He handed the paper to Harken, so Harken set aside his tea and read.

His face went hard, his eyes to blue ice.

"Like the evil witch in the storybooks, she likes to devil children."

"An archetype, isn't she then? And it may be her and her like are the base of the stories."

"It's dark magicks she weaves, black as they come."

"That I can see for myself, brother."

"You need a shield against it. One that goes in as well as around. Aisling—"

"I know it's superstition." Keegan cut him off. "But I don't want to take something so dark around her when she's so close to the birthing."

"No, superstition or not, you're right there. A potion and a protective spell, I'm thinking. For the inside and the out, and the words to power both. She's stronger than Yscult, is Breen, so Yseult crafted a spell wicked and deep to strike at her."

"Not to kill, but worse. A living death, one filled with pain, so Odran can drink her dry. The pain? That's Yseult's revenge."

"She'll have a plan to use it."

"Aye, and soon, I think, soon. What better time to strike than a time of joy? The solstice and Yule, a wedding, a birth."

He took the paper back. "Shana carries Odran's child."

The hard anger on Harken's face faded. "Ah, I'm sorry for it. Not for her, I can't find it in me. She tried to bespell you, hurt a friend. She tried to take Breen's life, and nearly did take the life of a young boy. She killed the man who loved her. The choices she made were hers."

"They were, and she'll pay a terrible price for them. For now, we deal with what we can. I'll send a falcon asking our mother to come on dragon-back to help make the shields."

"I'll do that. Amish is close. Morena's still sleeping, but he'll come to me and carry the message."

"Good. I'll go speak with Marg. I'll come back when I can."

When Keegan went out, Harken sat to write the message. Then he picked up his cooling tea to call the hawk before he got to the morning milking.

Keegan spent an hour huddled with Marg, then called Cróga and flew off to barter with the Trolls for specifics Marg wanted for the immunity.

When he got back, he found his mother sitting at Marg's kitchen table as the two of them discussed details.

"You made quick time."

"I did." Tarryn lifted her face for his greeting kiss. "And confess I'd nearly forgotten the thrill of a dragon flight. Did you get what Marg asked for?"

"I did, and they'd take nothing in trade."

With a surprised laugh, Tarryn sat back. "The Trolls refused a trade?"

"They did. Sul wouldn't have it. Nothing in trade for anything needed to keep the Daughter of the Fey safe."

"Breen made an impression." Marg smiled. "And how does Sul fare?"

"Very well, she says, and looks it. She already . . ." He held his hands in front of his stomach. "She asked when Breen has time if she'd visit her."

"So she will," Marg said. "And we'll want her for this."

"To help what's for her?"

"More power," Tarryn confirmed. "More light. Harken as well, and you. Two more of your choosing. Not Aisling."

"Not Aisling, no. And when this is done, the seven will go to the ruins where the spirits walk, trapped. It's time we released them, send them to the light or to the dark."

"Not the homecoming I'd have wished for you."

"But I'm home." She reached up to take his hand. "And with this done, we'll take all the joy."

"What time do you want the coven, and where?"

"We want this first done in the light, so an hour before sunset." Marg looked at Tarryn, got a nod. "And I know that's your training time with her, but it's the right time."

"She'll make it up."

"Sure and you'll see to that. Do you think by the bay, Tarryn, full open?"

"I do, aye, in the open, with the water element, the light, the earth beneath, the air around, and the fire we make. I'll go to Aisling now, see the children." After patting a hand on Marg's, Tarryn rose. "I'll be back to help you prepare. And don't worry, we'll see your girl safe."

"I know it, as I know you."

"Walk with me, Keegan, before you're off on all your duties."

He helped her on with her cloak, and since they were there, snagged a biscuit from the plate.

"A bright day," Tarryn said as they walked outside. "Cold and brisk and bright, just as it should be. I won't ask you how plans for the wedding go, as you'll know nothing of it."

"I know some things."

She hooked an arm through his. "Tell your ma."

"Harken's singing like a magpie all the day and half the night. And there's Morena, who's never given two thoughts on such things, worrying about boots and hair bobs and so on. They fill my ears with it when I'm around long enough. There'll be music, and Marco's a part of that. The food, and he's part of that as well."

"He's made himself part of the valley."

"He's a good man, Marco. And Morena's family?"

"This wedding is a gift from the gods, I swear. They grieve, but this joining lifts the heart. It lifts mine to know the happy life my boy will make with the woman he loves, one I love as well. As you do."

"She's been a sister to me all her life, so this just makes it official. I'm grateful you came so quick, Ma. Now I ask are you sure you want to take all of this on at once? The spirits have walked and moaned in that cursed place all this time."

"And may have walked among us, taking lives on Samhain if Breen hadn't gone to her father's grave that day, felt what she felt. We sealed it, aye, but that seal wasn't meant to last much longer than this. I planned for the solstice, and now a wedding instead. So we do it, and be done with it. Unless you wish it otherwise, Taoiseach."

"No. It's best done. You've the right of it. I need to leave you." He kissed both her cheeks, found it not quite enough, so gathered her in for a hug. "I'll choose two more before I do what else needs doing."

He called Cróga, as he planned to check on the Far West, and flew off. Tarryn walked on, then stopped, hands on hips, smile huge when she saw her oldest grandson at a trot on his birthday horse around the paddock.

A good seat, he had, she thought, a fine seat indeed. And there her girl watching, a hand on the child that waited, the other on the shoulder of the child beside her.

In the saddle, Finian spotted her and waved one hand wildly. "Nan, Nan, Nan! Watch me, Nan."

Oh, I am, she thought.

Kavan let out a hoot, pulled away from Aisling. He started on a run, then lifted on his little wings.

So soon, she thought as she lifted a hand to cover her mouth. They grow so soon.

She held out her arms so he could fly into them.

Aisling stood, tears streaming. "It's his first time flying, truly flying. Oh, Ma, his first time."

"But not your last." Tarryn rained kisses over his face as she carried him toward the paddock. "Not your last, no, nor your brother's last happy trot. It's only the beginning for you, my sweet boys. And I swear by all the gods, we'll preserve the future for you."

When Breen stepped into Talamh with Marco and Bollocks, she saw the arrival. The horses and dragons, the faeries and riders from the Capital. She thought of the first time she'd seen them come and her nerves at meeting Keegan's mother and all the rest.

So different now, now that she recognized the faces.

She watched Tarryn hold the horse's bridle as Minga dismounted, and Flynn lift his son's widow and her infant from a dragon's back.

"Hey, there's Hugh." Marco lifted a hand in salute. "Wonder how his wife's doing up north."

"Go ahead and ask."

"I'll just wait until some of those big-ass dragons move on."

"Fraidy-cat."

"Meow."

Laughing, she left him to climb over the wall and greet Sinead.

"Welcome to the valley," Breen said, and held her close.

"You've been missed, even in such a short time. And look at this one." Sinead hugged Morena to her side. "Already glowing like the bride she's about to be."

"Ma."

"Well now, you are, aren't you? And here's the lucky groom." Sinead shot up both arms to take Harken in.

"As lucky a man as ever born," he agreed. "And welcome to you, Mother. I'm thinking Noreen will be a bit tired after the journey. We've tea waiting, and all your rooms ready, if you'd want to take her and the babe inside, settle them up."

"You've a kind heart and good sense. I'll do just that. The girl's a treasure to me."

Because her eyes filled with the words, Harken kissed her again. "And to us all, as you are."

"I'll go with you," Breen began.

"Actually, you're needed elsewhere. But I'm hoping we can ask Marco . . ." Looking over, Harken signaled to him, got a sheepish smile, a shrug. "Still wary of the dragons, is he? I'll go to him then. Morena, you'll help get the family settled, won't you?"

"I will, of course. We're after having a feast tonight," she continued as she nudged Sinead along. "If Marco's willing."

Flynn came over to embrace Breen, with Seamus, Maura, the children with him. As she greeted them all, she noted Harken in what looked like deep consult with Marco.

And despite the dragons, Marco climbed over the low stone wall.

"We're imposing on Marco to make one of his far-famed feasts." Harken gave Marco a friendly punch on the shoulder. "Finola's on her way to help, and you'll have Sinead poking into it."

"Cooking's never an imposition for Marco." But there was something. "What's going on?"

"You're needed elsewhere. Ah, and here's my mother now."

"A welcome sight you are, Breen Siobhan, and you, Marco. I'm told we can look forward to your kitchen brilliance tonight."

Because she always dazzled him, Marco took her hand, kissed it. "You're so beautiful."

"Ah, sure I wish you'd come live at the castle so you could say the same to me every day. You and I will take some time later to spill the tea, but for now I'm needed elsewhere."

"That's really going around," Breen murmured.

"So it is. Come now." She gave Breen a pat on the back before giving the excited Bollocks a pet. "We'd best be on our way."

"I'd really like to know what's going on."

"It's time for magicks," Tarryn told her as dragons took to the sky with a sweep of wings. "Light and bright. Your dream, darling girl. Marg and I have worked it out, all we need to counter Yseult."

Breen glanced back to see Marco still standing, watching her go.

"You didn't want Marco to go with me."

"He'd be welcome, of course, as he is welcome anywhere in Talamh. But he's of better use at the farm, keeping Sinead and the family occupied."

"Morena knows," Harken added. "But we felt bringing worry to the family solves nothing. Let them have a happy time without the worry for now."

"Yes, all right, yes. And Noreen did look tired. What do you need me to do?"

"We'll be seven," Tarryn told her, and explained.

As they approached the turn to Marg's cottage, Breen stopped. "You want to do both, one after the other? The immunity or shield or whatever it is for me, and the release and consecration at the old Pious Prayer House?"

Tarryn lifted an eyebrow—imperiously. "Do you think we can't manage both?"

"It's just—both major castings. The one for me could wait. I'm careful, and I beat her once already, so—"

"No, and I speak to you as the mother of the taoiseach, and as his hand. You were given the watching dream as a warning, and the warning must be heeded without delay. You risk all by accepting your duty and destiny, and we will protect you as much as we are able.

"I ask to do the second because we'll be gathered, we'll have called on the powers and hold them and only be stronger for it. I ask because what Yseult planned for Samhain she may push again at the solstice. My son will have his wedding, my daughter will have her child, and no dark hag will interfere. I won't have it."

Harken simply kissed the top of his mother's head. "Best fall in line, *deirfiúr*. When she says she won't have it, there's the end of it."

Breen fell in line.

With the sun still shining, she walked from the cottage to the bay. She understood the spell now, and her part in it. And she trusted the coven Tarryn and Keegan had chosen to hold strong.

She spotted the children she thought of as the Gang of Six playing their game with a red ball and sticks in a fallow field and a doe with her shaggy-coated fawn slipping into the trees. On the ledge of the mountain above, Trolls trooped home after a day of mining.

At a near cottage, crystals and bells glimmered on trees in anticipation of Yule.

Ordinary things, she thought, on a brisk December afternoon.

But what they would do on the beach near the lap of the bay wouldn't be ordinary.

With the breeze streaming through her hair, Marg stepped up beside Breen and waited.

"This is for you," Tarryn told Marg, and Keegan nodded.

"This is for you."

With a nod of her own, Marg took another step forward.

"I thank you for lending your power and your faith, bringing your light here to strike against the dark. This Daughter of the Fey is precious to all, but more to me as the daughter of my son. I'm grateful to you, all who stand here."

Rowan from the Capital stepped forward. "We are seven, and we are one in this."

Each in turn did and said the same. And each set the candle they held on the shale beach to form a circle.

They cast the circle, calling on the Guardians of the East, West, North, and South. As they ringed inside it, the candles flamed on. As they flamed on, Breen felt the power in her, around her, begin to beat.

Keegan laid a stone in the center. "And here the stone, brought from the deep caves and sacred to the Troll tribe. An offering of strength."

Tarryn set a cauldron of hammered copper on the stone.

"And here the cauldron forged by their tribe for use in high ritual. An offering of purpose."

Harken placed three white crystals and a handful of faerie dust on the stone beside the cauldron. "And here the dust and crystals, given by the Sidhe, offerings of light."

"And here a bough of pine and acorns three from the Quiet Wood and the Elfin tribe. An offering of life." Rowan placed them.

"And here the feathers and the fur, given by the Were tribe. An offering of spirit."

"And here three shells, and the pearls from within them, precious to the tribe of Mer." Tarryn placed them. "An offering of faith."

Once again, Keegan stepped forward, and placed a red stone. "And here a dragon's heart, placed here by my hand as rider. An offering of loyalty."

"And here," the seven said together, "we, of the Wise, offer the power, sacred and precious, given us to bind all together. An offer of unity."

As Breen stepped forward, it pulsed on her skin, pulsed under it, what rose within the circle.

"I am the Daughter of the Fey, Daughter of man, Daughter of gods. I am of Talamh and the bridge to the world beyond it. I am a child and a servant of the light. Under the light, I ask for protection against the dark magicks conjured against me by one who corrupts the craft and gift. I ask not for my own life but for all, that I may fight back against the dark and bring peace to the worlds. If this is my place, my purpose, my destiny, I join, one of seven, seven into one, to cast this spell."

As she spoke, the stone beneath the cauldron turned to flame.

The wind rose, whirling around her, but the flame stone and the candles burned bright.

"Gods of the light," Marg called out, "witness our faith, one of seven, seven in one, so what we do here cannot be undone."

"Not by magicks born in the dark." Without hesitation, Tarryn reached into the flame to take an offering from the stone and lift it into the cauldron.

"Not by any who bear Odran's mark." Keegan did the same.

And each in turn spoke the words and reached into the fire.

It ran so hot and strong through her that Breen felt she became the flame as she stretched her hands into it.

Yet she felt no burn, only the searing power.

"Come earth, come air, come fire, come water, to protect and shield your humble daughter. Stir and boil to conjure a shield against the poison dreams revealed. At this hour and in this place, I pledge to you all my faith. We stand for the light; against the dark we fight. One of seven and seven as one, tribe by tribe until it's done.

"All of Talamh call to thee. As you will, so mote it be."

Thunder clapped once. The flames rushed up her arms, engulfed her, gold, red, blue. She felt their heat like an embrace, so strong it took her breath.

A thousand voices sang in her ears.

Then they died away, and the stone was a stone. And still the power of it beat inside her.

Keegan took a cup, and lifting the cauldron, poured liquid—eerily green like the lake, like the river by the waterfall—into it.

"Drink, Daughter. This is also faith."

She took the cup, and with her eyes on his, drank.

"So the gods will," Marg said. "And so the spell is done, and will not be undone."

"So close the circle, and bring the power arisen here with us to the next." Tarryn touched a hand to Breen's shoulder. "You did more than well."

"It felt—indescribable." Not like being one of seven, but one of all, of everything. "The sun's set."

"It took a bit of time."

"It didn't seem like it." She pushed a hand at her hair and discovered it had flown out of its band.

"I like it free." Keegan took her hand. "Come, call your dragon. We ride to finish the work. How did it taste? The potion."

"Like power. That's not really a taste, but—"

"It answers well enough."

The power rode with her as she flew from the shore of the bay to the ruins. They stood, gray and worn and eerily beautiful in their way under the light of the half-moons. The mirror moons sailed a sky where stars had awakened and shone white and hard over the headstones, the flowers, the high grasses of the graveyard, over the stone dance high on the hill, the spear of the round tower.

And the place where the Pious, turned dark with their fanaticism, tortured, tormented, and sacrificed the Fey.

Breen stood on the rise facing the stones she and Tarryn had sealed, with magicks, with their blood, and, to make the three, with blood from Bollocks's paw.

Beside her, Bollocks let out a low, warning growl. She laid a hand on his head to soothe him, but he quivered under it.

"A holy place once," Tarryn said. "Long, long ago. A place of prayer and good works, of intellect and compassion, all turned and turned and turned to bigotry and brutality in the name of false faith and false gods."

"And in the name of false faith and a dark god, black magicks plied to give the blood-soaked spirits form, once more to destroy the light. Never again," Marg continued, "said the Fey long, long ago. Never again, say the seven this night."

"It will be holy again." Keegan stood, a hand on the hilt of his sword. "We will not raze the stones here, but cleanse them, cleanse the ground beneath them, the very air around them, and leave this place to stand, as it was written, as a reminder of the corruption in the dark. So say the seven this night."

"We come to release the spirits sealed within." Harken spoke as he stood, with Keegan, flanking their mother. "To send them into the light or into the dark, as the lives they led deem. So say the seven this night."

"And with this pure heart, whose blood joined with mine and the mother of the taoiseach to make the seal as witness to this act, we come to break that seal. So say the seven this night."

Breen gave Bollocks one last stroke, then told him to sit, to stay as she, with the others, cast the circle.

She heard them, the moans and cries of the tormented, the howls and snarls of the torturers. And all of them, all within, pressed and pounded and pushed at the seal.

On the rise, within the circle, the seven joined hands, joined voices, joined power.

It shook inside her as she spoke the words.

"We come this night to bring the light, and here it spreads to reach the dead. Dark spirits trapped within, reap the dark you've chosen. Your sins are great, now meet your fate.

"Innocent souls, your suffering ends, and to the light the seven sends all tortured and slain by cruelty. This night, with the light, ends your misery."

And the light did spread, sweeping down the rise, covering the ground, gliding up the stones so it shined as bright as noon.

It breathed, and it sang, and on the high hill, the stone dance sang with it.

With the wind snapping at her cloak, Marg lifted her voice, strong and clear.

"What magicks shut, now magicks open. Let the seal be broken. Release all souls as we desire, into the light or into the fire."

When the ancient doors burst open, when the ground shook and cries ripped the air, Keegan unsheathed his sword.

"I am taoiseach, and this is Judgment. Come forth to take your peace or punishment." Flames engulfed Cosantoir, red as blood as he sliced it down toward the stones. "From this world you are set free. As we will, so mote it be."

They poured from the ruins, both beautiful and terrible. Forms only, white and dark. The white soared up, and Breen felt their desperate relief, even joy as they streaked from the ruins to the stone dance. The dark rushed or crawled, and unleashed shrieking cries, no longer human, as they turned to fire, then to ash, then to nothing at all.

The stone circle sang a welcoming on the high hill, and below the rise, fire roared. And like a statue, Keegan stood, the sword of the taoiseach lifted and flaming.

Then silence fell like thunder.

"So it is done," Keegan said, and sheathed his sword.

The cleansing and sanctifying rituals took time, but after the wild beat of power, Breen found the work both gentle and kind.

For the first time she walked inside the ruins, inside the great stone walls with its pillars and tombs, its winding stairs and altars.

"I can still feel them."

"Echoes only," Keegan told her. "Memories, and nothing more. What walked here, both the light and the dark, is gone, but the stones stand and will. We don't forget."

"I saw . . . Some of the spirits that went to the dance, they were so small, Keegan. Only children. And I thought, I thought I saw the form of a woman holding an infant. What drives anyone to torture and kill children?"

"Power drives all," he said simply. "For good or ill. They rest now because we had the power. Don't forget that."

How could she when that power had been a live thing inside her?

"I'm going to take a moment. My father."

When she walked out, she realized she could smell the grass again, the flowers, and air apple crisp. With Bollocks by her side, she stood at her father's grave.

"Did you believe I'd come here one day, that I'd help do this? I wish I knew. But you were there to welcome those we released. I felt it, and feeling it, felt close to you."

She watched Marg walk through the grass, around headstones, and waited for her.

"Did you feel him, Nan?"

"I did, aye, I did. And I felt his pride in you, *mo stór*, as I felt my own."

"I've never been part of something so far-reaching. There was such goodness here tonight, such love and care. I know we have to fight with swords and arrows—I know it takes violence—but it's that goodness that's going to win in the end. I absolutely believe that now. It sounds naïve."

"No. It's truth. Go now, have the meal Marco made, as I'm sure it's brilliant."

"Aren't you coming?"

"I'm for my own cottage, for Sedric, who waits for me, and a whiskey by the fire. I want my man tonight, the comfort of him, and the goodness."

"Then I'll see you both tomorrow."

"Blessed be, Breen Siobhan."

"Blessed be, Nan," she said as Marg's dragon glided down to the road.

Then she turned and watched Keegan, his leather duster billowing, stride toward her.

She wasn't sure if calling him her man was accurate, but she wanted him tonight. For the comfort and the goodness.

CHAPTER SIX

The morning of the solstice dawned cool and bright. In Fey Cottage, an early-rising Marco stayed busy in the kitchen creating what he called his Wedding Day Brunch Extravaganza.

Breen opted to stay out of his way, but instead of her usual routine went on a cleaning binge.

They'd host the bride, her mother, grandmother, sisters-in-law, mother-in-law, Marg, and Minga for the brunch, for hairstyling, dressing, wine drinking, and anything else that fit into the day.

She wanted the house to shine, in and out, and wanted an abundance of flowers, inside and out. They'd never had so many people in the cottage at one time—and she admitted the addition of the group from the Capital made her nervous.

Nothing less than perfect would do, not for her oldest friend's wedding day, or the home Marg had given her.

Marco—the only male (along with Bollocks) allowed—fussed for hours in the kitchen, so he clearly felt the same about his brunch.

At one point, he surfaced enough to glance over the stove at the table she'd just finished.

"Holy Martha Stewart, Breen, that looks like a freaking magazine."

She stepped back to study the centerpiece, a clear glass bowl filled with flowers and herbs on a bed of crystals, and the carefully scattered tea lights, the champagne flutes and water glasses, the multicolored rainbow of napkins artfully—and painfully—swirled over snow-white plates.

"It's not too much?"

"Girl, it's a wedding. Ain't nothing too much." He stepped out of the kitchen, glanced toward the living room. "Okay, wow time."

"But not too much? Not too many flowers? Did I go overboard with the flowers?"

"It's like a garden, and it's all that. All that and more. And, man, everything shines. You got the fire going, the candles going, flowers all over, pillows all plumped up. Christmas tree shining. It's total girl time. I'm privileged to be part of it."

He put an arm around her shoulders. "And just in time, because here come the ladies. I'm going to start pouring mimosas."

Breen went out to meet them, and Tarryn stopped to take in the cottage.

"Well, it couldn't be more charming, could it then? And look at your gardens! Blooming right through December."

"You've a lovely view, don't you?" Sinead pressed her hands together to look out at the bay. "A lovely view on a lovely day. And the sweetest dog." She bent down to kiss Bollocks on the nose as he wagged himself into delirium.

"Come in, and welcome."

They came in chattering, bright, happy voices with plenty to say.

"Mimosas for my ladies," Marco announced as he passed them out. "And for those with babies on board, a wedding day special."

"A toast to the bride," Tarryn began.

"Let me have the first toast, would you?" Morena lifted her glass. "To the very best of friends and family, who are one and the same, anyone could have. Thank you for making this a day I'll never forget. *Sláinte!*"

They drank, chattered some more, then carted wedding day finery to the bedrooms Breen assigned and settled the sleeping baby on the bed.

"She's so beautiful, Noreen."

"And angel sweet with it." Stepping back from the bed, Noreen turned to Breen. "She has her father's eyes, does Brenna. I can see him in them, and it comforts me. I miss him so hard, and every day, but it comforts me to see him in our daughter's eyes. And today I carry his happiness for his sister in me."

She looked around her. "It's kind of you to give over this room where you tell your stories to us for the day."

"It's our first real party. I hope you brought an appetite."

"If I hadn't, it would find me sure enough with all the grand scents in the air."

"Come sit, and we'll eat."

They feasted on frittatas with winter squash, candied bacon, tiny sticky buns, berries and cream, baked French toast, and more.

"How am I to fit into my wedding dress now? Marco." Morena sighed. "You're a kitchen magician."

"He is indeed, and as such, not allowed to wash a single dish." Finola wagged a finger at him. "We've more than enough hands to see to all this, but the cook and the bride are exempt."

"I'm all for that." Morena lifted her glass.

"If you're sure, I'll take Morena up and start on her hair."

"Oh, is it time? Oh aye, please. Make me beautiful, Marco."

"Not a challenge, since you already are."

That got a chorus of *ahh*s, as Marco led Morena away.

When, from the near bedroom, the baby let out a whimper, Maura waved Noreen back. She stood, tall and dark, her warrior's braid dangling from her short, sleek hair, and a short sword at her side. "I'll fetch her and bring her to you. And have a bit of a cuddle first."

"She likely needs changing."

"Sure I remember how it's done."

"Beat me to it, she did." Sinead shook her head. "I'll have my cuddle once she's changed and fed. Now you, Aisling, you keep Noreen company. Go in, the pair of you, with my beautiful granddaughter, and sit by the fire while we put all this to rights again."

In the way of women well used to the task, they dealt with platters, bowls, plates, pots, and skillets. Breen put music on low to add a tune to the voices, and laughed when Finola and Marg executed a quick little step dance.

"I didn't know you could do that! You have to teach me."

"Sure I will. And don't you look as happy as our bride."

"I never had this, all this." As she set another bottle of champagne in a bucket of ice on the table, she looked around. "We have friends in

Philadelphia, but . . . I never had a group of women I loved together like this in my place. All the flowers, and the candles, a Christmas tree, and a baby nursing in front of the fire. My friend upstairs where my friend is doing her hair for her wedding."

"She'll never forget you gave her this time, this gathering," Tarryn said. "Now." She clapped her hands together. "It's battle stations, ladies. Time for all the fuss and finery we can muster."

She heard laughter when she led the mother and grandmother of the bride, the mother of the groom to her bedroom.

Morena sat on a tall stool, back to the mirror, while Marco stood meticulously adding more braids to her sunny hair. Through them he wove a thin silver ribbon with tiny bells.

"Oh my God."

"Is that good or bad? He won't let me see."

"It's incredibly good," Breen assured Morena, as Sinead waved a hand in front of her face.

"My girl! I'm watering up again. You look a picture already, darling. Minga did mine and Tarryn's this morning, and I confess I worried you wouldn't be up to the task, Marco. But here you are, making my girl as beautiful as any bride could be in all the worlds."

"Ma."

"Ah, give me the day to weep and babble. Tarryn, give me a bit of a glamour, would you, that'll hold against the weeping."

Minga stepped in, carrying a case. "For your hair, Breen, if you'd like."

"Oh, that would be great. I never know what to do with it."

"For not knowing, you do very well. Do you have nothing in mind?"

"Not really."

"Well then, show me your dress, and if you'll trust me, we'll have at it."

Since Minga's hair fell in perfect dark curls, Breen gave her trust.

Later, she'd think of it as perfumed chaos. Hair and glamours or makeup tools, women stripping down without a thought as Marco continued to work.

Minga fashioned her hair, a few soft curls around her face, the rest swept back with a pair of flower pins, then glided away with her case to add touches to any who wanted them.

Finally, Marco stepped back and let out a huge breath. "Okay, you can look. I hope you like it. You've got a lot of hair, girl."

"At last!" Morena spun on the stool, then slapped her hands to her cheeks. "Gods, oh gods. Marco!"

"Good or bad?"

Dozens of braids rained down her back, shining with the thin ribbon. The layers of them looked like a waterfall of sunlight.

"It's just what I wanted. No, no, it's more." She leaped up, threw her arms around him, then jumped back to spin. "Look how I can toss them! Thank you, a thousand thanks. Here, I have something for you."

She took a little box from her pocket. "A gift from the bride. I hope you'll like it, and wear it."

"It's . . . a harp, like the one Breen gave me. Like my tat. A harp pin. You didn't have to— Hell with that—I'm glad you did. I love it, and I'm going to get out of here, get myself gorgeous, and pin this on."

He looked around, then focused on Breen. She stood in a velvet gown of deep, rich purple that flowed nearly to her ankles. Both the hem and the wide cuffs on the long sleeves sparkled.

"Wow, you already got your gorgeous on. All of you. I got my work cut out for me if I'm going to hit even close."

When he rushed out, Morena held out a second box. "A gift from the bride," she said to Breen. "With a thousand thanks for giving me this day in your home with so many I love."

Inside, Breen found a circular pendant holding a dragon symbol within.

"It's beautiful."

"I thought you might wear it with the dragon's heart, your father's ring on your chain. You're a rider."

"I will." She unhooked her chain, added it. "And wear it with pride. But today's been a gift for me, too."

"Before we all start weeping again," Tarryn said, "let's get the bride into her dress."

There was more weeping as the women helped Morena, and a little more when Sinead added the crown of flowers she and Finola had made to her head.

A bit more still along with the gasps when the bride walked downstairs. Bollocks, wearing a collar of flowers, thumped his tail in approval.

Because there wouldn't be photos in Talamh, Breen set her tablet on the patio table, and with all of them, Bollocks included, gathered, merged power and technology to memorialize the moment.

Together, they walked through the woods toward Talamh.

"Now Breen will wait with you while we go over." Sinead stroked Morena's cheek. "We'll be sure Harken's where he's meant to be so he doesn't see you until your da and I walk you to him. I love you so much, my darling girl."

"I love you."

When they went through, Bollocks looked at Breen.

"Go on with Nan and Marco. We won't be long."

"It's really happening. I'll be wed in no time at all now."

"Are you nervous?"

"Not a bit. Oh, let's go through, Breen, and start. I can't wait to start."

"Two minutes. I promised your mother when she said you'd say just that."

"She knows me too well. Did I tell you I'm getting a pup for Harken for Yule? A water spaniel, like Bollocks. Well then, no dog's like Bollocks, but from the cousin of his mother. A girl with the sweetest eyes."

"You didn't tell me. He'll love that."

"He will. There's been so much going on, I forgot to tell you. Gods, is two minutes over?"

"Nearly. You're so full of light right now I'm surprised it doesn't shine up the whole forest."

"I'm about to burst with it."

"Okay, close enough. We'll go slow and make it up."

She'd been told what to expect, but still it took Breen's breath away.

Pillars of white candles, tall as a man, created a path around the house, and flowers carpeted it. Overhead in a sky shimmering pink against blue with evening, faeries flew, sending a rain of sparkling dust. Dragons soared with them and sent out a bugling call as Morena spread her wings and flew to her waiting parents.

Flynn kissed his daughter's cheeks, and Sinead handed her a bouquet of flowers and herbs. And wept again.

"Bright blessings, sister," Breen said, and started toward the path.

Music began when she stepped on it. Pipes and harps filled the air, as faerie dust sprinkled onto her hair.

At the end of the path, with the hills and fields behind, with the snow-laced tips of mountains distant, Harken stood with Keegan and his mother. The men wore doublets and leather, formal white shirts, while Tarryn wore soft, dull silver.

As Breen smiled at Harken, who had eyes only for the woman who walked behind her, flanked by her parents, she realized she'd never seen him in anything but work clothes.

She stepped beside Keegan. On his other side, Tarryn took his hand and Harken's for a moment. Then released them.

"I am the mother of Harken, and so I welcome you, Morena, as my daughter."

"We are the mother and father of Morena, and so we welcome you, Harken, as our son."

"I come to you in love, Mother, Father, Wife." Harken held out a hand to Morena.

"I come to you in love, Mother, Husband."

Morena put her hand in Harken's, and together they walked under an arbor of flowers, turned to face each other.

"Here we go," Morena murmured. With a laugh, Harken pulled her to him, kissed her.

"That's for after!"

"Mind your own, Seamus," Morena called out to her brother without taking her eyes off Harken's.

"Do you have words for me, Harken?"

"I do have them, and give you this as well." He took a ring out of his pocket. "This ring, a circle that never ends. Will you have it from me and me with it, Morena? I've loved you your whole life, and pledge here, in front of all, to love you for all of our lives and beyond them. You're everything I want in all the worlds, and here I promise to treasure who you are in bright days, through dark nights. I give you all that I am and ever will be, and would take all you are and ever will be if you're willing. Be mine, as I am yours."

"I will. Ah, bugger it, you're better at this, and I've forgotten what I practiced to say."

She waited out the laughter, and took the ring tucked in her bouquet. "All right then. This ring, a circle that never ends. Will you have it from me and me with it, Harken? I've loved you as long as I can remember, and wasn't so happy about it some of the time. I don't know why, as I've never been happier in all my life than in this moment. You've been patient with me, which only made me love you more. I pledge to you all you've pledged to me. I won't promise to cook all the meals, as you're better at it, but I'll work this land beside you and tend all on it."

"A better bargain for both of us," he said.

"That it is. I promise I'll try that patience of yours, as I won't be able to help it, but I'll love you, Harken, through all that comes. You're all I want as well, and I give you all I am or ever will be, and take all of you if you're willing. Be mine, as I am yours."

"I'll take you, Morena."

Keegan moved under the arbor to wrap a white cord around their joined hands. "Brother, Sister, you are joined here as husband and wife. A pledge and promise of love and unity. Bright blessings on you, and all who come from you."

They kissed, to the cheers of all assembled, then kissed again before turning and lifting their joined hands.

"I am his wife."

"I am her husband."

Morena laughed when he scooped her up, spun her around.

So began the feasting and music, the cups lifted in toasts. Torches and candles lit bright as evening slipped toward the longest night.

Breen watched Morena and Harken take their first dance before others joined in. Some sat at tables ringing the blaze of the solstice fire, and more slipped inside to sip a whiskey by the hearth or rock a baby to sleep.

As the moons began their sail, a hush.

"Don't tell me we have to make speeches." Mildly panicked, Breen grabbed at Keegan's arm. "Nobody told me about speeches."

"No. Look." He gestured west.

A light bloomed, cool and white, spread up and out from the Far West.

"Fin's Dance," she remembered.

"Aye, as I told you, the moons give their light to the stones to mark the winter solstice, the longest night. Now listen."

In the hush she heard the stones, though miles away, softly singing. And the song, like the beat of angels' wings, spread like the light as every dance across Talamh answered.

They sang a song of peace and promise.

Marco moved beside her and groped for her hand. When she looked at him, she saw tears of wonder gleaming in his eyes and felt her own on her cheeks.

This is why, she thought as her heart filled, this is why we fight. So two people can pledge their love, and spread it. And for the light, for the song, for the wonder, for the beauty.

And she was part of it, part of the wonder and the song.

The solstice fire burned, the torches and candles blazed. For a moment trapped in time, all of Talamh stood united. Slowly, the light in the west quieted, and the song ended.

"So the wheel turns on the longest night." Keegan looked down at her. "A first for you in Talamh."

"Yes, a first for me. Anywhere. What do we do now?"

"Now. Well, we dance."

The music piped again, so she danced, and danced.

And she looked on in delight at her grandmother and Sedric's energetic step dance. She drank wine, and enough of it to agree to sing a couple of duets with Marco before she danced again with young Kavan, hooting along with the music, on her hip.

Bollocks danced on his hind legs to entertain children—and earned more scraps than a single dog could eat for his trouble.

As the night stretched out, she dropped down at a table by the solstice fire beside Aisling.

"My first wedding in Talamh. I'm not sure any that follows can hit this mark. Are they always so crazy happy?"

"Well, a wedding's a pledge with a fine party after. The marriage after that is the work. And they'll work, will Harken and Morena. Squabble some as all do, and love and love, then squabble some more. But they'll work."

Smiling, she rubbed circles on the mound of her belly. "I wonder could I ask a favor of you?"

"Of course."

"Would you fetch Mahon for me? He's out there dancing his feet off with Mina and the rest, and fetch my mother as well, if you will."

"Sure. Is something wrong?"

"Not wrong, no. Just time."

"Time for— Oh! Don't move, I'll—"

"Wait." Aisling held up a hand. "Wait this one out with me. Block yourself now, as I'm taking your hand. Block."

She didn't block in time and felt the contraction build. The rise of pain and pressure shocked her enough that the shield went up instinctively as Aisling gripped her hand and breathed.

"You're in labor. How far apart, how— I don't know why I'm asking, as I wouldn't have a clue. I'll get Mahon."

"Just another moment. Started coming on when we crossed over. Starting to mean it now, it is. There, all done for the moment. I'll want Marg as well, as she'll be midwifing."

"I'll get them."

"Oh, and ask Keegan if he'd see to the boys, would you? They've another hour or two in them before they tucker themselves."

"We'll look after them. Don't worry, don't worry about anything."

"Oh now, I'm not a bit worried." Aisling laughed it off with a toss of her hair. "It's my third time around, after all. I know what's coming."

Worried enough for both of them, Breen sprang up, bolted through the dancers to Mahon. "Aisling. Aisling says it's time. The baby, time for the baby."

"Is it?" The smile broke over his face. "I'll fetch her mother and Marg."

"No, just go. I'll get them, and see to the boys. Just, well, go."

"Thanks for that."

When he started toward Aisling, Breen darted off with Bollocks prancing at her heels. She spotted Tarryn carrying two more jugs of wine to the feasting table.

"Aisling, the baby. She says it's time."

"Is it? Ah now, that's lovely. And there, Mahon flying her to the cottage. Would you take these so I can go to her?"

"Yes, yes. And I'll find Marg, and we'll look after the boys. You should really go. She was having contractions."

"The only way to birth a babe, after all." With a quiet sigh, Tarryn looked around. "New lives starting. Harken and Morena starting theirs, and a new baby to be welcomed to the world."

She handed Breen the jugs before she walked away. "What a grand solstice."

Breen hugged the jugs to her, looked down at Bollocks. "Find Nan. You find Nan for me."

Because she'd spotted Keegan with a tankard of ale and a group of men, she aimed straight for him.

"Your sister's having the baby."

"Is she now?" He took the jugs from her, set them down. "A busy night for the O'Broins."

"I mean now, or really soon. I have to find Marg, we have to watch the boys." A spear of panic lanced straight through her. "I don't know where they are!"

"Around and about," he said easily. "Finian's with Liam and some others, into the stable to show off his horse, and Kavan . . ." He trailed off, scanned around. "Ah, there, tucked on Sedric's lap eating cake."

"Thank God. I have to find Nan. You watch them, Keegan!"

When she ran off, he shook his head, drank more ale.

Obviously pleased with himself, Bollocks strutted up to her with Marg beside him.

"Aisling."

"Ah, I've been waiting for her to tell me."

"Mahon took her home. Tarryn's gone over, too."

"And so will I. Would you tell Sedric for me? And if he wants bed before I'm done, I'll be home when I am."

A little wild-eyed, Breen made a beeline for Sedric.

"Where's Kavan? He was just here."

"The lad deserted me for a pretty, fair-haired girl." He nodded toward where Kavan, wings fluttering, danced with the bride.

"Okay, good. Aisling's having the baby, and Nan's gone to her."

"A solstice baby. Good luck that is."

She just stared at him. "Everybody's so casual about it."

"The Fey are creatures of nature, and birthing's a natural thing, after all."

"Spoken like a man."

Laughing, he rose, kissed her cheek. "I can't say you're wrong on it, but natural it is." He put a hand on her shoulder, looked toward the cottage where lights shined in windows and smoke curled into the night sky. "What's happening there is life and light and promise. At the end of the work, for labor it surely is, there's joy. Now, I'm for another cup of ale and a final toast to the bride and groom before I take myself home. Will you have one?"

"No. No, thanks. I need to watch Kavan and Finian."

"That's kind of you, and fine boys they are. Don't let the little one talk you into more cake. He'll have a bellyache for certain."

"No cake. Got it. Crap, there he goes. Bollocks, go after him, stay with him."

"Mab's around and about, too," Sedric reminded her when Bollocks ran off. "The wolfhound's a fine nursemaid. Don't worry yourself." He patted her shoulder, then wandered off.

Before she could rush after the boy—and she really needed to find his older brother—Morena intercepted her.

"And why aren't you dancing at my wedding?"

"I did, but Aisling's having the baby, and I'm trying to watch the boys, and—"

"Having the baby, is she? Did you hear that, Harken?" She gestured him over. "Your sister—our sister," she corrected, "is stealing our thunder and having the baby."

"She's not one to be outdone, is Aisling."

"I need to round up the boys so I can keep an eye on them."

"They're having a fine time," Harken told her. "See, there's Finian coming out of the stables with Liam—and Liam's good with the littles. I can tell you Kavan's wearing out, though he thinks otherwise. He'll be curled in someone's lap sleeping inside an hour."

"Let me fetch you a cup of wine."

"After I have both of them in my sights."

She left them, and nearly ran straight into Marco.

"Time for another song," he told her. "We've got requests."

"Can't. I'm trying to watch Aisling's kids because she's having the baby."

"Okay, after— What! Now? The baby? Now?"

"Finally!" Breen threw up her hands. "A normal reaction. I'm trying not to freak, but nobody's freaking even a little and it makes me have to try harder not to freak."

"Should we do something? Is somebody boiling water?"

"I don't know. Nan's with her." And oddly, Marco's reaction calmed her down again. "Nan and Tarryn and Mahon are all with her. It's fine." She blew out a breath. "It's all fine. I just have to watch the boys, and— Okay, I see Finian now. He's riding Keegan's shoulders. And now he's picking up Kavan, so corralled at last. I need to go do my part with them."

"I'm going to go tell Brian. We'll send vibes. That's a good thing, right?"

"Sure, whatever."

She made her way to Keegan.

"They're not a bit tired," he told her as Kavan's head drooped on his shoulder and Finian's heavy eyes struggled not to close.

"We're not!"

"I can see that." Breen transferred Kavan to her shoulder.

"Ma said we could stay up as long as we wanted because we all got married. And now the baby's coming."

"And how do you know that?" Keegan asked Finian.

"Because." Heavy eyes closing, he rested his cheek on Keegan's head. "Before midnight, and I can stay up and say welcome."

"We'll just walk you on home." Keegan reached back, shifted the boy into his arms.

"I don't know how far off midnight is, but he's not going to make it. He's already asleep."

"Not but an hour left on this side of the night. He'll say welcome in the morning."

They carried them in, and Keegan led the way to the room they shared. When they laid them on their cots, Keegan straightened. "I'll get them out of the jackets and boots. You should go over and let Aisling know we've got them abed."

"All right. Should we stay with them after?"

"No need. They're deep in sleep. But let her and Mahon know their boys are safe in bed."

She went out and down a little hall to where she heard voices, saw firelight flickering.

And stopping in the open doorway, stared.

Aisling, eyes glassy with pain and focus, sat naked on the bed with Mahon behind her, Marg between her updrawn knees, and Tarryn holding her hand.

"All right now," Marg said, "bear down, girl, and push."

Aisling sucked in air, pushed.

"There's the way, my brave one." Tarryn pressed her lips to Aisling's hand.

"A bit more, just a bit. That's fine, that's good. Stop, stop now and breathe."

When Aisling closed her eyes, leaned back against Mahon, Tarryn soothed her clammy face with a cloth. As Breen started to step back, Tarryn waved her in.

"No, come, come, take her other hand. We're so close now."

"Praise the gods," Mahon muttered and pressed a kiss to Aisling's shoulder. "You're a warrior, my darling."

Aisling grabbed Breen's hand. "Don't take any of it, you understand? It's for me. It's mine, but I'm going to squeeze tight. And now. Marg, I have to push!"

"All right, give us a good one. More now, that's right," she said as Aisling set her teeth and pushed. "Give us some pants now, hold off. The head comes with the next."

At that moment, Keegan stepped to the door. He simply said, "No," and stepped out again.

"Typical." Aisling leaned back against Mahon. "Gods, gods, all right, another."

Breen watched, stunned, as the baby's head—a full head of dark hair, long-lidded eyes—slid out.

"Pant now! Hold, hold."

"Look at that face. Do you see, Aisling?"

"Mahon's face, and his hair. Gods, gods, the rest wants out, and now."

"Push your babe into the world, into the light, mother." Marg placed her hands on the head, gently turning as Aisling pushed. As the shoulders appeared, and the torso, the new life let out a cry.

"Doesn't even wait to let the world know."

Into Marg's hands, into the light, the baby came, one fist shaking.

"A fine, healthy son," Marg announced as she cleaned the baby's face and kissed it. "With a good set of lungs."

"I'm bound to birth boys, beautiful, beautiful boys. Mahon, our son."

He wept as he pressed his cheek to hers. "A warrior. My love, my heart, my life. Thank you for our son."

Sitting back on her heels, Marg swiped at her forehead with the back of her hand. "You'll cut the cord, Tarryn."

"I will. With this you are born of love and are welcomed with joy." With light, she severed the cord, then lifting the baby, pressed a kiss to his brow before laying him in Aisling's arms.

"We've waited for you, my own, my love." She kissed him in turn, shifted him so his father could do the same. "And here you are, at last. You're Kelly."

She smiled at Breen's damp, stunned eyes. "In honor of the one who stood as my father when mine went to the gods. Will you kiss him in welcome, Breen?"

"Welcome to Talamh, and all the worlds, Kelly."

This is why, Breen thought as she bent down to touch her lips to the soft cheek. This is why we fight.

This is why we'll win.

CHAPTER SEVEN

Breen loved the way the Fey celebrated Christmas. For Talamh it stood as a time of joy and community, of gatherings and giving—and, as always, of light.

On the eve, from sunset till dawn, trees both inside and out would glow. Family and friends exchanged gifts, and stockings for the littles bulged with treats.

In the valley, many would gather at sunset to share the joy, to drink wassail as a representative from each tribe joined to sing the Welcoming Tree alight.

But her first Christmas in Talamh, in Ireland, couldn't leave out the family across the sea.

In Fey Cottage with Marco, she sat with their tree in the background and Sally and Derrick on-screen.

In Philadelphia, they wore Santa hats sparkling with glitter. Behind them, the tree—one of the half dozen in their home—glistened and gleamed from its red-carpeted base to its disco ball topper.

Across the miles they toasted each other.

"We miss you guys." Marco cuddled Breen a little closer. "First Christmas in a million years we haven't hung at Sally's."

"Tell everyone Merry Christmas from us," Breen added. "Send pictures!"

"We'll do that," Sally promised. "We loved the one of the bridal bash from your blog. You just need to tell your grandmother to send over the secret to her fountain of youth. She wins the Gorgeous Granny Award hands down."

"I'll tell her you said so. We're seeing her later for . . . the Christmas tree lighting." The best way to put it, she decided. "It's a community tradition."

"How's that book of yours coming, Breen?" Derrick asked her. "The big fantasy one. You know how I love fantasy."

"Pretty good, I think. Hope."

"Her agent wants her to send in a few chapters she's polished up." Breen elbowed Marco. "It's not ready yet."

"Won't let me read it either," he added.

"It's not ready yet. Marco's been working on his music but won't submit anything."

"Touché," he said, then shrugged. "Not ready yet."

"Our kids." Sally looked at Derrick with an exaggerated sigh.

They spent a happy hour talking, opening gifts.

Marco modeled his chocolate-brown leather duster.

"I can't believe it! This is beyond lit."

"Breen said you had a thing for Keegan's."

"Got it in one. I'm going to sleep in it!"

"It's damn sexy," Sally commented. "I bet that handsome artist of yours thinks so, too."

"Wait till he gets a load of me."

"I can't get over my boots!" Breen did a turn in the over-the-knee black leather with lacings up the side concealing the zipper. "They're amazing. I feel like a general."

"A smoking-hot one," Derrick told her. "Look at our cutie, Sally. She done gone and grown up."

"Girl." Marco put an arm around her waist, struck a pose. "We slay. We're wearing these tonight."

"Right there with you." She plopped back on the couch. "Your turn. It's from both of us to both of you."

"Been waiting." Derrick ripped at the festive paper as Sally winced.

"You know that kills me. All the trouble to wrap it up, make it beautiful, and you tear at it like a three-year-old."

"Everybody's three at Christmas."

Breen laughed. "That's what I say, and we hope what's inside's what counts."

Out of the sturdy shipping crate, they took a box. Polished to a near mirror shine, the cedar boasted gleaming copper hinges and an ornate latch. The lid held an intricate carving, meticulously painted with copper, of their names inside an infinity symbol.

It matched the ones etched on their wedding rings.

"It's gorgeous." Sally trailed a finger over their names. "The craftsmanship . . . It's just gorgeous."

"Sedric—I told you about him—helped us design it, and Seamus, he's an amazing craftsman, built it. It's a memory box," Breen added. "And a little more. You need to open it for the more."

When they did, Sally let out a watery laugh. Music streamed out. "It's our wedding song. We went with an old classic." He turned to Derrick, kissed him. "I got you, babe."

"I got you, babe."

"I've either got to get him really drunk or play this song to get the man to sing with me."

"I've got a voice like a sad trombone." Derrick cleared his throat. "This is precious, kids. Really precious."

"It gets just a little better. That's Marco playing the song."

"Get out! Child, that's wonderful! How'd you do that?" Sally demanded.

"We'll just call it magick." Because it had been.

But then it was a night for magick, Breen thought as she walked toward Talamh with Marco and Bollocks.

At Marco's insistence, Bollocks wore a Santa hat. To Breen's surprise, he loved it.

People had already gathered on the road, in the fields, on the low stone walls when they stepped through.

Some played music, of course, while others handed out cups of wassail. Morena greeted them with a hug and a whistle. "Look at the lot of you. Aye, your hat's most festive."

She gave it a nod of approval before Bollocks raced off to play with swarms of children. "And such a coat. Soft as a baby's arse," she proclaimed after stroking it. "But of all, I have to say I envy those boots."

"Who wouldn't? Merry Christmas—or Blessed Night of Lights."

"Either works. Well then, get yourself a cup of wassail, the sun sets soon."

"I want to see the baby first."

She made her way through the crowd, pleased she recognized faces and knew so many now by name. She found Tarryn beside Aisling, the baby swaddled in her arms.

"A Blessed Night of Lights to you, Breen Siobhan, and Merry Christmas with it. I see a bit of a wish in your eyes," Tarryn added, and held out the baby.

"Thanks." She breathed in the baby scent and cuddled. "You really do look like your da. When your wings come, green as the hills, you'll fly over land and sea, your voice raised in song pure with joy."

She blinked, looked up. "I'm sorry. I just—"

"No, no, it's lovely to hear. I saw the light of the Sidhe in him, but not the rest. Musical he'll be then." Aisling trailed a finger over Kelly's cheek. "It pleases me."

"All right now, give him over." Finola, in a bright, cherry-red cloak and matching boots, strutted up. "I need to practice, as I'm hoping Morena and Harken don't make me wait so long for a babe as they did to wed. Ah, they smell of magicks, new babes do."

"His brothers claim otherwise when he needs his nappy changed." Aisling glanced around, saw her boys playing and watched by Mab. "Ah, I see Bridie's got Marg in her clutches, and is surely bending her ear over her latest complaints. Breen, go save your nan—you could say I'm asking for her. New mothers get some indulgences."

"I'll do that."

She exchanged greetings as she went, and felt the lift as the sun dripped color across the sky. Soon, she thought, the trees would light, and voices would raise in goodwill and unity into the cold, clear air.

"Merry Christmas, Breen Siobhan."

She stopped, smiled at the woman. Young, pretty, soft brown hair in a thick braid, and face vaguely familiar. She dug for the name but couldn't quite reach it.

"It's the greeting on your side."

"On the other side, yes," she said, because both were hers. "And Blessed Night of Lights to you."

"Cait, Caitlyn Connelly you'd say, from the cottage near the ruins."

Now it clicked. "Yes, I've seen you walking when I visit my father."

"I've seen you as well. Have a cup of wassail, won't you? The sun sets soon."

"Thanks."

"A toast then, to Talamh on a joyful night."

The cup nearly reached her lips before Breen saw it, felt it, knew it. She started to upend the cup, then felt and knew more.

It was a time and a place for faith.

So she drank, and watched the hard smile gleam in Cait's eyes.

After drinking deep, she lowered the cup.

"You would choose such a night to do his dark work, and here, with so many gathered in peace and fellowship? With children playing. You would make this with my death that's not a death?"

"It will come in pain, and none will save you."

Bollocks raced to her side, growled, but Breen kept her gaze locked with Cait's.

"It will not come at all, and you will face Judgment for defiling your gifts. Hold!" She shot out a hand, and power she hadn't known she possessed. She caged the elf in place before Cait could run.

Eyes hot with fury, Cait squirmed against the bindings. "Why don't you drop!"

"Because my light smothers Yseult's dark, and always will. You've betrayed your people, Cait Connelly."

"Odran is my god, and the god of all. He will take back the power he granted you and burn this world and all in it to black."

People had begun to murmur, and some crowded close.

Breen's breath came short, but not from the poison. From anger, from sorrow. Here, on a night of light and kindness, Odran cast his shadow.

"Stay back, please. Keep the children clear, and send for the taoiseach."

"He's here." Keegan stepped beside her. "What is this?"

"Yseult's poison. She's Odran's."

"You were made for him. Made by him," Cait spat out. "And he will have you."

"I know you," Keegan said. "But now I see you and know your truth."

"Odran, god of dark, god of all, will drain her dry, and when Talamh is ash, he'll soak the ground with your blood."

"Sleep," Keegan ordered, and the woman crumpled to the ground. "You need to release her so they can move her away." Turning, he signaled to two wearing warrior's braids before bending down and taking a vial from Cait's pocket. "So small a thing," he murmured, then stood again. "I'll need the cup as well," he told Breen.

"Carry her off, guard her, for she meant to poison the Daughter with a sleeping potion at Odran's command."

His words brought more than mutters, but shouts of outrage, cries of shock.

"After the rite," he continued, "take her and these on dragon-back to the Capital and have her held for Judgment."

He gripped Breen's hand, lifted his voice over the rest. "She will be judged, and by our laws. But not this night. This dark act will not dim the light, it will not silence the bells."

He gestured west where the sun sank. "Talamh will shine on the Night of Lights. Come with me," he murmured to Breen. "Where is my nephew?" he called out. "Where is Finian, son of Mahon and Aisling?"

"I'm here." Finian stood, eyes wide as Keegan approached, as people parted to let him pass.

"Here is a child of the Fey, a son of Talamh." He hefted Finian onto his shoulders. "Lift up your young so they see the light that is ours. So they and all see this child of Talamh send the first light to the Tree of Welcome."

Finian leaned down to Keegan's ear and whispered, "I've done it only with a candle, with Ma, and a few times."

"Remember it's light, not fire you're sending. It's in you, bright as the day. But if you need help, you'll have it. Send the light, lad, one only."

Finian straightened, looked toward his family, then at the Welcoming Tree. "I—I send a light on this night to shine bright . . ."

"For all good and right," Keegan prompted.

"For all good and right."

The hand Finian held out toward the tree trembled a little. But a tiny light flickered on a sweeping branch, then strengthened, then glowed strong.

"Do you know the rest?" Keegan asked him.

"I think I might, but . . ."

"Say it with me, Fin, and strong now so all can hear."

Together, they said, "Now all who stand upon this land, every son and daughter who swim the waters, all who fly across the sky, send your light through this night. So every tree shines with the joy that's yours and mine until comes the sun, and this night is done."

The tree blazed with light, as did the forests, the orchards, the lone chestnuts or oaks in fields.

Voices raised in a song of peace and joy and fellowship.

As it flowed around her, Breen thought there could be nowhere in all the worlds as pure or as beautiful as Talamh on Christmas Eve.

"*Maith thú.*" Keegan lifted Finian from his shoulders, then gave him a high toss in the air. "Well done indeed. You've earned a dragon ride."

"Now?"

He started to put it off, then thought better of it. "If it's now, Kavan will have a ride as well."

"I don't mind."

"Call your dragon," Keegan told Breen. "You'll take Kavan."

"I—I will?"

"Go fetch your brother." Keegan set Finian down. "Let them see us both, and the light we'll stream over the sky. Let Odran and Yseult feel it and know they failed. It's a gift we'll give to Talamh, and a bloody kick in the balls to Odran."

With Bollocks and Kavan with her on Lonrach's back, she flew up beside Cróga. Kavan let out his hoots and babbles, and raising his arms, spinning his hands in the air, sent out rains of faerie dust.

When Keegan swept an arm, a white rainbow bloomed over the

sky. Breen did the same, while below Talamh glowed with countless points of light.

Since the incident with Caitlyn Connelly put Breen off wassail, she stuck with wine for the gift exchange at Fey Cottage. Though she'd seen some of Brian's quick sketches, saw talent in them, the painting he gave her, one of the bay at sunrise, took her breath.

"It's so beautiful, all the colors, the mists. You even have Bollocks splashing in the water."

"It seems a favorite time of yours, the break of dawn, and I wanted to give you that moment, with thanks for opening your home to me."

"It's Marco's home, too. But this?" She looked up and over to where he and Marco squeezed together in one of the big chairs near the fire. Like kids, she thought. Like lovers. "I'm going to be selfish with it," she decided. "I'm hanging it in the room I use to write. A constant inspiration."

She rose to walk over and kiss him before handing him a package. "Now that I have this, your gift might be a little self-serving."

He opened it to find an artist's case filled with pencils, paints, chalks, a sketch pad, and two small canvases.

"This is brilliant."

"I thought having some extra supplies here at the cottage would be handy."

"It's grand, truly."

She chose another package, walked back to give it to Keegan. "Merry Christmas."

"Thanks." Like Derrick, he pulled off the fancy ribbon, tore the pretty paper.

She'd made it, with considerable care, the band of leather and the single central stone, the labradorite she'd carved magickally in the shape of a dragon in flight.

"I know you don't generally wear—"

"I'll wear this," he interrupted. "It's Cróga."

"I had a lot of help with that from Sedric and Nan."

"It's very like, and means much." He put it on, twisted the ties to secure it. "He'll be pleased as well. You'll have yours then." Rising, he retrieved a long cloth sack from behind the tree. "I'm not one for wrapping."

"So I get a pretty bag." She untied the cord, pulled out a sheathed sword.

"That's going to rank high on the unusual gift list." With a half chuckle, Marco drank more wassail.

Amused herself, Breen ran a finger over the carvings on the sheath. "Beautiful, intricate."

"And I had a bit of help there on the design, thanks to Brian and Sedric as well. You have the symbols of the Fey, all the tribes represented, and the symbol for man, and for the goddess."

"And the twin moons of Talamh." She traced them. "Oh, and a shamrock, for Ireland." Delighted now, she scanned symbols. "Marco, there's a Liberty Bell, crack and all, for Philadelphia."

"Okay, points for that."

"The apple," Keegan told her, "for New York, as you have business there, and the dragon, as you're a rider. You need a sword of your own, not one borrowed. In tradition, a sword is passed down when it can be, but your father's is too heavy to suit you. This is cast to your hand and arm, your size."

She gripped the hilt and felt the difference. Just a bit smaller than the one she used for training, and when she drew it out, felt, too, the slight difference in weight.

"Careful, girl, you could put someone's eye out with that."

But she only stared at the blade, and the word carved into it. *Misneach.*

"Thank you." She sheathed the sword, then kissed him. "It means much."

Later, when the fire burned low, they went upstairs. She sat to take off her boots.

"That's clever, isn't it?" Keegan commented when she tugged down the hidden zipper. "Makes for an easy on and off. They're . . . provocative."

She glanced up. "Are they?"

"As well you know. Makes a man wonder how you'd look wearing them and little else."

"Marco decreed an oversize man's shirt with them. Maybe I'll try one of yours one day."

"That'd be a picture for certain." He paced to the window, back again. "Breen, I know the day of Christmas is important for you, but I have to go to the Capital and deal with the Judgment on this woman. I can't let it wait."

"Oh. Yes, you're right. We'll leave in the morning."

"There's no need for you to travel. We have the vial, the cup, her own damning words. And the truth is, she won't deny it, as she took pride in the attempt."

"She did, didn't she?" Breen murmured.

"Why did you drink the poison? Why did you risk it if you knew?"

"I nearly didn't." She rose to put the boots away. "Then I understood I needed to trust. You, Marg, the coven, the magicks, and the light. I had to trust what I felt inside me, that it was stronger than Yseult. And to believe in what I've become. So I made the choice."

"I'd have stopped you, and that would've been wrong. Yet I'd do that again if I had the chance."

"I can't play whatever part I'm needed to play against Odran, for Talamh and the rest, if I don't believe."

"You've the right of it, and yet."

"Are you saying I don't need to go tomorrow because you think I'm safer here?"

"I'm not, no. And if you're needed after all, I'll send a falcon and expect you to come. She has a family, you know, Cait does, and someone who hoped to pledge to her. Now their hearts are broken. How he turned her, I'll never know. I never know, for certain, how any of us can turn."

He grieved, she thought. For the loss of one of his own, for what he needed to do to right that loss. "You'll banish her, and that weighs on you."

"Her sister, Janna, wore a warrior's braid and came from the valley for the Battle of the Dark Portal. And gave her life there. Now her family has lost two to Odran, and one bears responsibility for the death of her sister. How much did Janna tell Cait about patrols, strategies, plans, as one sister might talk to another? How much did Cait pass to Odran, and how much of that beat the path of her own sister's death?"

He shook his head. "It won't weigh so very much."

But it would, she knew, whatever he said now.

"Will her family go to the Capital for the Judgment?"

"I gave them time to see and speak with her here before she was taken east. Aisling needs more time with our mother, and our mother needs more time with Aisling and the children. I'll be obliged to stay in the Capital, at least till the turn of the year."

"You have duties, Keegan. I understand them. Do you have to leave tonight?"

"I want tonight with you, what's left of it. I want to lie with you." He pulled off her sweater, tossed it aside. "I want to feel you under me, over me, around me."

He scooped his hands through her hair. "I like it loose. I like there's so much of it. I like when it goes a bit wild."

She thought of how she'd once spent what seemed like hours straightening that wild, covering the red with brown because her mother had drilled into her that she needed to blend in. To just disappear.

Never again.

She boosted herself up, locked her legs around his waist. And took his mouth with hers.

"I want you over me, and under me. I want you inside me. The nights are still long." She nipped at his throat. "We'll take all the rest of it. We'll take each other."

Gripping his hair, she dragged his mouth back to hers.

Hunger cut deep, hunger for her all but took him to the ground. The taste of her, suddenly so potent, so strong, so rich, only widened the wound.

With a single desperate thought, he stripped her, then himself, and hot skin to hot skin, pressed her back against the wall. His fingers dug into her hips, but he gave no thought to bruises as he plunged into her. Her gasps only fueled the fire burning in him as he drove deep, and deeper.

With his eyes on hers, he saw the gray darken, saw each shock of pleasure in them. Her legs, velvet chains, tightened around him, and her hips pumped strong.

She could only hold on while the air swirled hot around them. In the hearth, the simmering fire snapped into a blaze, and the blaze sent out a roar.

Every candle in the room shot into flame.

When she breathed, she breathed him. And what he was filled her, the power of it, the need, searing, exciting. Dangerous.

She gave herself to it, rushed to meet it, to take it all, sensation by electric sensation.

It ripped through her, the fire and flame. He smothered her cry with his mouth, feasting there as her body trembled, as her body went limp. Drove into her and into her until he emptied.

And even empty, she filled him.

Though her muscles had turned to water, she stayed wrapped around him. Her heart thudded so hard, she wondered it didn't sound in all the worlds.

As she tried to find her breath again, she spotted Bollocks on his bed by the fire, curled in a ball, his back very deliberately toward them.

"We lit all the candles, the fire's still roaring. And I think we embarrassed the dog."

"I like how you look in firelight, in candlelight. And the dog, he'll learn to live with it." Keegan turned his face into her hair. "Sure this wasn't the plan."

"You had a plan?"

"I thought to take some time, some care. You seduced me, so it's on your head, isn't it?"

Oh, how she loved the idea she could seduce him.

"We didn't use much of the night. Plenty of time left to implement your plan."

He shifted her so he could look at her. "I know where you came from, but I often wonder what turn of the path sent you to me."

"I often wonder what turn put you on my path. Then I decide I don't need to know, because I'm fine with it."

"I'm more fine than I ever thought to be, and still I wonder. But since it seems we're on the same path, let me show you my plan."

CHAPTER EIGHT

Because he needed the time, and the feel of his horse under him, Keegan mounted Merlin for the trip to the Capital. He left before daybreak, before even Harken started his daily tasks, and with Cróga soaring overhead, set off in the cool dark at a full gallop.

He wanted the solitude and the speed, with the only sound the stallion's hooves ringing on the hard-packed road. In the silence, he could think.

Odran had found a way to slip Yseult's potion into Talamh, and into the hands of one of his supplicants. The portals, though guarded well, remained vulnerable. He might have sent a raven through, or a Were in its spirit animal form. Yseult herself may have bespelled the guards long enough to slither in and out again.

They could, and would, hold back an army, but a lone spy or messenger presented a different challenge. After all, he himself sent spies into Odran's world.

They'd weakened Odran's forces in the Battle of the Dark Portal, but full victory remained elusive.

And if he looked at the long river of history, it would remain elusive until Odran's death.

Weakening him wasn't enough; containing him only offered respites from the war. It wouldn't end, it couldn't end, until Odran ended.

And only Breen could end him.

The sword of the taoiseach and all it stood for couldn't strike the blow, at least not from his hand. Gods knew Eian had wielded it with purpose and skill, but had failed and given his life in the effort.

Every song, every story on that long river of history put the weight of it all on the Daughter of the Fey, and nothing he did changed it.

And now, because he loved where he'd vowed he wouldn't, he feared for her. And fear clouded judgment when it must remain keen. It rocked the heart when the heart must stay steady, and troubled the mind when the mind must hold cool and clear.

So he rode at a gallop toward the first break of light in the east until the distance from her, from the other side, even from the valley helped the keen and steady, the cool and clear.

Around him as they slowed to a strong trot, the land began to wake. Lights glowed in cottages and farmhouses; animals stirred in the fields. Birds chorused the dawn.

He saw the waking sun glint off the snow icing the high mountains and mists rising from streams and curtaining the deep forests. A six-point buck, regal in his winter coat, waded through the mists, lifted his head to scent the air. When he crossed to the stream, a small herd followed, sliding silent through the curtain.

A pair of hawks, calling to each other, circled the sky on the hunt for breakfast. A red fox streamed across a field and into the forest shadows and its den, done with its night's work.

Small magicks, he often thought, as essential to life, a good life, as breath.

He saw a young boy trudging behind his father toward a barn, still half-asleep, no doubt, on the way to chores. Then a woman bundled in blue, tossing feed for chickens with the as yet empty basket for their eggs slung over her shoulder.

Released from the stalls, a buckskin foal frolicked in the field with infectious joy.

He caught the tang of peat smoke, heard a female voice (a bit out of tune) raised in song as she went about her work, the lowing of cattle, the sigh of the wind.

He'd been right to ride, he thought. On Cróga's back he could view all of Talamh. But on Merlin's he stayed part of it all. And he'd needed this time to help him remember, whatever his fears, he stood for this, he fought for this. He would give his life for this if asked.

Leaning down, he rubbed Merlin's strong neck. "Ready?"

In answer, Merlin leaped into a gallop.

Though he hadn't sent a falcon, and rode into the Capital without escort, they came out to call greetings, to tip a cap, lift a hand in welcome.

Children, free from school until the turn of the year, swarmed, and those gathered around the well, for a gossip as much as water, paused as he rode by.

He spotted Morena's nephew Bran as the boy raced toward him. After he crossed the bridge, Keegan slowed Merlin from trot to walk.

"They said you'd come, but not today for certain. I saw Cróga, so I came out to wait."

"For me or my dragon?"

Bran dipped his head but couldn't hide the grin. "For both, and the stallion as well, since you weren't on your dragon. I can take him to the stables for you and give him a good rubdown, as he's had a long ride."

"Can you now?"

"Sure I can." Ever eager, Bran trotted alongside the horse. "And water him, and all the rest."

"And the barter for your services would be?"

"Such a service for the taoiseach doesn't need a trade." But his eyes rolled up, full of hope, to Keegan's. "And Merlin worked up a good sweat."

"Both of us have, despite the chill in the air." After dismounting, Keegan handed the reins to the boy. "Take care with him, for he's earned that and a carrot besides. You'll have your ride on Cróga—if you get your ma or da's leave for it."

"They won't say no!"

"Likely not, but you'll ask all the same. How goes your family, Bran, and you?"

Bran stroked Merlin's cheek. "My uncle was brave and true, and I know he's in the light. But . . . I miss his laugh."

"As do I." Keegan laid a hand on the boy's head. "As do we all."

"We're sad, and sometimes it hurts in my belly when I think of him, and never seeing him again. But my ma says you look to the stars, and you'll see one especially. That's his light. I know it's just a story, but—"

"It's a fine one, and true enough, as when you look at that star you think of him. That makes it true. Cróga will come when you call."

Bran's eyes popped wide. "When I call?"

"He'll know, as I'll tell him. Take good care of my horse, ask permission, and the dragon comes at your call."

"I'll take care, I promise!" He split off toward the stables, turned, walking backward as he beamed at Keegan. "I trained this morning with my mother, as there's no school. I trained hard, Taoiseach, and I'll be ready to take my place against Odran and all the dark who come against Talamh."

"Please gods," Keegan murmured as Bran led Merlin away, "please all the gods and goddesses, let him never be called on for it."

He walked past the fountain toward the castle with its banner snapping in the wind. And tried, as he always did, not to feel confined the minute he walked through the doors.

He took time in his rooms to wash and change before meeting with members of the council and others who had needs or complaints, hopes or ideas. And knew before the end of the day, after a meal with Morena's family—his family now as well—he'd have to stay more than a handful of days.

His mother needed more time with Aisling and the children, and had more than earned it.

So he closed himself in to more meetings, made decisions on the day-to-day, the routine tasks he so often left in Tarryn's more than capable—and entirely more patient—hands. Though he refused to send for Mahon, as a new father needed time as well, he huddled with warriors and with scholars in the Map Room.

He made use of his own workshop, conjuring spells, mixing potions, searching for visions to help him keep Talamh, all who lived there, and all the worlds safe.

On the final day of the year, he called for the Judgment.

"They fill the room," Flynn told him, "as we expected. Many of them hope to see Breen, and no doubt witness her rising as she did on the Day of Judgment with Toric of the Pious."

"They'll be disappointed there. No need for her to come," he said, as he'd said before. "You yourself were witness, and no one would doubt your word. I've brought others who saw the same. More, Flynn, she won't deny it. She has pride in the attempt."

"I've spoken to her, as you asked, so I know you've the right of it. Still, they'll be sorry not to see Breen take this one on. I'm not shamed to admit I'm a bit sorry for it myself. She's a wonder, is Breen."

"She is." And he'd tried hard not to think of her the last days, with little success. Now he reached for the staff. "Have her brought up so all can hear the words."

The room, as full as Flynn reported, fell into a hush when Keegan walked in. Young and old and all between filled the seats.

When he sat in the Chair of Justice, he felt its weight fall on him. Here, whatever his feelings, whatever anger brewed in their depths, his blood must stay cool, his mind must stay clear.

Here, duty left no room.

The murmurs spread when Flynn brought her in.

So young, Keegan thought. A pretty young girl of good family who, gods help him, looked pleased with the attention.

What twist had knotted inside her for such careless evil?

They'd bound her Elfin gifts, but he wondered, looking at her eager face, if she'd have used them to try to escape the Judgment.

And he thought not.

"Caitlyn O'Conghaile, you are accused of treachery against Talamh, against all who dwell here. You are accused of betraying your birthright and our laws to do Odran's bidding. You are accused of attempting to poison Breen O'Ceallaigh with a potion brewed with dark magicks that would have taken her to the edge of death. And so you plotted to deliver her to Odran to destroy. What say you?"

"I am a handmaiden of Odran the Magnificent." Her face glowed, fervent, as she spoke. "What he wills is the law. There is no law but Odran's law, no way but Odran's way."

In the seats, her mother buried her face against her husband's shoulder, her own shoulders shaking with tears.

"You don't deny these accusations?"

"Why should I? You're nothing to me with your foolish staff and your weak sword. Odran could burn you to ash with a thought."

"He hasn't as yet."

"In his time," Cait said slyly.

"Though you admit all, deny nothing, we will hear the account from a witness. Flynn Mac an Ghaill, will you speak?"

"I will. On the night before the Yule, when in the valley many came to congregate, to share community and song and celebration, I witnessed this woman offer Breen O'Ceallaigh a cup, as if in friendship. I saw you, Taoiseach, begin to move quickly toward them as if alarmed when Breen hesitated, when she drank. I saw, as all did, and heard, as all did, the accused's shock, her demands for Breen to fall, her anger that Breen's light was stronger than the dark magicks in the cup."

"It was the witch's fault, not mine! The witch's magicks were weak!"

"Whom do you speak of?" Keegan asked Cait.

"Yseult! She failed, and she'll pay for it. I did what I was bid, but she failed, not I! So I'll tell Odran."

"How do you know the potion came from Yseult's hand?"

"Well, she sent it to me, didn't she?" Cait shook her head in disgust. "Through the portal, by raven, and in my dreams Odran spoke and promised me all I wished if I did this task."

"How do you know it was Odran and not simply a dream? How do you know his face, his voice?"

As if speaking to children, Cait slapped her hands to her hips.

"Sure I've stood before him, haven't I? In his world, in the black castle that shines with jewels, and the thunder claps when he calls it and the sea boils at his whim."

"What portal, and how would you pass through?"

She sighed now. "You with your guards and your weak minds. Torian took me through. Dig the potatoes, pick the cabbage." She spoke in singsong as she glanced back with a sneer at her grieving family. "Feed the chickens. Always the same, then Torian came and said there was more, and showed me, and flew me through the portals, one by one, to show me. And all the way to Odran, who blessed me and promised me all the more, and I would be wife to Torian when Odran ruled, not to some mewling one from Talamh. But you killed him."

"Whom did I kill?"

"Torian, you bastard! When he flew, strong and brave, and grabbed the mongrel witch, who could kick and scream and nothing more, from her weak father's grave. You severed his head, and I cursed you. Your dragon turned him to ash, and I cursed him. I curse you now."

The dark faerie, Keegan remembered, the one he'd fought the first time he'd met Breen.

"Torian was with you when he saw Breen at her father's grave?"

"With me, and we would have been rewarded for delivering her then. He should have killed you, and this would be done. I would have avenged him and served Odran, but the witch's magicks were small, too small. I pledged to Torian. I am pledged to Odran, and you will pay, Keegan O'Broin, I swear it. You will all pay."

She whirled to face her family and all the others.

"You'll be slaves and sacrifices, and I will dance to the music of your screams."

"Oh, enough, Taoiseach." Cait's mother fell to her knees. "I beg you, enough."

"Aye, it's enough. Caitlyn O'Conghaile, by your own words and your actions done willing, you've damned yourself. You have broken sacred trusts. You have broken sacred laws."

"I spit on your laws." And she did, literally, on the floor at Keegan's feet, drawing gasps from the onlookers.

"You are banished to the Dark World, where you will be taken and sealed for all time. This is the Judgment."

He brought down his staff.

"He'll crush you, and he'll free me, and all you've sent to that place will rise against any and all of you."

"You've betrayed your family, one who loved and cared for you. I feel nothing but pity for you now. Take her now to the dolmen."

Feeling that pity, he brought down his staff again and got to his feet. "So it is done."

"You'll all bleed and burn," Cait shouted out as Flynn pulled her from the room. "Odran will drain the Daughter of the Fey dry, and rule."

Ignoring her, Keegan went to Cait's mother, lifted her to her feet.

"You're not to blame for this, your family is blameless in this."

"She's my child."

"No longer, and I'm sorry for it, *Máthair*. He took your child, and I swear by all I am I'll make him pay for it. I ask that you not come to the dolmen but go with your family. Go back to the valley, and I'll come to you as soon as I can."

"She was lost," her mother wept. "She was lost."

"Aye, she was lost. I grieve with you for this loss." He signaled two dragon riders. "Take them home. See them home safe."

And he'd use the mirror to speak to his mother so she'd be waiting to comfort them.

But now he walked back to the chair. He didn't sit but stood as the family left the room.

"There is no blame," he repeated. "If any light a candle tonight, let it be for those grieving and broken hearts. Go now, to your own families, to those you love, and give thanks for them. The Judgment is done."

He did his duty and sent the defiant woman to a world of darkness and misery. Then he called Cróga and flew into the high thin air above the clouds, where he could simply be, where he saw nothing but the startling cold blue and the layer of white below.

He'd wanted to be a warrior, he thought, and had trained with pride and determination. He would have worked the land with Harken with pride if not as much determination as his brother.

Fate had handed him the sword and the staff, and so he'd carry them and all they stood for until his death.

But there were days like this when he wished, with all his heart, for a simpler life.

He yearned to just fly west, to home, to the valley, and, he couldn't deny it, to Breen.

To simply bury himself in her and forget everything else for one blessed hour.

As he rode that cold, thin air he heard her voice, bell-clear through the silence.

Choice turns out to be duty for both of us. But I'm here, and I'll wait. That's a choice, too, but it's not duty. I love you. It makes me afraid, and it makes me strong, but either way, I love you. So I'm here, and I'll wait.

"Gods, that she'd speak to me now, say those words now. Or not," he decided, as it might have been his own mind conjuring them up. "Down we go, Cróga. Today's duties aren't yet done."

The feast and celebration ending and beginning the year equaled duty. He couldn't shirk it.

He sat at the long table in the front of the banquet room. He ate, drank ale, had conversations he largely forgot five minutes afterward. He danced for duty.

Minga's daughter, Kiara, held out a hand to him.

"You look lovely, as always."

Smiling, she gave her head a little shake so the black curls and velvet ribbons cascading from the crown of her head danced like the people around them.

"For the compliment I'll ask if we might step out in the air instead of taking the dance."

"Now I owe you a dozen compliments."

"I told Aiden I'd help you escape for a few moments."

"Are you happy with him?" Keegan asked as they went out on a terrace festooned with colored lights for the celebration.

"So happy. I thought I would have a flirt with him, then he had my heart. I have his." She looked out to where the bonfire burned gold. "It's different now, everything for me. I know what love is, and I didn't, I think. Not this kind. I thought . . . I was in the Judgment today."

"Aye."

"I thought, when I looked at her, listened . . . she's like Shana. All my life I believed I knew Shana, and I loved her as a sister. I believed she felt the same for me. But never did she, not in truth. Like the girl at the Judgment felt no love for her own family."

"Odran corrupted her."

"Aye, aye, but doesn't there have to be something inside them, something that's inside Shana, to open them to him that way?"

"I think there is. We're not all made the same, Kiara."

"I used to believe we were, inside, I mean. Sure there's some that laugh more or cry more, or talk more. I'm one of those."

He kissed her knuckles. "Never."

And made her laugh.

"I thought, in our hearts and spirits, we were all good. We're Fey or, like my mother, just good. But I know that's not so, and because I know, the words you said today to the family? They spoke to me as well."

"To you?"

"The blame, that there was none. I've felt blame about Shana, how I'd often help her in her little schemes. They seemed harmless, and for fun. But under it, they weren't at all harmless. She isn't harmless."

"You're not to blame for that."

"I'm not, no, and I felt that today clear. Her parents aren't to blame. Sure they'd spoiled her, but in the way of loving. She was never my true friend, never a loving one. I was only of use to her."

Turning to him, she took both his hands in hers. "I say this to you, Keegan, to warn you to be careful, vigilant. She'll hurt you if she can. You above all others she would hurt. She'll do all she can to cause you harm, to cause harm to Breen, your family. Whatever you love, she'll strike at it. I saw that in her far too late, but I saw it clear."

"As I did, far too late. I'll say the same to you, Kiara—be careful, be vigilant."

"So I will. Will my mother come home soon?"

"Only a few days more and she'll be home, I promise you."

"We miss her, my father and I. Well now, I've kept you long enough. Will you give Breen my good wishes when you see her?"

"I will, of course. I know the valley isn't your home, but you're welcome in mine anytime."

He kissed her, made her smile.

"Now go dance, as your pretty red dress was made for it."

"So it was. And it nears midnight, so I'll find Aiden. Happy New Year to you, Taoiseach."

"And to you."

Rather than go back inside to the music and the dancing, Keegan walked to the balefire. Over its bright crackle, he heard the voices raised in song and celebration. As they should be, he thought.

He'd join them, as he should. But he'd take a moment or two in the last breaths of the dying year for himself.

Overhead the stars shined winter cold, and the moons hung in the black sky like beacons, gifting their light to all of Talamh.

The sea surged and ebbed, surged and ebbed, a song of its own.

Within the gold flames, the core of the fire glowed red as a dragon's heart.

And there, though he hadn't realized he'd looked, he saw her.

She wore a dress the color of emeralds, one that left most of her legs bare and sparkled like faerie dust. Her shoes, glittering gold, had heels like thin spikes.

He'd never seen her wear something so . . . provocative.

She sang with Marco, and, ah, Harken as well. Though he couldn't hear, he knew it was a happy tune from the light on her face. She'd left that glorious hair down so those marvelous curls fell as they wished.

He saw his sister dancing with Mahon, and his mother keeping time and laughing.

He imagined that the music in the farmhouse, the stomping of feet, and the voices raised sang loud enough to have long-lost spirits joining in.

It warmed him, as the fire warmed him. And still, it ached in him, the longing for home, for family, for the woman in the sparkling green dress. But he watched, and smiled as he did, sharing for a moment their joy.

Then the song ended as the year ended, and he imagined the cheers in the valley echoed those around him in the Capital, a welcome to the birth of the new.

In that moment she looked, and she saw him. Through the smoke and flame, their eyes met and held. When her lips curved, they curved for him. She touched two fingers to them, then held them toward him. And he, who'd never thought himself a sentimental sort, did the same.

Overhead, the sky exploded as faeries shot and showered bold jewels of light. In the castle, in the village below, and across the land, bells rang.

But he saw only her.

Then Marco lifted her off her feet, swung her, kissed her.

The vision vanished into smoke.

He stayed a moment longer, then turned to walk back to duty. Another toast or two, another dance or two, he promised himself, before he slipped away to the peace and quiet of his rooms.

Seamus, the lost Phelin's brother, met him on the terrace and held out a tankard of ale.

"Thanks for this, but why aren't you kissing your wife?"

"So I did, and well. Now she's dancing with my father. So welcome to the new, Taoiseach."

"Welcome to the new."

"Some look for you inside."

"Ah well." Keegan drank. "Of course."

"I toasted my taoiseach, and now I'll speak to my friend. Go home, Keegan."

"Ready to be rid of me?"

"To my friend of a lifetime, I say you've done all you need to do here, for the time, and more time will come for doing more. Go home to the valley, your farm, your family, your woman. We hold the Capital for you, and for Talamh."

"I know you do." He drank again. "She's not altogether in the way of being mine."

Shaking his head, Seamus lifted his tankard, drank deep. "*Mo dheartháir*, you may say it, and even in your way believe it, but that doesn't change the truth. Ah well. What I'm saying to you is take the time you need. You've given and will give again. When we lost Phelin, gods rest him, you gave us your shoulder, your hand, your heart."

"He was mine as well. A lifetime friend, as you are."

"That I know. So you gave to all what they needed. We stood when we needed, we fought, and we held. We will again. Today's Judgment was, well, a bloody bitch of a duty, and well done. And so done, Keegan.

"Was it home you saw in the balefire?"

"It was, aye, and that will hold me for another day or two. Three, I think, for the shagging meetings and bleeding diplomacy. But beyond that fecking shite, I want your counsel once more, and your father's, and others I know and trust to speak of what the traitor told us in the Judgment. There's much there to pick at."

He looked back toward the fire. "There are others like her, small and weak minds or greedy hearts or simply with some dark need inside. We have to root them out, Seamus, though gods know I find no joy in sending any to the eternal dark."

For a moment, silence held between them. Then Seamus spoke.

"I leaped in the lake that day along with you, and envied you, so envied you when you lifted the sword. Oh, so bright it shined in the morning sun. But that was the innocence of youth in my eyes."

Seamus clasped a hand on Keegan's shoulder. "Now, by all the gods, I don't envy you the sword or staff. We'll dig out those rotten roots, Taoiseach, and when you bring down the staff in Judgment on them, you'll bring it down with honor."

"Families will mourn, as Shana's does, as this Cait's does."

"They will, aye, and that blame lies with the ones who betrayed their families and the Fey."

"It does, so we'll meet. Not tomorrow, as too many will have sick heads and considerable regret they drank themselves drunk this night. I envy *that*," he realized. "I think I'd like a good drunk myself."

"Say the word." Seamus clapped him firmly on the shoulder again. "And I'll join you in one."

"Not this night," Keegan said with a laugh. "I've the First Day duties among others. But soon I'll take you up on it, be certain. Now, I've got two more dances in me before I can get away."

"Bridie Mag Aoidh's got her eye out for one."

"Is that the one with the strawberry hair and the odd sort of giggling?"

"That would be her sister, Maveen. Bridie's the blonde with a voice like rusty pipes."

"Ah gods, she's feet like long boats and clumsy with it."

Seamus gave Keegan another clap on the shoulder as they went back into the music and voices. "No indeed, I've no envy in me for you."

CHAPTER NINE

January winds blew cold, and they blew damp. Breen spent the mornings of the new year snuggled in her office. She blogged, then toggled between Bollocks's second adventure and the adult fantasy novel. She felt confident—and how she loved that sensation—she'd have Bollocks's book ready by spring.

She second-guessed the fantasy every time she sat down with it, then found herself just falling in until it was time to change gears and leave for Talamh.

And there, she filled her afternoons with magicks and training, with flights on Lonrach and rides on the ever-dependable Boy. In the evenings, she had the cottage and Marco, often Brian.

She might take an hour or two in her room, with Bollocks sleeping by the fire, to work a little more.

She couldn't say the nights were lonely, though they stretched long and she missed knowing Keegan slept beside her.

She took time for herself, visiting with Aisling and her boys, with Finola and Seamus, walking with Morena and watching the flight of the hawk.

She thought about her future, even set aside thoughts of Odran and war, and considered what her life might be like after.

After.

At the end of the first week of the new year, she walked with Marg, Tarryn, and Minga through the ruins.

Echoes, she thought, the echoes remained, but not the dark.

"It will stand," Tarryn said. "A memorial of a kind. What you forget to remember, you too often repeat, I think. So we remember what was done here in the name of faith, and we remember never to allow it to happen again."

She turned a circle, a woman in tall boots with her sun-kissed hair in a simple tail that flowed down her back. "More will walk here now, and remember."

"In my world, history speaks." Minga, wide-legged pants flowing, stepped out on a colonnade. "And it speaks of a time when those who ruled, and those under that rule, were judged by color."

She ran her fingers down the golden skin on the back of her hand. "This color would study and rise, would own the land and whatever riches they wished. This color would work the land and pay a portion to the rulers. This color would sew and craft and build. And this color would toil as slaves. So year by year this was law and custom."

She wandered up the curve of stone steps, looked out through an opening. "Then many, of all the colors, said no, no more. We share blood and heart and world and land. There were wars across Largus, and blood shed. Red blood, all the same under the skin. So the laws and customs changed. Some learned and remembered, others never do."

She walked down again.

"In every world, I think, all who can must learn and remember and stand against those who never do."

"This, *mo dheirfiúr*, is why you're on the council." Tarryn took her hand, then turned. "What do you feel here, Breen?"

"A lingering sorrow for wrongs done, but clean air. And . . . relief that what was done is finished."

"The spirits we freed," Marg added, "to the light and to the dark are on the next journey. As it should be. And if their time comes round again, there will be the fresh, the new, and that journey offers more choices."

She smiled, nodded, took Breen's hand and Minga's as Tarryn took Breen's other hand.

"We did good work, work of justice, of kindness. Work of the light. Blessed be to all," Marg said, "on this new journey, in this new year."

Bollocks trotted ahead, and the women walked out together.

Breen wondered she hadn't felt him, or known. Keegan sat on the big black stallion, who cropped at the tall grass in the graveyard.

Her heart gave a quick leap, and however foolish, the day seemed brighter. He dismounted, leaving Merlin to graze with the other mounts. He bent to greet the happy dog.

The winter wind stirred his hair, flapped his duster as he walked through the stones.

He greeted his mother first, as was proper, with a kiss she turned into a quick embrace.

"Welcome home, *mo chroí*. You made good time."

"The roads are hard and dry all the way west."

He kissed Marg, then Minga, in turn, before staring at Breen.

"Ah gods." Tarryn cast her eyes to the heavens. "Kiss the girl, for feck's sake, you great eejit."

"So I will."

He swept her right off her feet so she felt like the heroine in every romance novel she'd ever read. Then the world spun and spun when his mouth took hers.

"Well done," his mother approved. "And now, Breen, I bid you goodbye until the next." She cupped Breen's flushed cheeks in her hands, kissed her lightly.

"You're leaving?"

"It's time."

"Deaglan and Bria wait at the farm with their dragons to take you back." Keegan enfolded his mother. "Aisling will curse me for taking you away."

"She knows better. And we have the fire and the mirror until I come next to visit."

"Be safe, and you, Minga," Breen added. "Tell Kiara hello for me."

"I will."

"I'll ride with you to see you off." Marg gave Breen's hand a squeeze. "I'll see you tomorrow."

She stood with Keegan as they mounted, and watched cloaks fly as the three women set off at a gallop.

Bollocks raced behind them, barking his goodbyes. Then ran back again.

"I didn't know you were coming, or they were going."

"I hoped yesterday, even the day before, but it all took longer. There were . . . circumstances."

"You don't have to explain."

He let out a sound of frustration. "How am I to know this in here?" He tapped a finger on the side of her head. "To know what to explain and what not?"

She just smiled. "Why don't I just say I'm really happy to see you? Then you can kiss me again."

"That'll do fine."

He lifted her again, and she locked her arms around his neck as their mouths met.

Then, with his brow against hers, he held her a bit longer.

"Have you had time here with your father?"

"Yes, before we went in. It's clean, Keegan. Sad still, but clean. Do you want to walk through, or take time with your father and mine?"

"Not today." He glanced over, beyond the road, beyond the field, to the cottage.

"Oh. The Connellys. You need to go to them."

"I've been, before coming here. They said you went with my mother. They're grateful. As I am."

He eased back.

"Will you walk awhile? I've been in the saddle long enough for now."

"I'd like to walk." She gave Bollocks a pat on the head. "We'd like a walk."

They went to the horses, gathered the reins, and began to walk away from the stones.

"I saw you, New Year's Eve. Right at midnight."

"Aye. I took a moment in the air by the balefire, and there you were. It looked like a fine ceilidh."

"It was."

"Your dress that night. I hadn't seen it before."

"A bon voyage gift from Sally and Derrick when we first left for Ireland. Marco wouldn't take no. 'Girl, if you can't wear that killer on New Year's Eve, then when?'" She tipped her head up toward him. "You didn't like it?"

"I liked it quite a bit. What there was of it, I liked."

"The celebration in the Capital must've been wonderful."

He shrugged and took the stick Bollocks hunted up, gave it a long, hard toss. "Good craic for most. Sure I danced more than I wanted to, drank less. Kiara sends her best wishes."

"How is she?"

"She's well, truly. I find I misjudged her as I did Shana. And it may be I did because of Shana. I thought Kiara sweet, aye, and more than a bit foolish. She has the sweet, right enough, but not the foolish. She's life in her. She's filled with life."

He thought of her in her pretty red dress and dancing ribbons. Life, he thought again, and surprising strength.

"What Shana broke in her has mended only stronger."

He tossed the stick a second time, then walked awhile in silence.

"When I left, I thought a few days, a week if that. And I'd go back after another few at home to give my mother more time with Aisling and the children. But . . ."

"Circumstances."

"Aye. I'd tell you of them. It's not explaining, it's telling."

"Okay."

"Some is just . . . the small, the necessary. The bloody politics and diplomacy."

He threw the stick harder this time, as if throwing politics and diplomacy.

"My mother handles this with a light touch. I have to work harder to approach that touch. There's no need to talk about all that. It is. And the meetings with scholars and warriors and trainers—all needed to prepare or refine strategies. It's the Judgment I'll tell you of, as you should know."

"She didn't deny any of it or plead for mercy."

His brow furrowed as he looked at her. "You know this already?"

"I saw it in her that night. The fervor. Like Toric. Not as violent or overt, I think, but the fervor."

"You have the right of it. And a pride for her actions. More a contempt for her family, no shame in it. A contempt for all of Talamh, but so much for her family I all but heard her mother's heart break."

Breen reached for his hand, and Bollocks, stick clamped in his teeth, fell into step with them.

"But with the pride, the fervor, as you said, the contempt, she told us a great deal. More than I'd thought I'd pry from her she gave freely. Yseult sent the potion by raven, so we'll do what we can to watch for this."

"How did he indoctrinate her?" Breen wondered. "Turn her? How did Odran find her to know he could turn her?"

"I think Yseult, in her many guises, has come through many times over the years. And the scouts and spies. No one can pass through the Welcoming Tree who would do harm, but this is the only portal that can't be breached. We use protection," he explained. "But this can be worn away, like the sea against the shore, over time with magicks and focus and purpose."

"Like the breach under the waterfall."

"Aye. And this way they hunt for the weak or the unhappy, the angry. Gods know. This girl said she'd gone through to Odran's world."

"He brought her in?"

"So she said, and it was a pride that rang true. He lured her to him with promises of riches and more, with a lover. The dark faerie who tried to take you the day Marg brought you to your father's grave."

"That—" She shivered as she remembered being dragged into the air, the shock compounded when Keegan flew, sword singing, on his dragon. The fall to the ground, then the severed head thudding and rolling.

"It was months ago," she murmured.

"She's been with them longer, for certain. He saw you, left her to come for you."

"You killed him. My fault, your fault," she concluded. "That's been brewing in her, too. And she'd have gotten word to Odran. So he knew I was here, and sent Yseult. But—"

She stopped, turned to him. "There have to be more, more like her, and the one on Samhain, more like Toric and the Pious who were with him."

"You've the right of that, too. So it all took longer. Now we hunt them and we dig out those who'd betray their tribes, their families. And digging them out, use them or banish them as seems best."

"Use them. Like counterintelligence, I think. Feeding them false information or information you want passed on."

"Aye." Still walking, he gave her a considering look. "That's quick of you, and saves the explaining."

"Doesn't make it suck less," she muttered. "Knowing there are people you've sworn to protect, you've fought for, my father and yours died for, who'd betray everything for an asshole god who would slit them open in sacrifice without a second thought. And why?"

As temper snapped in her, she threw a hand in the air. Tiny sparks sizzled.

"Because they want more power when they've been given so much already? More riches when they live in something as close to freaking paradise as it gets? Or because they get sucked into worshipping the cruelty Odran represents?"

"You're right raging over it," Keegan said after a moment.

"Damn right I am. The Fey are peaceful, generous, joyful. I know that because I feel it in me. I'm part of it. We're brave and loyal. Flawed, sure, like anything alive, but to choose that over this?"

She took a breath.

"Some learn and remember," she said, thinking of Minga's words. "Others never do."

"There you have it in a . . ." He lifted a hand, wiggled his fingers. And somehow she understood, and understanding, calmed again.

"Nutshell."

"That, aye. Even gods make mistakes, and he made one with Cait. He picked one too angry to be smart. We'll find others." He gave her a long look. "It's odd for me, I find, to have walked and talked and not be annoyed with the talking. You're a sensible sort most of the time, Breen Siobhan."

"Most of the time?"

"Most," he repeated. "It warmed me to see all of you in the fire. You the most for all that. I couldn't hear the song you sang, but I felt the pleasure of it. Did you see me before that?"

"On New Year's Eve?"

"After the Judgment, after I sent the girl through and sealed her in the Dark World. I flew above the clouds on Cróga. Did you see me, speak to me?"

"No. Why do you ask?"

"I heard you. You spoke to me, as you did in the lake all those years ago. I heard you but didn't see you."

"I didn't . . . What did I say?"

"You said—" Now he hesitated, and hedged more than a little. "You said for such as us, choice was often duty. You said words I needed to hear at that time, in that place. Or I imagined you did."

"You'll always choose duty. It's who you are."

"And you?"

"I think—I hope—it's who I've become. Is that all I said?"

He shrugged, and though he knew he evaded, he told himself he'd talked more than enough. "You said what I needed to hear. We'll ride now and see how well you do at a gallop."

She did just fine, though he was—as usual—stingy with his praise.

She found Morena with the two older boys, schooling them in the art of hawking while the new puppy Harken called Darling leaped on and scrambled around the ever-stoic Mab.

"Welcome home to you," Morena said to Keegan. "Your brother's in the barn doing what he does, and Mahon's on a patrol. I'm giving Aisling a bit of a rest with the babe and entertaining myself with the boys."

She bent to rub Bollocks, who darted away to prance and play with the puppy.

Breen heard Mab's quiet sigh of relief in her head.

"And I'm escaping from whatever Harken's doing in the barn," Morena told them, "and minding the pup, who'll rarely leave Harken's side. We saw Tarryn and Minga off. And then? Well, Marco gathered up my nan, and yours, Breen, along with Sedric. They're having a baking contest over on the other side. I wasn't invited."

"Why don't I invite you to the results?"

"Accepted."

"I don't suppose he'd be thinking about making a meal while he's at it?" Keegan wondered.

"He's always thinking about making a meal. He put a pot of something on before we came over."

"I'll look forward to that, assuming I'm asked."

"I missed you," Breen said simply.

"Good," he said, equally simply, and walked away.

"Now Bollocks has two girlfriends," Breen observed.

"She's a whirlwind, is Darling. And darling enough with it I'm working on forgiving her for chewing a hole in one of my best socks. I may forgive Harken for pointing out she wouldn't have if I hadn't left them on the floor. Which *I* wouldn't have done if I hadn't stripped myself naked in a rush to have a tumble with him in the first place."

"And so goes your married life."

"I'm prizing every moment, and that's the truth of it. That's the way, Fin! Well done! Now give your brother a turn."

So Breen watched the boy help his little brother with the glove while Kavan danced in place, so delighted his little wings came out to flutter. And her dog, equally delighted, rolled in the grass with the inexhaustible pup.

Just perfect, she thought as Kavan, still dancing, lifted his gloved arm. The hawk soared toward it, a sweep of wide wings that folded when he landed. Kavan's arm dropped inches with the weight, but he held, and turned to Morena with a smile that would've lit the world.

"And well done, lad, well done indeed."

"Amish is amused."

Morena nodded. "You read him well, as he's all of that. Well now, look there." She gestured as Kavan, without prompting, lifted his arm to send Amish off. Then he raced away from his brother, flew up out of reach, and laughing as he hovered, lifted his arm for the hawk.

"There's a skill I hadn't yet taught him," she said as Amish flew back to sit quietly on the boy's arm. "And wouldn't have tried for another year or more."

"He's born for it." And through the scene before her, Breen saw another. "They'll both fly one day, Kavan with his wings, Finian on his dragon, and with hawks that come from your own on their arms."

"You see that? Know it?"

"So clearly, for just a moment." A moment that left her heart skipping as it opened. "Don't tell them. I think . . . I think some things should just come."

"Then I won't." Nudging back her cap, Morena studied the boys. "But knowing it, I'll put more time into training them for what's to come."

"Breen Siobhan."

She turned, and more from luck than skill caught the unsheathed sword Keegan tossed to her.

"Defend," he ordered, and killed her before she managed to take her stance.

"I'll be moving well away," Morena decided.

"I wasn't ready."

"And so you're dead, as you must always be ready. Pick up your sword, woman. Defend."

This time, steel met steel, and the clash rang through the winter air.

He was relentless, he and the phantom enemies he conjured for her to battle. Dark faeries, demon dogs, crazed elves sprang up again and again.

Obviously it proved entertaining enough to bring Harken out of the barn so he stood with Morena and Finian, the pup—finally tuckered—between his legs and Kavan on his hip.

At some point while sweat ran into her eyes, Mahon flew over and dropped down to join the audience. Though the onlookers rooted for her enthusiastically, it didn't do much to help.

She lost count of the number of times she perished.

She fought with sword, with magicks, with fists and feet. Though the blades striking couldn't cut or gash, the fangs snapping, the claws raking couldn't pierce skin, they bloody well stung.

By the time the day dropped into dusk, her whole body ached.

While she stood panting, her sword lowered with an arm she feared couldn't lift a handful of feathers, he sheathed his own.

"You're out of practice," he decreed.

"I trained every damn day."

"With this lot." He gestured to their audience. "And they're too easy on you, that's clear enough."

"You had her taking on five at a go," Aisling called out. She, with the baby bundled into a sling, had come out to join the others.

"She's the grand prize, isn't she now? And if there's a chance to separate and surround her, they'll do just that. Coddling doesn't sharpen skills."

"Coddling my arse," Harken objected. "She trained hard."

"Not hard enough. She'll do better tomorrow."

"Ah, bugger it and you with it, Keegan. Come into the house, Breen," Aisling invited. "Warm yourself by the fire and I'll fix you something that'll ease the aches you're feeling."

"I'm fine, but thanks." Pride wouldn't allow the *coddling*. "I need to get home."

"You did fine work against the were-bear and the fanged demon as well."

"Thank you, Mahon." She shoved the sword at Keegan. "Good night, everyone. Let's go, Bollocks."

She started across the road and prayed she could climb over the low wall without moaning out loud.

Keegan came up behind her and simply lifted her over.

"You should be training now with your own sword. You need to start wearing it when you come to Talamh."

"I'm not a warrior." She gritted her teeth as she climbed the steps to the tree, willed her legs to lift up to the low curving branch. "I don't need to go strutting around with a sword."

He passed through with her and into a misting rain.

"We have rotted roots yet to dig out, Breen. Being armed isn't strutting about."

"I am armed." She flicked a hand, held a ball of fire. Then crushed it out. "All the time."

"Fair enough, but the sword adds protection." He stopped, and in the dim light, took her by the shoulders. "I gave you the sword because you've earned it. It's no small thing in our tradition to forge a sword for someone and give it."

"And I appreciate it, I do, but—"

"You're not understanding me. I wouldn't have given it if you hadn't earned it. It would diminish the blade and you, and myself for all that. You've trained, and no, you'll never have a brilliant hand with a sword, but you work at it. You came through a battle with courage. So no, not a warrior, not by choice, but you stand and you fight, you train and you try. You earned the sword, one made for your hand, one that bears your mark. I ask you to wear it."

He soothed her aches as he spoke, and even her pride and lingering resentment couldn't pull her away from the relief.

"They didn't coddle me. They're not as hard on me as you are—who is? But that's a long way from being coddled."

"We see that differently. I will say Mahon had it right. You handled the Were well enough."

She looked him dead in the eye while Bollocks sat, head turning toward one, then the other.

"You're saying that because you want a meal and sex."

"Of course I'm wanting those, and plan to have them. But you handled the Were well enough."

She decided to take it. "I don't have a belt for the sword."

"Bring it over tomorrow. I'll make one for you." Now he lowered his hands to her hips. "I know the size of you."

Mollified a bit, she walked on. As she started to toss out some light, Bollocks let out a bark—a happy one—and raced ahead.

Lights danced down the path, with voices following them.

She heard Marg.

"There's that fine boy, aye, you're a fine one. And where's our girl?"

She watched them come through the mists, the tiny lights flickering all around them.

Bollocks pranced proudly beside Marg, with Finola laughing on the way and Sedric just behind them. All carried baskets, and the scent of their contents wafted seductively down the path.

And she thought they looked as giddy as teenagers on their way to a party.

"You missed a grand afternoon," Finola told them.

One with plenty of wine, unless Breen missed her guess. "Who won?" she wanted to know.

"We decided on a draw," Sedric told her, very seriously. "After much debate and discussion, and the sampling of the goods themselves."

"Enough sampling we'll likely give the evening meal a miss. And still." Marg lifted her basket. "We've enough to fill sweet teeth in half the valley."

"I wouldn't say no to a sample myself."

"And sure you'll have plenty at the cottage." Finola tapped a finger on Keegan's chest. "We'll be dropping some off at the farm, and for Aisling and the boys as well."

"You've still a bit of flour just here." Keegan kissed her cheek.

"Oh, you sly one." Laughing, she reached in her basket. "One biscuit, and that's the end of it."

"Save the sweets," Sedric advised, "as Marco has what he calls pozole in the pot. We had a sample there as well."

"Spicy." Finola wiggled her eyebrows. "Like the cook himself. I have a dish in here to take my Seamus, as he likes the spicy."

"And with the spicy and the sweet, we surely had a vat of wine." Marg leaned her head toward Sedric. "What a fine time we had. Now off with you, out of this wet, and have a fine time yourselves."

When they continued down the path, Keegan looked after them. "They're all of them a bit scuttered, and happy with it."

"Scuttered?"

"Drunk. A little." He bit into the biscuit. "And still the lot of them bake like gods."

When he offered Breen the second half, she shook her head. "I'll wait. I've had Marco's pozole before, so that'll come first for me."

"And what's this pozole?"

"Incredible," she assured him.

The minute he walked in the cottage, into the scents, he knew she spoke truth.

"Well now, Marco, it seems you've done it yet again."

"Welcome back!" With his dish towel over his shoulder, Marco came out of the kitchen to give Keegan a solid hug.

"Brother, I'm wet."

"Then take off your coat. You, too, Breen. Wine or beer?"

"Whatever's handy," Keegan told him.

"I've got a wine that goes with the pozole, so start there. I hope you're hungry."

"If I wasn't, whatever's cooking there would change that. A pie as well, I see."

"Deep-dish apple, with currants. I tried my hand at a flan, too, because pozole. I didn't want to go head-to-head with Sedric on shortcake biscuits. His are the best, but we've got some of his, and some of Finola's cream cake, Nan's winter berry tarts. And more. Jesus, what a great day."

All but babbling, he poured wine while Breen filled the food and water bowls for Bollocks.

"We're going to do it every month, like a round robin. At Nan's, at Finola's, here."

"This is Sidhe wine," Keegan said after he drank.

"Finola brought it, said it went with everything."

"She's right there. No finer in the whole of Talamh."

"Tell me. We drank two bottles while we baked. I might just sprout wings. I had the *best* time."

Breen set the table while they talked, while they drank. She watched Keegan as he leaned against the counter and laughed as Marco recounted the great baking contest. Music played, as she imagined it had all through the afternoon.

She lit candles while Bollocks curled up by the fire for a nap.

They'd share a meal, and likely gorge on pie. Later, Keegan would share her bed, and when he returned from duty, Brian would share Marco's.

Despite the training and the countless defeats she'd suffered during it, she had to agree, it had been a damn good day.

Like Morena, she'd prize every moment.

CHAPTER TEN

It rained for five full days, pouring and soaking and drenching on both sides of the portal. The roads went to mud; the bays held as leaden gray as the sky.

And the green glowed like polished emeralds.

Keegan rode or flew through it every day, checking portals from west to east and back again. He gave time to Harken and the farm when he had it to spare and consulted with his mother daily through the mirror.

The hunt for Odran's spies and scouts remained constant.

Though she'd have preferred to stay snuggled in the cottage with her work, Marco's music, and whatever culinary magic he conjured in the kitchen drifting through the air, Keegan pushed her through daily training.

Every evening, she trudged back to the cottage wet, muddy, and bruised. She wore the sword and almost grew used to it.

On the first day some blue broke through the gray, she came out of her office to where Marco sat working.

She got herself a Coke, let Bollocks out for a run to the bay, then sat. She waited as Marco held up a finger.

"Another minute. Solid blog this morning, by the way."

She said nothing, just studied him as he worked.

He had his long braids tied back and wore the red sweater Finola had knitted him. His black high-tops tapped to some inner tune as his clever fingers raced over the keyboard.

"And there we go. Got your daily social media posts up. I'm thinking if they can bring Darling over one day, I'd get some shots of her and Bollocks, 'cause I'm betting you're going to add her to one of his adventures sometime soon."

"You know me so well, and that's a great idea. I couldn't do this without you, Marco Polo."

"Oh hell, girl, you'd write the books and the blog." He picked up his tall glass of fizzy water. "But you sure wouldn't shine as bright on Twitter."

"You're going to do a cookbook."

"I am?"

"You read the comments on the blog, and the asks for recipes whenever I mention something you've cooked or baked. I can help you—not with the cooking and baking, but with the text and the photos—and I've already asked my agent what she thought."

"Well, Jesus, Breen." He scrubbed at his face. "You know how I cook. Try this, try that, how's it look, smell, and all that."

"And that's just how you should do it, and Carlee agrees. I don't want it to be work—more work for you. But I think you could have fun with it. Just think about it."

"I guess I could think about it, but—"

"No buts. Just think. Anyway, a couple other things, if you've got the time for it."

"We need to start over pretty soon."

"I know, but a few things first. I should have Bollocks's next book ready to submit in another six or eight weeks. Maybe. Pretty sure. Hope."

"That's great."

"And I have an idea I can outline—I think—for the third. And yeah, it'll introduce Darling."

"I knew it!" He bopped his shoulders up and down. "You really need to let me read the one you're finishing up. I can work little hints into social. Nothing major because we're still seeding the first, and we want that to drop before we start seeding the second."

"Listen to you with your publishing talk."

"I like it. Never saw myself doing this for a living, but I like it."

"It shows, and that's good, because that leads me to one of the other things. I think, hope again, maybe early April we could take a couple days. We could surprise Sally for his birthday."

His eyes popped. "Go to Philadelphia?"

"For a start, yes. See Sally and Derrick. And I'll go to see my mother."

He took her hand. "I'll go with you."

"No, I'll be fine, and I'll be ready. Then we'll take the train to New York."

His eyes popped again, and this time his mouth fell open. "Do what? New York? Are you messing with me?"

"It's time you met the people you're working with in person, and they met you. And, of course, if we had the basic concept of your fabulous and unique cookbook worked out . . ."

"By April." He pushed up, paced a circle. "You're scaring me some here."

"If," she said again. "We could open the portal into the apartment, go that way, since Keegan has one of the Fey there. And I want to meet her, too. It saves time and trouble, so we'd have a day with Sally and Derrick, a day in New York. It all depends on . . ."

"War and peace."

"I can't go, even for a couple of days, if I'm needed here. I'm talking to you first. I have to talk to Keegan and Nan. But I wanted to see how you felt about it. And you'd want to see how Brian felt about it."

"Yeah, yeah. All of that."

"Things have been quiet, but they won't stay that way. I'd say we'd go right now, while they are, but I feel like it's not the right time. And I don't know if that's because it's not, or because I want to finish the book first."

"When you say go, we go. Brian's going to be fine with it. We've all got our work, right? This is yours and mine. Now I've got a question."

"I had another thing."

"Me first. How about the big book? When are you going to send that one off?"

"It's not ready."

"I've been hearing that for a while now." He held up a hand before she could speak. "And I know, like you know, Carlee's given you nudges—in her really gentle way—to send a chunk of it. When are you gonna do that? Pull that trigger, honey."

This time she pushed up. This time she paced. "I'm so stupid nervous, Marco. I didn't think I'd be this nervous again. I don't feel so shaky about the second YA, but it's familiar territory, and god, so much fun for me. But the other . . . I can't even settle on a title."

"What is it now?"

"Well, this week it's *Magicks Dark and Light*. But maybe—"

"It's strong. Leave it. And let me read some of what's after it. The first chapter. No, the first two. Let me read them tonight."

"It's not—" She hissed when he pointed at her. "Give me two more weeks. I'll let you read that much in two more weeks."

He rose, held out his hand, crooked his little finger. "Pinky swear."

"Shit!" She hissed again but hooked her pinky with his. "Two more weeks."

"Pinky sworn and sealed. Now, let's go. Maybe it's cleared up in Talamh, too. Put the whammy on the pot roast, will you?"

"Is that what it is? Smells great. But I had another thing."

"Talk to me on the way."

She strapped on the sword, which still felt weird, grabbed a jacket, a scarf.

"It's warmer," she said when they went out. "Still winter, but it's already turning warmer." When Bollocks bounded up to them, she dried him, then stood a moment.

"The bay's pale blue instead of gray, and everything smells fresh, clean." She took Marco's hand, squeezed it before they started toward the woods.

"Have you and Brian talked about after? After all of this?"

"Yeah, and that's us, together. Wherever, and I have to figure that's here. Not the other side, Talamh, not to live. I need my damn broadband and hot showers. I gotta have a freaking dishwasher. But you're here, and I know you're staying. Truth? I think I knew that the first time you saw the cottage. You cried. You cried because it was exactly what you wanted."

"It is."

"We've got Sally and Derrick back in Philly, and my sister. But we can visit. The rest of my family . . . I had to accept they'll never accept. And they'd never accept Brian either. So we talked some about finding a place on this side, close to you, close to Talamh—where I've got so many people I care about now."

"You'd be happy here, in Ireland?"

"Loved it since I first set eyes on it. Never figured to live here, but never figured on Brian either. He's my everything, and I'm his."

"It's just beautiful to see that, Marco. To feel it, to know it."

"First sight." He sighed with it, a quietly happy sound. "Never believed in that until it happened to me. On the, you know, practical side of it, as long as I'm connected, I can work anywhere."

He gave her hand a quick, hard squeeze. "And until the after, girl, I'm with you."

"I know that, and I love you. And if you're sure about the rest, I thought I could ask Nan about adding onto the cottage."

"Breen."

"Just hear me out. You'd both have your own space. Or, if it's better, and I think it would be for you, there's enough land to build another cottage. Yours and Brian's. We'd be neighbors."

"Neighbors," he murmured.

"You could get your own horse on the other side, and Harken would keep it at the farm. I know he would. You love riding, and you could have your own. You could design your own kitchen, and the king of showers. You could have a music room and write and play."

He stopped on the path, wrapped her in his arms. "I love you, Breen."

"I love you, Marco. Please say yes. If you stay, stay close, close to me, close to Talamh."

"Can't say yes till I talk to Brian, but it couldn't be more what I'd want. Now I'm gonna cry all over you."

"It couldn't be more what I want either." She kissed his wet cheek, hugged him tight. "We'll get through the rest, Marco. We'll get to the after, and we'll have what couldn't be more what we want."

They found Marg with Sedric outside the kitchen. Both wore trousers and sweaters with Sedric's hair shining silver and Marg's red glory bundled up under a knit cap. When they went out to join them, Breen saw a huge pot smoking over a fire while the two of them cubed a mountain of apples on a worktable.

"Oh, and welcome. Breen, *mo stór*, go in and get our boy his biscuit, as my hands are full."

"Applesauce?" Marco guessed as Breen went for the jar.

"Apple wine," Sedric told him. "My young cousin brought the apples to barter, and it seemed a fine use for them."

"Yeah?" Marco checked the pot, found what looked like clear water. "How do you do it? You can't just boil them down."

"More to it than that, and a good job of work, as the rain's finally left us for a while."

Breen brought out the biscuit. Bollocks decided the best place to chomp it down was under the table by Marg's feet.

"Do you want some help?"

"We've near to worked through the apples here, but the company's welcome."

"That's a kind of fermenter, right?" Marco walked down the table to another pot with a spout near the bottom.

"It is indeed. Aren't you the clever one?"

"We'll tie up the apples in this straining bag here," Sedric explained, "good and tight, and into the fermenter, then the boiling water with it, then water to cool it. And it all sits for a time before you do the science of it."

"And after the science, and a bit of magick, after all, comes the patience. A good wine takes time."

Once they'd tied up the cubed apples, Sedric lifted them into the fermenter.

"Let me get some gloves, cart that big-ass pot over. It's gotta be heavy."

"No need for that. You stand back a bit, Marco." So saying, Marg lifted her hands toward the pot. An arch of bubbling water rose into the air, streamed from pot to pot.

"You could fill that bucket there from the well." Sedric gestured. "And that way you'll have a hand in the making of it."

"And once Marco adds the cooling, we'll take ourselves off to the workshop and leave the men to their devices."

"I'd like to talk to you about some things first. Right after I get over the shock and amusement of watching Marco fill a bucket from a well. It fits, actually," Breen decided. "Because I guess it won't be the last time. He's going to stay in Ireland. He and Brian talked it out, and—I'm just calling it *after*—and after, they'll live on the other side, in Ireland, so Brian can go back and forth easily."

"Oh, I'm more than pleased, so much more than pleased to hear that. We were hoping, weren't we?" She reached for Sedric's hand.

"That we were. Here now, neighbor, pour it in slow." Sedric supervised, nodded as Marco added the water from the bucket. "And that's that until it's not."

"I was going to take a ride. Can I come back in an hour or two and see what's next?"

"I wouldn't mind a ride myself. We'll do that, then do what's next."

"I'm so glad you're staying close, you and Brian." Marg cupped Marco's face in her hands. "I'm happy to know I'll see your face often, and happy to know you'll be near to Breen, as a finer friend she couldn't have."

"I'd like it if it could be really close. Would you be all right if we added a cottage for Marco and Brian by the bay, near Fey Cottage?"

"A better idea I've never heard. Have you, Sedric?"

"If I have, I can't think of it."

"It's your land, *mo stór*, to do with as you like."

"I wouldn't have the land or the cottage if it wasn't for you."

"Oh, what a time we'll have doing it up—close enough for friends and neighbors, but with enough distance to be private for all. We'll get Seamus on it, as he's got the way. You'll talk to him, Marco, about what you and Brian want in your home, and trust me, Finola will have plenty to say about it. As will this one."

"Opinions, of course. But the right ones," Sedric said firmly. "It'll be the kitchen, for certain, at the heart of it. You'll want a place for your music, and one for Brian's art and such."

"I'm choking up again." Marco swiped at his eyes. "I gotta say something before I blubber. Back in Philadelphia, my family's Sally and Derrick because my, well, my family-family, except for my sister, we—they—I'm gay, and that just doesn't work for them."

"I'm sorry for them," Marg murmured. "And will hope one day the locks on their hearts break open."

"Wouldn't count on it. But the thing is, I've got family right here. The two of you, you're Breen's, but you're mine, too. That's how I feel. I really love you."

"And are loved. There now, sweet boy." Marg enfolded him. "*Garmhac*. Grandson. You're ours. Now, off to the farm with you with your grandda for horses, and have your ride."

"Okay. It feels like another really good day."

"It does, aye, and we'll hold tight to them."

Breen watched them go. "It means so much to him, to me, to do this."

"Love costs nothing. I wonder at those who can't feel it, or won't give or take it. Ah well, we've more than enough to spare, don't we?" Marg said to Bollocks when he rubbed against her legs.

"I wanted to talk to you about something else," Breen began as they walked into the trees toward the workshop. "I wanted to take a few days, with Marco, maybe in April. A day in Philadelphia, another in New York."

"To see the mother of your heart, and then for business."

"Yes. I won't go if I'm needed, if things aren't—quiet the way they are right now. I know all of this is more important."

"Your family on the other side and your work are important, and of course you should go. Why do you wait until spring?"

"It's Sally's birthday, and it's the book. I want to finish Bollocks's next book."

At his name, he wagged all over, then leaped into the stream to splash.

"Of course. I'd like to send a gift for him when you go. He gave you love when I couldn't." On the bridge Marg paused, as she often did. "Now, tell me what you feel."

"I feel the trees, resting before the spring, as the earth rests. And . . . four doe with three young. Yearlings. They'll wait until Bollocks is inside to come and drink. There's a dragon and rider flying east from the Far West. And Lonrach, he's with your Dilis near the lake. And there's . . ."

Her breath caught.

"Nan." She groped for Marg's hand. "Odran. Blood. Blood magicks. I can't see where, only feel it. So deep and dark. Not the waterfall. I can't see."

"Does he feel you?"

"I— No."

"Hold the curtain closed, *mo stór.*"

"It's hard. He's stronger now. I can feel his anger, and it feeds him like the blood feeds him."

"Step back from him, step back."

"I need to see."

"Step back, and look. I'm with you. The curtain is closed to him. Step back, and look."

She felt Marg's light strengthen her own, suddenly felt Bollocks by her side. Felt both, saw herself with them as if looking through a glass. Though the urge to step forward came strong, she stepped back. And through the curtain, thin but steady, she saw.

He stood naked in a circle of black candles. He had a small scar on his chest over his heart. Smoke and chanting filled the air, rising and rising, and through it she heard the sound of waves crashing, a raging beat. On an altar of stone, the sacrifice lay, naked like her god, with her skin smeared with blood.

Breen felt no fear from her, but a terrible excitement.

He mounted her, and as the chants grew deeper, darker, took her with a kind of brutality that had Breen's hand trembling in Marg's.

"Stay strong," Marg said in her head. "Stay quiet."

And she saw through him what seemed to be claws, claws that pierced the faerie's flesh, drew blood to drip on the stone.

She screamed, not in pain, but in exultation.

When he finished, she lay, her eyes locked with his, and his glowed red.

"I give myself to your glory, Odran the Only. I give my body, my life, my soul."

"And so I take."

He sliced a claw over her throat, and while the chants grew deafening, drank.

She felt glee, so much glee, then saw Shana outside the circle, dressed in gold, dripping with jewels, hands clapping.

She saw more there that twisted inside her.

And saw the curtain shake.

"Enough!" Marg snapped it out. "Control it. Come back from it. Enough."

"It's gone. It's gone. I need to sit down."

"Inside. You've gone cold and pale. Lean on me now." She waved a hand at the workshop door to throw it open, and again to have the fire in the hearth blazing.

"You'll sit," she said as she took Breen's weight. "I'll get you a potion to warm and soothe you."

"Did you see? God, did you see? You were there with me. You and Bollocks. I could see us."

"I saw some, through you, but not all, I think. Here now, here, by the fire. You're shivering."

Marg tucked a throw around her, and Bollocks laid his head on her knee.

"I'm all right." But the cold, the cold pierced down to the bone. "It was just—so much. I could've gone through the curtain, Nan. I think I could've gone through and tried to stop it."

"Gone where I couldn't follow, alone, against so many? You'd not have stopped it, *mo stór*. Here, drink."

She brought Breen a cup warmed by her own hands.

"In the end, I saw Shana. Did you?"

"I didn't, no. The curtain was thinning, and I had to hold it for you. What of her?"

"What's inside her, Nan, it's not right. What he put inside her, the baby? It's dark like him, twisted like her, and it's not growing—I don't know—right. Deformed, somehow. I don't know."

"She made her choice, Breen."

"I know." She sipped, felt the worst of the chill ebb. "The Sidhe on the altar, you saw?"

"I did."

"She wanted what he did to her, all of it. She felt honored, excited. When he was on her, in her, did you see what he was?"

"I know what he is."

"No, no, did you see his eyes, did you see the claws?"

Marg's breath caught. "This I didn't."

"He's not just a god, Nan, not only a god. There's demon in him. I saw it, I felt it." Her eyes filled as she looked into Marg's. "There's demon in him, so it's in me."

"You're sure of this?"

"I'm sure. Oh, Nan, if that part of me turns."

"Don't be foolish." The quick dismissal left Breen speechless. "You mistake if you think all demons are dark and evil. Like anything else, it's choice. Many embrace the dark, but you never have and never will."

"Did you know? Did you?"

"Not before this, and I think you feared it, so hid it and well. Let me tell you this, and know it—as I love you—as truth. This makes you stronger. It makes you more. And remember, if this passed to you, it passed to your father. Does that change who he was?"

"No. Do you think he knew?"

"I think he didn't, and you wouldn't if you hadn't seen what you were meant to see so we'd know these things. Will you open for me now, let me see? I'd send you to Harken, who has more skill with this, but you're mine, so that's enough."

The cold had gone to ice, and the ice coated her belly.

"If it's bad, you have to tell me. We have to find a way to suppress it."

"Give me your hands now." Marg took the cup, set it aside. "Give me your hands, and open."

"Promise me first."

"You have my promise. I'll never lie to you."

Breen put her hands in Marg's. "I think you have to help. I'm not sure I can do it."

"You can, but I'll help. Look at me, see only me, as I see only you. Open to one who loves you. Ah, there you are, that's the way."

Breen felt herself drift on Marg's voice.

"There's my darling, there's my love. Such light. So much. Strength, courage still so new, power still growing, such heart. And there's fierce in it."

"Is it bad? Is it bad?"

"Bright and light, every part of you. There's nothing in you for you to fear. Not any more than this sweet boy looking at you with love has to fear the demon dog he sprang from."

"I forgot. I forgot." On a wave of relief, she leaned down to hug Bollocks. "My water demon. I forgot. Something else in common."

"He'll have another biscuit for it." Rising, Nan went for the jar, and had Bollocks wagging again.

"You'll tell Keegan all of this, as it's more than useful. But first we'll do some bright magicks here to balance out the dark."

Nodding, Breen rose. "Yes, I need to practice. I don't think this quiet time will last much longer."

"Listen to me, my darling girl, child of my child, light of my heart. Listen and believe. He's no match for you. I know that with everything I am."

"I want to believe that." Struggling to steady, Breen let out a long breath. "Let's make sure of it. Let's make the bright."

Bollocks started the bright by dancing on his hind legs for the biscuit.

PART II
LIFE

Life is a pure flame,
and we live by an invisible sun within us.

–Sir Thomas Browne

To be what we are, and to become what we are
capable of becoming, is the only end of life.

–Robert Louis Stevenson

CHAPTER ELEVEN

After leaving her grandmother, Breen called her dragon, and with Bollocks, flew west over the sea. She'd steadied—Marg had seen to it—but needed the flight, the communion with Lonrach and with Bollocks's unbounded joy.

She circled back, soaring over the hills and the Troll camp. On impulse, she took Lonrach down, landed just above the camp.

Children stopped playing; others around the fires or about their work stopped as well.

Rather than dismount or let Bollocks race down, she remembered formalities.

"Greetings to all. I haven't come to trade today but hope I'm welcome."

She watched Sul, tall, arms like battering rams, and the mound of her belly under her rough shirt and trousers, get to her feet.

"Ya are welcome, Daughter of the O'Ceallaigh, Daughter of the Fey, Warrior of the Battle of the Dark Portal." She angled her head, warrior braid swaying. "As is yer dog. We've heard tales of Bollocks the Brave and True."

"Thank you." Breen dismounted, told Bollocks to stay by her side as was polite. "Greetings to you, Sul, Mother of the Trolls, and to Loga and all your kin."

She looked down at Bollocks as she crossed the encampment to the stone huts. "Bollocks would like to greet your young. They have permission to touch him, and we ask he be permitted the same."

"Granted." Then Sul held out a hand, gripped Breen's forearm.

"Loga is in the mines. I can send for him if ya wish to speak with him."

Children, and those not so young, surrounded Bollocks to stroke and laugh.

"I came to see you, particularly. To see how you're doing. Please give Loga my thanks. I know he and others of your tribe traveled to the battle to fight when they were sorely needed."

"No thanks is necessary. We are of Talamh. Wine for the daughter," she shouted, and, knowing her duty, Breen sat on the ground outside Sul's hut. "It's kind of ya to come, to take yer time to see me."

"Your burn's healed well."

"With yer help."

Breen accepted the cup. "And you're well otherwise?"

"Strong and well, and so is this gift of a child, though he's put me off my mead. Ya have my permission."

"Thank you." Reaching out, Breen laid a hand on Sul and the child. Then closed her eyes, sighed. "Strong and well and bright. I had reasons inside me to know the strong and well and bright stirring in his mother."

She looked back as Bollocks raced tirelessly after the stick the kids took turns—more or less—tossing. "And to see young, happy faces. I can't stay long now. I have duties. But when I come again, I'll bring sweets to trade."

"Yer always welcome here." Sul smiled. "And so are the sweets."

She felt lighter when she left, and flew to the farm a solid hour earlier than expected.

She noticed first the targets set up near the wooded area well behind the house. So Keegan planned for archery training, which she found very slightly preferable to work with the sword. What she didn't notice as she landed was anyone.

No Harken in the field or Morena, no kids out playing or Keegan. Dismounting, stroking a hand over Lonrach's scales, she listened to the quiet.

Some horses grazing, but none in the paddocks. Sheep, cows, and now listening closer, the rutting of pigs, the hum of chickens.

She thought of the first time she'd stepped into Talamh—stumbled in, she corrected. The quiet, much like this, but with Harken singing as he walked behind a plow and plow horse.

Not even a year ago, she realized, though it felt like a lifetime. It felt like her life the way Philadelphia never had.

Whatever happened with that life, she'd have no regrets, as it had given her what she'd searched for when she'd titled her blog.

She'd found herself.

"And so much more," she murmured with one hand on the sassy topknot of her dog, the other on the smooth scales of her dragon.

For a moment, she pressed her cheek to Lonrach's sinuous neck. He'd fly to the mountaintop, to Dragon's Nest. She felt that from him. And she had only to call to bring him back.

"We'd go with you if we could."

But she stepped back. He turned his head, those amber eyes bright on hers. Then he rose up and up, shimmering red against the blue, and soared through the layers of clouds.

She turned toward the house, but Bollocks scampered away, raced toward the stables and back, away and back.

"Okay then, the stables it is."

She walked away from the house over grass thick and springy and still wet from the days of rain. As she got closer, she saw the stable doors stood open, and she heard singing from inside.

She took it for Harken, who often sang as he worked, but realized even before she got to the open doors, Keegan sang, and sang softly and beautifully, in Talamhish.

She smelled hay, manure, sweat, leather, felt the contentment of the pregnant mare, Eryn, in a near stall as she stood half dreaming. She felt pleasure from Merlin, two stalls down. And the slyness of a pair of barn cats, waiting for a mouse to chance a race to the bit of dropped grain it coveted.

To her regret, the singing stopped when Bollocks raced ahead of her.

"Come to visit, have you?" Keegan greeted the dog with a rare and easy cheer. "And timed it well, as we're barely back from a long, hard ride."

He stood, legs spread, boots and trousers muddy, his duster, splattered as well, tossed over the open stall door. His hair, windswept, fell past his collar as he ran a brush over Merlin's flank.

He looked happy, Breen thought, a man thoroughly pleased with the mud and the work.

"And brought your lady as well, I see. You're early for a change of things."

She would spoil this cheer, this contentment, she realized, and postponed it for just a few minutes.

"What was the song?"

"Ah, one that tells the tale of a heart broken by a fair-haired woman. You should learn the language. Marg might be the one for it, as I'd never have the patience."

"I've picked up a little. *Brisfaidh me di magairl.*"

He stopped, leaned against Merlin. His mouth curved, just a little. "And what, I have to wonder, have I done lately that you'd want to break my balls over? Sure you mangled the pronunciation more than a little, but the meaning came through."

"Morena gave me that one. It's handy."

"Well then, you can't truly speak a language until you can speak its curses, can you now? You'll be after your carrot now, won't you?" he said to Merlin. He got one out of a bin, offered it. "And you've earned your nap as well."

As he grabbed his duster and stepped back, Bollocks thundered by after two streaking cats.

"You'll regret it, *mo chara*, if they get their claws in you," Keegan called out.

"*Mo chara.* My friend. I've picked up a little more than swear words and curses." And she found herself amused the mouse had the grain after all. "Where did you ride?"

"Here, there, then the other, and back again." He tossed on the muddy duster, then closed the stall door. "Into the midlands to have a look at the spy we dug out of his snug cottage by a stream."

She gripped his arm. "You found one? You're sure?"

"I am now that I've seen him myself, and the shrine to Odran he had behind a locked door. From the other side he is, near to your part of it. Came over from the land of Alabama, near a dozen years past. Had a woman once, an elf called Minia who loved him, so he came with her and was welcome."

He stopped by the mare, looked in her eyes, stroked her cheek, then reached in another bin for an apple, carved it in halves with his knife. "Two children they had, I'm told, before she took them and left him, as he grew surly and too lazy to work."

He fed the horse half the apple, offered Breen the rest. When she shook her head, he bit into it himself as he strode toward the stable doors. "It seems in his bitterness and solitude, as he had little truck with his neighbors, he turned to Odran."

"How did you find him?"

Keegan secured the stable doors. "It was Uwin, Shana's father, who told one of the scouts we might have a look there. So they watched, and saw the man send a raven and receive another. It's Odran who uses ravens, as we use hawks."

"Yes, I know."

He looked out at the hills. "It's a twisty road, is fate. If Uwin hadn't been so indulgent, so trusting, and told Shana council business, made her useful in that way to Odran, and if she hadn't tried what she tried to do to you, to me, I wouldn't have sent them from the Capital. My mother wouldn't have found a cottage for them, and one that sat close enough to this man for Uwin to wonder."

"You'll take him in for Judgment."

"Aye."

"Banishment."

"It might be that."

"What else?"

"If we find no doubt of the treachery, it may be the Dark World. But as we've yet to find he's done violence to any, it may be to send him back over, bespelled so his memory's clouded."

"Like mine was."

He turned to her. "A bit like that, but with no way for him to find a way back. Talamh is barred to him, whatever the Judgment. He could've gone back when he found himself discontented here, and instead he chose to follow a path that would have destroyed his own children. For his wife to have taken the children and left? This is a serious matter of itself."

"Divorce. It's the first I've heard of it here."

"It's not altogether like that." Frowning, he shrugged. "Not with laws and judgments and all of it, as it's a thing personal, intimate, and of the heart. The Fey don't take the pledge or the ending of it lightly. I spoke with her myself, and though the love for him had died in her, she wept for the father of her children. She wept though she told me, and others confirmed, he'd refused to so much as lay eyes on his son and daughter these past four years."

"When will you go?"

"Tomorrow, but giving time for any who may know more to come forward, so a few days at the Capital." He looked down at her. "But this I don't have to explain."

"No, you don't."

"Well then, I'll fetch the bows and quivers, and we'll see if you can come close to hitting the target."

"Keegan. I came early for a reason."

"You need the practice, right enough."

"Not that reason. I had a vision. I saw Odran, in his world. I need to tell you. I— No."

"No, you're not telling me?"

"I need to tell the council. The one we made here. The council in the valley, you said. I don't know where the others are."

"Harken and Morena are up turning the peat. Mahon's on patrol. Aisling's likely in the cottage, as the boys were out and about when I got back. If you'd tell me—"

"It would be easier to say it all once. I can get Nan and Sedric."

His eyes, that deep, intense green, bored into hers. "It's that important then?"

"Yes. I really think it's that important."

"Then get Marg and Sedric and Aisling, and I'll call Cróga and round up the rest."

It took time, but once more they gathered around the big table in the farmhouse. Since Marco came back, expecting a training session, he kept the boys occupied with games and dogs. Aisling settled the baby in the living room, then stood with her hands on her hips.

"You've tracked mud clean through, the lot of you men, and Morena as well. I've a boy only three who knows better."

"We'll clean it up again. Bloody hell, Aisling, sit down." Keegan yanked back a chair. "We've more important matters than a bit of mud."

She folded her arms, gave him a hard glare, but she sat.

"You've called us together, Breen, so tell us why."

"All right." She clasped her hands under the table. "I had a vision."

She told it straight through, every detail now as clear as it had been then.

"You'll want to tell the council in the Capital," she finished.

"Sure and I will."

"I want to ask something before we go on with this. I know we're not supposed to talk about what we talk about here with anyone, but I want to tell Marco about what I saw. I don't feel right not telling him."

"I've something to say about that." Morena spoke before anyone else could. "We've Minga on the council in the Capital. She's not a Fey, and not from Talamh, not from birth, but she's true. Marco's proved as true as any could, and he deserves to know this."

"Aye." Harken nodded, and so it went around the table.

"I appreciate it. I didn't know. I didn't know about the demon in him, in me. Nan looked, and she says there's no dark in me, that not all demons are. I don't know enough, but she looked. Harken can look now, so everyone's sure."

"None here would doubt Marg's word, or yours," Harken told her. "And I don't have to look to know."

"No more nonsense." Reaching over, Aisling took Breen's hand. "No more of it."

"You're taoiseach, and responsible for everyone."

Keegan just lifted a hand. "Did you hear my sister? And do I look like a growl to you?"

"I don't know what that is."

"A good step down from an eejit," Morena supplied. "And to speak truth, we all know he can be a right growl at times, but not this time. Put it aside, Breen, so we can get to the meat of it, for I never remember a story that puts demon in him."

"But it explains much, doesn't it then?" Keegan studied Breen as he spoke. "Not that gods can't go dark. Others have, but Odran the worst of them. And not slain for his sins but cast out."

"The demon blood," Mahon agreed. "So never fully one of them. Not worthy for slaying. Worse than death, to be deemed so unimportant and tossed aside."

"So the anger and bitterness and the thirst for power and vengeance grew." Marg picked up her tea, but simply stared into it. "To rule all the worlds, and maybe, one day, to wage war on the very gods who dismissed him as beneath them."

"But there are other demigods, aren't there?"

"Oh, we've scores of them," Harken told Breen cheerfully. "If the songs and stories hold true. But he broke their laws, and broke the peace brokered between the gods and the Fey. Blood sacrifices, of Fey and Man and god, to stir up the dark, to feed on it."

"To rise above them," Keegan concluded. "And rule all worlds, even the world of the gods. He's hidden this part of himself, shamed of it he might be. Or not wishing those who worship or follow him to know he's not pure."

"Both seem true." Morena frowned at Breen. "And you only saw the demon, the signs of one, when he was in sex with the offering?"

"Yes. His hands were claws and dug into her. She bled. His eyes turned red, and his teeth got longer, sharper." She shut her eyes to bring it back. "It wasn't rape. She was part of it, and I think . . . I think she saw or felt, but it didn't matter to her. If the others, the ones who watched, saw, it didn't matter. Or more . . ."

Looking back, looking in. "More it was like being drunk or mesmerized. All smoke and blood, her screams, the chanting. Frenzied, and when he killed her, when he slit her throat and drank her blood, like an animal feeding, they called his name over and over.

"She applauded, like you would at a performance."

"She?" Keegan repeated.

"Shana. Keegan, what's inside her, it's not growing right. It's deformed and diseased, and so dark. It's not innocent."

"I'm sorry for that, for it had no choice. But she did."

"He was so pleased when Eian was born." Marg set the tea aside. "I wonder now how many he tried to bring into the world before and since, who weren't right, weren't healthy and strong and innocent." She turned to Breen. "That life he helped make through me, one he thought to use and destroy? It will, through you, *mo stór*, be the undoing of him."

"I'll talk to the council, and more, to the scholars when I go to the Capital. We'll see if any have heard even a whisper of this, and how we can use it."

"Dorcas, the Old Mother."

Keegan sent Marg a pained look. "Ah gods, Marg, she'll talk the hind legs off a donkey, and ply you with her houndberry tea until your teeth ache."

"That she will, and I've suffered both, but no one remembers more swimming in the mists of time than Mother Dorcas."

"And I'd hoped tucking her up in a pretty cottage with her pack of cats would spare me any more of it. I'll speak with her, feck it all, for you're right. If any know of anything, she will."

The thought of it had him scrubbing his hands over his face. "All right then. We know more than we did, and we'll learn more yet. You say this wasn't by the portal in the falls?"

"No, not there. I couldn't tell where. It was dark, but because he brought the dark. I know it happened while I watched. I saw some trees, and I heard the sea. Fires, candles, smoke, the altar—stone, black stone, black candles around the circle."

She tipped her head, eyes narrowing as she pushed. "The smoke. Something in the smoke? Like the fog, Yseult's fog. I could smell it. I didn't think of it, Nan, it was so visual, I didn't think. I could smell something—a little too sweet? Like fruit that's going over—like that, but not. The fog, that's what it reminds me of. I hadn't realized."

"So he needs that," Marg said. "He needs Yseult's magicks to keep them in that state."

"And it may be to make the sacrifice so willing," Keegan finished.

"Even the choices they've made aren't enough for him. And his power isn't enough, on its own, for them. He still needs his witch."

"More of you than one of her," Morena pointed out. "And whatever other Wise have gone to him, she holds the most power."

"She's failed him, but he hasn't killed her. Because he needs her," Breen said. "He still needs her."

"As she serves him, is fervent, she'll try again to bring him what he covets. And she'll fail again." Keegan spoke with absolute confidence. "Her end comes with his, if not before."

He glanced out the window, flicked a hand to light candles as the sun slid down toward dusk. "We've lost the training time, so while we're here, I'll tell you we've found a spy in the midlands."

He went through it before he rose.

"Now, what I'm hoping is Marco's got a hot meal planned."

"I can tell you he does, and that I'd like to go over with him first, explain all of this."

"All right then. Brian should be coming along soon. I'll wait for him."

"Appreciate it."

"I need to go back to the Capital, deal with the spy and his Judgment. I'll be leaving the targets up, Harken, and hope either you or Morena can take Breen through some training there tomorrow."

"I'll see to that," Morena told him. "And with Marco as well, as he could use the practice there. When you see my family, give them love."

"Sure I will. I'll be a few days, I expect. Not as long as the last time." He looked at Breen as he spoke. "But a few days."

"You'll take Mahon with you." Aisling waved a hand. "I know you've had him stay close for the past weeks, and I'm grateful. But we're all fine, and he should be with you for this."

"She's the right of it. And only said it before I said it myself," Mahon told him.

"I won't argue with that, as I could use you. At daybreak then. Three or four days," he told Aisling. "No more."

"I'll fetch Kelly, and if you'd free Marco from our hooligans, Breen, tell them their da and I are coming. Safe travels to you."

She stepped to Keegan, kissed his cheek.

"Thanks to everyone for making the time." Breen laid a hand on Marg's shoulder. "I'll see you tomorrow."

She got her jacket and went out to see Marco, with Kavan riding his back, dancing like a lunatic to whatever crazed tune Finian played on the harmonica Marco had given him for his birthday.

Would Marco and Brian make a family one day? she wondered. Find a child who needed love and that family?

She hoped so.

"It's time for Marco to go home."

"But he's teaching me to play!"

"You keep practicing." Marco gave Finian's hair a tousle before sliding Kavan to the ground. "And we'll have another lesson soon. You got skills, kid."

"I heard them myself. Your ma and da are coming. We'll return tomorrow."

"I'll make a new song."

"I can't wait to hear it. Come on, Bollocks."

He raced a circle around the boys, bowled the pup over, and gave Mab a series of adoring licks all before racing ahead.

"They never run out of juice," Marco observed. "The kids or the dogs. It sure keeps the energy up. And I bet I sleep like a pile of rocks tonight. Hey, isn't Keegan coming?"

"Yeah, he'll be along." They crossed field, road, field, and started up the steps, where Bollocks waited for them. "You're not going to ask what we all talked about."

"I know it's super secret stuff."

She took his hand as they crossed from one world to another.

"Not so much this time, and I can tell you they've caught one of Odran's spies and taken him in for Judgment."

"No shit? That's pretty quick, right?"

"One of those twists, I guess. He lived in the midlands, near where Shana's parents are now. Her father led them to him. He came here from this side, Marco. Years ago, he came here from America, and was welcome, and he does this."

She gave him the bare bones of it.

"Got kids and everything." Caught between sorrow and disgust, Marco shook his head. "You know, if somebody's going to suck out loud, Breen, it don't matter a damn where they start out. It's where they end up."

"One place he won't end up is Talamh. Keegan's got to go back east for a few days. But there's more, and it's going to be harder to tell."

"The kind of hard that says it's glass-of-wine-thirty?"

"Boy, that'd be nice. When I was with Nan this afternoon, I had a vision."

"Was it bad? Are you okay?"

"It was bad, but I'm okay." When they came out of the woods, she stopped, just to take in the cottage. Her cottage.

"One day soon, you and Brian should pick your spot."

"I still gotta tell him. Keegan give the go?"

"With all the rest, I didn't have a chance to tell him. We'll tell them both tonight. Anyway, the vision."

She started as they walked to the cottage, continued as she set the fires to light and Marco poured wine. And finished as they sat drinking it in front of the fire.

"He's not just evil," Marco concluded. "He's one sick son of a bitch. He just, like, sucked the blood out of her throat? Like a vampire?"

"Sort of. He didn't bite it, use fangs. He slit it open with a claw, then drank it from . . . the source."

"So not like a vampire god—which doesn't make sense anyway because that would make him undead, and he's not. Is he?"

"No. No, he's alive. But he does have demon in him, Marco. That means I do, too."

"Yeah, sure, I get it. There are all kinds of demons. I used to figure they were just fun fiction stuff, but I guess most fun fiction stuff had to start somewhere. So whatever demon's in him wants to drink blood. You don't."

"No! Ew."

"I'm saying"—Marco gestured wildly with his glass—"you won't even eat a rare steak. Much less a little tartare."

"Because ew."

"You're so wrong about that, but I'm saying the demon part of him wants it, or needs it, and yours doesn't. Because he likes it." Now Marco shot up a finger. "The whole Odran psycho gets off on it. And you know what Spike said."

"Buffy's Spike?"

He shot her a deadly serious look. "There's only one Spike, girl. Blood's life. It's always about the blood, has to be blood and all like that. You know why?"

"Because Spike's a vampire?"

"Yes, and no. Because when Odran takes blood, he's taking life from somebody else. Because that's his life, and his psycho shit, and it's power and, you know, it's ritual. And it's a fucking show on top of it. A goddamn performance for the crowd, Breen."

She stared at him, then sat back. "Holy crap, Marco Olsen. That's just completely . . . right. That's all of it. That's exactly. He needs it for all of that, and he needs to do this horrible thing in front of an audience, in front of his cult to keep them loyal, excited, in awe."

"But like you said, he hides the demon so they only see the god. Some of that cult, they're demons, and if he shows he's sort of one of them—"

"It diminishes him." She punched him lightly in the shoulder. "Hammer. Nail. Head."

Looking smug, he gave a shoulder wiggle. "I got some skills."

"I'll say. How come you're not even a little weirded out that I've got some demon in me?"

"Maybe because I jumped into another world with you, or because I'm crazy in love with a guy who can sprout wings and rides a freaking dragon, or maybe because you lit that fire there without a match. Stuff like that. But mostly?"

Turning to her, he gripped her chin, gave it a quick wag. "Who knows you like I know you?"

"Nobody. Nobody in any world anywhere."

"My best friend's a demon witch. Or it's probably witch demon, because there's more of the witch."

"There's Sidhe and human, too."

"That's a big punch in one package." He patted his knee so Bollocks came over to put his head on it. "And she's got the best demon dog ever."

"Who's waited patiently for his supper until I got through this. I'll take care of that and set the table."

"Great. I want to make some biscuits—not cookies—to go with the roast." He rose with her, and sensing what was coming, Bollocks raced into the kitchen to sit by his bowls.

"We make a good team," Breen said.

"Always have, always will."

CHAPTER TWELVE

She saw Keegan off before dawn, and watched Bollocks take his first swim of the day as the light began to shimmer in the east. She imagined Keegan flying on dragon-back toward the sun.

She'd miss him, but she couldn't deny the archery practice would be more pleasant under Morena's gentler touch.

She stood, her cloak wrapped around her pajamas, drinking coffee as the early light began to play on the mists spiraling up from the bay.

She heard the cottage door open, glanced back as Brian stepped out. As he did whenever they crossed paths in the morning, he brought her a piece of toast.

"Thanks."

"I have early duty the next few days, and I wanted a moment with you."

"Sure."

"I couldn't find the words last night. I still search for them. The cottage you offer."

Distress came first. "You don't want it?"

"I do," he said quickly. "We do. This is the answer to everything, for both of us. I can't find the words to thank you. That you'd do this for him."

"Not just for him, and for you, but for me. As much for me."

"I know this." He let out a breath that whisked away into fog. "And knowing it makes the gift even more, so I can't find the words."

"I think all of those work just fine." And started her day off on a bright note. "We're all going to live in two worlds, and that's a strange balancing act. But at the same time, we can have the best of both of them. After."

"I'd go anywhere with Marco. That it can be here is another gift. I want to take him to meet my family. They know of him, of course. I've told them I found the one, and so they want to meet him. And when they have, I would ask him to pledge to me, and me to him."

She shot out both hands, pushed them against the morning air.

"Wait, wait! You want to marry him? Oh my God, oh my God." She turned two circles, sent the rest of the coffee sloshing. "Now I can't find my words. Oh, oh, *yes!*"

Heart in his eyes, Brian grinned. "You approve. I thought you might think it too fast."

"Oh, hell with that. I can't tell him, can I? Crap, crap, I can't spoil the big moment. Give me a second." She shoved the nearly empty mug at him, then turned more circles. "Okay, it's zipped." She mimed zipping her lips. "In the vault. Not a word. I swear, pinky swear, cross my heart, whatever it takes."

"I wanted your approval because you're his family."

"Gold seal, stamped, done. Big, giant approval. Gift-wrapped-with-a-shiny-bow approval. Oh, but . . . Sally and Derrick, and Marco's sister. They'd want to be there for a wedding."

"It must wait, I think, for the after, as you call it. It would be best. To have the vows said both in Talamh and in this world."

"Marco gets two weddings?"

After throwing her arms around Brian, she stepped back to dance in place.

"Okay, that just tops everything. If anybody deserves it twice, it's Marco. Damn it, why didn't I ever learn to do a cartwheel? I'm doing many brilliantly executed mental cartwheels right now."

"You fill my heart, Breen Siobhan," Brian murmured.

"Two weddings for Marco! And meanwhile, you'll be pledged. I know how much that means to the Fey. And I can promise it'll mean everything to Marco."

"And you a bridge, again, Breen Siobhan, who'll be with us for both."

"You bet your ass. I'm so happy." Giddy, she waved her hands in the air. "Okay, crap. He's going to see that, but I can say the book's going really well and keeping me way up there. Tell me you're doing this soon so I don't explode."

"I need to ask the taoiseach for the time. Marco won't fly on my Hero. When I tried to convince him, he said . . ."

Brian cocked his head and spouted an American accent, close enough to Marco's to make her laugh.

"Dude! I love you down to my balls, but that's one big negativo. As in no way and no how."

"You've got him, all right."

"And intend to keep him. So a day to ride there, a day to ride back, and two days at my family home. But we worry about leaving you so much alone here."

"Dude." And made him laugh in turn. "I lived here alone most of last summer and was just fine. Get the time and go."

Then she pressed her fingers to her teary eyes. "Brian, I've known Marco since we were kids. He's a romantic down to the core. All he's ever wanted was to love and be loved. He has that with you. Get the time and go."

"I'll speak to Keegan when he comes back from the Capital. I have to go, take my duty."

"You started my morning off with a bang. And that's a good thing." She took the mug back. "I'll see you later. And . . ."

Once again, she zipped her lips. Then called to Bollocks to start the rest of her morning.

She kept those lips zipped, though it took a lot of willpower. Keeping busy helped, so she added more hours writing in the evenings while Keegan saw to his duties at the Capital.

When Mahon returned three days later without Keegan, she struggled against impatience. The sooner he came back to the valley, the sooner Brian would ask for the time.

And the sooner she could unzip her lips with a shout of congratulations.

But duty remained duty and another three days passed.

Seamus showed her how to plant seeds in holding beds to give them a head start on spring. Morena gave her hawking lessons, which Marco studiously avoided, and with Marg she practiced the craft religiously.

If more visions remained elusive, she didn't complain. As long as the curtain and the boundaries held, she could prepare, she could get better, stronger, smarter.

On a fine afternoon when the rain held off and the temperatures crept up, she rode with Marco. He rode a new mount, a pretty young pinto mare with black-and-white markings and a high-stepping gait that Marco claimed said spunk right out loud.

"Harken calls her Álainn because it means pretty, and she sure is."

"And she knows it. Right now she's thinking she looks even prettier with you in the saddle."

"For real? What do you think?" Lifting his chin, he struck a pose. "Do we look lit or what?"

"You do. She's a good size for you, and as long as you understand she expects to be pleased as much as please, you'll do fine."

"Who wouldn't want to please such a pretty girl?" He leaned over to stroke her neck. "I'm getting serious about having a horse of my own, and when I talked to Harken, he said I should ride her for a few days, see if we fit. I already feel like we do, and if we do, I'm going to barter for her. But I don't know what I've got or can get that Harken needs or wants."

"Are you kidding me? First, you could help him out at the farm. I don't know exactly how it works or when, but spring planting's bound to start soon. And more, cook. He does most of that, with Morena taking a couple nights a week, but say you did enough for them when you do your usual, and added to it for them when you bake?"

"Well, I sort of do that off and on already. It's just being friends and, you know, neighbors."

"Exactly how it works."

Already more than half in love, he stroked the mare again.

"It seems so damn simple. You know, Breen, how we used to always have to worry about making ends meet up, every damn month it felt like. Now, we've got all we could want, and all we have to do is live and share and do what we love anyway."

"You haven't dealt with the Trolls yet." But she said it with a laugh as she looked up and saw some of the mine workers taking their break on the ledges of the mountain. "They drive a hard bargain."

"I can always bake more cookies. How about we ride to the waterfall? Sedric and I rode there once, and I'd like to see it again."

"It or Brian?"

"It can be both. Never saw a real waterfall before we came to Ireland, and never saw one like this anywhere, anytime."

"It's unique."

He heard it in her voice, so shot her a quick look. "If it gives you bad vibes, we can skip it."

"It doesn't. It does," she corrected. "It gives me all kinds of vibes. We should go. Vibes are something I should go toward rather than avoid."

"It was always in you." Marco tapped his wrist in the spot where Breen had her tattoo. "You just had to find it."

Courage, she thought. She had to remind herself to hold on to it, every day. She sent Bollocks a glance, a suggestion.

He raced ahead.

"How about we see what that pretty girl can do against Boy in a race?"

Before Marco answered, she kicked into a gallop.

Imagine it, imagine it, she thought. The two of them racing horses with the wind streaming and the sun flashing bright to warm the winter-cold ground. She watched Bollocks streak into the woods for his shortcut. She heard the call of a magpie just before a pair flew across her vision.

Two is for joy.

They reached their own turn into the woods almost neck and neck.

"You had a head start."

"Boy and I held back some so you could catch up."

"Maybe." Marco stroked the mare again, and Breen recognized love. "But my girl can *move*."

"She likes apples."

"Yeah? I'll get her one."

They walked the horses through the trees, and the trees changed. The light changed from bright and light to soft and green, a kind of pulse drawn from the moss-covered bark and stones.

The thunder of the waterfall rumbled in the air as the river, eerily green like the light, ribboned its way.

"Spooky place, but excellent spooky." Wide-eyed and enchanted, Marco looked all around. "Gives me the vibes, too, but like I get when I settle in to watch a really good spooky movie."

No movie here, she thought. Odran had trapped the child she'd been in a glass cage in this river. Yseult had lured her here with the drugging fog.

Yet she'd seen Lonrach here the first time in a dream, and been part of sealing the breach in the portal under the falls—however reluctantly.

She couldn't deny its beauty, the showering light through the canopy of trees, the life and lichen in the nurse logs that scattered here and there, the span of another as it formed a kind of bridge over the river.

Elves and others who lived here might use that natural bridge to cross. Squirrels and birds nested in the thickly coated trees. Deer came to drink, foxes and owls to hunt.

She felt them now, the beating hearts, as she felt the beating heart of the trees, of the earth, of the river.

All connected, all part of the whole, as she was.

And magicks thrived here.

A deer slid out of the trees, became a woman.

"Good day to you, Breen O'Ceallaigh, and to you, Marco."

"Hey, Mary Kate! You gave me a jolt."

She tossed back her dark oak braids—the one over her shoulder, and the warrior's as well—and grinned at him. "Ah now, Marco, darling. I'm Mary Kate on two legs or four. Your dog's already up ahead, Breen, so we knew you'd be coming. He's swimming around the falls like a fish."

"All's well then?"

"It is, aye. A long quiet day, so your visit's very welcome indeed. I'll go on ahead, let Brian and the rest know you're on your way."

She slid into deer form as another might into comfortable shoes and bounded out.

"Ain't never getting used to that." Marco shook his head. "It's always going to give me that jolt."

"Not a bad thing," Breen decided. "That way you keep the wonder of it. You go on ahead, grab some Brian time." She dismounted. "I'm going to walk awhile."

"You sure? If it's bad memories—"

"They're not all bad, and I've got the urge to walk a little while. Mary Kate's not the only one patrolling the woods," she told him. "I'm fine."

"If you're sure, but stay along the river, okay? If you want to go off exploring, come get me and we'll go together."

"Just a walk, along the water."

When he trotted off, she stood listening.

The drum of water falling, falling to beat against water. The sweep in the air of birds on the wing, the bare whisper of Elfin feet on patrol deeper in the trees.

She walked Boy, following the river's curves, taking her time, following an instinct she didn't understand. Time for alone, time to feel, time to look.

And alone, feeling the life all around, she looked. And saw the glint in the green water.

Walking toward it, she saw the bright gold chain with its bold red stone. She'd seen it before, she remembered now, in dreams before she'd come to Ireland, before Talamh.

And . . . on the Day of Judgment, in the portrait of her grandmother. Nan wore this pendant that gleamed and beckoned under the clear green water.

She'd meant to ask her about it—why hadn't she?

Because she'd forgotten it.

She knelt down, reached out. It had seemed so close, but now lay beyond the stretch of her fingers.

How could it be there, glinting, glimmering, when she'd seen it around her grandmother's neck in the portrait?

Had Nan lost it?

She needed to reach it, to take it out of the water, take it back to Nan. It was precious. She *knew* it was precious, important, it mattered.

But as she inched closer, reached farther, she slipped. And scrambled back to keep from falling in.

She couldn't go into the water, not here—no, not here, not alone. Not where she'd beat her hands to blood and cried for her father.

With her heart pounding, she reached out with an unsteady hand. She tried to focus her will, her power, to pull the pendant to her, to lift it up, out of the water.

But it only glimmered and gleamed, and waited.

"I'll get Marco. He's got a longer reach."

She crawled back, pushed up. Taking up the reins again, she walked toward the sound of the falls.

She heard voices now and felt Bollocks's pleasure as some generous soul tossed him a bite of cheese.

The great white water fell from its great height, foamed and boiled, then spread into the serene green of the river.

Pixies fluttered above the shallows and their colorful polished rocks. Guards flanked either side of the thundering falls with more of their number on both sides of the riverbank.

The pretty mare grazed as Marco sat on a stump chatting away with Brian and Mary Kate.

She started to call out, ask him to walk back with her to that curve where the pendant lay out of her reach.

Then something drew her eye up.

She saw it like a shadow, high up, on the edge of the falls. Like a small parting of water, here then gone. Then a shadow out of the shadow. And the bird it became, the raven that winged overhead.

"Brian!" She shouted it, shot her hand up.

When he looked where she pointed, he lurched to his feet. "Duncan!"

Across the bank a man—hardly more than a boy with a thatch of straw-colored hair and a braid that barely reached his ear—folded his arms.

Became a hawk.

"Follow! Don't intercept."

"I didn't see." An elf blurred up to Brian. "I swear to all the gods I had my eyes trained for a breach. And Gwain beside me as well."

"I didn't see." Brian looked toward Breen as she hurried to him. "When you called me, pointed, for an instant, and an instant more, I didn't see. Only sky, trees. Then the bird, already flying. It came through?"

"It was like a shadow, barely a ripple on the edge of the falls. I think it's . . . I need to get closer."

"The rocks are wet and slick with it. If you'll trust me, I'll take you closer."

"I do trust you, and if you'd come with me. But I think I need to . . ." She closed her eyes. "I need to take myself. One against one, light against dark. Power to power. Hers and mine meeting."

As she spoke, she began to rise off the ground. Slowly, fighting the fear that hounded her of falling in, she rose by inches.

Marco sprang to his feet. "Oh man, oh shit. Go up with her."

"I've not seen her do this before, quite like this."

A foot now, then another, and she felt it pounding in her like the water pounding on water.

The spray drenched her face, her clothes, even as the power swam through her. So strong, the thunder of it inside her drowned out the roar of the falls.

"Just a ripple, just a crack, opened and closed, closed and opened." Her eyes, open and deep now, focused as she hovered twenty feet above the river. "Her magicks, bloody and black, claw it open, claw it closed. Small and shadowed, shadowed and cloaked. See the fog here, I see. So thin. Just enough, just enough to blind the eye. I see, I see, I see. She doesn't, not yet."

"I don't see it." Brian spoke from beside her.

"I see, I see, I see. Light in the dark. Her dark. Odran's dark. I can close it, as I close my fist."

When she lifted her arm, closed her hand into a fist, Brian swore he heard a snap.

With her eyes still dark and deep, Breen smiled. "Now wonder, witch, and wonder how your magicks failed here. How the crack sealed, no more to be clawed open. Wonder and fear. Fear the day that comes when I crush you." She opened her hand, fisted it again. "When I crush you and your blood-soaked god. *Ar shaol m'athar, swear mé é.*"

When her eyes rolled up, her head fell back, Brian caught her.

"Don't let me fall in the water."

"I have you." He cradled her as he flew to the riverbank. "Bring water!"

"I'm okay. I just got dizzy for a minute and lost my focus."

"You drink some of this now." Marco held a skin of water to her lips. "At this moment you're the whitest white girl I've ever seen. And how the hell did you forget to tell me you could fly?"

"I can't. I didn't. It's like levitating, and I never did more than a few inches before. With Nan there. Remember?"

"Hell of a lot more than a few inches this time. You gotta stop scaring the crap out of me, girl. And this boy here, too."

She wrapped an arm around Bollocks as he pressed hard against her.

"I could feel it, up there. I had to get close." Realizing Brian still held her, she put a hand on his chest. "I'm okay, I promise. I really have to thank you for not letting me fall."

"Do you remember?" He set her carefully on her feet.

"Yeah. I had to really focus. I felt more—I mean more than I do now. And I felt her spell. I knew I could break it, close the crack."

"So you did, with this." Brian took her hand, closed it into a fist. "And the words you spoke, there was such power, and a kind of music in them. You glowed like the sun with your eyes dark as new moons.

"And when you smiled—"

"I smiled? I don't remember that part."

"You smiled like a warrior when the battle's won. And spoke in Talamhish."

"I did?" She pushed at her wet hair. "I know a few words."

"Ar shaol m'athar, swear mé é."

"I don't know those. What do they mean?"

"You said, in your tongue, you would crush her—the witch—and her god with her. Then you said those words. They mean: On my father's life, I swear it."

"I don't remember, but I must've meant them."

"I had no doubt of it."

"I'm going to take you home, no bullshit training today." Marco put an arm around her. "I'm going to tuck you up by the fire, and I don't want any sass from you about it."

"Best to listen," Brian advised.

"Duncan's coming back." But she leaned against Marco, kept a hand on Bollocks as she looked up.

The falcon danced through the trees, swooped across the river, and dropped to the ground as a man.

"I followed the raven to the Troll camp, and to the hut where he took the scroll. The one who lives there is called Thar. With the scroll, Brian, the raven brought a knife. I saw Elfin markings on it. And he read the scroll out loud, as if to push it all into himself. It tells him to use the knife on Loga of the Trolls and leave it in him. Leave it, and claim he saw an elf attack and run. The elf is Argo, from the valley."

"Mara, call your dragon, and get word of this to the taoiseach. Tell him I'll go to the Troll camp even now."

"I'm going with you. Marco," Breen snapped before he could protest, "they know me, trust me. I have Sul's ear, and that could be important in this."

"I have to take one of their own, so, aye, it would be. You'll trust me with her, Marco," Brian said.

"Damn it. Okay, all right. We'll wait at the farm. I'll take Bollocks and the horses."

Brian turned to him, kissed him. "I'll bring her back safe."

"Bring both of you back safe."

"I have you," Brian said again, and, picking Breen up, flew.

"I know you're the warrior, and one of Keegan's right hands, but I'm going to ask you to let me do the talking—at least try to—at the start."

"I'll do that, but if this Thar tries to harm you or any, I'll stop him. If he tries to run, I'll stop him. If any Troll objects, I'll stop them."

"We need to ask permission to—"

"We won't be after standing on ceremony," Brian said grimly. "And they'll have to deal with that."

He flew straight into the Troll camp. Everyone in it rose to their feet. Children stopped playing, others stopped cooking or drinking or hammering.

Not a single one looked pleased.

"We apologize for the intrusion," Breen began. "We have urgent business with Loga. Please, it's urgent."

Sul strode up the path Breen remembered led to stables, and beyond to the caves.

She stopped, hands on hips, and sent Brian a hard look.

"This is not the way to welcome."

"It's urgent," Breen repeated. "Where is Loga—please. His life's in danger."

"Why would ya say such things? I left him not ten minutes past after he finished a bartering."

"Where is the one called Thar?" Brian demanded.

"And what business is that of yers, Sidhe?"

"He means to kill Loga. Sul, I swear it. He took a raven from Odran, and a knife with Elfin markings."

"Ya call my son a murderer?" A woman pushed forward. "Ya lie, and are no longer welcome."

Sul rounded on her. "I say who is welcome here. Where is Thar, and we'll end all this."

"He went down toward the caves," a boy called out.

"I'da seen him," Sul said.

"I tell ya, Ma, I saw him going that way just before they came."

"Loga's in the caves?"

Sul nodded at Breen. "Or coming back from them by now."

Sul turned on her heel and ran.

She moved fast for a big woman several months pregnant. Breen moved faster and passed her as Brian soared overhead. Others thundered behind them as horns sounded an alarm.

Breen saw as she rounded a turn on the path the dark-faced Troll with wild red hair leap at Loga and plunge a knife into his side.

Still running, she hurled power and sent the attacker flying back. As Brian swooped down, flew him up out of reach, the knife fell out of his hand.

Blood spilled out of Loga's side when Breen reached him to lay a hand on the wound. While overhead, Thar shouted and cursed, Loga, barely conscious, stared at Breen with eyes glazed with pain and shock.

"I didn't give ya permission," he choked out.

"Please, Father of the Trolls, grant it."

"It's a—it's a scratch."

"Grant it so I can heal the scratch to soothe my own nerves."

"Grant it." Sul dropped down beside him, gripped Loga's hand, and pressed it to her belly. "Ya stubborn old fool. Feel this life kicking in me and grant it."

"So I do. To soothe female nerves," he added, and passed out.

"Release me, Sidhe bastard. He's in league with the elf assassin who attacked Loga!" Thar shouted. "He let him escape!"

Behind them more than one Troll nocked an arrow.

"He's lying." Breen shot one quick glance at Sul. "I saw him use the knife. I swear it."

"I didn't see. Heal my man."

She shifted, turned to those behind ready to fight, attack, defend. "Hold, every one of ya! The Daughter of the O'Ceallaigh accuses Thar of this treachery."

"She lies! She lies! Would ya take the word of this outsider, this spawn of man over one of yer own? I tell ya the elf Argo killed Loga. There's his knife, still bloody."

"He's not dead." Breen lifted her voice over the shouting, the rumblings. "He won't die."

Then she shut them out, the voices. She shut out the fury, the anger, the fear.

Not just a scratch, no, though not as deep as she'd feared. But deep enough. And so much blood already lost.

It hurt, oh it hurt, that struggle to heal flesh and muscle, to slow the flow of blood. Loga stirred under her hands, fighting back against the pain and the fiery heat she pushed into him.

"Ya give him pain," Sul snapped.

"I'm sorry, I'm sorry." Unsure, Breen eased back. "If you'd send for Aisling, or my grandmother—"

"Give him pain if pain it takes to save his life. Do what needs doing." Fiercely, she gripped Breen's arm. "And stop playing at it."

"Quit yer whacking at her, woman." Eyes still closed, breath shallow, Loga managed a whisper. "A scratch is all."

"Hold that tongue of yers." A tear slid down Sul's wide face. "I'll whack any who need whacking."

"It's closing. I have to— It's slow. I'm not as good as . . . Jesus, so much muscle."

"Would I choose a weakling for my mate? To father my children?"

"Who chose who?" Loga's eyes fluttered open, looked into Sul's. "That's enough of the fussing."

"Just another minute. If I don't, it'll open again. You're so strong, what would be a killing wound is only a scratch. But still, it was a fierce one. You lost a lot of blood, and need a potion, and Sul, a balm for the wound. I don't have anything with me."

"We have medicinals. Tell us what."

"Away now, back away now. Do ya think I'm going to lie here on the ground?" Loga shoved the women back and pushed to his feet.

He'd lost color as well as blood but planted those feet and stared up at Brian and Thar.

"Bring him down, Sidhe."

"He'll be taken to the Capital for Judgment. That's the law, the law for all Fey."

"Ya think I don't know the law?" He looked around at his tribe, the ones who'd run from the village, those who'd poured out of the mines at the call of alarm. "We know the law, and we honor it. Put those weapons down, ya bunch of eejits. He'll face Judgment right enough, and none here will stop ya. But I'll have a bloody word first. It's my right."

"It is, aye."

Brian brought him down but held him fast.

"Put a knife in me, would ya, Thar? Eaten at my fire, haven't ya? Shared my food, my drink, and put a knife in the Father?"

"Not my father. My father's dead, gone fighting for this one's." He spat at Breen's feet.

"And a warrior he was, brave and true." Sul looked back, nodded to some of the women to give comfort to Thar's mother as she wept. "Ya disgrace him and bring shame to the one who birthed ya."

"Loga's weak, all of ya, weak who follow him, who follow the taoiseach. What do we get but huts on the stone and breaking our backs in the caves and mines? When Odran comes, and he will come, I'll lead the strong ones, and the weak will beg for my mercy."

"Take him to Judgment, and tell the taoiseach I will come for it as well. He is no longer of the tribe. Whatever Judgment is said at the Capital, he is banished from this camp and from the tribe. We do not know him from this day on."

"So I will. I will call my dragon and take him. Breen—"

"Go. I'll call Lonrach. I need to see to the potion, the balm first. I'll call Lonrach as soon as I'm finished."

"She's under our protection here," Loga told him, "and in all of Talamh. This is my word."

They bound Thar with rope, and when Hero hovered, Brian flew him up. "I'll tell Marco you're coming soon," he called, then soared east.

"Ya'll come to the caves," Loga told Breen. "Take payment for healing my scratch."

"I won't. I healed a friend. I won't trade or take payment for healing a friend."

His eyes narrowed on hers, and she worried she'd insulted him and the rest. Worried considerably more when he drew his knife.

"Will you give me your hand?"

Hoping for the best, she held it out. He scored his palm, then hers. Then gripped their hands together strongly enough to make her wince.

"Now we share blood. Witness this, all of ya! The Daughter of the O'Ceallaigh shares blood with the tribe. She is one of us from this day. She is Daughter of the Trolls, and is welcome here as she wishes, without permission. This is my word."

"I'm honored."

"Well, ya should be." He grinned at her. "Now ya'll finish your fussing for yer nerves, and have ale. Oh no, it's wine ya like, isn't it? Ale for me."

She got the potion into him, chose the balm. When she called for Lonrach, a young woman stepped up to her.

"I'm Narl, the oldest daughter of Loga and Sul."

"I see your mother in your eyes."

Narl held out a thin band of hammered gold studded with dragon hearts. "This is a gift from all the children of Loga and Sul, and the one yet to come, from their children, and all yet to come. This isn't a trade or payment, but a gift. It's a thanks."

"It's beautiful."

"Wear it into battle, see?" She set it on Breen's head. "It's protection, and a warning, a warning the one who wears it is fierce with the blood of the Trolls though she has no braid."

With a nod, Narl stepped back. "We're sisters now, so when ya fight, fight fierce. When ya stand, stand strong."

"I'll treasure the gift and wear it with pride. Troll pride," she added, and made Narl smile.

CHAPTER THIRTEEN

On the flight from the Troll camp to the farm, Breen stretched out on Lonrach's neck and closed her eyes. Everything in her let go, every muscle went lax, every thought hazed.

It had been the deepest healing she'd ever attempted, and one that sucked her dry. She'd washed Loga's blood—so much blood—from her hands. But she could still smell it.

She felt the wind snap at her, and a quick damp when they streamed through a cloud, but lay limp. She'd probably been more tired in her life, but at the moment, she couldn't remember when.

Trusting Lonrach wouldn't let her fall, she half dozed until she felt him descend.

As she let herself slide off, Marco hurried out of the house with Morena and Bollocks on his heels.

"Brian did a flyby—literally—and called down you were coming. That was awhile ago. Girl, we were about to send out a search party."

Her tongue felt limp, barely able to move to help form words. "It took awhile."

"Hey, you're wearing a Wonder Woman crown—diadem," he corrected.

"With Troll markings," Morena added, fascinated. "Only members of their tribe are allowed to wear one."

"I'm an honorary Troll now." Her head spun a little as she bent down to pet Bollocks because he whined at her feet.

"There's a story I want to hear, but not now, I'm thinking." Morena took hold of Breen's arm to steady her. "You look worn well past the bone. Come inside and sit. We'll get you some food, some tea."

"Honestly, I just want to go home, go home and lie down for a few minutes. It's been a lot."

"I can see it has been. Take her on to the cottage, Marco, get some food into her if you can. Do you want me to help?"

"I've got her." He slid an arm around Breen's waist. "We've got her, right, Bollocks? Morena, you give that stew a stir now and again, then garnish it like I told you when you and Harken are ready to eat it."

"Leave it to me now that you've done all the rest of it. You rest yourself, Breen. We'll talk tomorrow."

"Tomorrow."

Instead of dashing ahead, Bollocks stayed by Breen's side as they crossed to the Welcoming Tree. Marco hauled her up the steps, over the branches and rock, then into Ireland.

"Brian said you saved Loga's life—that's head Troll, right?"

"Yes, but I don't know as I'd go as far as saving his life. He was hurt, and he needed attention, but he's really strong. It was awful pain, Marco, and he barely flinched, even when he came to."

"You feel some of it, too. The pain, right? Isn't that how it works?"

"Scared me. There was so much blood. Blood all over my hands," she murmured, leaning on him. "And I was afraid I wasn't going to be enough. I felt a little off still from the waterfall. But—"

"You did what you had to do."

"We were almost too late. If Brian hadn't gotten us there so fast, Thar might have stabbed him again and left him to bleed out. The rest of the tribe might have believed him."

"Didn't happen. You and Brian made sure of it. Why that elf guy? Why hang it on him?"

It felt like a dream, walking in the chilly air, hearing the burble of the stream.

"Argo and Loga got into it a few days ago over a trade. Insults were hurled, punches exchanged. Apparently it happens sometimes, and they all shrug it off. But it made for a scapegoat. Sul thinks— and I agree with her—Thar likely sent a raven letting Odran know all of that. It's just all screwed up, Marco."

"Yeah, it is." Almost home, he thought, again and again, and kept his voice cheerful as worry for her hounded him. "And you got yourself a Troll crown."

"Wear it into battle to show I'm Troll fierce."

"Uh-huh." When they broke through the trees, he simply picked her up and carried her the rest of the way.

"Just need to sleep."

"That's what you're gonna do."

He got her inside, laid her on the sofa, where he and Bollocks could keep their eyes on her. He crouched down to build a fire, but the peat sparked, then flamed.

She smiled. "I still got it," she murmured. Then closed her eyes and slept.

"Yeah, my Breen, you still got it."

He slid a pillow under her head, gently removed the diadem. Then tucked a throw around her.

Bollocks sat to take first watch.

"That's a good boy. You do that, and I'll go put something together so she has herself a good meal when she wakes up."

Watching her just a little longer, he brushed the hair back from her face.

"All that magick, it puts something in you, but it sure can take something out."

When she woke, the fire simmered, the lamps glowed on low, and candles flickered. Music played, as low and warm as the lamps. She smelled something wonderful, something merging with the peat fire and candlewax that reminded her stomach she hadn't eaten since breakfast.

And she found, tucked against her neck, the little stuffed lamb that was Bollocks's current favorite sleeping companion.

She saw Marco, his head haloed in the light, sitting in a chair, his feet up on the coffee table and a book in his hand.

Bollocks curled by the fire, dozing, but as she surfaced, his eyes opened. His tail wagged as he uncurled to prance to her and lick her face.

"And there she is! Sugar pie, you went out like a light and stayed there."

She sat up, tried to stretch and nuzzle the eager Bollocks at the same time. "How long?"

He picked up his phone from the table to check the time. "Four solid."

"Four *hours*? That's a nap squared."

"You needed it. You had us worried, girl. Harken and Morena came over about an hour after you crashed to check on you, and Harken said the sleep was the best thing. I guess he had it right, 'cause your color's all rosy Breen again."

"I'm sorry all of you worried, and honestly, I feel great now. Starving, but great. What is that turning the cottage into heaven?"

"Beef bourguignon, Marco style. It's gonna be about ready. I figured you need some red meat. Since Brian doesn't figure to make it back tonight, it's just you and me and our pal here. Stay."

He pointed at her, not the dog, and rose to go into the kitchen.

On his way back with what Breen recognized as one of his famed charcuteries, he opened the door. And tossed Bollocks a bite of meat on the dog's race out.

"He wouldn't go out the whole time you were," Marco told her. "Went upstairs to get his lamb and laid it up there with you when I came in to sit and read, but that's it.

"Best dog in dog history."

"I've got the best friends in friend history."

"Stay," he repeated, and went back for wine and glasses. "We're going to sit here, have some wine while you fill the hole some off that tray. It'll give our dinner time to finish up while you tell me what the hell went down up there with the Trolls."

She grabbed finger food, stuffed it in. "Good. God. Good. Let's start by saying I'm glad Brian was with me. I don't know how I'd have managed without him. Thar? He was a lot like that girl Cait Connelly. Bitter."

She took the wine, sipped, then told the tale.

At the Capital, Keegan took a meal with Brian in his quarters.

"You give me an excuse to have a meal in peace instead of the banquet hall. Even if bringing the Troll means it'll be another day or two until I can go back to the valley."

"I'm sorry for that part of it."

"You'll bear witness at the Judgment, and we'll wait for that until Loga comes. You think he's well enough to travel?"

"He was on his feet and holding his own when I left. I don't think the wound was a mortal one—the single wound Odran's assassin put into Loga before Breen stopped him. And stop him she did, sending him six feet in the air. Made it easy for me to grab him up and hold him."

He washed down a bite of rack of lamb with ale. "She had the right of it, Keegan, when she said they'd trust her. Sul did just that, or I might've found myself dodging Troll arrows."

"Thar's father fought with Eian against Odran and fell as Eian did. I remember this, though I didn't know him well. So I remember Thar was at the lake, and in it, the day I lifted the sword."

"And hopes to take it from you."

Though Keegan's lips curved, humor played no part. "Well now, he'll have to keep hoping, won't he? There's only one Judgment for an attempt to take a life. You'll have your say, as will Loga and any other he chooses to bring. As will Thar himself."

"Three now, well, four with the one from Samhain, and there's Toric and his like. How many more like them, I wonder, living with us?"

"I'm hoping not many. You said the raven came through the portal."

"I came straight from the Troll camp to the Capital," Brian told him. "As you needed to know about Thar's attempt on Loga's life. It was Breen who saw the raven, so Duncan could follow and learn."

"How is it she saw and none of you?"

"Yseult, she said."

As Brian went through it, Keegan rose, paced, threw open doors for air, sat again. Drank again.

"I've never seen anyone do what she did. Well, no one without wings," Brian clarified. "Can you?"

"I've never tried it. It's a simple enough matter, with focus, to rise a few inches, a foot perhaps. But it's been more of a giving. To the air. To merge with the element. Not as much a purpose. It would've taken power, will, and purpose."

"And how she spoke, Keegan. Full of that power, will, and purpose. In herself and out of herself at once, if that makes sense."

He'd seen it in her before. "Sense enough."

"When she spoke the last words, in Talamhish? I swear to you they shook through me. And I confess here to you, if they'd been meant for me? I would fear."

Misneach, he thought. It meant both courage and spirit. She had both.

"And the breach is sealed. We'll check all the others for this crack she saw. One that opens and closes."

"Even when I was beside her, in the air, I didn't see what she saw."

"Yseult's magicks, but knowing that, and them, I'm forewarned. We won't close the others should we find them." He lifted a brow when Brian nodded. "You think as I do."

"If we close them, a raven can't get through, and we can't follow as Duncan did today."

"Aye." Sipping his ale, Keegan considered. "We could prevent a message getting to a spy—by that means in any case—but we wouldn't find the spy so easy. Or stop a plan such as the one to take Loga's life and point at another for murder. Odran hopes to set us on each other, that's clear enough now. And this tells me he's not so sure he can defeat the Fey as we stand together."

"We will stand together."

"That we will, aye." Keegan lifted his tankard in toast. "For one and all."

Later, well into the night, and alone, Keegan roamed his rooms.

He thought of calling Cróga, a flight to break this confinement. But he knew himself, and knew once on Cróga's back, he'd fly west.

He'd fly to the valley, and through the portal.

And to her.

Though he wanted that, just that, more than he could say, it struck as too much what he'd done with Shana.

An itch to be scratched, a need to be met. Mutual, aye, and yet . . .

He wouldn't fly to Breen for an hour or two, the pleasure of a tumble, the comfort of her body under his or beside his in sleep.

She meant more, and while that was a tangle he needed to unknot, she simply meant more.

So he wandered his rooms, a cat in a cage, and considered the council meeting he'd called for in the morning, the Judgment that waited for Loga's arrival, the patrols, the training, and all the rest.

For his own curiosity, he stood still, closed his eyes, and let himself drift into the mild trance self-levitation demanded.

His focus arrowed in, then arrowed out.

He was the air; the air was him.

He let the heat flow in, the cool flow out.

In and out, all around, and under.

He felt himself rise, an inch. He held his arms up, palms up.

Another inch, and one more as he poured himself out, drew himself in.

He opened his eyes, found himself level with the top of the candle-stands on the mantel, so pushed and floated up another foot.

Though his mind stayed clear, his heart began to pound, his breath to labor as it might if he carried a heavy weight up a very high, steep hill.

He felt the sweat of it ride its way down his back as he fought to hold that focus. But it broke, and he dropped easily six feet. He stayed in the crouch as he'd landed until his breath came steady again.

"Well, bugger it. That takes a toll. We'll practice that until we've sharpened that blade. It could be useful."

He poured water rather than ale and drank deep.

She had Sidhe in her, he considered, but then so did he. The next time he tried it, he'd do what he could to draw on that part of his blood and see where it took him.

He stripped down, lay on the bed with the mural of Talamh overhead.

He found the valley on it, and missed it with a physical ache. He wound over to the Welcoming Tree painted above him in full summer green.

He imagined himself going through it, and to her cottage. Did she sleep now? Surely she slept, the good dog by the fire, as it was late.

He thought of how she slept, her hair loose fire over the pillow, how if the moonlight slid through the windows, it would glow on her face.

Seeing it in his mind, he drifted.

Then she was there. Not in her bed sleeping but standing by his.

"I'm dreaming," she said. "Are you?"

"I was awake. I thought of you."

"I'm dreaming, and dreamed of you. Am I here?"

He sat up. She stood in a pair of the pants and baggy shirt she often slept in. Certainly not the stuff of dreams.

And he wanted her like he wanted his next breath.

"Am I here?" she repeated, and reached out to lay a hand on his chest. "I feel you, I feel your heart beating. I must be here. Can you feel my hand?"

"Aye." He covered it with his own. "If it's a dream for us, let's not waste it. I've a longing for you, Breen Siobhan."

She knelt on the bed beside him, twined her arms around his neck. "Show me what we can do in dreams."

Mouths met, softly seeking the warmth, the taste, the promise already given. And with the kiss, the dream spun out, spun on. Held close, body to body, they gave themselves to it, to each other, while the fire simmered and the twin moons shed light through the dark.

Murmuring to her, he slipped her shirt away, so now they were skin to skin, warm flesh to warm flesh. He stroked the line of her back, drew in the scent of her hair. All there, all real, all his.

Indulging himself, he tasted more, taking his lips over her face, her throat, her shoulders, then sipping her sigh when their mouths met again.

Her breasts under his hands, so soft, so firm. Her quiet sigh of pleasure as he touched her, wherever he touched her. The sweetness of her lips as they brushed his, then lingered.

All his.

She shifted, pressing him back and down. For a long moment, she lay over him to feel that hard warrior's body under hers. The shape of him, the strength, the scent of his skin enticed her. She felt the beat of his heart inside her own and shifted once more to press her lips to it.

Now she indulged, and took more. Slowly, floating on the dream, she took her hands, her lips over him.

Shoulders broad, muscles taut, jaw a strong line under rough stubble. Skin surprisingly smooth over a tough, ruthlessly disciplined body.

All hers.

As she explored, inside her heart his heartbeat thickened. Though his hands both soothed and seduced, inside her body she felt his need for her. He wanted, yet he waited, and nothing could have aroused her more.

With a thought, she stripped the flannel away before she rose up to straddle him.

She saw his eyes in the moonslight, the way they looked at her. Only her. Lifting his hands, she brought them to her breasts, to her heart. And took him into her, slow, slow, slow, her breath, her body shuddering.

She held him there, held them both while the sensation saturated. Still he waited.

When she began to move, undulating, fluid as water, she ruled him. His body ached, his blood burned, and the pleasure swamped all. Bewitched, bespelled, he watched her, the tumble of hair a glow of fire in the fractured light. Her eyes, locked on his, so dark now with the power she held.

She lifted her arms high as her head fell back, as she took him as no one had, as he hadn't known any could. Light glowed around her now, a dream within a dream. She took him with her, beyond wants, beyond needs, beyond self.

More than a mating, this, a kind of merging so he felt her pleasure even as he felt his own. He rose as she rose, and felt, within himself, the long, keen, welcome release inside her.

When she ran her hands down her own body, he reared up. Seizing her hair in his fists, he crushed his mouth to hers.

She answered, and she chained her arms around him, her hips moving still. Driving him mad, driving him deep.

Crazed words poured out of him, words she wouldn't know, words his clouded mind barely understood.

Then at last, at last, he reached the edge. When he fell over it, it seemed he fell into her.

He held on to her as he lay back, held her as once more she lay over him.

"I know we have to wake up." She sighed the words out. "But I'd rather not."

His hands tangled in her hair again. Here was peace, he thought, such utter peace she brought to him.

"Did you work a spell to bring the dream?"

"No." She lifted her head. "No, I wouldn't—"

"I'd have been grateful. I thought of you, as I said. I thought of you."

"I thought you might fly back, for a few hours, like this."

"To have you? As I did with Shana? No." He twined her hair around his fingers, released it, twined again. "You're not Shana. You're nothing like Shana."

Smiling, she tipped her head. "In all the time I've known you, that's the most romantic thing you've ever said to me."

"Then your view of romance is very odd."

"Maybe. And still." She turned to look back at the fire. "Did you hear that?"

"What?"

"I— Oh, it's Bollocks." She turned back to him. "Come back soon."

"Wait."

But she was gone, and he was left with the fire burning low and the mural of Talamh spread overhead.

It took two days to hold the Judgment, two days before Keegan listened to the words—hot but clear from Loga, hot and bitter from the assassin Thar.

Two days before he once more brought down his staff for banishment.

When it was done, when the portal to the Dark World opened and sealed again, he met with Loga in the village at the Smiling Cat.

"I've bartered for the ale already, so ya'll drink yer fill."

"I thank you for it." Keegan joined him at the scarred and sturdy table where a tankard already waited. "And hope it washes the taste of Judgment out of my throat."

"Chose a heavy weight to lift when ya picked up the sword, didn't ya?" Loga brooded into his own ale.

He wore a polished, undented helmet and breastplate to show respect for the solemnity of the day. His wide, craggy face carried shadows under his eyes.

"Knew Thar since his first breath. Thought once he and my Narl might make the pledge, but she had an eye for Neill. Narl and Neill? I says to her." Rolling his shadowed eyes, he made Keegan laugh.

"Still, a good mate he is, a good father to their children. And the gods know, as I do now, Thar would've broken her heart as he's broken his ma's."

"She didn't come for the Judgment."

"Wouldn't. Sul tells me she weeps all through the night, but she won't speak his name in the light of day. Under my nose he was, I tell ya, and I never saw it in him. But when I look in the backward way, aye, it was there, clear enough."

"The girl Caitlyn O'Conghaile had parents, a brother and sister. Not just sharing a camp, but a cottage. She had a man who loved her. Not one saw it in her. Some hide the truth of themselves very well indeed."

"How many more, do ya think? Every Troll in Talamh will hunt with and for ya on this."

"I can't say." Someone struck up a tune on a pipe, and hands clapped the time. "That's the hard truth of it."

"Without the Daughter of the O'Ceallaigh, we wouldn't have known of Thar, and I'd be dead. She's the key, and there's no doubt of it. Wouldn't take payment for healing my scratch." He brooded over that. "Puts me obliged to her, I find. Not used to that."

Then he shrugged his big shoulders and drank some more. "Sul says if the one she's carrying comes out a girl, she'll have the name of Breen. Arguing with a woman most times gives ya a head worse than a night of drinking bad ale. But argue with a pregnant one, and ya'll have your balls kicked blue."

"As my own sister's had three, I can't argue with that point. Is she well, Sul? She didn't come with you."

"She's too far along with the new one for so long a journey, and I risked my balls saying so, as she was bound to come. But as up in temper as she was over all of it, she's a woman of sense. Had to bring three with me to stop her nagging, but it's company on the traveling."

"You and your party will have a meal with me tonight, and rooms at the castle until you journey west again."

"We'll take the meal, but we're not ones for bedding down in a castle. We'll camp in the fields and ride back at first light."

He looked around the pub, where a mandolin had joined the pipe and the air smelled of spiced meat and fresh bread.

"Been some years since I've been to the Capital. Too low to the ground for my liking, and too many in it, but this pub serves a good ale. Not my first Judgment, but the first I've seen ya holding the staff. Ya do well enough there, and a credit to yer da, who I knew. He could play a tune and swing a sword, could Kavan O'Broin."

"That he could."

"So we'll have another round"—Loga signaled—"and raise a cup to him."

CHAPTER FOURTEEN

On a day when the rain came and went, Breen walked with Bollocks from Marg's to the farm.

She'd seen Marco and Brian off that morning, on the trip to Meet the Family.

"He should probably be there by now, or nearly," she said to Bollocks. "He was so nervous! How many times did he change his mind about what to wear, what to take? I lost count. And tonight, tomorrow for sure, Brian's going to ask him."

Beside her, Bollocks executed a full-body wag to show enthusiasm.

"I feel the same way! But we kept it zipped, right? As promised. Thank *God* that's almost over. Looks like just you and me tonight." She reached down to tousle his topknot. "What do you say, popcorn and a movie? We'll get all cozied up and—"

She broke off when Bollocks leaped into a dance, let out joyful barks, then sprinted ahead.

She expected to see Aisling's boys in the field, and there they were. So was Keegan.

And so, she noted, were the archery targets.

As she watched, Harken came out of the barn with the pup prancing beside him.

Darling and Bollocks tore toward each other as if it had been weeks rather than hours since they'd last met. As they wrestled, and the boys raced to them to join in, Keegan turned.

"He's got you set up—barely back, and already at it," Harken said as they crossed paths.

"So I see. He's just back?"

"Not an hour ago. He's tired. He won't say it, but I can see it clear enough. You might have to call out some patience, as he can get snappy when he's tired out."

"Oh well."

"I'll be well out of the way of it." He gave her a pat on the shoulder. "Morena's giving Finola and Seamus a hand with things today, and Finola's taking pity on us by sending some of her roast chicken and such. So I've the excuse of going in to clean up."

He rubbed at a smear of grease on his trousers.

"Good luck to you."

"Thanks."

She waved to the boys as she walked to where Keegan waited.

"You're late," he said by way of greeting.

"Brian thought you wouldn't be back until tomorrow or the day after, so I planned to work with Aisling on my healing skills."

"You were skilled enough to heal Loga."

"I'm not sure I could have if it had been worse than a single wound, and on a Troll as strong as Harken's prize bull."

"Skilled enough there, so Aisling can wait for another day. With bow, you're lacking."

Tired, she reminded herself, because she could see it just as Harken could. And still.

"How do you know I'm still lacking? You haven't been around the last week."

"Fine then, show me."

He handed her a quiver of arrows, and when she'd strapped it on, a bow.

"I had duties." A bit snappy, as Harken warned, Keegan shoved his hands in the pockets of his duster. "I'd have come back sooner if I could have."

"I know."

She started to reach back for an arrow, but he caught her face in his hands, laid his lips on hers. Then searched her face.

"Were you there, or was the dream mine alone?"

"I was there."

He rested his forehead on hers. "All right then." And stepped back. "All right then. Now show me your great skill."

She nocked the arrow, took her stance, slowly and smoothly drew back. When she loosed the arrow, it nipped the outer ring of the target.

"I didn't say great," she muttered.

"By all the sweet goddesses, you've eyes. Use them."

"Nothing's wrong with my eyes. And you're just . . . crowding me." She waved him back. She tried again, and hit the other edge of the target.

"I watched a little not yet eight do better, and on her first go. Steady your arm, woman. Adjust your stance."

"Steady your arm. Adjust your stance," she repeated.

She'd missed him, she reminded herself. She'd wanted him back.

She went through another six arrows and managed to hit halfway between the edge of the target and the center twice.

"Just save it," she snapped at him. "I do better with Morena. You can ask her. It's you."

"It's me, is it?"

"It's you standing there glowering at me."

"Sure the one coming at you to do you harm will wear the most pleasant of smiles as he cuts you down."

She wouldn't need a damn bow and arrow to stop an attacker, she thought. She had other ways.

Other ways, it dawned on her.

She took some calming breaths, then readied another arrow. She thought of the point, thought of the center.

Bull's-eye.

She sent Keegan a smug look as he frowned. "Glower at that, *mo chara*."

"Anyone can have a bit of luck. Do it again."

She did, then a third time, nesting the arrows point to point to point in the target center.

Enjoying herself now, she reached back for another. Keegan stilled her hand.

"You're using power."

"And it works. I don't know why I didn't think of it before. Why didn't you say to?"

"I never— Because it's not the way of it. It's—"

"What? Cheating? Maybe on a hunt, yeah, or in a contest. Not fair. But all's fair in war, right? If I'm defending myself or another, why wouldn't I use any and all weapons at hand?"

She could see she'd baffled him.

"It's not the way," he repeated.

"And you're not the Mandalorian. It works."

She stepped laterally in front of the next target, pulled another arrow. She didn't bother with the bow this time, just held it out, then sent it flying into the target.

Dead center.

Behind her, the boys cheered. She turned to take a bow, and saw Harken had come out, and stood with the kids, grinning.

"You don't learn the skill," Keegan argued, "if you rely on magicks."

"So I'll practice without them, but I know what I can do if I need to. Sometimes, Taoiseach, you make another way."

She used one target for the power boost, the second for without.

Without, by the end of the session, she'd improved. Marginally. With? She decided the Avengers' Hawkeye couldn't do better.

"You're in luck," she told Keegan as they started to the cottage at dusk.

"Am I?"

"Marco made jambalaya last night, and we have leftovers."

"I haven't had this. It's good?"

"It's excellent. I'm glad you could give Brian this time to introduce Marco to his family."

"He earned every hour of it. They'll agree to pledge, I think."

She nearly stumbled over a branch as they moved into Ireland. "Why do you say that?"

"Brian takes him to meet family, and in a way that has meaning clear enough. And he had nerves. Brian isn't one for nerves. So they'll likely pledge."

"Thank God! It doesn't feel like I have to zip it if you've got that much."

"Zip what?"

"He asked for my approval. Brian. It was so sweet!" Remembering, she crossed her hands over her heart. "I promised I wouldn't tell anyone, and I'd rather shoot arrows for six hours than have to hold that back again. He's going to ask him. Maybe tonight. And we'll have two weddings."

Thrilled, she hooked an arm through Keegan's as Bollocks raced back and forth.

"One here—or in Talamh, that is. And one in Philadelphia for Sally and Derrick and Marco's sister."

"What of his parents? Marco's."

"No. No, they wouldn't come. I'm going to ask them. I won't tell Marco, but I'll go and talk to his mother. But they won't come."

"Then the flaw is in them."

"It doesn't matter. We'll have it at Sally's. I know that's what Marco's going to want. And everyone who loves him will be there. Oh, it'll be amazing. You'll come, won't you? You'll be there for both?"

When he hesitated, she pressed.

"It'll be after. When the rest is done. However long it takes, that wedding, at least, will be after."

"I'd want to be there."

"Good enough."

"You'll make plans, some of them, when you go in the spring."

"You can count on that." They stepped out of the woods; Bollocks streaked to the bay. "I appreciate you not putting up any obstacles over that."

"You have your family and your work."

"I do, but I won't go if I'm needed."

"So you said before."

Inside, he tossed his duster on the peg, took her jacket to do the same.

"We can have some wine—or a beer for you, if you'd rather—while I heat up the leftovers."

Even as the words were out, he lifted her off her feet.

"Those can wait. Light the fire, *mo bandia*. Here." He stopped by the living room sofa. "This is far enough."

"Works for me."

"I would have come back sooner."

"I know."

That he would have, she thought as he laid her on the sofa, was all she needed to know.

Later that night, Marco sat on a hill, wrapped in a blanket with Brian, drinking sparkling Sidhe wine. A fire blazed in a circle of stones while the moons—two halves he imagined nudging together for one big-ass ball of white—competed with the stars to shed light.

A midnight picnic, Brian had said, and Marco figured there was a first time for everything.

"I really, really like your family."

"They love you already."

"They sure love you. And they made me feel so welcome. Two minutes in, I forgot to be nervous. Ten minutes in, it's like I've known them my whole life."

He turned, brushed his lips to Brian's.

"And there you are, charming them head to toe and back again. Saying to my father how you see now where I get my good looks, and to my mother how you see where I got my good brain. That was clever of you."

"How I saw it, so that made it easy."

He tipped his head toward Brian's, watched the fog of their breath merge, then whisk away.

"Now I'm sitting here with you, midnight picnic, a sky full of stars and moons. I'm looking down at where you were born, where you grew up, and down there at the tree you climbed to stuff yourself with green apples until you got the mother of all bellyaches."

"Ah, my ma and her stories."

As happy as he'd ever been, Marco snuggled closer.

"Can't wait to hear the rest of them. Like I can't wait for you to meet Sally and Derrick in person instead of just over FaceTime. They're going to love you, Brian, like I do. They're my real family, along with Breen. And my sister."

"And will there be stories?"

"Oh yeah."

"It's important to meet family, to be part of the whole of it, and the history of it. And for me, to see the smile in my mother's eyes when she met you, and the look she gave to me that said, so clear: Aye, of course. I see why you love him."

"She already knew why I love you."

"Well now, of course. What's that you say? What's not to love?"

Laughing, Marco poured more wine for both of them.

"It's important to make family as well. To find the one you love and want and see yourself with through the years to come. And there your own becomes a part of that whole, and that history."

He took Marco's hand, brought it to his lips. "Make that family with me, Marco, be a part of that whole and that history with me. Will you pledge to me here, where I was born, and take my pledge to you?"

Marco's breath simply stopped, and everything went still. The night, the air, the world, and all the worlds beyond.

"Are you . . . are you asking me to marry you?"

"I am, and now all the nerves I felt on it seem foolish, as the asking is the simplest thing in all the worlds."

Turning Marco's hand over, Brian pressed his lips to the center of his palm. "I promise to love you and stand with you, and build a life with you that brings you joy. I know it may seem quick, but—"

"No, no, it doesn't. Brian Kelly, my Sidhe warrior, my lover, my friend. It feels like I've waited for you all my life, and that night we stood by the bay, everything just clicked into place. You're the one, and you're always going to be."

He all but threw himself into the kiss, into the rightness of it, the joy already begun.

"So you will? You will?" Brian said as his lips rushed over Marco's face.

"I was going to ask you. Man, just hold on to me a minute, I'm shaking. After meeting your family, I was going to talk to Breen."

Holding tight, holding on, Marco closed his eyes. "She's my north star, you know? I wanted to figure out how to ask you, make it special."

Easing back, Brian cupped Marco's face. And saw his whole world, his entire life in those beautiful eyes. "You would ask me?"

"All my life I wanted someone to love me like you do, wanted to love someone like I love you. I wanted to ask you to marry me, but you beat me to it."

"Say to me: Aye, Brian, I'll pledge to you."

"Aye, Brian, I'll pledge to you."

"And I say to you, aye, Marco, I'll marry you."

The kiss sealed the promise, and a loving step into the future.

"I found you," Marco murmured. "I found you. All I had to do was walk into another world, and there you were."

In the afternoon that brought more rain, Breen stepped out of her office and the work. She let Bollocks out, as rain or not, he wanted a run, then went into the empty kitchen for a Coke.

She'd have to get used to it again, she reminded herself. To the quiet and the alone, to not finding Marco at the table working, or in the kitchen cooking.

He'd have his own kitchen, his own table before too much longer. And she wanted that for him, a home of his own with someone he loved.

She wandered to the doors, looking out at the rain, the way it—and Bollocks—stirred up the bay. She loved the look of it, in the rain, in the sun, in everything between.

She'd seen it in summer, in fall, and now in winter. In a matter of weeks, she'd stand here, just like this, and watch spring come.

But no rush, she thought. With spring, she'd go through the portal again, but to Philadelphia. As much as she wanted to see Sally and Derrick, spring meant facing her mother again.

And it meant facing the fact she couldn't keep dragging her feet on submitting the book.

"It's good enough or it's not, Breen," she told herself. "Either way, you wrote it, and that's more than you ever thought you'd do."

If it wasn't good enough, she'd try to make it better.

"Like I made myself better." She turned up her wrist.

"*Misneach*, and don't you forget it."

She had a life here, and in Talamh. And in both she felt productive and happy. She was damn well going to keep that life, that productivity, and that happy.

All she had to do to make sure of it was defeat a god.

The following afternoon, as the rain continued, she followed Marco's recipes to the letter—such as they were. At least for the Italian bread he had very specific amounts. The red sauce for the lasagna she planned for his welcome home dinner proved more problematic.

"I've seen him do it countless times," she told Bollocks as he sat and watched her chop herbs. "And he's not coming home from getting engaged—and I *know* he's coming home engaged—and making dinner."

She added the herbs, stirred the pot, and resisted the temptation to do a spell that turned her sauce into Marco's.

"It's not really cheating, but it could go wrong."

She uncovered the bread dough she'd formed into very, very careful football-shaped loaves for the final rising.

Saw the pair of them had somehow merged together into a fat, puffy blob with a slight fork at the top.

"Shit, shit, shit! Why? We'll fix it."

She started to use her fingers, then imagined the loaves deflating like balloons.

"It's not cheating," she insisted, and just held her hands over the mass, gently, slowly separating them. "I did all the work, and no shortcuts, so it's not cheating."

She slid them into the oven, over a shallow bowl of water already steaming—for reasons she didn't understand, but Marco had in the recipe.

She set the timer and hoped for the best.

"Now we clean up." And, Jesus, she'd made a mess.

By the time she'd dealt with the dishes, taken out the bread—and it looked pretty good—she heaved out a huge breath.

"It's exhausting! How can he love doing this all the time? Let's get the hell out of here, Bollocks."

She grabbed her rain jacket, tossed up her hood.

After the heat and terror of the kitchen, the cool and wet felt like a blessing.

The rain—if it rained in Talamh—might delay his travel.

Even as she thought it, he walked down the path toward her.

"Marco Polo!" She and Bollocks ran to him together. She jumped into a hug while Bollocks just jumped.

"I was just thinking you might not get back for a few hours because of the rain."

"Sun's shining in Talamh. Sure is pouring here." He gave her a hard squeeze before he drew back.

And when she saw the light in his eyes, she bounced like Bollocks.

"Tell me, tell me, tell me."

"Brian said he told you he was gonna. And you didn't say a word."

"It *killed* me. Now tell me, tell me everything! How did he ask, where, when?"

"Don't you want to know if I said yes?"

"As if you said anything else."

"Let me go toss the bag in the house, and I'll walk back with you."

She waved a hand, and the bag vanished. "In your room. Done. Tell before I explode."

"Midnight picnic."

"Oh, oh, oh!" She punctuated by slapping a hand to her heart on each syllable.

He told her as they walked, and as her tears fell like the rain.

"It's all so beautiful, so romantic and perfect. So you and Brian."

"His mother cried like you are—that kind of crying. They're just like super great, Breen. I cried some, too, when she said I should call her Ma. If I wanted."

"I love her already."

"Brian said you told him I'd want two weddings, one here, one at Sally's. You really know me, girl."

"No one better."

"We're thinking maybe September for the one here, around when we met, like an anniversary."

"And the romance keeps coming."

"His mom wants a big splash."

"I told you I love her already."

"Oh man, me, too! The way she's talking it'd be a lot like Morena and Harken's. A big-ass Fey wedding.

"For the one at Sally's, we'll see if we go before or after that. Because after, right? He really shouldn't leave until after. So maybe more like November, or over into January."

"You know, earlier I was thinking how I've got more than I ever thought I could, how my life is so big now, so good, and if I could just put off the rest. And now? I want the damn after to hurry up."

"Doesn't matter when, Breen."

Everything about him glowed as he spoke, and it made Breen tear up again.

"We're pledged. Brian asked his brother to stand for him at the wedding at his home, and he was going to ask Keegan if he'd do it, if he'd come and stand for him at Sally's. You'll stand for me for both, won't you?"

As the rain poured, she turned to him, wrapped around him, and wept.

"Come on." He kissed her hair. "Let's get into the sunshine. When we get back, we'll FaceTime Sally and Derrick."

"Oh yes!"

"I'll go back a little early," he said as they stepped onto the branch. "You could help me barter for some fish, maybe. I can make some fish and chips."

"Nope. I've taken care of dinner."

Stunned, he looked at her and barely noticed the change from rain to sun. "You what now?"

"I'm making lasagna, and I baked freaking bread."

"Now I'm gonna cry."

"You might when you eat it, but if it's not good, lie."

She clasped hands with him as they went down the steps with Bollocks waiting for them at the wall. "What a beautiful day. What an absolutely perfectly beautiful day. Now let's go spread the word."

Even the thought of training didn't spoil her mood as she walked from a lovely time of celebration and magicks at Marg's toward whatever torture Keegan planned for her at the farm.

No doubt Marco had celebrated at the farm, and at Finola's. And they'd celebrate again at the cottage when Brian joined them.

"A really, really good day, Bollocks. Like the start of a new chapter in a book you can't wait to read. I can't wait to see Sally's face when we tell him."

Buoyed by the image, she strolled on.

Ahead, just ahead, a gray cloud swirled on the road. The cloud became a form—a faerie, a dark one, with wings edged in black.

Recognizing wraith, she cursed Keegan, and fumbled for her sword.

"Breen Siobhan O'Ceallaigh, I am from Odran, god of all."

"Yeah, yeah, yeah."

Beside her, Bollocks growled, low and fierce.

"Through my eyes he sees; through my mouth he speaks."

"Clever," Breen muttered. "Sneaky clever, Taoiseach."

She started to toss out power rather than strike with the sword, but the voice came. And the voice was Odran's.

"The sand is low in the glass for you, and when the last grain falls, all this will burn. Burn and bleed. Should I show you now, with this foolish dog?"

"No! Sit." She snapped it so fiercely at Bollocks, his rump hit the ground with a thud. And she stood in front of him.

"You won't touch him."

"I could spare him, and a handful of others of your choosing, if you come to me now."

"You'd spare nothing and no one. Death is all you know. And I'll never come to you."

"This choice runs out as the grains of sand run out. Come through the portal in the Tree of Snakes. Unseal it and come before the turn of the moons, or all burn and bleed. All curse your name as they burn and bleed. Come and you'll sit by my side, a treasured granddaughter. Feed me your power and live, honored for the gift. Refuse and I take all you are, and you live only long enough to see the worlds so precious to you die."

He brought her fear, she wouldn't deny it. But neither would she fall to fear.

"You threaten me through a phantom, an illusion. Your power's weak and stinks of your desperation. Here's my choice."

When she struck out at the wraith, steel met steel. She saw the fury in its eyes, Odran's eyes, and something like pleasure.

Before she could block, the opposing blade struck her arm, and sliced through flesh.

Pain and shock ripped a cry from her as she stumbled back. Bollocks, too furious to obey, leaped. And leaped straight through the wraith.

"Your blood. Such is my power strong and yours weak. Now watch this mongrel die for you."

"No."

As Bollocks charged again, and the wraith lifted the sword, Breen shot fire. An inferno, one that erupted in her through twin sparks of fear and rage.

As the wraith burned, she dropped to her knees on ground stained with her own blood.

"Choose!" The voice thundered so the ground shook under her. "Life or death."

Then all that was left was smoldering ash.

"Don't! Don't go near it."

Whining, Bollocks came to her, nuzzling against her as she clutched her wounded arm. "Salt, we need salt. I can't think. I might be in shock. I need to get up, get up. Can't pass out. Have to heal this. Can't think."

She heard the horse, coming fast, and struggled to stand.

Defend.

And saw Keegan, bareback on Merlin.

"Salt," she said again, and went back to her knees.

He dropped down beside her before the horse stopped.

"Salt. Salt the ash."

"You're bleeding. Gods, this is deep. Be still, let me do what I can first."

"I thought— Jesus, that burns!"

"I know, I know. I need to stop the bleeding. We'll leave the rest to Aisling. Hold quiet, brave one, let me do what I can."

She shut her eyes, bore down. "I thought you'd sent the wraith, a sneak attack for training. I was pissed. That's enough, isn't that enough? It's worse than the gash."

"Almost."

"We have to salt the ash. Someone might come. One of the kids might—"

"We'll see to it. Here comes Harken now."

"How did you know? How did you know I needed you?"

"The fucking bastard shouted loud enough to wake the dead. See, here's Marg and Sedric as well, riding double on Igraine. Harken! Go fetch salt for that stinking ash. We'll need to take it and bury it at the Bitter Caves."

"Let me see her first."

Like Keegan, he dropped from the horse, and with gentle hands took her wounded arm. "How bad was it?" And only nodded when Keegan looked at him. "You've done well then. Marg can have a look, so stop now."

"Yes, please."

"*Mo stór, mo stór.*" Marg knelt beside her.

"I'm all right." Better, she thought, since the burning stopped. But, God, her arm throbbed.

"I'll send him to hell myself for this. It was Odran?"

"Not exactly."

"I stopped the bleeding, but she needs more."

"Aye, aye, and this comes first. Aisling and I will see to the rest."

"The salt, Harken, and let Aisling know she's needed."

"I'll lift her up to you. No, darling, don't try to stand yet." Sedric picked her up in his arms. "I'll stay here until the salting's done so none go near the ash."

Before he set her on the stallion in front of Keegan, Sedric kissed her. "You're in fine hands now, not to worry a bit about it."

"Bollocks."

"We're right behind you," Marg promised, and mounted Igraine.

"I've got you."

Merlin took off at a gallop, and the movement made her stomach pitch and roll.

"I thought you'd sent it."

"So you said, and a fine idea that would've been."

"Then I knew. He was going to kill Bollocks, just to hurt me."

"I'd wager that'd be harder than he thinks. The dog's a champion."

Her head, so heavy, lolled back. "It said it saw with Odran's eyes, spoke with his mouth. And it did."

"Strong magicks, strong enough for that, and for the sword to slice."

"What happened? What happened? I heard—" Marco ran hands over Breen's face when Keegan pulled up. "I didn't know where to find her."

"Take her now, brother. She's hurt, but already healing. Take her inside, and Marg and Aisling will see to the rest."

"Okay, all right. It's all good now, baby, Marco's here."

"Bring her in, lay her down." At the door of the farmhouse, Aisling snapped out orders. "Lay her down on the divan, Marco, and take the baby."

As she shoved the whimpering Kelly into Marco's hands, she pulled pins out of her pocket to bundle up the tail of her hair.

"He's fussing, walk him around, jiggle him. He wants his supper, and he'll have to wait a bit. We'll get that jacket off, and the sweater as well, and see what's what, won't we?

"Keegan, the potion, the blue bottle, the squat one with the yellow topper. Seven drops in two fingers of whiskey."

"I don't like whiskey."

"You'll drink it, like or no. Here's Marg. You'll get the potion, won't you, so Keegan doesn't muck it up."

"I wouldn't muck it up."

"Be useful and hold her hand while I see to this. Ah, the flaming bastard. Marco, would you step out for just a moment, and tell those boys I said stay outside if they know what's good for them."

"I wish I could snap out orders like you." Breen gave Aisling a vague smile, then closed her eyes. "General Hannigan."

She took Breen's other hand. "Outnumbered by men, you learn. Keegan, fetch a candle."

"Do I hold her hand or fetch a candle?"

"Do both! And Breen, you'll look at the candle, at the flame. Look at the light. This will hurt a bit."

"It already hurts."

"A bit more. Now look at the candle, the light. Into the light, see it. Feel it. Be it. Into the light where it's warm. It soothes, the warm does."

She felt the pain as Aisling worked, but distantly, like a dream pain. She heard her grandmother's voice join Aisling's, both as soothing as the candle flame. Easy, quiet, and she drifted on them.

Once, twice, a third time her breath caught as the pain snuck closer, then it faded.

"Drink this now, there's a girl. Every drop."

"It burns my throat. And it's bitter."

"The potion's on the bitter side," Aisling agreed, and swiped the back of a blood-streaked hand over her brow. "But it works well. Now just lie still for a moment or two."

She focused on Aisling's face now, and on Marg's, saw they both carried the sweat sheen of effort.

"It hurt, what you did. It hurt you, taking on the pain."

"Healing's a gift." Aisling spoke briskly as she got to her feet. "But not without a price, and the price is given willingly."

"I need to see to my horse." Keegan shoved to his feet, walked out.

"Right pissed, he is," Aisling noted.

"I know he's angry with me, but I—"

"Not with you." As she might one of her boys, Aisling gave Breen a light cuff on the head. "Don't be stupid. Here now, Kelly, here—give him over, Marco."

When he did, she flapped open her shirt and set his greedy mouth on her breast.

"When you've rested a bit, and Keegan works off the mad, we'll all have a drink not bitter, and you'll tell us what the devil happened."

CHAPTER FIFTEEN

Breen learned Morena had come on wings and had flown to the farm just as Marco stepped out to warn the boys to stay outside. Assured Breen was in good hands, she flew off to help Harken deal with the ash.

Finola and Seamus had rushed from home as well. It seemed half the valley or more had hurried to defend whatever and whoever needed defending.

She sat at the big table now, with her arm healed and unscarred—though Aisling warned it would throb a bit off and on for a day or two—and with those closest to her.

Most took whiskey, or tea with a healthy dollop of whiskey in it, but she gratefully took a glass of wine, sipping slowly as she related the story.

"Bold of him," Sedric commented. "Bold and rash with it."

"He's both of those. He'd know of the wraiths in your training from those who spied for him," Marg added, "so used that for his. Sly. Something else he is."

"He bargains with you," Morena pointed out. "Do this, or I do that. But if he could do that, he would."

"He wanted to scare me, and hurt me. He did both, so missions accomplished. But I think he really believes I'll be lured, not just with threats, but with promises."

"Many are."

She glanced at Keegan. "He could have killed me—maybe—but he doesn't want me dead. Not until he gets what he wants out of me.

But he couldn't take me, or that. Not through the wraith. I know I wasn't as good with the sword as I should've been, and maybe at least part of that was me believing his couldn't really hurt me."

"Any weapon's to be treated with respect."

"Lesson fully learned. He doesn't. Learn, I mean, or he's too full of himself to learn. When I was a teacher, I'd have students like that sometimes. The kind that didn't really pay any price for not learning the lessons, so they didn't really learn from a mistake or a bad grade."

"Kids with 'tude," Marco put in. "He ain't no kid."

"Yet for all the time he's existed, he keeps reaching for the same thing and failing."

"Definition of insanity." Now Marco shrugged. "Psycho, like I said before."

"He never had a prize such as you as a goal before." At the table's head, Keegan turned the cup of whiskey in his hand. "As you're our key, you're his as well, and this he knows. He makes it a choice, a false one, but a choice come to that. And shed your blood this day to show you what it could cost you to make the choice against him."

"He's made of lies." Harken spoke quietly. "This choice he offers is just one more."

"I'm not a warrior." His hair in tufts, as he'd taken off his work cap for his seat at the table, Seamus looked around that table. "Or one for heavy thoughts as most here have weigh on them. But I wonder why it is Odran spoke through this wraith, a dark Sidhe, you say, Breen darling. Why not the illusion of himself? Wouldn't that hold more power and bring more fear with it?"

"A fine question, isn't it?" Mahon turned from the window where he'd stood watching his boys and the dogs.

"I'm wondering if any with more knowledge on the matter can answer it."

"It's still beyond his reach," Marg said simply. "And Yseult's. He sits in his black castle unable, as yet, to come through. And I'm thinking—and it is a fine question, Seamus—the wraith was not only a wraith."

"I don't get it." Baffled, Marco hunched his shoulders. "But first, look, I don't really get most of this stuff anyway. Breen's doing good here, so I can go out and keep an eye on the kids if you want."

"They're fine." Mahon took a last look out the window before returning to the table. "They've Mab and Bollocks and the fierce pup to watch them, as well as Liam. He's a solid lad, is Liam. You've a seat at this table, Marco."

"What was sent to Breen is salted ash and buried," Morena reminded him. "I'm of the Sidhe, but I know enough about the craft to understand what came for Breen took much power, and concentrated, you could say. She destroyed it, and destroying it, shattered the power. Would that be the right of it?"

"Right enough." Keegan continued to turn the cup in his hand. "And no, Odran doesn't have the power, as yet, to bring himself through. But more than that, he wanted to bring through a weapon that could—and did—slice flesh, shed blood. A wraith alone can't."

"Now I don't get it, because he sure as hell did." In response, Breen closed a hand over her healed wound.

"Then study more and deeper."

Breen felt the punch of Keegan's words. Before she could counterpunch, Harken waded in.

"She's had months, not years. It would take a merging," he explained. "Or would as I see it. The Sidhe you faced was real, but on Odran's side. A strong spell, a blood spell, to form the wraith in that image here, and only possible if the Sidhe was born here. To merge, the Sidhe becomes only a vessel that Odran fills."

"And the sword?" As she spoke, Finola covered Marg's hand with hers for comfort.

Marg turned her hand over, linked fingers with her friend. "Must have its origins here as well. And another spell brewed up to give it the power to harm. An illusion still, but one that can kill. He had a message to deliver to you, *mo stór*, and a lesson with it."

"Message received; lesson learned. Bollocks leaped right through it when he tried to protect me. But when I struck out with my sword, and his met it, I felt the block. I heard the clash of steel. After he cut me, and I used fire, he burned. How—"

Then it came home to her. "The Sidhe, the flesh and blood one in Odran's world. I killed him. I burned him alive. I—"

"Finally had the sense to do what you should've done at the start," Keegan said flatly. "Used power as well as the blade against an enemy wielding both."

"Your own blood added to what you used against him." Sedric's tone struck a gentler note. "Odran knew if you used your power, the wraith would burn, and so the vessel. Such a life means nothing to him."

"He wanted to watch you, gauge you," Keegan added, "as much as deliver the message and the lesson. He doesn't have your blood, as the sword smeared with it would have burned as the hand holding it burned. There's a disappointment for him."

"My blood. All right, I see that. To use in a spell, to add even a little to his own power. It would be worth whatever it cost him to gain even that. And all right, watch me, gauge me, but that goes both ways. I saw him, too.

"He could've struck when Bollocks jumped at him—through him as it turned out. But he didn't, because he wasn't expecting it, because he'd focused on me. And he needed me to go up against him, sword to sword, because yeah, he'd be a lot better with one. And he wanted my blood. Covets it, but needs it, too."

"I wonder if I could ask another question? How did he know where to come at you, and when for all that?"

"I could use such as you asking the good questions on the council."

Seamus laughed. "Oh no, not the Capital or councils for me, not even for you, my boy. I'm just a curious sort."

"Routines." Marco shrugged when eyes turned to him. "You know, like how cops say how she jogged that route every morning, or he walked the dog around that block every night around seven. So the bad guy got a handle on their routine. Breen usually walks to the farm from Nan's most days around that time, right?"

"So she does. And comes through with you and the dog near the same time daily. And the training," Keegan added, "there's a routine as well. So she wasn't as prepared as she should've been, as she's gotten too used to how it goes. That we'll change, right enough. As for the rest, we'll change that as well. Some days, you'll train first, others work with Marg. We'll not hold with routine."

"Destroy the pattern. Okay, but we're agreed doing what he did today took a lot. I don't see him repeating it."

"He'll always have a vessel, willing or no," Marg told her. "Best to have a care."

"So training first tomorrow. I'll bring her to you when it's done." Keegan pushed to his feet. "We'll go to the other side now. It's going dark, and there's rain coming in."

He was right about the rain, of course. The wind blew in and brought the first drops as Breen stepped outside.

She watched Aisling and Mahon gather up their boys, and Liam race off on two legs that became four.

And her grandmother, agile as a teenager, mount the mare while Sedric transformed into a cat to leap up with her.

"I'll help you put a meal together, Morena, while your da gives Harken a hand with the milking and such. A wet night we're in for." Finola gathered Breen into a hug, whispered in her ear, "You have that care now, darling."

"I will."

Flanked by Marco and Keegan, she walked through the rain—picking up fast—and thought how she'd walked to the tree from the other side in rain hours before.

And as she had when she'd stepped from Ireland into Talamh, she stepped back into clear air. Cool, on the damp side, but with no rain pelting down.

She had things to say, but kept quiet on the walk back.

"You feeling okay, my Breen?" Marco took her hand in his.

"Absolutely." Though her arm throbbed a little, as Aisling had warned her.

"Scared me."

"Me, too. But he's the one burned to ash—or his wraith and his vessel are.

"You're going to stop worrying, because tonight's about celebrating." She tossed out little beams of light. "You're staying out of the kitchen, going straight upstairs, and taking the shower I know you've been wanting since you rode back. You're going to unpack because it drives you crazy not to, then when Brian gets home, we're going to have the dinner I made."

When they stepped out of the woods, she looked down at Bollocks, since he stuck with her instead of racing for the bay.

"And you stop worrying, too. You go swim. Go on."

He ran off but shot several looks back to be sure before he leaped in the water.

"Something smells good," Marco began the minute they walked into the cottage.

"No." Folding her arms, she blocked his path. "Not one foot in the kitchen."

"I'm just gonna—"

"No. You're just gonna go upstairs."

"Bossy pants." He sent an anxious look toward the kitchen but obeyed.

"You can start the fire," she told Keegan as she stripped off her jacket—one her grandmother had cleaned of blood and mended. "Then you can explain why you felt it necessary to take that shot at me."

She marched into the kitchen; Keegan flicked a hand at the fire and followed.

"What shot?"

"How I finally did what I should've done in the first place. I did my best." She got a pot, slammed it into the sink to fill it with water for the pasta.

"But you didn't, and not doing your best let him open you up, here to here." He traced a finger—and not gently—from above her elbow nearly to her shoulder.

"I stood my ground, I fought back. I burned someone alive. What the hell else was I supposed to do?"

"Defend, by whatever means." He took an open bottle of wine— one she'd used in making the sauce—and poured it near to the rim of a glass, then got a beer for himself.

"Tell me how it is you fought in a battle where many fell on both sides, and came out with barely a scratch, but today, you faced one and your blood stained the ground."

"Because he's a *god*, for fuck's sake." She grabbed the glass, gulped down wine.

"As are you."

"It's not the same. You know it, you know it! It's mixed in me, with everything else."

"You feared him."

"Damn right I did. Do."

"There's no shame in that. But you thought of your fear, your worry, your doubts, and didn't act."

"I did act."

"Not with what's inside you, with your keenest weapon. What did you say to me when you put the arrows in the center of the target?"

"What did you say to me?" she countered.

"I'm saying now I was wrong. And I'm saying the fault, at least some of the fault, for what happened today is mine."

That put a hitch in her mad stride. "How?"

"I'm responsible for your training, and I found you bleeding on the ground. What he sent shouldn't have been enough to harm you, not like that, and yet . . . So I've done a poor job with your training."

"Oh, that's bullshit." She started to lift the pot out of the sink, but he nudged her aside, hefted it out himself.

"Where does it go?"

She stared at him. "Guess."

With a shrug, he set it on the stove. She added salt to the water, as Marco did, then turned on the burner.

She pressed her fingers to her eyes, then picked up her glass again. "If you were any better at training, I'd be black and blue from head to toe every stupid day. No, no, that's backward. I used to be black and blue every stupid day. I'm better at avoiding that now because of the training. And I do study, Keegan. I study the magicks as hard as I train."

"That was, perhaps, harsh."

"Perhaps?" She sighed again, then stirred the pot of sauce. And it did smell good, damn it. "If I don't know enough about the black magicks, I will study harder and deeper."

"I was wrong to say that. I was angry at what happened."

She moved past him to get the cheeses for the filling. "I'm going to say you weren't completely wrong."

He took a slow sip of his beer. "I wasn't, no."

"I was distracted, thinking about Marco and Brian, and it was such a gorgeous day. I can't live on edge every minute, Keegan. No one can. Not even you. But."

She turned to him again. "I did think too much. When I saw his eyes, heard his voice . . . I thought too much when I should've met power with power. But I thought, wraith, and it—he—they—couldn't really hurt me."

"Yet you stood in front of the dog, you said. There you acted."

"You're right. That was instinct. And it was instinct—and shock—that had me using power after he hurt me. I wasn't fooled by his lies, but the illusion? Well, a trick's a trick, and this was a damn good one. I fell for it."

"He'll have other tricks, other ways to try."

"But I saw him. And I saw, felt, a kind of desperation along with the greed, and the pride and the need. He doesn't know what I see. When he looks at me, Keegan, he sees the prize, like you said. The key, the power he craves. But he doesn't see me, just enough to know some weaknesses. Like Bollocks."

Sensing him at the door, she waved a hand to open it for him. "Dry him off, will you? He knows I love, but he doesn't understand love," she continued. "It's just a soft spot for him to exploit."

After he'd dried the dog, Keegan filled his bowls.

She slid the pasta in to boil.

"But it's not a soft spot, or not only," she added. "It's strength, it's a reason. If I made a mistake today, well, I'm human, too. You're just going to have to suck that one up."

"The human in you makes you what you are. It's not a flaw, but another strength. Another power. Another gift."

He put his hands on her shoulders as she worked. "I had your blood on my hands, Breen. And feeling it, seeing it, it may be I thought too much."

"I'd say all's well that ends well, but it hasn't ended yet."

"For tonight, it has." He turned her. "Take a moment, drink your wine, then tell me what I can do to help with whatever the hell it is you're doing here."

"Do you know how to make lasagna?"

"I don't, but I like to eat it."

"We're in the same position on that. You could stir those noodles so they don't stick together." When he circled a finger in the air to stir the pot, she rolled her eyes. "Not that way. Oh hell, that way's fine. You can make the salad."

"Can I now?"

"I'll walk you through it. That's something I can actually pull off. And I'm going to pull off this meal." She strode over to get a colander and a casserole dish. "Then I'm turning this kitchen back over to Marco for the duration."

She had it under control when Marco came down, so she just pointed a finger. "Stay out."

"I'm just going to get myself a glass of wine in anticipation of this fine meal."

"Keegan will get you a glass of wine. Stay out."

Though his face registered some sympathy, Keegan poured the wine, handed it to Marco. "Leave it to her, brother. Best let her have her way on this."

"Smells great." But Marco paced around the dining room. Before she could snap at him for it, his face lit up. "Here's Brian."

Breen paused long enough to watch the newly pledged couple greet each other with a strong kiss.

"Breen's cooking."

"So I see." Brian smiled at her as he wandered over. "Are you feeling all yourself then?"

"Because I'm cooking I don't feel all myself?"

"No indeed. Word's gone out far and wide about Odran's attack. Are you healing well?"

"Yes, thanks."

"We heard his bellow. I'm surprised if they didn't hear it in the Far North. I couldn't leave my post but sent Duncan, and he came back full of reports of how, even wounded, you burned the wraith vessel to ash, defeating the god and sending him crawling back to his own with a warning the next you met he'd burn."

"It wasn't exactly like—"

"Mara's got a song started on it. 'The Ballad of Breen and the Wraith.'"

She couldn't say the sound Keegan made was a snicker, but it came damn close.

"I didn't really—"

"But you did." Keegan poured wine all around. "Or close enough. And the Fey need their songs and stories. So a toast to Breen Siobhan for her victory on the field of battle and, we hope, in the kitchen."

"Ha," she said, and mentally crossing her fingers, pulled the lasagna out of the oven.

"That looks . . ." With some astonishment, Marco finished, "Perfect."

"We were going to eat by candlelight if it didn't." When she reached for a long knife, Marco made a sound. "What?"

"You need to let it rest awhile, or it'll be all sloppy."

"Oh. Right. Forgot. We'll have the salad while that happens."

"I made the salad. I want the credit for it." So saying, Keegan carried the salad bowl to the table. "So sit, and another toast comes first. To friends, to men who have all my respect and my affection with it. May joy surround you and contentment latch your door, and may the gods send their blessings now and evermore."

"I'm going to water up again. It means a lot, the meal, the toast." Marco lifted his glass. "But especially the friends. *Sláinte.*"

She didn't doubt the salad—not really cooking—but held her breath when Marco sampled the bread. His eyes narrowed on her.

"Girl, where've you been hiding?"

"It worked." Finally, she risked a bite herself. "It worked! It has to rise *three* times. Why isn't once enough?"

"Chemistry. This is the sweetest thing, doing all this for me and Brian."

"It's not every day my best friend and my cousin pledge."

She rose for the big test and brought the lasagna to the table to serve.

"Is your family well then, Brian?" Keegan asked. "And happy for you?"

"All well, and couldn't be happier. They fell in love with Marco just as I did."

"Mutual, and man, the stories his mom told me."

"Oh now, don't start there."

"Gotta."

They dug into the lasagna with laughter as well as forks.

"It's really good, Breen. Really good."

She nodded at Marco, pleased as she ate. "It doesn't quite reach your level. But it's good. I didn't burn it, and don't have to pull out the frozen pizza."

"Marco, I think, has his own magick in the kitchen." Keegan scooped up more. "Still, if I hadn't sampled his, I'd say this is the best I've had."

"That's a ringing compliment, and I'll take it."

"Food's love." Brian lifted his glass to her again. "And I taste yours in every bite."

"Now I'm going to water up."

CHAPTER SIXTEEN

She trained and she studied and she practiced through the February winds and rain. True to his word, Keegan changed up her routine. And true to himself, he remained unrelenting.

She fought wraiths in the woods with mud sucking at her boots. She shot arrows from dragon-back, clashed swords on horseback, and ran what seemed miles with quiver, bow, and sword.

Then he took her to the base of a rocky hill north of the valley. Pointed up.

"Scale it."

"You want me to climb a damn mountain? I don't know how to rock climb. I don't have a harness."

"There's enemy above. They have prisoners, small children," he added, and made her roll her eyes. "Would you stand here and leave the littles to their fate? They'll be sacrificed unless you find your way to the top and defeat the enemy."

"Oh, bullshit. Why wouldn't I call my dragon, fly up there, and rain hell down on them?"

"Because that's not the training here. You must reach the top yourself, and with what you have."

"And if I fall, splat?"

He shrugged. "Don't fall."

"Don't fall," she muttered. "Sure, there it is. Why didn't I think of that?"

She reached up, trying for a handhold, then a foothold. It took her about fifteen minutes—with fingers already raw—to manage three feet.

"By the time you get there, they'd have roasted and eaten the children. Had the tiny, squalling babes for dessert."

"Oh, shut up!"

She reached up, muscles straining. She didn't hold back the squeal as she slipped a little. Didn't see the point of it.

"Now they know you're coming for certain, so mind the arrows that'll be winging down at you, and the faeries flying out with swords to hack off your hands."

She just pressed her face to the cool rock and breathed. Then, teeth gritted, she managed another three feet.

Sweat slid down her back, down her face, and into her eyes. It coated her hands, and she hissed when she saw that her raw fingers bled a little.

She should've refused, she realized. He couldn't force her. But, as usual, she just went along. And now she was stuck on the face of a damn mountain. After she glanced down, she clung to the rocks like a lizard with her heart pounding a wild tattoo in her head.

If she fell, she might not be high enough to splat, but she'd sure as hell break something.

Possibly her neck.

"Maybe they're bratty children, and nasty babies. Maybe they're all like this kid I had in class once. Trevor Kuhn. Miserable little—"

The rock she gripped gave way, and so did she.

She felt the shock of falling backward, a rush of air and helplessness. Then she hovered, holding the air as she had the rocks.

"And there it is."

To her shock, Keegan rose up to her until they were eye to eye.

"You—you can do this, too?"

"I've been practicing."

"Why didn't you say to do it this way?"

"I said reach the top with only what you have," he reminded her. "You chose the hard way, and the process of it was likely good for you. But sure when you slipped, you called on what you have."

"My fingers are bleeding, and I rapped my elbow twice."

"They'll heal. But you stay here complaining while the children cry for help."

She looked up. "It's really high. I've never gone that high."

"Sure I haven't either, but now, together."

He reached out for her hands.

"It really sucks the energy."

"A price, but less to pay if you breathe the air, ask it to lift you."

They rose up together, passed goats with curved horns that balanced on ledges, and the nests of hawks and eagles. She saw a low cave and wondered what made its den there, and felt an odd thrill as they slid through thin clouds.

When they reached the top, they lowered onto a rocky plateau. One, from the scattering of goat droppings, the mountain goats frequented.

"How high?" she wondered. "Fifty feet?"

"Near to seventy. I thought high enough for this first time."

"I don't feel as rocky as I did after the waterfall, but maybe that was a combination of things."

There was something . . . in the water, in the river. Something she couldn't reach with her hand, and now couldn't reach with her memory.

She shrugged it off.

"But it's enervating. Even with this incredible view, I could take a nap right here."

"Stay alert. Defend."

Later, she'd think she'd become Pavlov's dog. Keegan said *defend* and she drew her sword. And, she'd suppose later, that was the whole point.

But at the moment, she was too busy fighting off wraiths to think at all. Dark faeries, a Were that became some sort of mountain cat, two demon dogs, and a witch who hurled fire.

It surprised her to find herself fighting back-to-back with Keegan.

"We came together," he said, "we fight together. In battle, you know who fights with you and against you. Duck," he added, then astonished her by flipping over her back, landing on his feet, and taking the last two wraiths out with one strike.

"So that's done."

In response, she lay down on the rocks, closed her eyes.

"You're lying on the shite of goats."

"I don't care. Everything hurts. My fingers sting, my lungs burn. You said it's done, so we saved the poor innocent children and the sweet, tiny babies. I'm going to lie right here for a few minutes."

He crouched beside her. "And what if more enemy are hidden behind the rocks over there?"

"You'll take care of them. How do we get these imaginary children off the mountain?"

"It's more hill than mountain, and we'd call dragons to fly them safely home again."

"Good, consider I'm doing that while you destroy the last of the enemy."

She opened her eyes, looked at him. She thought he was a little winded, but that could've been wishful thinking.

"Tell me the training's finished for today."

"Well, we've still got to get down, then there's the ride back to the valley. But after that, it's done."

"Hallelujah. I want the world's longest shower, a gallon of wine, and the flank steak Marco's got marinating."

"Then you'd best get on your feet." Rising, he reached down to take her hand, pull her up. "You did well. There's improvement. Small, aye, very small with the sword, but improvement for all that."

"I'm trying to think less, act more. I'm never going to be a warrior—"

"A warrior trains. A warrior fights, risks death to protect, to defend. You've done that and will do that. You've earned the braid if you want it."

Stunned, she stared at him. Emotion filled her, chased by a quick and unexpected thrill. She let it ride through her as she turned, looked out at the spread of Talamh, the rise and fall, the green and brown, the gold and blue of it.

Breen Siobhan Kelly, she thought, warrior for the Fey.

"Those are words I never expected to hear you say to me."

"They're words I never expected to say to you when we started. But you train, all these months now. When you fail, you try again. You complain, that's for certain, but you keep trying. You've fought and bled, and still you pick up the sword. What else is a warrior but this?"

"I'm . . . surprisingly flattered. But no, I won't wear the braid. When this is over, I really hope to hang up my sword—in a place of honor, of course. But I don't think a warrior ever does."

"The choice is yours."

"I disappoint you."

"You don't, no, I promise you that. Come now." He took her hands again, kissed her fingers, healed them. "We'll go down as we came up."

"You said you practice." With absolute confidence, she walked to the edge and stepped off with him. "You hadn't levitated before."

"Inches as most can and do. But I thought of what you said. I have all the tribes of the Fey in me. So I called on the Sidhe in me, and the Wise, always, as that's the dominant."

They floated down, through the clouds, on the air. Of the air.

"A few feet at first, and tiring, I'll admit. Then more, and not so tiring. I like having the skill, and might never have thought to hone it if you hadn't said what you did."

"I like the skill," she agreed when her feet finally touched the ground. "But I'd rather take the air with a dragon under me, or stand on the solid ground. I guess you'll start trying out other skills, from other tribes."

"Ah well." He glanced to the woods toward the west, and ran.

In seconds she lost him in the trees, then he bolted back to her.

She let out a surprised and delighted laugh.

"Fast!"

"Not elf fast, but surely twice what I could do before I drew on it. You're fast as well, not fast as this," he added as they walked to the horses. "But fast, and with endurance. That's from the jumping around you do every morning as well as what the fates gave you."

"Cardio, and it's not just jumping about."

"You look good when you're at it, and wearing those snug little bits of things. And for all of that, good training."

Amused, she mounted. "Can you become a tree—or I guess it's more go into one?"

"Not for lack of trying. But I can feel it, and the stone, the earth, the way I couldn't before. Or never thought to."

"Were?"

"This is my form, and my only."

"It's a good form."

That had him grinning at her. "It's the dragon that calls me, as it does you. Now I find, with practice, with effort, I can call to them. Not only Cróga, though that's different. It's—"

"Intimate. A shared heart and mind."

"It is, aye, but I can call others now—those not bonded with another—and they come. This is, I think, from the Were blood in me. Not taking their form, but being one of them, in some way. I'm grateful to you for putting this thought in my head."

"I'd love to see you call them."

"We'll find time for that if you like."

"I'd very much like. That leaves Troll and Mer."

"As for the Mer, I'd as soon wait for warmer before testing the waters, so to speak, and seeing what might be. And I'd as soon keep my legs. For the Troll blood, it's strength I think's coming. If I put my mind on it, I can lift and carry more. At least a bit for now. Although . . ."

He glanced at her as they rode through the woods and toward the road beyond. "It's said a Troll is tireless with the mating. Recovering, so they say, so quick, you wouldn't notice there'd be a pause in the matter."

"Is that right?"

"So the stories go, and the bawdy sort of songs with them. Which may be no more than bragging. But I thought it wise to test that out soon."

"Reasonable. I suppose, being loyal to the Fey, I should help you out with the practice."

"I'd be grateful. And more if you'd wash first, as, *mo bandia*, you smell of goat."

When she sniffed at herself, winced, he laughed and kicked the stallion into a gallop.

If she hoped the brisk ride back to the farm would diffuse some of the aroma, Morena disabused her.

"You smell like Finnegan the goatherd, who forgets to wash more often than not."

"I'm going to shower, and as soon as possible. Where's Bollocks? I guess where's Marco, as I left them together."

"And together they've gone to the other side moments ago. Something to do with potatoes, and Keegan said you'd be a bit later today, as you had training out of the valley."

Helpfully, Morena pulled a hoof pick out of her pocket, leaned on Boy's leg, and began to clean the hoof while Breen unsaddled him.

"He wanted me to fight to save imaginary children from the evil clutches of the enemy who'd roast and eat them."

"I doubt they'd bother with the roasting first, the bloody devils."

As they rubbed down the gelding, Breen told her about the choice of the day's training.

"You must've been worn indeed to lie down right on goat shite. That's a high ways you took the air, the both of you. Can you only go up and down? I mean to say have you tried going forward or back for all that, once you're up?"

"I don't honestly know. It still takes considerable to go up. Down isn't as much for whatever reason."

"It seems to me you could, and if you could, it's in a way almost like flying. You so wanted wings when we were little." Vigorously, Morena brushed the gelding's coat. "I could lift you, just a bit off the ground for a short ways, and you loved it so. Ma made you pretend wings out of wire and—"

"Bright green cloth," Breen remembered. "With blue around the edges. Like a butterfly. I'd run through the fields and pretend I was flying with you."

"Then Phelin—" Morena broke off, laid her cheek on Boy's neck.

"He was such a tease," Breen said softly.

"He was, aye, he was. But he didn't mean to make you cry with teasing you about the pretend wings."

"He thought I'd get mad, and give it right back to him, and when he saw he'd hurt my feelings, he took me up and flew me all around and around. An honorary Sidhe, he said I was. And anytime I wanted to fly, he'd take me."

"It's a good memory." With a nod, Morena continued the grooming. "A good one, as he was good. The sad still comes and goes, and just yesterday I found my nan crying and my grandda holding her. She's started her spring cleaning and found a picture he'd drawn for her when he was just a little."

With a sigh, she set the brush aside. "But there's so many good memories."

Breen came around the horse. "I smell like goat shit, but I'm hugging you."

Morena returned the embrace. "Oh, but sure you do reek."

"Probably some top notes of sweat to go with it."

"Go, get your wash. I'll take Boy in for his feed. I'll take Merlin," she called to Keegan.

"He'll want his carrot."

"As if I wouldn't know that." Morena reached out to scratch Merlin between the ears as Keegan led him over. "And tomorrow's training?"

"Starts straight off."

"Of course it does," Breen muttered.

"We'll see you straight off then. Come on, my boys, your supper's waiting."

They followed her as she walked to the stables, as a line of cows followed Harken as he walked to the barn and the milking parlor.

"You could stay, give Harken a hand. I'm fine walking back alone."

"I did the morning milking, and swallowed down some of Morena's lumpy porridge after. Harken seemed fine, with the porridge, I mean." Obviously baffled, Keegan shrugged. "That's love for you."

"I wanted to ask if I could, or should, barter with Harken for Boy. Would he be willing to trade for him, and then for his—Boy's— stabling and feed and so on?"

"Is he the horse you want, for having, not just for training?"

"We're used to each other. We like each other and feel easy with each other. I can keep it at borrowing if Harken doesn't want to trade, but—"

"He chose him for you because you fit, so he'd make a gift of him to you."

"I know he would, but I'd like to give something in return. I just don't know what it should be."

"He could use a new plow harness, and that's the truth of it. He's patched and repaired the old one more times than you could count."

"Where would I get one?"

They crossed back into Ireland.

"We'll make the visit to the elf known for making such things as part of tomorrow's training."

"Okay, and what about the feed and the rest?"

"He won't take for that. You're a sister to Morena, so one to him. He'll take the harness and use it, and see it as thoughtful more than bartering. Spring planting's coming."

"Will you plant?"

"What I can, when I can. I'll need to spend some time at the Capital, and soon. But unless there's urgency, it can be a day or two here and there. You might come with me for one of those. It's good for those there to see you."

"All right."

"I know you have your own trip, so before that, I think. A day or two."

"Will you have a Judgment?"

"For small things. We've found no others, as yet, who spy for Odran. I hope to the gods there are no more to find." Face grim, he thrust his hands into his pockets. "I've banished more this year than in all the years before I sat in the chair. I still don't have the taste for it."

"I'd be sorry if you did."

When they came out of the woods, the door of the cottage opened. Bollocks raced out to greet her as if they'd been separated for months rather than hours.

"There's my sweet boy. Were you a good boy for Marco?"

"Good as they get," Marco called. "I got the taters in the oven, and I'm grilling asparagus from Seamus along with this steak when Brian gets here. Let's— Jesus and all the rest, what is that smell?"

"It's goat, or what comes out of them, and I'm going straight up and taking a shower."

"I hear that. But first, I need those two chapters."

"What?"

He planted his feet. "It's been more than the two weeks, but I cut you a break considering attack by psycho god, and a change in your training and all that. But we pinky swore, and I want the chapters. I'm going to curl right up with them tonight."

"I'd really rather you—"

He put on his serious-as-fuck face. "Pinky swear, girl."

"Damn it." She stomped off to her office.

"Her book? What is this pinky swear? I want to read it."

"No." She said it firmly as she stomped back out with a flash drive.

"Why can he and I can't?"

"Because he put me in a bind." She held the drive just out of reach. "Now you swear, Marco Polo. Not a page more than we agreed. There's more on here, but you stop at the end of the second chapter."

"Aw, Breen."

"Pinky swear."

"Fine, fine, fine." He hooked pinkies, then snatched the drive.

"This is an oath?" Keegan hooked his two pinkies. "Why is it an oath?"

"Why is anything? Trust and honor. Two chapters, then stop, and no reading them while I'm around. It'll make me crazy."

So saying, she headed straight for the stairs with Bollocks.

"Why does she smell like goat poop—that's goat poop, right? Because I think it's the first time I've smelled that smell."

"I'll tell you after I convince her to let me read what you read."

"Yeah, well, good luck with that."

She stripped down in the bathroom, tried not to think of anything but hot water and fragrant soap.

She'd barely stepped into the spray, into the jets, when the glass door opened.

"Really?" she said when Keegan stepped in with her.

"I'm after a shower as well." But he ran his hands up her as he pressed against her back. "And you. Hot water feels good, as you do."

He pressed his lips to her shoulder. "I want to pinky swear with you."

"No." But the way he said it made her laugh. "No and no."

"You have no trust in me, think I have no honor."

She turned, and as the water rained down, the steam rose, shoved her now wet hair back. "I have absolute trust in you, and know no one with more honor. And still no."

"Why do you let Marco?"

"Because he put me in a bind, and before I could get out of it, pinky swear. I'd hoped he'd forgotten."

"Then I'll put you in a bind." He poured some of the shower gel she'd made with Marg's help into his hand. "Then we'll pinky swear."

"No," she repeated.

But she didn't say no to the rest.

She woke with the fire simmering and Bollocks tapping his whip of a tail—his signal to get up, get moving.

Relaxed and content, she did. Shower sex, a really good meal she'd had no part in preparing, and a little music before a solid night's sleep. She couldn't ask for better.

She tugged on boots as Bollocks danced by the side of the bed.

"We're going, we're going," she told him, and grabbed her robe.

Following habit, she went down, straight to the door. Where he streamed out into the predawn in his race to the bay. And she aimed straight for coffee. On the way, she boosted the fire in the living room from simmer to blaze.

Still half dreaming, she carried the coffee outside. Could she actually smell the early hints of spring coming? Maybe just wishful thinking, she decided, but either way she liked it.

She'd check on her seedlings later and start making real plans for the little cutting garden she'd talked through with Seamus. And vegetables, too—a small patch. Maybe overkill, since she could get all they needed from the farm or Nan, but she thought Marco would enjoy stepping out and picking his own tomatoes and peppers.

Plus, fun.

And she liked, really liked, making these plans for a life she wanted.

The sun shimmered awake in the east as she drank her coffee and Bollocks splashed in the bay. Mists rose, caught that early light, and went to silver with hints of pink.

Dawn, she realized, always lifted her mood. It bloomed, every day, with promise and possibility.

She imagined on the other side Harken set about the morning chores. Or maybe Keegan perched on a three-legged stool, milking a cow.

She'd pay to see that one.

Soon, on both sides, parents would wake children for school. People would dress for work; families would share breakfast.

So much the same everywhere, she thought. Yet so much different. And as part of both, she had duties and pleasures on either side.

When Bollocks raced back to her, she dried him. And crouched, an arm around him, enjoyed sharing the break of a new day.

"Time for my workout. You already had yours, didn't you? But time for mine, so I have to gear up. Breakfast for you first," she promised, and kissed his sweet face.

She went back in, then nearly jumped a foot when she saw Marco sitting by the fire with his laptop.

"Jeez! You scared the crap out of me! What are you doing up at dawn?"

"Reading."

She remembered, said, "Oh," and retreated to the kitchen to feed the dog.

She poured a second mug of coffee but decided her now uneasy stomach couldn't handle her usual slice of toast.

"I'm going up to change, get my workout in."

Marco just looked at her, pointed to the cushion beside him. "Sit."

"Oh God. It's that bad? I didn't think it was that bad."

"Stop it. Sit."

"Okay."

She sat, braced, reminded herself she wanted honesty. "Maybe I started it off too fast. Or too slow. I could—"

"Stop it," he said again. He set the laptop aside and picked up his coffee. "I read the stingy two chapters you said I could, twice. I'm starting the third time through. You need to let me have more."

"If the first two don't work—"

"Did I say that? Don't be old Breen." He tapped a finger to the middle of her forehead. "I'm saying I'm up at this crazy hour because I want more. Because the first two chapters sucked me right in. Because it's good, Breen. It's damn good. And shut up," he added, "before you say something stupid like maybe I'm saying that because I love you."

"You do love me."

"Yeah, and because I do, if it wasn't so good, I'd say something like . . ." Considering, he rubbed a fingertip over his goatee. "I got it. I'd say: You really got something started here, girl, I bet you can fix it up and make it shine. Something encouraging, right? But I don't have to, because it already shines."

"You mean it?"

"Look at my face."

His brow beetled, his jaw firmed, his mouth set.

"It's your SAF face."

"That's the one. Handsome, but serious as fuck. You're going to let me read more."

"If you really want another chapter—"

"Uh-uh." Now, he ticktocked a finger in the air. "Three more, total of five. It's fair. It should give me a better handle on this big world you're building here. It's not Talamh—I see pieces of that, but it's bigger, like, with other countries and continents and seas and all that. Five chapters to give me a handle on the world, the characters—I know there's more coming."

"Three more." She let out a breath. "But if it doesn't hold up, you'll tell me. And I get something back. You write out three recipes for the cookbook—write them out your way, then I get to read them."

"I got recipes written out already."

"Add in the fun, Marco, the charm. Chat them up—and you know just what I mean. If it doesn't work, I'll tell you."

Saying nothing, he crooked his pinky.

On the oath, she rose. "I'm going to change. I really need the workout now."

When she came back down, he just held up a finger. "Don't bother me." So she went straight in, chose one of her more challenging workouts. Because it didn't fully sweat out her anxiety, she topped it off with a half hour of yoga.

She came out to the scent of bacon.

"Since I'm up, you're getting a solid breakfast before you head to your writing cave." He plated the bacon, cheese omelets, a poached pear half drizzled with honey.

She stood watching, fighting the urge to actively wring her hands.

He set the plates down, then turned, wrapped around her.

"Is this to soften the blow?"

"Breen, I'm so proud. When you let me read *Bollocks's Magic Adventures*, I laughed out loud. I saw that dog clear as can be before I ever met him. And this? This is different. I can hear you just like I could in the other, but its—*scope*'s the word, right?—its scope is so wide and, like, rich. If Mila doesn't make it through, it's gonna break my heart."

He pulled her back. "Girl, you've got It. Whatever the hell It is for writing, you've got It. I want it all."

"Marco—"

"I'm not gonna push for all at once, but I'm sure as hell gonna nag more out of you every day. Now, you're gonna listen to me."

"I am listening to you."

"You're gonna listen and trust me. Who was right about you writing a blog?"

"You were."

"Who was right about you sitting your ass down and doing what you always wanted? Writing books."

"You were."

"And who's right to tell you to send those five chapters off to Carlee, right now?"

"Oh, Marco, I haven't finished polishing or —"

"You're not standing there telling me what I just read isn't polished up."

She ended up wringing her hands after all. "I was going to go over it one more time after I finish going over what's left to go over."

"And who knows you well enough to know damn well that's not because it needs it but because you're afraid to let it go?"

She sighed hugely. "You do. I was just going to take a couple more weeks. Or so."

"Go on in there, do it now. Now." He put on his serious-as-fuck face, pulled a weak laugh out of her. "And make it fast before your breakfast gets cold."

"If I do that, you'll sit down and write those recipes."

"Didn't I pinky swear? You go pull the trigger, and after breakfast, I'll pull mine."

CHAPTER SEVENTEEN

She didn't hear from Carlee for two days, and filled her time to the brim and beyond so she wouldn't obsess.

She obsessed anyway.

She worked with Marco on his recipes, just some fine-tuning. When it came to cooking, talking about cooking, writing about cooking, he had that elusive It.

When the call from New York came, she took the phone into her office while Marco put the finishing touches on the homemade pizza they'd share.

Just the two of them, as Keegan had business at the Capital and had taken Brian with him.

She walked back in just as Marco slid the pizza into the oven. "That is gonna be *good*."

"That was Carlee."

He stopped. "And?"

"She liked it. Whew. Big exhale. She liked it."

"Because she's not a fool." He opened his arms, then grabbed her up into them.

"It's too soon to celebrate. Well, maybe a little," she added.

"Never too soon. I say we break out the faerie wine instead of the store-bought."

"No, no, let's stick with the store-bought. She said she'd like to send it to my editor, my publisher—and saying that's never going to get old—if I'd send her a synopsis on the rest."

"You can do that. That's what you do. Look, if you want to take your pizza and go in and work—"

"No, you, me, Bollocks, pizza, wine, a movie. That's what we planned, and just what I want. I told her to give me two more weeks."

"Oh, girl."

"No, no, no. Two weeks so I could polish up the rest, then send it to her. All of it. I just need the time to make sure it's the best I can do."

He smiled; he nodded. "That's my girl. That sounds smart. And you're going to give me five more chapters to read tonight so I'm not all lonely in my empty bed with Brian away."

"Now I really need that wine."

"Coming right up." He smiled at her. "So proud, Breen."

"Me, too. And I told her, in two weeks, you'd send in a selection of recipes that'll give her a sense of the style you're going for."

"Oh, girl," he repeated.

Breen just wiggled her pinky finger.

She spent two weeks focused like a laser on the book before crossing into Talamh to focus on magicks and training. If her life spread over two worlds, she'd do her best in both of them.

At the end of two weeks, she presented Harken with the new harness. He studied it, ran his hands over it like another might a precious jewel.

"Oh, this is fine. More than fine."

"So's he." Breen pressed her cheek to Boy's. "I'd hoped to get it to you before you started plowing for spring, but the craftsman was very particular."

"Oh, he's all that. And this is a harness my children may use one day, and theirs after." He stroked it as he might one of those beloved children. "You've had our family name put on it."

"Keegan's idea."

"It means much." He pushed back his cap as he looked at her. "You know, Boy's been yours since first you swung up on him."

"I wouldn't have called that a swing, not the first time. But I felt that connection. Thank you, Harken, for knowing it before I did. I'm sorry I can't take him with me tomorrow, but we'll only be gone a day or two."

"We'll take good care of him for you. Enjoy the Capital, and the flight over. Spring's coming," he said as he looked around his fields. "And the bloom of it."

Trust a farmer, Breen thought when they took flight the next morning. The air, unquestionably warmer than her last trip east, carried the promise of spring.

With Bollocks, topknot fluttering in the wind, she rode Lonrach, with Keegan on Cróga beside them. On her other side, Mahon's wings spread.

And below, she saw others plowing the earth, turning that rich brown for seed and seedlings. She'd do the same on her return, now that the air and earth warmed to welcome the rebirth.

She'd have the time, she thought, and wanted that work as well as her work on Bollocks's next book, now that she'd sent her manuscript to New York, along with Marco's sampling for the cookbook.

Sent them, she admitted, late the night before so with the time difference Carlee wouldn't see them until into the morning in New York.

Just as she'd left Marco the entire book while he slept.

She'd done the very best she could, and told herself to put it aside, put it away. She had work to do here, in Talamh, and whatever duties waited at the Capital.

When Cróga veered north over the green roll of the midlands, she glanced toward Keegan, but he looked down where he guided the dragon.

"He means to stop at a portal here, for a check on things, and on those who stand guard," Mahon told her. "It's good for those here to see the taoiseach, and you now."

"Oh."

She'd dressed for the flight, not for being seen, in leggings and boots, a sweater and jacket. Though she'd tied back her hair, she knew the wind had already done a number on it.

Keegan landed in a field separated from the next by a line of long-limbed trees. Their bare branches showed the faint haze of the green to come.

Three stood, swords at their sides, one with a quiver on his back. She recognized a Sidhe, a Were, and an Elfin.

"Welcome, Taoiseach." The Sidhe stepped forward, a slender woman with a honeycomb cap of hair and a warrior's braid. "And to you, Mahon, and to the Daughter. Peace holds here."

"I'm glad of it." Keegan scanned the tree line.

"We're on the watch for ravens or any else, but there's been none since the last."

"You'll keep sharp, I know," Keegan said, and turned to Breen, lifted his brows.

Now she was supposed to say something?

"Um. Talamh and all the worlds are grateful for your vigilance."

"We're honored to stand."

"And how's that brother of yours, Lisbet?" Mahon asked, and got a quick grin.

"Traveling from pub to pub with his voice and his harp and happy as two pigs rutting."

Keegan took time to speak to all three, then again turned to Breen. "Do you see the shadow of it?"

Now a test—in front of the guards. But the nerves that rose dropped away again as she looked.

She *felt* the portal, felt its seal, strongly charmed and locked. And as she looked, as she opened, she saw the faint blur of shadow.

"There." She pointed up to a bare branch. "Clawed open for the raven and the message carried. Clawed closed again. No bigger than my fist, and shut tight again. It costs to open it, blood and power, and the payment wanted in return never came. But blood, they'll always have it to spend, so stand watch for Talamh and all the worlds."

"And so we will." Lisbet murmured it. "I climbed the tree to where the raven flew through, and barely saw the shadow when I stood on the branch a handspan away that you see from here."

Next they flew north, where winter clung tight. Keegan repeated the process, this time to the guards on a snow-topped hill.

She saw the shadow in the hill.

At every portal, she realized. Scratching and clawing at every one.

"I don't understand strategies or tactics when it comes to war and battles." She turned to Keegan as she remounted Lonrach, and Bollocks leaped up with her. "But I do know it takes a lot of effort to put those cracks in the portals. To open and close them so a raven can get through. Wouldn't one, even two be enough? It may take longer for the bird to get where it's going and back, but it would get there."

"I understand strategies and tactics very well." He glanced back as they lifted into the air. "First, can it be done, this small shadow of a breach? Pitting magicks against magicks, and likely slow and careful on the other sides. And where each portal opens, wouldn't he have those who follow him to aid in this?"

"Okay, yes, I can see that, but—"

"We go through to trade and travel, though not so free and easy these past months. If I'm Odran, I use the time—the time upon time he has—to think of this, to plan this, to work the magicks. Aye, one would do for spying, if spying was the end of it."

Riding the wind, he looked ahead to the east. "So I ask myself the very question you ask me now."

"And what's the answer?"

"If you find you can make this crack, the size, you said, of your own fist, in time, with purpose, with blood magicks, you'd work on a way to make a bigger one, and bigger yet. To make them big enough for armies to pass through, as they did in the South, as they did at the Tree of Snakes."

"To—to break through them all, all the portals, all at once?"

"It's what I'd do, had I time upon time and no quibble about the blood spilled for it."

"But what will you do about it?"

"What needs doing. The Capital," he said, gesturing ahead. "We'll talk of it later."

The castle stood, stone sturdy and strong on its hill, its banner of the red dragon on a white field flying. Behind it, the sea thrashed, heaving itself against the rocks before drawing back to heave again.

The village bustled below the castle and its towers, beyond the river and the bridges that spanned it.

When she'd last left, some of the land had still lay churned from the battle. Now it spread green and lush or brown and rich from the plow.

Smoke curled up from the chimneys of cottages and farms, shops and pubs.

On the far side of the castle, the woods loomed where the battle had begun.

They landed on the green, where on that day she'd faced Yseult, had bested her, bloodied her. But in her rage had failed to end her.

Now she knew that because in that rage she'd wanted Yseult's pain more than that end, Odran's witch would spell and scheme to cause more death.

Water towered and spilled from the fountain, and though the air held a lingering chill, flowers thrived.

Bollocks sent a longing look toward the river—a favorite for his swims—but walked with Breen toward the massive doors of the castle. When they opened, Minga stood in brown leggings and a white tunic belted in copper to greet them.

"Welcome, Taoiseach. Breen and Mahon." She took both Breen's hands, kissed her cheeks. "The air runs cool yet. You'll want a fire. And welcome to you as well." She stroked a hand over Bollocks. "Tarryn mediates a minor disagreement but shouldn't be much longer. Your rooms are ready whenever you want them."

Even as she spoke, a young elf rushed over to take Breen's bag, then blurred away up the central stairs with it.

"I have some duties to see to and need Mahon for the first of them." Keegan turned to Breen. "We'll sup with my mother tonight, a quiet meal, thank the gods."

"All right. Is there anything I should do?"

"There will be. If you'd stay close, I'll find you when you're needed. Mahon."

When they walked off, Minga smiled. "He's not one for wasting time. Come, I'll take you up. You'll have some tea and get settled. And there'll be a biscuit for you, of course."

The word *biscuit* sent Bollocks's tail ticktocking.

"And how are Aisling and the boys? I know Tarryn's counting the days until she can see them all again."

"They're great. Morena's teaching them falconry. Well, not Kelly, who somehow gets more adorable every day."

They started up the stairs, a grand focus of the entrance hall, and one, Breen knew, that became a high stone platform in times of battle and defense.

"And your family?"

"All well," Minga told her, "I'm grateful to say. It's a quiet time, for now, this edge between winter and spring. And Marco? I'll tell you there was deep disappointment he wouldn't visit with you, especially in the kitchens."

"He's pledged."

"Ah, I'd heard this! To Brian Kelly—such a good man, is Brian. When he does visit again, we'll have a celebration."

She climbed beyond the wing where Breen and Marco had stayed on their first visit and continued up to the chambers of the taoiseach.

"Brigid asked to tend to you again. I thought you'd enjoy that."

"Yes, thanks. I'd like to see her again."

Minga opened the door. "And I see she's already got the fire going and some food and drink. As I see you've already got a visitor."

"I couldn't wait." Laughing, Kiara ran forward to hug Breen. "I saw the dragons and came right up. Please say you don't mind."

She had her mother's coloring, the deep golden skin, the thick black hair. But in place of Minga's steady dignity, an infectious cheer lived in Kiara.

"I more than don't mind. I'm so happy to see you."

"Then I'll leave you to it. Don't talk the ears off the sides of her head, Kiara."

"But I have so much to say!" Laughing again, Kiara knelt right down to hug Bollocks. "Oh, you're bigger, aren't you? And with the same sweet face. I've been helping tend to the littles, so I'm in my rough clothes, as I didn't take time to change."

The rough, on Kiara's scale, equaled plum-colored trousers with matching boots and a flowing lavender shirt. Gold drops dangled from her ears.

"You look wonderful." Nothing less than the truth. "I love your hair that way."

"Do you?" She skimmed a hand over the multitude of narrow braids spanning the crown of her head before they exploded into a curling cloud. "I wanted to try something new."

"It's gorgeous. Come, sit down, have tea with me. And spill some."

No one had better castle and village gossip than Minga's daughter.

In minutes, with Kiara's rapid-fire tales, Breen had laughed off the chill of the flight. Replete from his promised biscuit, Bollocks curled by the fire for a nap.

"Now, you have a turn here. I want to hear all about Marco and Brian pledging. Which asked which, if that's the way of it, and how and where. Do you know?"

"I do. Brian did the asking, though it seems Marco was planning to. Brian took him home to meet his family."

"They loved him, of course. I don't know them, but I know Brian, and he's not a fool, so I'm saying his family shouldn't be."

"They're not, and they did. After they'd met him and loved him— which is mutual—Brian did the asking."

"Oh, don't say in front of the family!" Bouncing, Kiara wiped her hands in the air. "That's sweet, but it's not at all, even a bit, romantic, is it?"

"Not in front of the family. Just the two of them. On a midnight picnic."

"Oh!" Kiara fell back in her chair with her hands crossed over her heart. "I'm melting right here. You'll tell them both how happy I am for them, and if Marco doesn't invite me to the wedding itself, well, I'll cry a river of tears."

"I'll tell him—if you promise to do my hair for it."

"I can hardly wait to get my hands on your hair again, so an easier promise there couldn't be. Now, I promised I wouldn't stay long, and I already have. But I've something for you before I go."

She got up and walked into the bedroom. She came back with a large box. "It's a gift I hope pleases you."

"A gift?"

"Open it, won't you? I've nearly died waiting to give it."

Breen pulled off the faerie-dusted bow and the gold paper to open the lid. Inside the froth of tissue, she found leather the color of the copper belt Minga wore.

"Oh! God!"

"Take it out! Try it on! Oh, I can't stand the waiting."

Because she couldn't, Kiara pulled out the knee-length coat, then pulled Breen to her feet. "It has to fit, or I'll kick Daryn's ass so hard it'll ram his balls. Oh, it fits, it fits! It's perfect. Go, look in the glass. The color with your hair? It's perfect. Oh, oh, it's so what I wanted for you, and I hope it's what you want for yourself."

Stunned, Breen walked to the tall mirror, stared. The coat hit just above her knees, all butter soft with deep slash pockets and a lining of antique gold silk.

"Kiara—"

"It's a coat fit for a dragon rider. Turn, turn, see how the back cinches at the waist? Feminine as well to show you've a fine shape."

"It's absolutely stunning. But, Kiara—"

"You did more than save my life." The bubbling excitement in the voice turned quiet, and here was her mother's steady dignity. "You turned it so I could change it. You showed me true friendship doesn't always ask and prod, it doesn't lie and use, all while manipulating feelings and heart. Without you, and Bollocks as well, I might have died that day, and left my family grieving. More, I might have died being deceived, being played a fool by one I believed cared about me and for me.

"Please accept it, Breen. It would make me so proud to see you wear what I helped make. Well, I didn't do much of the making, truth be told, but I told Daryn how it must look and deviled him over it."

"It's the most beautiful coat I've ever owned, or ever hope to."

"Truly?"

"Truly. Thank you." She moved in to hug. "Thank you for the amazing gift, and just as amazing, being the first friend I made in the Capital when I felt so odd and out of place."

Alone, she started to hang the coat—reverently—in the wardrobe where the speedy elf had already put the few things she'd brought for the trip.

Then she stepped back. "Hey, Bollocks, let's take this fabulous coat out for a walk. And yes, you can have a swim. A short one," she said when he jumped up.

They walked the grounds, watched those still training on the fields below. She glanced toward the woods. Part of her wanted to go in, check the portals there, but Keegan had asked her to stay close.

So she walked to the bridge instead and let a very happy dog jump off and into the water.

Keegan found her there just as Bollocks scrambled up the bank.

"It all took longer than I hoped, but then it always does. Come, we—" He broke off, frowned at her. And skimmed a finger down the coat. "Where did you get this? You've been to the village? Why is it shopping is what most women must do first and last and in between?"

"Breen, you look stunning in that coat. Some men might think to say that. In reverse order," she continued, "I don't shop first, last, and in between. No, I haven't been to the village. And Kiara gave me the coat. A surprising and generous and thoughtful gift."

"Ah, she did very well. The coat suits you."

"Suits me." She could only cast her eyes to the clouds.

"I'll say the coat looks stunning on you, as it's only a thing, but you're wearing it and that lifts it up."

"All right, now I can say you did very well. Where are we going?" she asked as he pulled her along.

"You're not council here, and where you are, that's not altogether official in the way of things. But it's time you meet all who are."

"Now?" Instant nerves shot straight through her. "But haven't I met them?"

"You haven't met Neo of the Mers, Nila, the elf who replaced Uwin, or Sean of the Weres, or Bok of the Trolls. I've called them to the council chamber, where I'll make the introduction, and as my mother insists is proper, there'll be some refreshment and chatting about. In that way I can put off the bloody council meeting until morning."

"So you're using me to skip out on a council meeting?"

"I don't skip. Littles skip. And it's time, true enough, you've met the whole of them, and they you."

"Fine. Just let me go up and change first."

"Why? You're fine. You have your stunning coat, don't you?"

"Yes, but—"

"You'll drink some tea, make some chatter, let them have some time with the Daughter of the Fey when she's not bringing a traitor to his knees at Judgment or wielding a sword in battle."

She had her first look at the council chamber with its roaring fire, its long table and high-backed chairs.

And those who would sit in them to advise the taoiseach.

A diverse group, she thought, with every tribe represented, and Minga with them. And Tarryn, Keegan's mother, as his hand.

"I bring to you Breen Siobhan O'Ceallaigh, Daughter of the O'Ceallaigh, Daughter of the Fey."

Tarryn, in slim pants and boots, shirt and vest, her sun-washed hair in a thick braid, crossed the room to take her hand, to kiss her cheek.

"Welcome back. I'm sorry I couldn't greet you." She leaned in for a second kiss. "You wear Kiara's gift," she whispered. "And please her mother very much."

She drew back, then led Breen forward. "Flynn, you know, of course. Flynn of the Sidhe."

"Little red rabbit." He lifted her off her feet in a hug and washed away half the nerves. Then he stepped back, and though he shook her hand in a formal way, his eyes twinkled at her. "The Sidhe welcome the Daughter."

"The Daughter thanks the Sidhe, and . . . pledges her loyalty."

She saw by Tarryn's nod she'd said the right thing.

"Neo of the Mer."

He stepped to her on the legs he wore on land. "The Mer welcome the Daughter."

So it went with every member until Minga took her hand.

"Talamh, that has welcomed me, welcomes the Daughter."

"I thank Talamh, that has welcomed me home, and pledge my loyalty."

She thought she managed the chatter, since most of it was politely formal—and Tarryn ran interference without seeming to.

"We meet in the morning," Keegan announced. "My thanks to you all."

Breen waited until he'd guided her out of earshot. "I didn't notice you doing a lot of the chatter."

"They've all heard me before, haven't they? It's you they wanted to see and hear—now they have. And now, thank the gods, we'll have that quiet meal, and I can down a damn ale."

"I need to change."

"What is this obsession with changing clothes all the bloody time? Why put something on you only want to take off again?"

"If we're having dinner with your mother—"

"It's a family meal. You're fine."

"I don't need the coat to have dinner."

He shot her an impatient glance. "Then you'll take it off."

"You never change." She muttered it as he pulled her up a curve of stone steps.

"I change daily." Then he glanced down. "Ah, I get your meaning. Why would I change when . . . No, that's not the truth. I explain much more than I did, and that's a change."

"You didn't bother to explain we'd make stops on the way here so I'd meet and talk to people. Or how I'd meet the council and have to talk to them. I could've used a heads-up. Advance warning."

"No, you do better without it. Not so much time to think and worry yourself over it."

Since she couldn't say he was wrong, she said nothing.

"And you did more than well on both things. Now you can talk as little or as much as you like, as this is family."

He turned at an archway. "And I'll wager a Troll bag of stones my mother doesn't change."

CHAPTER EIGHTEEN

Breen wouldn't have called the room cozy, but at a fraction of the size of the banquet hall, it didn't intimidate.

It held the warmth of a fire, the charm of dozens of candles. While the table would seat a group of fifteen easily, four plates sat at one end. It gleamed, as did the chairs, the beautifully crafted buffet, the floors.

And smelled of fresh oranges and vanilla.

Keegan went straight to a serving counter, poured wine in a glass, ale in a tankard.

"We've both earned it," he said, handing her the wine.

She took it and wandered to admire the two arched windows of stained glass, each depicting a dragon in flight. And the intricate tapestries of land, of sea, of villages, of farms.

"One from every tribe in Talamh," he told her. "They've hung on these walls as long as these walls have stood."

"They look as if they could've been done yesterday. The colors are so vivid. I wonder, did I eat here when I came as a child for the Judgment?"

"You didn't, no. Your mother wouldn't have it. Your father gave it over to my family during those few days. It was kind of him, as we were grieving, and the room has warmth and privacy. And quiet. You may have before that, but I can't tell you."

"Maybe. It doesn't feel familiar, but I can imagine him here. With Nan when she was taoiseach, and later when he lifted the sword. And your father, too, because they were brothers in all but blood."

"Aye, they were."

Tarryn came in on Mahon's arm, and Breen noted Keegan would have won his bet.

"Ah, what a pleasure this room is after all that. Well done, Breen. Neo, who can be difficult to sway or impress, was very taken with you. And I'll say this, wearing that coat gave you the look of a woman who knows her business and means it as well."

With an unmistakable smirk, Keegan drank some ale. "What'll you have, Ma?"

"I'll go with Breen and the wine. I expect Mahon's ready for a tankard."

"You know me."

"I do indeed. Let's sit or they'll never bring in the food, and I'm half-starved. I missed tea, as I was listening to a pair of foolish females spatting over the wool of a sheep not yet sheared. Now they'll each get half and be glad of any." She sat, smiled at Keegan. "So it is done."

"You've more patience than any cat ever born, and more wisdom than all the owls in Talamh."

"He gives me sweet words so he doesn't have to listen to foolishness."

"Oh now, I hear plenty of it." He set the wine in front of her when she sat.

"Come sit beside me, Breen, so you can give me news from the valley. Mahon's proved a dry well when it comes to Brian and Marco and the weddings to come."

It was easy, and quiet. Conversation flowed with family things and bright stories as they dined on roasted chicken and potatoes and vegetables fresh from a Sidhe farm.

Relaxed, Breen drank wine and felt the day melt away.

When the plates were cleared and a platter of cream-filled cakes offered, Keegan sat back.

"Sure I'm sorry to have to talk of it, but it needs talk between us before the council meets in the morning."

"We're here," his mother reminded him, "not only because we're family, but because we stand for the Fey, for Talamh, and all the worlds beyond it. We won't shy from hard talk."

"Then I'll tell you that but for the Welcoming Tree and the Tree of Snakes, every portal in Talamh carries the shadow, the opening driven through by Odran and Yseult, and whatever other dark magicks brew there. And I won't feel sure about the two until Breen's had a look."

"The Welcoming Tree?"

He shrugged at Breen. "I can't see any way possible for a breach there. The magicks that protect it are older than Talamh, and to unwind them? More than he has, I think. More than you, or any."

"There's logistics as well," Mahon added. "Where it stands is beyond him. He'd need a powerful force in Talamh or Ireland, one that could push through all protections to begin to unwind. And this we'd know. But the Tree of Snakes, well, he breached it once."

"The seal's stronger now." But Tarryn frowned as she rose to pour tea. "What of the portal to the Dark World?"

"I want Breen to look there as well. What lies beyond it? None of the banished have power there, but if I'm Odran, there is where I would push, and hard. Find the way to release those who've already broken sacred laws, taken lives, those who followed him? They'd add to his numbers.

"All of this I'll say to the council tomorrow," he added. "And more. If it takes so much blood and power, weighing on this side of the scale"—he held one hand down to demonstrate—"and the benefit is a handful of spies giving and getting some information?"

He held his other hand high. "It's foolish to spend so much for so little. But if the aim is to widen those breaches, and break through all at once?"

He reversed his hands.

"A small price to pay for an army flooding across Talamh from all directions. I think it may be the breaches—the South, the Tree of Snakes—served as a kind of practice for what's to come."

"Is it possible?" Tarryn reached out to lay a hand on Keegan's arm. "What you're saying, the power of it, the coordination, the numbers?"

"I can't say, but I know he'd spill an ocean of blood to try. Worlds beyond the portals. How many in them might follow him for riches or the thirst to kill and conquer, how many might be true believers as

Toric and his ilk? So I say we move on as if he can and will. The Fey won't be caught unprepared."

"We'll fight to the last breath, there's no question. How do you want to prepare?" Mahon asked him.

"We'll move strategically." Keegan glanced toward Breen. "As we did in the South, as we failed to do until nearly too late here. We'll be shifting some training grounds and placing the seasoned and the green near every portal. We need the green to ripen."

"You don't mean the littles, Keegan."

"Ma." The distress on her face sliced through him. "He would cut them down, or worse. Those too young for a sword or a bow, or too old for all that, well, there's power. It's sparked in Finian. What he has, it's best he learn how to use. I'm sorry for it. I wish—"

"No, no, don't. You're right, of course. I swear by all I am there'll come a day a child is only a child and there's no thought of war. But what of those who can't fight?"

"We'll have shelters for them, secure as we can make, and shields around them. I've spent bloody hours in the Map Room, going over all of this, the wheres and the hows."

"What if— I'm sorry," Breen began, "I really don't know anything about how to do any of this, but I take it you're banking on surprise, like you did in the South."

"It would be a fine advantage—which is just what he believes he'll have."

"But if you're moving troops and training grounds, and he gets any spies or scouts through, he'd know, wouldn't he?"

"That's a good question from someone who says she knows nothing of tactics or strategies. It's all to freshen things up, you see. Change routines, move some closer to home, and others who may need some discipline that distance can bring, away a bit. To give areas who haven't had the troops and training nearby the benefit. For custom and trade, for help with spring planting, with the stock."

"A kind of rotation."

"A kind of that."

He rose, held up both hands. On the wall a mural, not unlike the one over his bed, formed. "Here is Talamh, and here, the portals. A farmer has a field resting, fallow for the season. Ah well, we'll make use of it. This village could use a bit of help thatching roofs or repairing walls, what have you. We'll train there, and when not training, lend the hands. These woods, here, here, here, who notices if more make camp in them, or hunt there?"

"Fresh troops in the South." Mahon nodded as he studied Keegan's map. "A prime duty, and so in the Far North, not as warm and balmy, and don't some need a bit of toughening up?"

"And a chance for those who rarely wander far from home," Tarryn added, "to see the world. So by the shifting, the increased numbers don't show as much as they might."

"I wonder if . . ."

"Ah, speak, woman," Keegan said impatiently when Breen hesitated.

"I know it might sound frivolous, but if you planned—announced— festivals, contests? Archery and races, horsemanship, that sort of thing."

She cast her mind back to Renaissance fairs. "Crafts, demonstrations of crafting, games for children, music. One in all those areas. A kind of reward for the training. When I was teaching, the kids usually worked harder if they thought they'd get something or could show off. Then it would look like you're—we're just going about as usual. More, planning fairs and celebrations."

"Nothing of tactics, is it? That's bloody brilliant. Food, music," Keegan speculated. "Contests, shagging jugglers, and the like. We're all just lambs for the slaughter, aren't we? The Capital, the midlands, the Far North, the valley, the South, the Far West, the Troll camps, the elf camps, and so on and on."

"He'd see it, and we could make certain he does," Mahon added, "as the Fey dancing their way to their end."

"We stopped him in the South, and here." Now Tarryn nodded as she studied the mural. "We have the Daughter safe from every attempt made on her. With spring comes the blooming, the planting. We train, of course, as always, but we've held the peace."

"And with the summer comes the fruit and the plenty," Keegan continued. "So we celebrate, we reward the skilled, we dance to the pipes. A year it'll be since the Daughter returned. So festivals across Talamh. The Return of the Daughter."

"Oh, Keegan—"

"It's good tactics." He interrupted Breen's automatic protest and just rolled on. "Wouldn't I, as taoiseach, want to mark the year? It shows confidence. Wouldn't Talamh, after all the loss and grief, want this time of music and dance? If he strikes sooner, we'll be prepared. But if he waits, and oh, I surely would, for that ripe moment, to destroy all at its happiest? If he waits, we'll end this, and him, by all the gods, by the solstice when the light is ours."

She went with Keegan, Bollocks by her side, at first light. Into the wood where she'd fought and bled and killed, where so many had fallen.

She knew the way, realized she could have found it in the dark. Bollocks didn't prance, didn't stray, and she felt him remember, just as she did.

When she stood in front of the tree that wasn't a tree, he didn't sit, but stayed on alert.

"There's nothing to fear here now," Keegan began, but she shook her head.

"Everything. He's so close, I can almost hear him breathing."

Keegan took her hand. "Don't be drawn over as you were before. I have you. You're anchored here."

"We shared a vision of the other side, his side. Of him pushing. Spring or early summer."

"I remember."

"A portent? I still don't know. But he works here, Keegan, close. This, like the waterfall in the valley. Those are keys to him. This, the seat of power. And the valley, where my father was conceived, where I was born. Where you were born. He's started here."

"I don't see a shadow. I look every time I come east, and see nothing."

"I feel it, like I feel him. He needs this . . . position? And more, this, like the waterfall, is direct. He doesn't have to go through other worlds, other portals to reach those two. An ocean of blood, you said," she murmured. "He'd use every drop to open this again."

"All right. We'll prepare for that. I need you to do the same on the portal to the Dark World. I see, and feel, nothing of this there."

"But you feel?" she said as he began to lead her.

"I feel the despair, the fury, the bitter, the thirst for blood. And the hate. What's bound there has nothing else."

And yet the woods held such beauty, such promise. The sharp scent of pine, the buds on branches not yet formed, still sleeping. Light and shadow danced together here, and a hawk—red-tailed and swift—flew through both on a hunt.

When they came to the portal and the stone that marked it, she shuddered. The cool air went frigid and sharp; the light dimmed so shadows swirled.

And in them she felt all Keegan had said, and more.

"Step back. In here." He pressed a hand to her heart. "You can't take their pain. And know, any one of them would slit your throat for a chance to escape."

"How many?"

"One is too many, and more than one. Step back, *mo bandia*."

"They kill each other when they can. For sport."

"I know it."

"They'll never know the light again." She stepped back. "He knows that, too. All of it. He feeds on their rage and fears. The weaker minds, so many, he uses. Whispering threats, promises in equal measure. Worship me, bow to me, and I will one day grant you your vengeance."

"Breen."

Because her eyes, her voice, had deepened, Keegan started to pull her back. She shook him off.

"He rules there, in his way. Distant in his high castle. Reveling in the suffering, preening as so many still take the knee for him. Only him. Whispers and threats. Whispers and promises during their fitful sleep or raging wakefulness. Kill the next you see and paint the rocks with their blood. I will lead the worthy out come the day, and you will rape and burn through all the worlds. You will know my glory and bathe in blood.

"Say my name!" She shouted it. "For I am Odran, god of all."

She fell to her knees, with Bollocks shivering as he pressed against her. Breathless, she pointed up. "The shadow. It's there."

"Come away now."

"I'm all right. He rules in the dark, Keegan. Don't open it again. He wants you to. It widens when you do. The ones you found, and sent there after Judgment, not failures for him. Because he used the ritual to widen the crack."

"Then I won't." Kneeling with her, he put his hands on her face. "You're like ice. Come away now."

"I need to . . ." She looked back at the stone. "They're damned there. Some go mad, others just exist on their fury. But none, not one, repents. Is that the word? Not one. Don't open it again, not while Odran exists. He'll use it and them."

"My word on it. Now, for gods' sake, come away."

He dragged her to her feet, half carried her out of the clearing.

"He can't hear me over them. I think. Or it's more . . . Their screams and curses are like music to him. Slow down, I'm okay. It was just so cold there, and so wretched. I'm okay. We're okay."

She stopped to rub her hands over Bollocks, to warm and soothe. And looked up at Keegan. "Banishments are rare—I know you've had more than your share in the last weeks, but over history, they're rare."

"They are."

"And still, every one is a moment of great joy to him. I think Marco's right. He's insane. But he's evil with it, and the evil of others is candy for him. Both portals in these woods lead to the dark, and both are more his than ours."

"When this is done, the woods here will be cleansed and consecrated. The Tree of Snakes destroyed."

"I don't think you'll have to destroy it. I . . . it blooms again, Keegan. When the light takes the dark, it blooms again. It bears fruit. *Réalta milis.*"

He stopped to stare at her. "Where did you learn of *réalta milis?*"

"I have no idea. It's very sweet? Is that right? Blue like the sky, pear shaped with a white star on its base when ripe. Is it real?"

"I thought not before this. Something in myth, a fruit for the gods. No tree like this exists in Talamh."

"Maybe it will."

"Maybe. I know this: When it's done, I pray to all the gods I never again have the duty to send anyone to the Dark World. For now, if there is Judgment that demands it, it will hold."

He rubbed her hands to warm them. "It cost you, and I'm sorry for it. But you've given me more to take to the council. I'll postpone the meeting until later in the day."

"Don't. I'm all right. Really. If you're going to do all you're planning, you need to start."

When they stepped out of the woods, she looked down at the training field. "The young ones, Keegan. The children."

"Will be defended. But if lines break, Breen, I want the young ones to have the means to defend themselves. Look here, look here now."

Deliberately, he turned her so she faced the village below.

"Here you see life—too much of it for my taste, all crowded together in one place. But here people do no harm. Ah, petty squabbling to be sure, but no harm. They create things, build things, grow things, including that one there, growing another life inside her, as one she already made clings to her hand while they walk to market.

"You see wagons ready for trade, stalls and shops opening up for the same. The colors of sweaters, scarves, things as simple as warm socks or as fine as a crystal bowl. Pubs offering a hot meal for the traveler. And there, smoke from the chimney of the schoolhouse, where those who teach warm it for the children who'll soon trudge their way there wishing it was a holiday instead of one for sitting and learning. And there, by the well, drawing gossip and water both, more life."

She saw, as he did, and knew—however he spoke of its being too crowded—he loved, and he honored.

He tipped her head up, pointed. "Dragons and their riders in a sky open to all and any who fly. This is yours as it's mine, Breen, as it's theirs. And there's too much of it for Odran to take. We will not lose this."

"You make me believe it."

"As you should. You're the key, the bridge, but as much as that, and it may be more than that, you're Fey."

His eyes held hers, intense, and greener than the hills around them.

"This life is yours. Beyond the power in you and the duty with it, it's a walk along the river, a gossip at the well, a ride on a good horse. It's a life well lived. Whatever comes, it's all of that."

Loving him, knowing all he'd said was only one of the reasons why she loved, she took his face in her hands. "Chosen and choosing well, Taoiseach. Go to your meeting. We've got a world to save and a life to live."

"I'll find you when I'm done, though it may be some time. I hope by all the gods we're for home tomorrow."

When he left her, she wandered, let herself feel that life. She watched Bollocks swim in the river, then with him crossed the bridge into the village.

It did teem, she supposed, by Keegan's standards. As always she found it charming, colorful, enjoyed the mix of voices. And when she saw Kiara with a baby on her hip and a market basket on her arm, she waved and changed direction.

"And who is this pretty girl?"

"Ah, this is Fi, Katie's young one. I said as I was going back to help with the very littles, I'd take Fi along. Are you after some shopping, as I could take awhile longer and go with you."

"Actually . . . I wonder if I can ask you a favor."

"You can, of course."

"Could Bollocks go with you, play with the kids and other dogs for an hour?"

"We'd love to have him. Where are you off to then?"

"I'm hoping you can tell me how to find Dorcas's cottage. The Old Mother?"

"I can, but gods, Breen, she'll talk till you fall unconscious, or wish for it. And she's so many cats you'll wade through them like a furry river."

"That's why I'd like you to take Bollocks. There's something I want to ask her."

"If she doesn't know, no one does. I'll send my pity with you. Well, there, see the road running past those stalls and bending left? You take that, then the first path you see on the right behind the yellow cottage. You take that straight into the woods and stick right to it. When it forks, take the left, and you'll see Dorcas's cottage. Cozy-looking in the trees, it is, and likely half a dozen cats slinking about. A pretty garden despite them, and a bright red door."

"Thanks. You go with Kiara now, Bollocks, and play. I won't be too long."

"She'll keep you until next year if she can manage it. She'll give you tea and biscuits," Kiara called out as Breen started on the road. "And both a horrible thing indeed."

It couldn't be that bad, Breen thought. Besides, it was a lovely walk. All she knew from Keegan was he'd talked to Dorcas—and suffered through it. She hadn't known for certain about the demon in Odran but had promised to pore through her books and look for answers.

Maybe she'd found some. Maybe they'd offer some new way to fight Odran.

At worst, she'd spend an hour listening to the rambles of a very old woman and dealing with a houseful of cats.

She liked cats.

She liked the pretty yellow cottage with the young woman in a blue dress and many-colored shawls hanging out wash. She liked the bumpy green field where a stubby gray donkey stood guard with sheep forming a single wooly cloud behind him.

She followed Kiara's directions and took the path into the woods. The light streamed stronger now that the morning moved on.

She felt life in the woods as Keegan had pointed out life in the village. A sleeping fox, a brown rabbit scratching its ear with a busy hind foot, a scurrying mouse, two deer grazing, a horned owl dozing in his tree burrow.

Enjoying the beats and rustles, she took the fork. A narrow stream ribboned along, tinkling out music as it tumbled over rocks worn smooth by its constant passage.

A dragon soared overhead, great wings spread, scales like polished amethyst. Beneath the wings a young dragon flew. Barely fledged, Breen realized, and testing his own wings.

She didn't hear birds calling, but felt them, in the trees, on the wing. A chipmunk scurrying with an acorn tight in its cheek. Away from a cat, she thought. No, two cats.

Four. Four cats, she realized, as she came through the trees and saw the cottage with its bright red door.

And three more cats curled up on the tiny porch. Another perched on the edge of the thatched roof like a gargoyle.

Then the woman in the long gray dress, white apron, and faded blue shawl lifting a bucket of water from a well.

Her hair, as gray as her dress, spilled down her back past her waist in a tangle. Her arms, thin as straw but roped with muscle, hauled up the bucket while more cats swarmed around her.

Her black boots had pointed toes and heels stubby like the donkey guarding the field. Her chin, just as pointed, lifted when she caught sight of Breen. Blue eyes blazed out of a face as wrinkled as old paper and as brown as an acorn.

Breen's first thought was she had a story here for sometime in the future. Some twist on a classic fairy tale. The witch with her many familiars in her woodland cottage.

Bespelled or bespelling?

Something to think about later.

When Dorcas spoke, her voice rasped on the cool air.

"Well now, it's the Daughter of the O'Ceallaigh, and a fine and good one he was indeed. Gods rest him through all his journeys."

Though husky with age, her voice carried strength, like her eyes.

"Sure ye've the look of him and of Mairghread, that's for certain. It's been too long since I've seen Marg. She's well, I hope, and Sedric, that fine cat, with her?"

"She is, and they are, thank you, Old Mother. Let me help you with the pail."

"Aye, ye've younger arms than I, so welcome to it. I've a kettle on the hob. I had a pricking in my fingers this morning. Then didn't the broom fall? A visitor coming, I told my friends here. So we've biscuits fresh and tea to go with them."

Dorcas walked through the cats, who meowed and purred. Carrying the pail, Breen did her best not to step on any tails as she followed Dorcas to the red door.

Pausing, Dorcas tapped her knuckles on the door three times. "Tap three to welcome thee."

"Ah, thank you."

Dodging cats, Breen stepped through the red door.

CHAPTER NINETEEN

Breen would have called the cottage a dollhouse with its tiny rooms and small-scale furniture. And leaning toward Chucky, considering the dim light filtered through windows crowded with herbs hung for drying. Stones, bits of wood, books, and perching cats jammed the narrow sills.

More cats draped over chairs like living throws, curled on cushions, ribboned through rickety chair legs. Two sat on the thick, artfully painted mantel above the roaring fire like statues among the dozen half-burned candles, and more books.

Considering the sheer multitude of felines, Breen expected the tiny cottage to reek of them. Instead, it smelled of the herbs, the candles, dust, and surprisingly the orange blossoms smothering a potted tree no more than twelve inches high blooming fiercely on a shelf. Along with countless books.

"Set the pail there, just there." Dorcas waded through the cats and into a kind of kitchen, where the squat black stove also blazed hot. "Didn't I make biscuits fresh this morning for the company to come? Sure I didn't know it would be ye, the O'Ceallaigh's daughter. Sit now, sit, and we'll have a cuppa and a chat."

Where? was Breen's first thought, but Dorcas wagged a finger at the cat curled on the cushion of one of the little wooden chairs. The orange tabby spilled out of it like water from a cup.

When Breen sat, the cat leaped on her lap, kneaded its way around a circle, then curled back to sleep.

"That one's Rory, and a fine mouser he is for all he'd sleep both day and night away. Good company, cats," she continued as she measured out something from a jar into a squat brown pot and poured water from the steaming kettle into it. "I find in my advancing age they have more to say with sense than some on two legs. A kind word, a good stroke of the hand now and then, food when they need it, and we all go along fine as ye please."

From another jar she took biscuits, nearly as brown as the teapot. They clinked like stones against the dark green plate.

"It's a dog for ye, isn't it then? A water spaniel. That's what I hear."

"Yes, I—"

"Dogs are fine companions as well, though they lack a cat's independence. And slyness. I'm an admirer of slyness myself. Not much of that in ye, is there, Daughter? Take a lesson from the cat and find some, for it's a fine tool, it is."

Dorcas moved a teetering pile of books, and the cat sitting on it, from a table to the floor, and set the plate of biscuits down.

"Young Keegan came to see me not long ago."

"Yes. He—"

"A demon in the god, he tells me—so ye say to him. So in ye as well. Ye'd find some slyness in that, if ye need it."

She poured the tea into two red cups, carried them to the little table.

"Thank you. I was wondering—"

"I told young Keegan—oh, and there's a handsome one, and I've seen handsome in my time. Yer father among them. Ah, such a voice he had as well. I'm told ye have that, for the singing. I'm an admirer of a good singing voice. The cats sing to me oft times. Ye there, Mary, give us a tune."

A sleek black cat lifted her head from a cushion and sang. Yowled, Breen supposed, but she couldn't deny it was tuneful and rather sweet.

When she laughed, Dorcas broke into a grin showing a strong set of teeth.

"If I get out my squeeze box—and there's the beginning and end of my musical talents—the whole lot of them will have a go. That was fine, Mary, and thanks. Have a biscuit now, Daughter, and yer tea. Ye're after learning what young Keegan hoped to learn."

"He said you didn't know for certain, but would research. I saw—"

"Aye, aye, ye saw the demon in him, and during a dark ritual, a sacrifice. Handsome is Odran as well—I laid my eyes on him more than once when Marg was taoiseach. But the handsome there is a lie. Not a mask, as a mask is for folly or a simple sort of deceit. His handsome is lies, like the rest of him. It hides the beast within."

Breen's throat tightened. "The demon?"

"Ah, ye fret over a beast in ye, a darkness, a creature of cruelty and lust for blood. Demons aren't so simple as that, child, as none living are so simple. Ye've had blood on those pretty hands, from the healing, and from the battle as well. Did ye think to taste it? Did hunger for it stir in ye?"

"No." Shocked by the question and the—yes, it was slyness—in Dorcas's eyes, Breen bit into a cookie.

It had the consistency of gravel, and tasted like sawdust.

"Not even a sip, just a tiny lick?"

"No."

"And there ye have it. What rides in ye hasn't the bloodlust. Odran had his own before the demon. It's a lust for power that only comes through blood, taking it, spilling it, consuming it."

"Before the demon? I don't understand."

To wash the sawdust out of her throat, Breen sipped some tea.

That added the taste of leaves soaked in muddy water.

"Didn't I do as young Keegan asked? Even if he weren't handsome, weren't taoiseach, I have the curiosity, don't I? A scholar I've been since I drew my first breath, and a scholar I'll be until I take my last. I'm in no hurry for that," she added, and ate a biscuit with obvious enjoyment.

"Did you find something, Old Mother?"

"I did indeed, and only this morning, after the broom fell. And so I got to making the biscuits for the company to come, and all the while thinking: Wasn't there something, long ago? A story. Just a story in an old book full of them. Legends, we'd say. Myths curled out of mists with heroes and villains. But something, my mind pricked at me along with my fingers, that may be, as many stories are, rooted in truth."

Sipping her tea, she sat back. "And here ye are, coming to ask me, so no need to send a message to handsome young Keegan. And though I'm pleased to have ye here, Daughter, I'm still female, and my heart young as spring. So it's sorry I am he won't come to share my biscuits. Share his bed, don't ye?"

"I . . . Yes."

"Ah, there I can enjoy some envy, as I see vigorous in him as well as handsome and a fine, strong form he has. I recall, very well, a good and vigorous mating. I had one of young Keegan's grandfathers as a lover once, in our prime."

"Oh. His grandfather?"

"Not as you mean it. How many times grandfather I couldn't say unless I counted back, and counting back is a sad business. But he was vigorous, and we had each other for a night. A very long, vigorous night."

She let out a cackling laugh. "Owain was his name, if my memory serves, and he left me a rosebud before back to the valley he went. More tea?"

"No, thank you. I'm fine. You found something about the demon. In Odran?"

"This very morning, sun barely up, and my fingers pricking, the broom falling. And I'm after making the biscuits for the company to come, and my mind says: Wait, now, Dorcas, wait. Wasn't there a story, read long ago? In my childhood, I'm thinking. So I hunt through the oldest of my books, as already I've been through all I can think to look through at the castle's great library. But this is one of my own, I'm thinking, and written way and well back by one who came before me. In the old tongue."

She poured more tea for herself. "So sit ye back, Daughter, finish yer biscuit, and I'll tell ye the tale of the god and the demon who loved him."

Taking it as a requirement, Breen suffered through another bite of the biscuit.

"In the long, long ago, before Talamh was Talamh, when the worlds of gods and men and Fey lived peaceably enough and magicks thrived in all, there was one in the world of gods who thought himself above the rest. Above the worlds of man, of Fey, and of gods. He was born of lust, with no care, no fondness. A mating of greed, and born through a mother, though one of the Tuatha Dé Danann, whose heart was hard and cold as stone. But the child softened it, toward him only, and so she reared him with great privilege, rocked him with tales of his greatness, his destiny to rule."

Dorcas paused long enough to slurp at her tea.

"He suckled milk from that hard heart and grew bold and proud. Well then, gods are often so, are they not? And though his mother loved him, and him alone, and pampered him and spoiled him, granting his every wish, it was not enough, ye see.

"She schemed with him for more, but he grew restless with her clinging fingers. He had no love for the one who'd carried him, birthed him, did he, but only the lust, and the lust was for power and blood. Even this, breaking the law of gods and men and Fey and all, she granted him. Sacrificing the living in secret to feed that lust to him. Though he drank the blood of man and Fey, it didn't slake the thirst."

Odran, Breen thought, but didn't interrupt.

"So there was a demon, a female and comely in her way. Young and proud to take any form she wished. There was no evil in her, so the tale goes, and she lived happy enough in her world, doing no harm.

"And the mother of the god saw this and saw the power in this young demon, and she told the son, who looked on her. A maiden she was, and pure, and powerful, and young. The god went to the demon world, wooed her, seduced her. But she, though she loved, wouldn't leave her family. He took her, unwilling, and while the cry went up for the abduction of this young maid, he, with the mother's aid, lashed her to an altar, and the dark ritual began."

Dorcas paused to drink again, jutted her pointed chin at Breen.

"Seen this ritual, I think. The vision ye had of the god and the demon in him."

"He raped her, this young demon, killed her, drank her blood?"

"All that, aye, all that, while she cried out for love of him, for mercy, cried out for her family, for her life. Until she could cry no more, for he consumed her. Do ye understand? Her blood, her flesh, her bones, her essence. All. And the mother, seeing this, how he feasted like a beast on the flesh and bone, understood, too late, what she'd borne and raised. She begged him to stop. Beyond reason, he slew his mother, and drank of her blood that spilled on the altar. Drank the blood of his mother, the blood of a god, consumed the body of a demon, and so with the ritual, with this lust, with this feasting beyond all the laws, took the demon into him, a part of him now. Blood in his blood, bone in his bone, flesh in his flesh."

It made Breen want to shudder because she could see it. She could see it so clearly. "Do you believe this?"

"I'll tell ye I do, and I'll tell ye the rest. Her cries were heard, Daughter. The gods broke through the spell wall and into the secret place of ritual to find the dead mother, the god beast, and the simple dress the god beast had ripped from the young maid.

"In the story they say they slew him where he had done his evil, that they brought the justice of gods down on him in lightning and fire. But this I think is not true. In the tales of Odran, all I know, they speak of the casting out, when they find he's broken all laws, done blood sacrifices to gain power. Consuming blood, and some say flesh. Of man and Fey and of other worlds, all in his thirst for more. This, I think, is the true ending of the first story I told ye. There is none I know that tells of Odran with a demon in his ancestry."

"You say she was pure, did no harm, was young and good. But what I saw in him—"

She cut Breen off with a wag of a bony finger. "Was the corruption, the choice, the evil done to another for the joy of it. The beast ye saw in him is what he made of it. And though they cast him out, Daughter, what was done formed the first cracks in the worlds, in the trust, in the time upon time of unity. This is what I know. As I know until he's destroyed, no world is safe from that lust. He thirsts for ye, Daughter."

"I know."

"Do ye know how to destroy him?"

"I . . . Do you?"

"This comes from ye and not from me. The songs and stories call for ye, and say his end is by the hand of the Daughter. But this is hope. The act must be of ye, from ye, for ye. The god slays the god, and it may be the demon at last frees the demon."

She smiled then. "Have another biscuit."

"Thank you, Mother, but I should get back. I need to tell Keegan all you've told me."

"Well then, take the book." She rose to wade through cats who'd crowded around like children listening to the story. "And if the taoiseach can't read the old tongue, the shame is his. I'll have it back," she told Breen as she pulled a thin book bound in worn brown leather from a pile. "Be sure of that."

"I'll make sure of it."

Dorcas laid a bony hand on Breen's. "My eyes still see, and see ye clear. Not a maid, but pure enough. Use what ye are, take what ye need, trust in yer gifts. He has only the dark and those who walk in it. Ye have the dark and the light, and both will serve ye."

"Thank you, Mother. I'll keep the book safe."

"See that ye do."

She stepped out into the blessedly cool air and, clutching the book, started down the path.

"Mate vigorously, Daughter!"

Laughing, Breen looked back to see Dorcas in the doorway, a cat on her shoulders and others swarming around her feet. "I'll do my best."

She carried the book, the story, a million impressions back to the castle. Before she could reach her mind out to Bollocks, she saw him with Kiara and two others along with Sinead, a brood of young children, and a small pack of dogs playing a game that made her think of Duck, Duck, Goose on the green lawns.

Even as she started over, Bollocks raced toward her. He ran a circle around her, then stopped, his eyes going huge. He went on an orgy of sniffing, her boots, her pants.

"Cats," she told him. "As I'm sure you've already detected. But in your dreams you couldn't come up with so many." She bent to pet him all over. "You'll always be my first love."

Sinead crossed over to her. "What a fine day it's turned out to be, and what a joy it is to see the littles so happy."

"Is it Duck, Duck, Goose?"

"It is! How I remember seeing you and Morena and all the others playing the same game."

"She'd take wing and fly around the circle when I chased her."

"So she did. And now I'm reminded I have something for you if you've time to come to my rooms for a moment."

"Of course." She'd make it quick, she thought, holding the book close.

"Were you off for a quiet reading time?"

"Oh, this? No. I need to take it to Keegan. I've just come from talking to Dorcas, and it's hers."

"Dorcas? Ah, child, did she ply you with biscuits and tea while the cats swam around you?"

"I don't know that they could reasonably be called biscuits, or tea. But yeah."

"Then, as I know Keegan's with Seamus and Flynn even now, you'll have time to have a real cup and a real biscuit to kill the horror of it."

"I won't say no. She's fascinating, though, Sinead. So are the cats." She glanced down as they walked; Bollocks continued to sniff at her. "I see my dog feels the same."

"A fount of information is Dorcas the Scholar, but I swear I'd rather go uninformed entirely than suffer through a round of her tea and biscuits. If you go again," Sinead continued as they went inside and started up the stairs, "take a bottle of wine and some sweet—biscuits, tarts, little cakes. She'll be grateful and honor bound to share them with you."

"Now, why didn't I think of that?"

"A lesson I learned hard over the years. I'm told you'll likely go back to the valley tomorrow." Sinead hooked her arm with Breen's as they walked. "So I'm glad to steal a bit of your time."

"It's not stealing when I want to spend it with you."

They went into Sinead's cozy sitting room. And a bigger contrast to Dorcas's cottage Breen couldn't think of.

Soft fabrics, pretty colors, soft cushions. And not a cat in sight. Flowers sat in a trio of vases; crystals dangled in windows to shoot rainbows.

"Sit now. We'll have some sugar biscuits and tea with honey."

Because she remembered Sinead liked to fuss, Breen sat while Bollocks settled, sniffing still, at her feet. "It's so pretty in here. It's so like you."

Sinead's cheeks flushed with pleasure as she opened a tin. "Flynn says I'd stack cushions on cushions if I had my way. He's not wrong on it."

She'd done her summer-sun hair in a long, thick braid with a pink ribbon wound through it. Her dress, a deeper pink, skimmed just over her ankles to show off boots that matched the ribbon. Crystals dangled from her ears as they did at the windows.

"You always had the prettiest clothes. I remember asking you to do my hair. My mother never got a handle on it, and if Nan wasn't around to do it, I'd come running to you. I always felt pretty after you did my hair."

"How I loved playing with it. Oh, so red, all those curls. My only girl with hair as straight as rain." Sinead brought over the tea, settled on a cushion. "You remember more and more?"

"Like I never forgot. And so clear. Clearer than you'd think possible considering I was only three when I left."

"I think the taking away has the memories coming back strong. It hurt your da to take those memories, darling. He took them so you wouldn't hurt."

"I know. Oh, this is wonderful. You always made amazing biscuits."

"I don't have the type Bollocks usually has, but I don't think just one of these would hurt him, do you?"

"He'd love one."

"Well now, you enjoy, the both of you. And I'll get what I have for you."

Happy, Breen thought. The room held happiness. It soothed her heart to know Sinead could find happiness after her loss.

"I spoke with Morena through the mirror only this morning, and she told me you remembered these."

Breen looked and saw the little wings in Sinead's hands. Bold green edged in blue. Like a butterfly.

"Oh! My wings! You kept them."

"Sure and I kept them. You were so very fond of them, and couldn't take them with you to the other side. I thought you might like to have them now. Just a little thing from when you were a little."

"Not a little thing, not little at all." Breen cupped them in her hands as the memories flooded her mind, her heart.

"Sure they won't be fitting you now, but, well, one day you'll have littles of your own."

"I remember when you first put them on me. You said pretending was as good as doing, and often better, as you could go and do and be anything you wanted in the pretending. You were right."

She shifted to take Sinead into a hug. "I have a mother in Philadelphia. His name is Sally."

"I know of him, and I'm glad."

"I have Nan in the valley. And I have you here. I have you here, as I had you when I needed you. How many women can say they have three mothers?"

"Ah, my sweet girl. You're making me cry."

"I'll treasure these. When I get back to the valley, I'm going to ask Seamus if he can make me a frame. Like a shadow box for them. And I'll hang them in the cottage."

"Ah, they're only made of some old cloth, and faded some for all that."

"Oh, no. No, they're made of love, and as bright as the sun to me."

She spent an hour with Sinead, then took the book and the wings to Keegan's rooms. She'd barely set the wings, reverently, on a table, finally opened the book to satisfy her curiosity, when he strode in.

"I've just started hunting for you," he began.

"I've been with Sinead. She told me you were with Seamus and Flynn."

"So I was, after the endless council meeting. Since here you are, I'm taking a bloody moment and having some ale. You'll have wine, I suppose."

She didn't have a clue what time it was, then decided what the hell did it matter. "All right. Then if we could sit down a minute, I—"

"I've barely more than that, as I'm damned determined we'll leave tomorrow, and I've enough left to do to fill the rest of the day and half the bloody night."

"You'll want to take this minute, and it's going to be more than one. I went to see Dorcas."

"Dorcas the Scholar? What in hell did you subject yourself to that for? Are you after paying for some grievous sin?"

"Stop. She's not that bad. Well, her tea and biscuits are that bad."

"You have all my pity. But you were after asking for it, weren't you? I told you she didn't remember anything about a demon in Odran, and would study on it, and tell me if something came to mind."

"Something did."

Amusement fled; impatience replaced it. "Then why didn't she send for me?"

"Just this morning, after her fingers pricked and the broom fell."

"Company coming."

"And anticipating that, she made biscuits—which are horrible—but she remembered some old story, from a childhood book."

Breen picked it up. "On loan—with a promise to get it back to her. It's written in the old tongue, which I take to mean predates Talamhish."

"It does."

Frowning, ale forgotten, he opened it, turned a page, then another. "Children's stories."

"If you consider rape and murder and drinking blood stories suitable for children."

Amused again, he glanced at her. "And what do you think are the roots of the fairy tales you tell children on the other side?"

"There's a point," she muttered, and poured the ale and the wine herself. "Can you read it?"

"I can, aye, and will, despite the bloody headache that'll give me. Did she tell you any of what she remembered?"

"All of it."

"Then I'll take more than the minute, and as much as you need to tell me. I'll read it myself as well, but that's a miserable process. Sit." Now he picked up the ale. "Tell the tale."

He didn't sit while she related it as carefully as she could, but paced. Bollocks watched him for a while, then stretched out long by the fire for a doze.

He didn't interrupt or speak at all, even when she paused to drink or to think through the next part.

"Then she gave me the book," Breen finished, "so you could read it for yourself."

"And so I will. Why, I wonder, has this tale never been told that I know of?"

"It's my impression it's only in that book, and one that was passed down in her family, as those children's stories. It may be just that, Keegan."

He shook his head. "It has the ring of truth in it. There are tales of Odran's mother, and they vary. She was stolen and taken by force by a lustful god, or she gave another a sleeping potion and stole his essence to make her child. And all between those. But none have that ring of truth as this does."

"But it ends with him being put to death."

"And there you have the child's story. The punishment for evil deeds, harsh and final. Not the half measures. And put to death he wasn't, was he? Cast out, banished, stripped of the luxuries the gods enjoy. It may not be precisely what's written in that book, but the heart of it—or lack of heart—that has the ring. Consuming the demon, and a maid at that."

"It's always a virgin."

"Well, it's a matter of purity, however unjust. An abduction, a rape, a murder—the gods are known to sometimes dally in those. But all of that, and the devouring of another? All for power?"

He shook his head as he paced to the window, back again.

"No, that's beyond what could stand, be excused, be punished in small ways. And for power coveted over them, the gods, as well as all else. Aye, there's the answer to that."

"Okay, it has to be asked. Why don't they stop him now? Or why haven't they?"

"It's for us." As if it was the simplest of matters, he shrugged. "They've passed their Judgment on him. And it's for us to pass ours for his crimes against the rest. The worlds are separate now. Dorcas may be in the right that this was the beginning of that. But they're separate, and while it may be the gods themselves will go at him if he destroys us, that's for their own reasons. You're the key, and that's all they'll give."

"That's stupidly shortsighted."

"Or slyly, very long."

She opened her mouth, closed it.

Or slyly, she thought, very long.

"I'll read the story for myself when I've finished what I need to do yet. And doom some poor messenger to get it back to Dorcas safe tomorrow."

"She and your grandfather had a one-night stand."

"On what did they stand?"

"No, they were lovers, for a night."

He looked sincerely horrified. "My grandfather?"

"Actually, there would be several *great*s there. An ancestor, great—however many—grandfather. She thinks his name was Owain. He was vigorous."

He pressed his fingers to his eyes. "I call on the gods of all goodness to spare me from such as this."

She laughed until her sides ached. "She also says you're handsome and she's sure equally vigorous."

"Sweet gods."

"Though she envies me a little on that score, she wishes us vigorous mating."

He stared at her, then breathed out. "I'm wiping this entire part of things from my mind and leaving."

When he strode out as he'd strode in, she smiled. She hadn't known he could be embarrassed by anything.

CHAPTER TWENTY

They had the family meal and spoke of all the serious matters.

"In a child's book." Tarryn studied her wine as she spoke. "And not, as we believe or can find, in another. In the old tongue as well. And yet, I believe as you, Keegan, it has the ring of truth. A loud, clear bell."

"I'm with you on that." Mahon nodded. "There are countless tales of the gods having their way with others, of their own, the Fey, from the world of man and beyond. Even taking lives, though always with the cover of war or some justification."

"It was my sense that the blood sacrifice and cannibalism crossed the line," Breen put in, "and was enough to have him cast out."

"So it's been told," Tarryn agreed, "and yet, you yourself saw the demon in him. And you say, and Marg confirms, he had a mark here." She touched a finger to her heart. "This he doesn't hide, or can't."

"Can't, it says to me. He is vain," Keegan pointed out. "Carrying a mark or scar? It's not perfection. If you follow it through, the gods cast him out, but also marked him. A mark of a demon, the mark of the beast."

"What does this tell us? It's a weakness." Thoughtful, Tarryn lifted her glass. "This mark he can't hide even with his power, with Yseult's. You've read the story?"

"I have, and can say it goes as Breen told me, as was told to her."

"I'll read it before Dorcas has it back."

"It's in the old tongue."

Her eyebrows winged high. "And who taught you the first words of it? I'll read it. You'll speak to the council of it?"

"I don't see a way around it, but early morning. We go west no later than midday."

"I'll bring it to the council, then take it safe back to Dorcas."

"Wading through the scribbles and scratches of the story is task enough, Ma. I'll send someone to take it."

"I'll take it," she insisted, "and take a basket of sweets and a good wine."

"That's what Sinead said to do."

With a laugh, Tarryn turned to Breen. "As both of us learned after suffering too many of her biscuits. It will please her, Keegan, that the hand of the taoiseach pays the call. The duty's mine. It was good of you to visit with her, Breen."

"Well worth it, for the story and the book. And she's actually fascinating." Because she couldn't help herself, she related the sexual connection.

"Must you?" Keegan demanded as his mother roared with laughter. "Did you know of this?" he asked Tarryn.

"How would I? Well before my time, I'd say. If I remember the tree branches well enough, I think there were Owains on my branches as well as your da's. So I can't say which side of things gave her this . . . vigorous night, and surely a century ago if a day."

"How old is she?" Breen wondered.

"Ah, she's coy about it, but I'd say easily half through her second century. She chose to have no child," Tarryn went on as Breen boggled at the idea she'd sat with someone who might be a hundred and fifty. Or more. "She preferred her studies and her cats. But it's well known she took many lovers, so it's not surprising one might have been a family connection."

"He left her a rosebud when he left."

"A romantic as well." Tarryn sighed, then gave Keegan a poke in the arm. "Take a lesson."

"I'll vow if I have a vigorous night with Dorcas the Scholar to leave a rosebud behind."

"I feel I should say—confess? Inform," Mahon decided. "It's told in my family my own grandfather, when young and still untried in the ways of . . . romance, we'll say in polite company, had—by the accounts—a full three nights with Dorcas the Scholar. She'd have been aged enough to have been his grandmother, most likely, at the time of the lessons. It's said she took him to instruct him on the ways of pleasuring a woman. According to my grandmother, she's a fine teacher."

"Ah, and did those lessons pass down from father to son to son?"

Mahon smiled at his mother-in-law. "I feel it indiscreet to say more than I do all I know to keep your daughter happy."

"Well then, I say we lift a cup to Dorcas the Scholar, to her long life, her deep knowledge, and her very fine lessons."

They left for the valley just past noon and in a drizzling rain. The rain spread over the whole of Talamh, a mist here, a downpour there.

On the roads below, thawed from winter's grip and muddy from the rain, the troops and trainers assigned to the new fields made their way.

Breen stood in the rain, grateful for her new coat, when Keegan detoured to other portals and studied the shadow breaches.

More and more she saw the wisdom in his decision to lay new lines of defense.

As they approached the valley, the sun pushed through the clouds and sparkled on the rain that continued to fall. A rainbow arched, beautifully bright over the hills and fields, over the green and the freshly plowed brown.

Breen took it as a sign of welcome.

Another welcome came from Morena the moment the dragons and Mahon landed.

"Welcome home, travelers." Soaked to the skin, she came through the farmhouse gate. "It's rained buckets until moments ago, so you've brought the sun. The farmer I married had me out in the buckets, spreading manure, which you can smell right enough with every breath."

"Smells of spring," Keegan claimed.

"To the farmer and his brother. Did you get that in the Capital?" Morena reached out to touch Breen's coat. "I don't think I've seen finer."

"A gift from Kiara."

"Ah well, she has an eye for such things. I imagine your two oldest will be up from their naps and bursting outside any moment, Mahon."

"I'll go on to my family then, Keegan, if you have no need for me now."

"Not till morning. You'll tell Aisling what we learned and what we're doing. As part of the valley council."

"So I will. In the morning then."

"And what's all this?" Morena demanded when he flew toward his cottage.

"I'll tell you and Harken together—when I have an ale and a dry spot."

"Should I get Nan and Sedric?"

"They're at my nan's, along with Marco," Morena told her. "Having one of their baking parties. As it's my turn to see to the evening meal, more's the pity, we'll be grateful for whatever they send along."

"Tomorrow's soon enough. I've other things in the morning," Keegan continued, "so training later in the day."

"All right. I'd like to talk to Seamus. Your mother gave me my wings, Morena. I'm hoping Seamus can make a frame for them so I can hang them on a wall at the cottage."

"Oh, that would've pleased her to tears. It happens he should be at your cottage now. He wanted to fiddle with your garden."

"That's perfect. Let's go find him, Bollocks. Good luck with the cooking."

"Ah, easy for you to say, as I know Marco's bound to have something glorious already on the stove. And me, after spending half the day spreading shite."

"You married the farmer."

"Aye. What was I thinking?" Laughing, she tossed back her damp hair. "I'll fetch him, Keegan, and we'll get that ale and a dry spot for all three of us."

"I'll come when I'm done with what needs doing." Keegan looked toward the Welcoming Tree, where Bollocks already waited. "It's likely Marco will get there before me. You can share all this with him."

"Good. I'd feel better about it."

He pulled her into a kiss, then surprised her by running his hands over her to warm and dry her.

"No need to be wet," he said, and walked away.

He had his moments, Breen thought as she crossed the road. If you paid attention, he had his moments.

She walked into Ireland and sunshine, and though the scent wasn't manure, it definitely said spring. Even in the few days that had passed, she could see its progress. Leaf buds had grown fat, and some began their unfurling.

She thought of her seedlings, of the plans for a small patch for vegetables between her cottage and where Marco and Brian planned their own.

Still wet from the rain, Bollocks splashed into the stream and out again, then with a glance toward her, shot out of the woods.

His happy barks got their answer with Seamus's cheerful greeting.

"There's that good dog. Look here and know this spot's not for you to run through and dig."

She came out of the woods, and to her surprise, saw Seamus, his cap cocked on his head, gloved hands on his hips, standing at the edge of a small plowed patch.

The rich brown made a tidy square just in front of a hedgerow of fuchsia that separated the wide lawn from the field beyond.

As she hurried across to join him and Bollocks, she caught the sharp scent of manure.

Spring.

"Oh, Seamus, I didn't expect you to do all this!"

He turned to her, all merry blue eyes. "You wouldn't deny me my pleasures, would you then? Such a fine time I've had here while my cottage is filled with bakers."

He gave her a pat on the shoulder. "See here now. We've had some talks in the last days, Marco, Brian, and myself, and thought wouldn't it be a pretty thing to cut through the hedgerow right over there and make a kind of gateway, an arbor, open to their cottage and yours. With the hedgerow giving privacy to all. They'll have a fine view of the bay and the hills, and with the bit of a garden you wanted just here for sharing the work and the bounty. They gave me leave, hoping it would be a happy surprise for you."

"It is. It's perfect. It's exactly where I thought it should be. We've never grown vegetables, Marco or me."

"You'll have your tomatoes and peppers as you said. And we can put in some potatoes, some cabbage, some beans for snapping, and carrots as well. On the small scale, I'm thinking."

"You'll show me. You'll teach me."

"I will, and glad to. But you know more than you think. It's in you already. Come, we'll have a look at your seedlings. They've done well, and it's time to harden them off. We're done with frosts." He glanced at the sky as he spoke. "You can trust me on that."

"I do."

He showed her the line of boxes full of dirt and young plants he set by the cottage.

"They'll have the shelter and the warmth of the cottage as they grow used to the air and settle. When they're ready, you'll pot them up or plant them as you please."

She spent a delightful time talking gardening and plants while Bollocks splashed in the bay.

"You've done so much for me, and now I'm going to ask you for one more thing."

"Ask away."

She dug in her bag and took out the wings she'd carefully wrapped.

"Ah, don't I remember those! How you used to race around, flapping them."

"I remember, too, and how much they meant to me. I'd like to frame them, hang them in the cottage. Such a good memory."

"Ah, that's a grand thing, grand memories. A shadow box is what you're wanting here, so they're open and show well, not just flat in a frame."

"Yes, exactly. I thought you'd know the kind and size and the right wood."

"And the making of it will bring back good memories for me and for Finola as well."

He pulled off his gloves, rubbed his hands together to free them of any stray dirt before he took the wings in their wrapping.

When he left, she took Bollocks inside. Drew a deep breath of whatever Marco had in the oven.

She lit the fire, hung up her new coat, and just sighed.

"You know what, pal? You get a treat after a long journey, and I'm taking a hot shower. Then if we still have the place to ourselves when I'm done, I'm going to squeeze in some writing time."

She indulged in a long shower, then indulged herself with the lightest of glamours rather than fiddle with makeup. She tied her hair back and considered grooming done.

Downstairs she grabbed a Coke, and since it remained just her and Bollocks, they settled into her office.

"Time for your adventure," she told him, and booted up her laptop.

She spent the next hour rolling out the scenes she'd written in her head when she'd had time to think in the Capital.

Fun, some drama, a lot of high jinks.

The sound of her phone ringing shot her straight out of the story. For a moment she just stared at it, sitting on its charger—as if it was some strange and foreign device.

It had nearly become one.

She noted the name and number of the display and hesitated a moment longer.

How had she managed to forget she'd sent Carlee the manuscript?

She rubbed the tattoo on her wrist and answered.

"Hello."

"Breen. It's Carlee. I'm hoping I caught you after work and before dinner."

"You actually did." If she didn't count the fact she'd intended to work until someone came through the cottage door. "How are you?"

"Great. And I hope you have time to talk about *Magicks*."

Breen squeezed her eyes shut. "Sure."

When Marco walked in—strutted would be closer—carrying a box that smelled of sugar and vanilla, she sat at the table, a glass of wine in her hand.

"Hey, girl! Welcome back! Gotta hear all about it. Just let me check my roast. Garlic and rosemary pork roast."

"There's a lot of all about it."

"I bet! Had the best time. Baking party day at Finola's. Brought you some of Sedric's lemon biscuits and a whole lot of other goodies. Marg did the magicks so dinner would coast right along, and oh yeah, that looks and smells just right.

"How about I get me a glass of what you have and join you in the living room?"

"How about you do? Marco—"

"Whoa! Where'd you get that coat? Holy crap." He rushed right over to the peg. "This is what it's about. This is lit, and lit all the way up. Girl, how'd you know to get this when I wasn't there to make you?"

"Kiara gave it to me."

"Sure she did, it's got her good fashion sense all over it. Get up! Put it on. Let me see."

"Can you sit first?"

"Oh, baby, something's wrong."

"No, no." She got up, wandered in to the sofa. "A lot of strange things to tell you, and I'm going to go backward because I really need to talk to you about the last thing. Get your wine and sit so I can work it out in my head."

She kept stroking Bollocks, who sat right beside her while Marco brought a glass of wine and sat on her other side.

"Tell Marco."

"Okay, back to front. Carlee called just a little while ago."

"She read it—good and fast. Okay, let's hear it."

"Back to front," she repeated. "And the last thing we talked about was the recipes you sent. She really liked how you presented them, the fun way, the story, or the bits of music you connected to each one."

"You did most of that."

"No, I helped with that, but they were your stories, and it's your music, and it's your style. Anyway, she gave them to another agent in-house, Yvonne Kramer, because she's represented three well-received cookbooks, and actually cooks. Yvonne, Carlee said, tried out your spaghetti and meatballs. And big success. Then she tried out your applesauce cake. Same thing. Yvonne wants to meet with you when we go to New York."

"Holy shit!" He actually goggled, open-mouthed, bugged-out eyes. "You're not kidding me?"

"Holy shit, I'm not kidding you. Marco, I think you might just have an agent, and one who wants to see more."

He shoved up, walked all around the living room.

"I never really figured anybody would, you know, want to go with it."

"Marco, don't tell me you don't want to do this!"

He stopped, pointed at himself. "Is this the face of a dumbass?"

"It is not." And grinning, she jumped up to hug him.

"I gotta figure out what to do for more. My brain's kinda—" He made the sound of an electric sizzle. "I just never . . . I don't know how any of this works."

"Yvonne knows. It's like you keep saying to me. Trust Carlee. Now you trust Yvonne. I have her contact information, and she'd like you to get in touch tomorrow."

"Okay, wow. I need to sit down again. A freaking cookbook," he said as he sat. "Ain't that a kick in the ass? I need to let it all settle in, and I'm going to find the fun in it, Breen. That's what I'm going to do."

"You always find the fun."

"Settling," he said. "Tell me the next—back to front."

"Okay. Deep breath. Carlee likes the book. My book."

"Didn't I tell you!" He poked her arm. "Didn't I?"

"She really likes it, Marco. She said she's sure she can sell it."

"Damn right. So why are you sitting here instead of dancing?"

"I'm trying to get it through. She said we didn't have to offer it to my publisher first because it's not a YA, it's not a Bollocks book, but she thought we should. That it's the right thing to do because, you know, good relations."

"That's not what you want?"

"No, no, she knows best, and besides, I really like my editor, and you know all the people on your end, and I— She really liked it, Marco. She wanted my go-ahead to send it over. I said okay."

"Because you're not a dumbass."

"My brain's doing that thing yours did. And I don't know what to think."

"Let me pause and consider." Head tilted, he held a finger in the air. "Oh yeah, I got it. How about: I wrote a damn good book. Two," he corrected. "You're two for two."

"She hasn't sold it yet, so let's not get ahead of things. But she liked it. She could even talk to me about some of it, so I know she meant it. Marco, a year ago this was all still a dream. A dream that only started to open up when I found out about the money my father and Nan sent me. When you asked me what I wanted, and I said to come here, to Ireland. And it's all happened so fast. So much, so fast."

"Has it really, my Breen?" Wine in one hand, he ran his other over her hair. "That book, I think some of that's been rolling around in your head for a really long time. You just needed to, like, you know, pop the cork. And the rest, it was all in there. It was just corked up, too."

"I could see the world I wrote about, so clear, Marco. A lot like Talamh, I know. I think some might have been memories buried in me, or wishes. And it all just poured out. I don't know if I can ever do that again, but—"

"Stop it. I mean it. Did you write a book about this most excellent dog here?"

In response, Bollocks whipped his tail.

"Yeah."

"And are you writing another one?"

"Yeah, it's going pretty well."

"And do you write a good, solid, and popular blog on a damn near daily basis?"

She let out a huge breath. "I really needed you to come home."

"Are we going to dance now?"

"I don't want to dance until we know it's sold. Actually sold. Then I want to dance like maniacs over that, and your amazing cookbook."

"Okay, no jinxies. We'll hold off on the dancing."

"I really needed you to come home," she repeated. "And now that I can breathe again . . . When I got home, Seamus was here. He's started our garden—the veg garden."

"He did what? Seriously?" He popped up, hurried to the window. "Look at that! Seamus is the *man!*"

"It's going to be perfect, and the idea about the opening in the fuchsias, and where you're going to put the cottage. It's all perfect. I want it all so much. When I first saw this cottage it just blew through me: what I always wanted. But even then, I couldn't imagine the rest."

She circled her arms in the air as she rose to join him at the window.

"You right here, you having Brian and being through the hedgerow. Me writing books, and having this really, really exceptional dog. Having Talamh, and Nan and everyone. A place, Marco, a family, a purpose.

"And sometimes, like after I talked to Carlee, it all just hits me, blows through me again so I can't think. Or I start thinking: Can this be real? Or am I in some sort of weird dream? Or a coma?"

"Am I in one, too? 'Cause, girl, I have everything I ever wanted and more right along with you."

"Well, if we're in some sort of mutual coma, let's just stay in it." Smiling, finally smiling, she tapped her glass to his. "I got lots more, like about a woman named Dorcas who's at least a hundred and fifty years old—"

"Get out."

"At least, according to Tarryn— Oh, and I like Keegan's mom so much, Marco. Even if Keegan and I weren't—whatever—I know I'd just really like her. Anyway."

Taking his hand, she walked back to sit. "Dorcas the Scholar. She has a million cats. Okay, that's an exaggeration, but I'd bet on a hundred. And she lives in this sort of spooky fairy-tale cottage in the woods near the village at the Capital."

"Is she a good guy or a bad guy?"

"A good guy. Strange, but a good guy. A respected scholar—the one Tarryn talked about when we all discussed the whole demon-god thing with Odran."

"Right, right. Keegan said something about crappy cookies."

"Beyond crappy. They taste like sawdust, and her tea tastes like tar, and I half expected Chucky to start cackling in one of the shadowy corners of her tiny cottage."

He gave her a long look. "And she's a good guy?"

"Yeah, and despite everything I just said, she's so damn interesting. Anyway, she found a story in one of the books she's had since she was a little girl."

"Like a hundred and fifty years ago."

"Like that. I'm going to tell you what she told me, and why she believes, and Keegan believes, and everyone who's heard the story now believes it was about Odran and how he got the demon inside him."

Halfway through, Marco held up a hand. He went into the kitchen, brought back the wine bottle.

When she finished, he got up again to take out the roast and let it rest.

"I'm trying not to let this put me off this really good meal I've got going. You don't maybe think the whole eating-that-girl-demon is like a metaphor?"

"No, sorry. I think it's literal. A virgin—naturally—demon who could take any form she wished. He wanted that power, the demon element to add to his own. I don't know if she was the first he cannibalized, but I doubt she was the last."

"So he's the Hannibal Lecter of gods?"

"Only you, Marco. Besides, he wouldn't bother to chase it down with a nice Chianti."

"But the demon inside him is evil."

"Because he is, because he corrupted it."

"And this mark deal, the scar, whatever it is?"

"Is—maybe—a way in, a way out. A weakness."

"A way out for what?" he countered. "The demon? Now you've got some evil demon with evil god innards all over it. How's that an improvement?"

"Would it be evil if released? I don't know, Marco."

She pressed her fingers to her eyes. They'd gone from talking cookbooks and publishing to demons.

"I wonder if it's like releasing the trapped souls in the ruins, if this is like that. Something I'm meant to do. I can't know until . . . until I do what I'm supposed to do, however I'm supposed to do it."

She shoved at her hair. "Meanwhile—I forgot all of this—they've worked those cracks into every portal from Odran's side."

"Like in the waterfall one?"

"Yeah, like that. Except for the Welcoming Tree, which can't be breached. And Keegan— Wait, he's coming now. I'll let him go into all that battle-tactics stuff."

"Fine. If he's here, Brian won't be far behind. We'll have dinner while he explains."

Marco rose. "And you get to tell him about your book."

"It's not sold yet. And you get to talk about your cookbook."

"It's not written *or* sold yet." He just pointed at her. "But we're talking about it, all of it. It's good news, so we share it. We got plenty of the weird and strange, so we share the good along with it."

"All right." He'd argue it out of her anyway, she thought. "I'll tell him."

"Tell him what?" Keegan demanded. "I hope some of the telling is Marco saying whatever he's got for dinner is ready, as I'm more than half-starved. Brian'll be along by the time I wash up."

"You're in luck there." Marco lifted the roast onto a platter and began to surround it with potatoes, carrots, celery, onions, all roasted in herbs and the juices.

"Well now, that looks fairly amazing." Keegan scrubbed his hands in the sink. "If I hadn't been told Seamus started your garden, I'd have smelled it. So you don't have to tell me that. Is there more yet?"

"Breen's agent loved her book. The new one," Marco added while Breen rolled her eyes. "The one she just sent in."

"All right." Drying his hands, Keegan looked over at Breen. "Did you think she wouldn't?"

"I couldn't know until—"

"Didn't you like it?"

"Yes, of course, but—"

"And you let Marco read it, and he's a man of good judgment, and he liked it. Seems you fretted for nothing, but women will."

"Oh, really?"

He just shrugged. "Now you've no reason left, and you'll let me read it for myself. But not on the machine. I like the paper."

"I haven't—"

"I'll print it out for you. And here comes Brian." Marco carried the platter to the table, gave Breen a big, wide grin.

So she shot him one right back. "Marco's writing a cookbook, and has a meeting with an agent in New York who wants to represent him."

"Well done, Marco. It's a generous thing to share your talent for cooking with others."

"Still have to figure it all out. But meanwhile . . ." When Brian stepped in, Marco simply lit up. "Let's eat."

PART III
MISNEACH

*It is not the oath that makes us believe
the man, but the man the oath.*

–Aeschylus

*Courage is not simply one of the virtues,
but the form of every virtue at the testing point,
which means, at the point of highest reality.*

–C. S. Lewis

CHAPTER TWENTY-ONE

It didn't completely surprise her to find Keegan in the kitchen staring holes through the coffee maker in the morning. While most days he left to do what he did before she came down, occasionally he started later.

"You want coffee?"

"I dislike this machine a great deal, but I have a need."

"I'll take care of it." She let Bollocks out first, then dealt with coffee. "No morning milking for you?"

"I took the evening, and have other duties."

"Didn't you sleep well?"

"Well enough, not long enough. After our . . . vigorous mating," he said, and made her snicker, "you went out fast and full, so I thought to read a bit of your book, thanks to Marco and not so much to you."

She said, "Hmm," and handed him a mug.

"I read later into the night than I planned. I had a taste before, when I saw some papers you left sitting out. But this was more, and from the start of it. I saw home in what you painted, and you used strong colors for it."

She took her time with her own coffee. "I started it before I saw Talamh. Or, before I came back. Before I remembered. I wrote the start before that."

"Because your heart remembered."

She looked at him then. "I think it did."

"The woman you have at the center of it, or it seems to me she's the center of it. She's not you."

"No?" Intrigued, she still left the question in the air as she went to the door. She wanted the morning, the bay, the mists, and the tender beginning of light.

"She's not, and I thought you might make her so, as why not, after all. But she's not."

He followed her outside, where the sun barely winked awake in the east and the mists rose over the water like shadows.

"She's stronger of will than you were then, at the start of things. And angry with it. She's younger, I think, still forming. Searching, as you were, but already aware of her powers. Or what she sees of them, feels of them. The one you have teaching her, that's not Marg, or me for that matter, but an old, cynical one. I like him."

"Why?"

"Because he's seen much and learned more. I like that he teaches her not because he wants to but because she pulls at what he was, what he feels he's lost, and what he may still become."

She took a slow sip of coffee. "It matters that you understand that, you saw that in them both."

"I'm not an eejit, after all. It's right there in the words."

"I wanted it to be."

"And sure it is. Stop fretting about it. It's annoying."

She had to laugh again. "It's different. For you, as much weight as you carry, there's dark and light, right and wrong, what is and what can't be. What I do, with stories? It's subjective. And it matters, a lot to me, that you liked what you read."

He circled his neck on his shoulders. "Sure I'll be paying for it, as I didn't get near enough sleep. You've a gift, Breen, that's the truth of it. Embrace it, respect it, as you do the craft."

She took another slow sip of coffee. "I'm working on it."

"You'll go soon, to your Philadelphia and New York."

"Soon. Unless you tell me I'm needed."

"I think you'll go, and you'll come back. You'll see your family, as is right. You'll do the business of your work, which is right, then you'll come back."

"I don't suppose you could go with us."

"I can't. I'm sorry for it."

"No, don't be. I understand."

"I am sorry. I liked your Sally, and his place, and the music. They serve good beer. If I could take a day away for that, with you, I would."

She watched Bollocks come out of the water and shake so drops scattered.

"He liked you."

"I know Brian would like, very much, to meet Marco's family— Sally, I mean, and the one he loves."

"Derrick."

"Aye." He looked down at her. "I would give him this if I could, but the time isn't right."

"Understood, completely. I'm going to see my mother while I'm there."

He said nothing for a moment, just watched the mists take on the light. "Then I'm all the more sorry I can't be there, and go with you."

She heard the regret in his voice, and it touched her. That sneaky kindness of his always would.

"No, it's something I need to do, myself, then it's done."

"You'll use the portal I made into your apartment. Meabh will leave it for that time."

"It's not necessary. I booked us into a hotel for the night, and we'll take the train into New York the next morning."

"Still, she'll leave it for you. You can use the portal in New York to come back."

"What? Wait. There's a portal in New York?"

He turned to stare at her. "It's an important city in that world. When you're ready to come back, Sedric will guide you. This is his gift, and he can bring you back through the Welcoming Tree. How do you not know this?"

"Maybe because no one told me."

He huffed out a breath, drank the rest of the coffee. "Sure I'm explaining now, aren't I? He'll come to guide you when you're ready."

"Great. I can cancel the train tickets from New York to Philadelphia."

"I'm after making the portal to Philadelphia a permanent sort of thing, so you can go when you need. I have to take it up with the council, and bugger that."

There it was again, she thought. That sneaky kindness. Now she turned, embraced him. "That's very considerate, thank you."

"It's efficient." But he wrapped around her in turn. "I have to go, the morning's wasting."

"Brian?"

"He has the day, as he starts night duty tonight. Breen." He cupped her face. "You'll speak to Marg and Sedric, as my time is crowded."

"Yes, I'll speak to them both today, tell them all we know."

"Good. You don't have to add the business about my ancestor and Dorcas."

Now she smiled, even batted her lashes. "Maybe I don't have to, but I will because it's excellent spilled tea."

"Bugger it." He kissed her anyway. Then strode off into the woods and toward Talamh without another word.

That, she thought, might be why she'd fallen so hard for him. He was, very simply, who he was. Light against the dark, right against the wrong.

She held the empty mug he'd thrust at her, finished off her own coffee.

And with Bollocks now at her side, watched the new day dawn bright.

With the workday done, Breen moved from bright to bright with Marco and Bollocks. The sky in Talamh was bluebonnet blue and nearly cloudless as the sun beamed on the fields.

"Now, this looks like a day and a half." Pleased, Marco put on his sunglasses. "It's almost warm on top of it. And there's a sight you don't see every day, unless you're us."

Morena, on the wing, sowed seeds in a freshly plowed field while Harken tamped them in. In another, young plants, greenhouse started, rose out of the brown toward the blue.

"They've had a busy morning."

"Maybe I'll give them a hand while you're at Nan's. Give me a lesson on what we're doing in our own patch. Still smells pretty strong," he added. "I guess you get used to it."

In the distance, Aisling and her boys worked their kitchen garden with the baby in a sling on her back.

"I'd say Aisling could use a hand more. Those two seem to have a rhythm going."

"Yeah."

As they crossed the road, Bollocks let out a greeting bark.

Hands waved, and the boys called out their own greetings that whisked away in the breeze.

"I'm gonna put on my Farmer Marco. Catch you later."

"And he'll have fun," Breen told Bollocks as she boosted over the stone wall. "Who'd have thought it?"

She wandered down the road, and yes, she could see a few more signs of spring in the green haze on the trees, a few brave wildflowers drinking in the sunlight.

"This'll make all four seasons for me, Bollocks. Just about a year ago now, my life changed. Marco's, too, as it turns out. That bus ride to my mother's to go through that ridiculous routine she insisted on. Sort the mail, open every damn window, water all the plants. The first time I saw Sedric. He made me so nervous. God, I was so unhappy."

She dropped a hand to brush over his topknot as they walked. "Honestly, I don't think I knew how deeply unhappy until I broke away from all of that. Until I finally found me. And you, of course."

When he wagged in agreement, she spread her arms wide as if to pull in all she had, all she knew, all she felt.

"Marco's right. This is a day and a half."

They made the turn to Marg's cottage, and she thought of the first time she'd walked this path. Still a little dazed at stumbling through the portal after the puppy Bollocks had been.

And the shock of recognition, and so many nerves, when her grandmother stepped into the open doorway.

It stood open now, a welcome. Delighted to accept, Bollocks dashed ahead. And Marg came into the doorway.

She wore her glorious hair bundled back. The rough trousers and frayed sweater told Breen she'd been at work, either indoors or out.

"A fine bright day for the gardening," Marg called out. "And haven't we just come in from it to have some tea, and here you are, back from the Capital."

"With a lot to tell both of you."

"Come in and sit. We've biscuits aplenty after yesterday's baking. And for you as well." She bent to pet Bollocks. "Always for you as well. The coat suits you perfectly, I see."

"You knew about the gift from Kiara?"

"She consulted me on it." Marg welcomed Breen with a hug and a kiss on both cheeks. "And sure don't you look as bright as the day?"

"I was just thinking how spring comes early here—or earlier than I'm used to. And with it I'll have seen all four seasons in Talamh, and Ireland. So many firsts for me, Nan. So I feel bright."

She moved into the kitchen, where Sedric, in baggy trousers, poured the tea. She greeted him as Marg had greeted her. He smelled of fresh earth and green.

"The first time I saw you, on the bus. Part of me must have known you, or had some inkling. It made me so anxious. You made that wind come up, so all the papers from the file cabinets scattered. So I'd find out about the money my father and Nan left me. My life changed in that moment."

"It wasn't the money itself so much."

"It didn't hurt. Jesus, we scraped by every month. But no, it was learning he hadn't just walked away from me. If it had just been the—literal—windfall, I wouldn't have come to Ireland. Without Ireland, I wouldn't have come here. So I'm feeling bright, even though I have a dark story to tell you. It's one Dorcas the Scholar told me."

"You went to Dorcas's cottage? Sedric, let's get this girl some tea and biscuits to wipe that part of the visit away."

She sat and let them fuss because she knew they enjoyed it.

In the cozy kitchen, with the windows open to the air and the fire keeping the air warm, she told them the tale, beginning to end.

"I marvel I've never heard a whisper of this before. Have you, Sedric?"

"I have, now with all this said." His silver hair gleamed as he bent his head, looked down at his own hands. "Long ago, a child myself. A story I took for frightening the littles, as I was, to behave, not to wander. I've given no thought to it since."

"This same tale?" Marg asked.

"Not the selfsame. It spoke of Odran, for even in my youth his name spread fears. But not of a demon, not that I recall. It was told to me and other littles by an Old Father traveling through. In this, he said Odran had been born out of dark magicks, a mother's pining for a son. And as in Dorcas's tale, she pampered and spoiled him and lifted him up high so he grew proud and greedy and, having the dark in him from the womb, embraced it.

"The demon mentioned only in that he learned from one, an evil one, the power gained in the drinking of living blood, and the pleasure of the taste of living flesh. He had a fondness, the Old Father said, for young meat, so hunted for the littles who wandered too far or refused to listen to their good mothers.

"In this way he feasted, year by year, in secret until the other gods learned of his crimes from a young witch who escaped his clutches. So they cast him out, and the mother, in her despair, threw herself after him, only to be dashed dead on the rocks of the Dark Sea."

He gave a ghost of a smile. "I had terrible dreams for nights after, with my own mother soothing me, telling me it was nonsense, just a tale conjured up to frighten children. So I believed, and now I think there was some truth in it."

"To do these things," Marg said slowly, "to consume another, and more, in a quest for power? The gods can be cold and they can be fickle, but this they could and would not forgive. A trust broken between worlds, and in those times to have cast him out but let him exist after such a crime? A trust that wouldn't mend easily. So the beginning of the end of the unity of the realms."

"That's what Dorcas said, and Keegan agreed. The beginning of the end."

"The demon in him makes him a demigod," Sedric pointed out. "As you are, Breen. He would not have this known, and this may be why the tale of it is obscure. His powers are diminished by what he took into himself. Not increased, as he craved, but diminished."

"So we're on more even ground?"

Marg shook her head. "It's never been so. You're the light to his dark. Dark may try to smother the light, and may dim it, even shut it off for a time. But light finds its way. He fears you because he knows this."

Rising, Marg went to the window, leaned out a little. "I think now drinking the power from my boy, my sweet babe, wouldn't have been enough. And I think what he would have done to my son if I hadn't waked that night."

"But you did wake." Sedric pushed away from the table to embrace her. "And you sent Odran back to the dark, so Eian grew strong. And his child sits here now, stronger yet."

"It's a weakness, Nan, and knowing it, we'll find a way to use it. There's more."

As she told them of Keegan's strategies, the plans for the cover of festivals, the aim to use the solstice, both came back to the table.

"The longest day," Marg noted. "The strongest light. He should know this as well as we, so it's a trap that must be well baited."

"My own Marg, he thinks us foolish and weak. But in the end, that's a mirror, his own reflection. The solstice is always celebrated across Talamh, but we have Breen here." With a glint in his eyes, Sedric patted Breen's hand. "A year, a way to mark this anniversary. Festivals, in her honor as well as the solstice celebration. I think he would find this irresistible."

"Is she the bait now as well as the key?" The moment she said it, Marg grabbed Sedric's hand. "Forgive me. I know you'd lay your life down for hers. A grandmother's weakness."

"No." He kissed the hand that gripped his. "Strength."

"It has to end, Nan. He has to end, and this may be the way, at least it may be the time. If he comes at us through every portal, and we don't end it there, when?"

She laid her hand over their joined ones. "If there's more to teach me, teach me."

"All right, aye, you've the right of it. There's always more, isn't there? And if this tale is true, the young demon girl, there's a path to explore. We'll take some steps on it."

"I'll find Keegan." Sedric rose again. "See if I can be of any use to him."

"You're always of use. Have a care, *mo chroí.*" Marg rose, kissed him.

When he left, Marg patted Breen's hand. "We'll go to the workshop then. I've things that might help the walk on this new path."

They started out, and as they approached the bridge, Bollocks sent Breen a hopeful look.

"Go ahead, splash away."

As he did, Breen hooked her arm through Marg's. "Don't worry, Nan. It's too pretty a day to worry. We'll explore," she decided. "And I have some good news—at least possible good news—on two fronts. The cookbook Marco started? Actually, it's more than a cookbook, with the little stories or anecdotes or music connected to every recipe. The agency in New York's very interested."

"Oh, this is grand news indeed!"

"It really is. And my agent read the book, and likes it. She thinks she can sell it."

"Oh! You've been here all this time and just now tell me!"

"It's not as important as—"

"Bugger that." Marg stopped on the bridge, took Breen's shoulders. "It's more than important. It's life, the shine of it. My granddaughter's a scribe, and our Marco a far-famed cook. I couldn't be more proud."

She held Breen tight. In the water below, Bollocks barked and swirled and shot water high.

Laughing, Breen looked down. And saw it.

"It's there. In the water."

"What is?"

"Just there. Don't you see?"

"I see only the dog, the water, the rock bed below, the little fish that swim. What do you see?"

"It's the pendant. The dragon's heart on a gold chain. So bright and beautiful. I've seen it before, but I keep forgetting to ask you. Don't you see it?"

"No." Marg's voice came soft and flat. "I don't see it."

"I . . . In the portrait, your portrait in the Justice Hall. You wore it. But I'd seen it before."

Struggling to pull it clear, she rubbed at her temple.

"I had a dream. I remember now. Before we left for Ireland, I dreamed I walked in the green light, the waterfall, the river, the moss. All so beautiful. And the pendant in the water. I wanted to pull it out, to take it out. It had to belong to someone. But I couldn't reach it, and I—I slipped. He kept me there, in a glass cage. I didn't know, I didn't know. I was drowning. I couldn't get to the surface, then Marco woke me."

She turned to Marg. "I dreamed of it."

"You never spoke of it."

"I kept forgetting. It's the oddest thing." Even now her head ached from trying to remember. "And—and after, after I came, I dreamed of it again, near the waterfall, in the river. I couldn't reach it, and started to slip. I couldn't fall in. I was so afraid I'd fall in."

Images circled in her mind, confusing, disjointed.

"But . . . Then I saw it, not dreaming. I went to the waterfall with Marco, the day I saw the shadow. But first I saw it again, in the water. Just out of reach. But . . . You wore it. In the portrait. It's yours."

"Not anymore, and not for some time. You see it there, in the stream?"

"Yes, I—" But when she looked again, she saw nothing but the dog. "It's gone. I saw it, but . . . What does it mean? Did you lose it, was it stolen?"

"No." Marg turned, walked away a few steps. And pressed her hands to her face. "Always they ask for more. Always more."

"Who asks?"

"The gods, the fates, the powers beyond us. Always more. I thought— hoped—what was given would be enough, and now they demand this last thing. This everything."

"I don't understand."

She turned back, weariness like a cloak around her. "Go to the farm for your horse, *mo stór*. I'll saddle Igraine. We'll ride to where you saw the pendant, in dreams and awake. And see it or not, I'll tell you what it means. Please, give me time to settle myself, and I'll tell you the whole of it."

"All right. I won't be long. Bollocks, stay with Nan."

Because she felt an urgency in herself as much as she'd seen her grandmother's weariness, she ran back to the farm. Then forced herself to slow to a walk before she came into view.

"Nan wants to ride," she called to Morena. "I'm going to saddle Boy."

"Save me!" Laughing, Morena clasped her hands together as she stood in the plowed field. "Take me with you."

"We're nearly done." Harken reached over to pull the brim of Morena's cap down over her eyes. "Another hour and I'll set her free. She'll find you."

She called to her horse, and because she knew she was distracted, took care with the saddle and bridle. She gave the fields a cheery wave and set off in an easy canter.

Marg and Bollocks waited for her at the head of the turn.

She told Bollocks where they meant to go so he could take one of his shortcuts.

"So I'll begin as we ride."

And still they'd ridden a quarter mile before Marg spoke again.

"It has no name, or none I've known, though some call it Fate's Mantle and others the Chain of Duty. It was forged from gold mined in these hills, and the stone, the heart stone, from the Dragon's Nest. A true dragon's heart, the heart of a great dragon—some say the first of his kind—upon his death, enspelled into a stone. Older than Talamh, it's said, a gift from the gods to seal the treaty between our worlds after Odran's fall."

"It has power."

"Great power, and a great price. The Fey closed it in glass, to honor the gift, and coveting it, as he covets all, Odran struck out from his world. The glass shattered, and the pendant was lost. Or so it was believed."

"You found it."

"I was not the first to find it. The gods were displeased by the loss, though it was Odran's greedy hand. There came a time of unrest until the treaty held again.

"So a coven of the Wise cast a spell to find the pendant, but no more to be closed in glass. They deemed whoever found it, lifted it from water, into the air, would wear it—if they chose, if they pledged."

"Pledged what?"

They turned the horses into the woods where the light spread green like the carpets of moss.

"Their loyalty to Talamh and the Fey, their respect for all the worlds and the laws in them. To stand for Talamh and the Fey in times of joy and in times of strife when strife might come."

She closed her eyes briefly. "And to give their life for Talamh and the Fey should it be asked. To give it willing, in the moment of asking."

"The moment of asking?"

"Not in the heat of battle, you see? But in that moment, a moment of choosing. All life over one life, all light over one light. To take it, lift it, wear it, and break this pledge will have all powers stripped from the one who breaks the vow. They may keep their life they chose as more precious, but all they are, whatever their gifts, die."

"You took this pledge."

"I did, and kept it. I would have given my life. I fought in battle, spilled blood, and shed it to defend the Fey and the worlds. Should the moment have come, I would never have hesitated. But not enough, no, not enough. They took you away from me, and still I honored my vow."

Marg dismounted, pressed her face against Igraine's neck. "Then it was my son's life lost. My precious boy. I wore it one last time, on the day Keegan took the sword from the lake. I wore it to honor the next taoiseach. And the night after I handed him the staff, I flew over the sea in the Far West and cast it in."

She straightened. "As others have, either in ceremony for the life given willing, or as I did, in grief for a life taken. Centuries might pass, Breen, before it shows itself again, and so I believed when I cast it into the sea. I never thought it would be now, it would be you."

"You dropped it into the sea, yet there it is." She pointed at the pendant gleaming under the clear green water.

"I can't see it. It's not for me. It was for me, a girl younger than you who walked not these woods but another, and in the stream where the dog splashed today, I saw it and knew it. I took it and pledged, and the very next day, I went into the lake with all the rest and lifted the sword. It brings change, it's said, it comes at times of great change."

She gripped both of Breen's hands. "You can leave it where it lies. There's no shame in that. We live by choice, and this is a choice. I would take it, wear it again if I could. I've lived my life. Yours has only begun."

"It has. It really has. A real life for me is not quite a year old. I fought, Nan. I spilled blood and shed it. But . . . it was the frenzy of the moment, kill or be killed. I've vowed to stand for Talamh, to do everything I can to defeat Odran and bring peace. And it's not enough?"

"It can wait for another."

Breen shook her head. "Before I came here, I dreamed of it, and the fear of dying. Did I remember it from childhood? Did you wear it, tell me the legend?"

"I wore it in battle, and for ceremony, not to bake biscuits for my granddaughter, or to tell her tales like this one."

"If it's my life, and I refuse to give it if—when—demanded, I lose everything. What I am. I don't want to die. I want to live, and write, and laugh. I want to have children and watch them grow. But I can't go back to being less."

"You'll never be less. Oh, *mo stór*, you've never been less."

"It's more than flicking on a fire, or casting spells. It's being a part of something."

When Marg gripped her hands, Breen felt the fear. In herself, in her grandmother.

"Leave it in the water, and lose nothing."

"It's mine," Breen murmured. "If I didn't feel that before, I do now. It's part of why I am, why I'm here, what I'm here to do. I'm afraid of it, of all of that, so I pulled back each time before instead of taking it."

She spun around. "He put me in a cage in this water. He'd have taken all I am. And because of that, all I am *was* taken from me for most of my life. So it comes to me here. You know that's why. You made the choice, Nan, made the pledge, a girl younger than me, you said. Her whole life ahead of her. But you took it because that's who you are. I can't be less."

She heard her own heart beating over the beat of the waterfall as she stepped to the bank, stared down at the pendant.

A choice, she thought. The choice. If she had to give her life, if it came to that, she'd had a year like no other. She'd lived.

She heard Bollocks whine and Marg sob once as she simply walked into the water. Reaching down, she closed her hand over the gold chain and lifted it and the stone free.

"I pledge my loyalty to Talamh and the Fey. I pledge my respect to all the worlds and the laws in them. I pledge to stand for the Fey in times of joy and of strife when strife comes. I pledge to give my life willing for Talamh and all the Fey should it be asked, in the moment of asking. All life over one life. All light over one light."

Trembling a little, she lifted the pendant high toward the sky, then draped the chain over her head. "If I break any of these vows, I'll lose my powers, my gifts. And I will deserve to."

Lightning cracked over the clear blue of the sky; thunder followed in a roar.

Then all stilled again as Breen stepped out of the water to take her weeping grandmother in her arms.

"Don't cry, Nan. It's mine. It's waited for me since they joined the stone with the chain. Everything Odran's done, through greed and thirst, ends with me."

One way, she thought, or another.

CHAPTER TWENTY-TWO

T hey rode back, out of the soft green light and into the bright.
"I would go by your father's grave site. A moment there, *mo stór*, for both of us."

"Yes, I'd like that, too."

Breen told Bollocks, but instead of dashing off, he kept pace with the horses and stuck close.

Breen felt the weight of the pendant, not merely the gold and stone but the symbol and the pledge. Would she grow used to it, she wondered, as she'd grown used—or nearly—to all the rest?

She lifted her face to the breeze as they rode. Today, she thought, the air held so much promise, and the earth offered the same with the scatter of starry white flowers along the roadside, the bold yellow of buttercups poking their heads above the green in the fields.

On the hills, mixed with the deep green of pine, she saw that tender wash where new life began.

She'd remember this day, she promised herself, for that, for all that as much as for what now hung around her neck.

She saw the ancient stone dance on the hill and the rambling spread of the ruins, now cleansed of the dark.

And she saw some black-faced sheep grazing close to the ruins as they hadn't before. She wondered if they came from the fields across the road, where a family had lost a daughter to her own weakness.

She dismounted, then tethered both horses before joining her grandmother at the grave.

The flowers they'd planted with love and magicks the summer before bloomed fiercely, and always would, Breen knew. The carpet of color spread over the grave of a man she'd had for so short a time but remembered so clearly.

"He's so proud of you. I feel that as I stand here. I feel his love and pride for you. When you were only hours old and your mother resting, I found him holding you and, though you slept content in his arms, singing to you.

"I have that memory of my son and his daughter, together in the light. A painting in my mind so vivid, Breen, and his voice through the painting so strong and clear."

"What did he sing, Nan?"

"Ah, an old, old song, and a sweet one of peace and beauty. A song of Talamh, and the light that comes with love."

"Will you teach it to me sometime?"

"I will." She took Breen's hand. "I gave you tears when I should have given you strength."

"Nan, you've taught me more of strength than anyone. You watched me when I was growing up. I wasn't strong."

"Stronger than you think."

"I gave in and gave up. I just never stood up, never fought back. I forgot how. You reminded me, and gave me the tools. This past year? It's been everything to me. I'd already chosen to stand for that, to fight for it. This?"

She closed her hand over the stone. "It's just the next step."

"They put such weight on you," Marg murmured. "I know this weight."

"Then you have to know, have to believe, I can carry it. Nan, you said you cast it into the sea."

"And that I did."

"But you have your powers."

"Never would I break my pledge. Never. I have fought, and will fight, will die willingly if it's asked of me. But they took my son when they could have taken me. And his child, taken as well to live unhappy on the other side? No, I would not wear this symbol.

"Had I known it would come to you, and damn the gods, I should have known, I would have worn it the rest of my days."

"It was always going to come to me, though, wasn't it?" She'd felt that, the certainty of that, as she stood on the bank, looking down at the pendant under the water. "All of this, everything, always was going to come down to me wearing this and all it stands for."

"I think now, aye, this is the way of it. They're cold, the gods, weaving their sticky webs."

"I have that in me, and I'm saying this as cold-bloodedly as I know how. I'll fight to live, Nan. I won't break the pledge, but I'll fight to live right up to that moment, if that moment comes."

Because he'd walked so far already, Breen called Bollocks up on Boy to ride with her. To ease his worry, because she felt it from him, she stopped by the bay when Marg rode home.

Two mermaids sat on rocks, combing their hair while a half dozen young played in the water.

"Go. They want to play with you, and I like to watch." Bending, she kissed him between his worried eyes. "I need the joy, too. Let's take the fun. I really want it."

So he ran into the water, where the young Mers welcomed him.

Watching the wonder of it, she leaned on Boy, felt his contentment in the breeze off the water.

"Daughter!" One of the mermaids, one with hair of gold and fire swirled together, called out to her. "Will you come closer?"

Breen walked to the edge of the water, then on impulse, pulled off her boots and waded into the shallows.

The one who spoke had eyes like deep, dark wells of green. "I am Alana, mother to Ala—and others who play here. Ala sometimes slips through to your side to play with the good dog in your bay there."

"I didn't know. I haven't seen her there. I didn't know that was possible."

"She's careful, and shy. Not with the good dog shy." Alana smiled. "The portal opens in the sea as well. We guard it for Talamh and for the worlds beyond. My sister Lyra wonders why you don't swim."

"I'm not dressed for it. And not as hardy as the Mers in water so cold. I like to watch your young swim and play."

"They have the curiosity about you." Lyra spoke now as she continued to run a luminous white comb through her ebony hair. "As do we all. I've traded with your friend, the human."

"Marco."

"Aye, and very, very handsome he is, for a human. He makes the young ones laugh with his jokes. He mates with the blue-eyed Sidhe, who is also handsome."

"Brian. Yes, they're pledged."

"A happy life to them. I will not pledge again for a very long time. My mate, a strong warrior, was taken to the Deep in the battle of the South."

"I'm sorry for your great loss."

"She tells you this," Alana put in, "because we see you wear the Mantle of Fate. You have pledged to give your life for Talamh, all lives above one, all light above one."

"Yes, I have."

Alana slipped a bracelet off her wrist. "We send these to you."

To Breen's surprise, the bracelet and Lyra's comb floated over the water to her.

The comb she saw now had tiny jewels crusted over the mother-of-pearl. The bracelet had polished stones, the palest of pink, between perfect white pearls.

"These are so beautiful. I have nothing with me to trade."

"You wear the pendant and took the pledge. These are thanks. We live our lives under the shadow of Odran. Our young live under that shadow. You have pledged to give your life if needed to lift that shadow. Daughter of the Fey you are, but your life lived on the other side. You have chosen, and we honor your choice."

"I'll treasure your gifts of thanks."

As if he knew it was time, Bollocks came out to her. She dried them both, put on her boots. "Tell Ala she's as welcome in my bay on the other side as she is here."

"And the Daughter will find welcome and protection on and in the sea for all the time of her life."

As she rode toward the farm, Breen thought, at least for a few minutes, the weight didn't feel so heavy.

She found Keegan waiting.

"You're late. Very late. Marco's already gone over to—"

He broke off as she dismounted.

"I'm sorry. There were circumstances."

He reached out, closed a hand over the stone around her neck. "Marg gives you this?"

"No. But she explained what it is when I took her to where I'd seen it before. First in dreams."

"Take it off. Give it to me."

She took a step back from the order and the angry tone. "You know better."

"I am taoiseach. The pledge is already mine, and so should this be. You'll give it to me, and all it asks."

"Taoiseach, as you've told me, isn't a king. I took it from the water, the river where Odran had once caged me in glass. I lifted it—by choice—just as you lifted the sword. I pledged, as you've pledged. How can you think so little of me to expect me to break that vow?"

He strode away from her, gripped his hands on the top rung of the paddock fence. "I knew better, from the start I knew. And yet. And yet."

He turned back. "I would not have this for you. You were rash. You should have spoken to me first. You should have told me you saw it in the water."

"I didn't remember. It kept slipping away. I think I was afraid so maybe I blocked it out. I don't know, but I did remember, and I chose. Not rashly, Keegan. I think . . . inevitably."

"Bugger that. Nothing is."

"Isn't it? Here I am, Keegan." She spread her arms. "When spring came to Talamh last year I was still miserable, afraid to reach for anything I really wanted. Only steps away from all that changing, but still. Now I'm here. You helped me awaken. Right here, on this damn stupid training field. You helped me become what I am. I made the choices along the way, and now I've made this one.

"It's mine, Keegan. If I took it off and put it in your hands, it would still be mine, and so would the pledge."

Emotions, all so hot, swirled in his eyes as he stared at her.

"I'd have it buried in the depths of the sea. The fates push us this way, that way."

"Maybe. Or maybe it's just life, forks in the road. You knew when I came here I might not make it through. You trained me to fight to give me a chance, even knowing the answer might be death."

"That was different."

"Why?"

"Because it bloody was." He gripped her shoulders, and she prepared for an onslaught of curses. Instead, he pulled her to him, held hard. "Can you see this leaves me without choice? If Odran somehow takes your life, what's left?"

"Talamh. I'm not just giving up, Keegan. Please don't give up on me."

He pressed his face into her hair. "If you die, I'll be very pissed off."

"Good. I'm going to do my best so you don't have to be very pissed off. It has weight, Keegan, but it also has power. I'll learn to use it."

He stepped back. "It's too late for training today. You'll train harder tomorrow."

He led Boy toward the paddock gate as Harken came out with a pail on his way to the well.

Something passed between the brothers—she saw that clearly. And Harken set the pail aside. "I'll see to Boy."

But he crossed to Breen first, his eyes on hers as he cupped her face, kissed it. "Nothing is written that can't be changed to read another way. Who'd know that better than you?"

"Come." Keegan grabbed her hand. "We'll get over before dark for a change."

With Bollocks leading the way, she started across the road. But glanced back at Harken, then up at Keegan.

"Tell me something I didn't think to ask until right now. Has anyone who's worn this lived a long and happy life?"

"Marg is alive and well as you know yourself."

"But lost her son. Don't bullshit around with me, okay?"

"Only two I know from song and story broke the pledge. Stripped of their powers, their gifts, stripping themselves of honor, their lives withered. Others, like Marg, lost not their life but one more precious to them than their own. And others fell."

"So death, dishonor, or the loss of someone loved." She crossed into

Ireland, then sat on one of the wide, sweeping branches. "I'm taking a minute."

"What Harken said is true."

"Okay, we'll go with that. And none of the others who put this on had god blood running through them. That should be advantage me."

He moved to sit beside her, but she waved him off.

"No, don't. Don't be kind and comforting just now. There's two ways this could go—I mean two most obvious ways. The first is all of this, from Odran's fall to now, skipping eons, to Nan falling for Odran's false face, having my father, and what followed that. My mother walking into the pub in Doolin the night my father, and yours, and Morena's, and their friend played. Her going to Talamh with him and having me. And all that followed that to me going into that same pub, and all the steps and choices since. All of that is one long, long story that ends with me giving my life to end Odran's, bringing peace to Talamh and saving the worlds."

"I won't accept that."

Her throat felt raw, as if she'd swallowed something jagged. But she did her best to think clearly and coldly.

"I'd rather not, but I've heard it said more than once the gods are cold and sly. But the other scenario—and I prefer it— is all I've just said, but the end remains largely true. But because advantage me, because there's the demon added in the mix, I use what I am, and whatever this pendant gives me, and end him. And live through it. Because there's been enough sacrifice and loss, and his time's just fucking up."

"I like that version a great deal more than the first."

"Me, too." She rubbed Bollocks, nudged him back so she could stand again. "I'd never really considered a tattoo. So not me—or the me I thought I was. But that day I walked right into that tattoo parlor and got this."

She turned her wrist over. "Why did I choose *courage*, why did I choose the Irish—and it turns out the Talamhish—word for courage? Maybe some part of me knew I'd need it to finish this."

"You'll be protected."

She nodded as they walked again. "You'd fight to protect me?"

"Aye, of course."

"You'd die to protect me and Talamh."

"I'm taoiseach—"

"The answer would be the same whether or not you'd lifted the sword. It's who you are as much as what. You'd die to protect me and Talamh."

"I would."

"Don't ask me to be less. However foolish it is, if I fear anything more than dying, it's being less. Don't say anything about this to Marco. I'm not going to tell him. He'll worry too much, and—"

Now Keegan stopped. "You'd lie to him? Lie to your friend, your brother?"

"Not saying anything about this isn't lying. I don't want to add this kind of stress."

"You'd shield him like a child? He's not a child. He's a man."

The words whipped out of him and took her back a step.

She'd seen him angry, but never quite like this. Not this hot, bubbling anger that didn't shout, but sliced straight through.

"Keegan, I—"

"You'll treat him like a man, by the gods, and with the respect he deserves. You'll treat him like the good man he is, or you shame him, and yourself. You make *him* less when you know how that cuts more than anyone."

She drew in a shaky breath, then rubbed her hands over her face. "You're right. I hate it that you're right. Not tonight, okay? Please. I don't think I can stand talking about it more tonight. And . . . I have people I need to speak with in America, and I need to think all that through, make some calls. Probably need to do some emails, and I can handle that part in the morning before he gets up. Then I'll tell him. When it's just him and me. It's better if it's just him and me."

She took the pendant off, slipped it into the pocket of her coat. "I'll tell him tomorrow, that's a promise. I'll tell him all of it because you're right. To hold back is a kind of lie, and worse, it makes him less. He doesn't deserve that from anyone, but especially from me."

She took a long breath as she saw the cottage through the trees.

"Do me a favor and keep him occupied while I go upstairs and make those calls?"

"Who do you call?"

"If I'm going to have the courage to do whatever I need to do, I need to have enough, and common sense with it, to make arrangements for if. I have a lot of money, my father and Nan saw to that. I need to make arrangements for it—it's important on this side."

"Make all the arrangements you like. You're going to live because you don't want to piss me off."

"That's absolutely the top reason I want to live."

It wouldn't be easy. She thought the conversations she'd had the evening before—broker, accountant, lawyer—had been fraught. Simply because it all struck her as so complicated. Telling Marco everything would be more fraught and more complicated.

In the morning, she read over drafts of legal documents, made changes or corrections, added a few things, answered questions, and shot emails back.

She thought she had a reasonable handle on it now, for a layperson, but expected it would take more rounds to firm it all up.

It all ate through the early hours of her morning. When she heard Marco in the kitchen, she waited awhile longer. He deserved to get some coffee in him, she told herself.

Finally, she read the word on her wrist and stiffened her spine.

"Hey, taking an early break?"

He wore an old sweatshirt with its sleeves cut off. She could see the tattoo of the harp on his biceps. He'd tied his braids up high on his head and padded around the kitchen in gym shorts and bare feet.

"How about I make you a good breakfast? Cheese and spinach omelets, some good thick Irish bacon, and some breakfast potatoes. Got some nice blueberries, too."

She wasn't sure she could eat, but admitted it delayed things enough to rewrite in her head—again—exactly how to tell him.

"Sounds amazing."

"We can get some fuel inside, then get to work."

She filled her role as assistant in the kitchen and listened to him talk about the upcoming trip to New York, about putting together another recipe or two for the proposed cookbook.

So excited, she thought as he worked. So looking forward to meeting in person all the people he'd worked with through emails and phone calls and Zoom calls.

He didn't know she'd bought tickets—orchestra seats—for a musical on the night they'd arrive. She held that surprise close.

"You nervous about the trip, my Breen? You're awful quiet."

"No, not nervous. Well, maybe a little about the book." No lie there.

"Waste of nerves," he declared. "We're going to burn that off with some shopping. New York City shopping. Been damn near a year since either of us did any serious-type shopping, and now we're going to do it in New York. You're getting a new outfit for meeting all these people."

"I have an outfit for that."

"Not a new one. Marco's Rules. Stores are open Sunday afternoon when we get there, and we're hitting them hard."

She argued about it because it kept them both occupied while they sat and ate.

She cleared and washed up—her rule—while he opened his laptop and started his workday.

Though she knew he really didn't want to go, she urged Bollocks outside.

Then she laid a hand on Marco's shoulder.

"I have to interrupt you. I need to get something, show you something, then talk to you."

He shoved the laptop aside. "You sound really serious."

"I know. Give me a second."

She went into her office, where she'd put the pendant next to the labradorite globe.

He'd closed his laptop, gotten each of them a Coke. And his eyes widened on the pendant she carried.

"Holy shit. Holy big-ass shit, Breen. That's . . . that's amazing. It looks old, in the high-class way of old."

"It's really old."

"Is it yours?"

"Yeah. It's mine."

"Put it on! I bet it makes that black sweater look like a frigging Oscar gown."

"Marco." She put a hand on his. "I need to tell you about it, what it is, what it means. I need you to listen and let me finish it."

The light in his eyes dimmed. "I'm not gonna like it, am I?"

"Just listen. Do you remember, the day you came home—we were leaving for Ireland—and I was having a nightmare?"

"Hard to forget that one. I thought you were having a seizure or something."

"I was having a dream. And it was about this."

She told him, and as she went through all of it, saw him fight the need to interrupt. To protest. She watched every emotion run over his face. Anger, fear, denial, grief.

When she'd finished it all, he got up, walked around the table. He went to the door, opened it for the dog, who waited, sad and patient.

He went into the kitchen, got a treat out of the jar.

"You're the best dog there is. Don't you worry."

Then he came back, sat, looked straight into Breen's eyes.

"You said you could've left it there, in that river."

"Yes, but—"

"That's a damn stupid thing to say. You never could. Not my Breen. All this bullshit about choice? It's not always true. Sometimes, and most times, it's just how you're made. Maybe you were afraid—who the hell wouldn't be? But when it came down to it, you picked it up and put it on. And you sure as hell didn't do that because it's pretty."

"Marco—"

"You just shut up a damn minute." Tears glimmered in his eyes, but he didn't shed them. And behind them lived heat. "I listened to you. I don't give a flying fuck what's written or not written, what some asshole gods say or don't. I know you. You got held down all those years, but you never let anybody down. And all that before you knew the truth. They're not going to beat you."

With the biscuit still clamped in his mouth, Bollocks came out to stand beside Marco. His tail whipped.

"You have to accept—"

"I don't have to accept a goddamn thing, and neither do you. You're a bitching powerful witch, a hell of a human being, and all the rest. And you listen to me, girl, and you listen *hard*. You're going to kick that psycho son of a bitch's ass, and after you do, we're going to fucking dance on whatever's left of him. Then we're going to live happy as all fuck after. That's not just what I believe. It's what I *know*. Now you'd better know it, too."

She let out a careful breath. "Of all I expected from you, it wasn't this."

"That's another stupid, and that's all you get. I believe in you, Breen. I believe in you."

It took a moment for her to compose herself enough to say the words. "And of all the things I needed to hear since I picked this up, you just said it. Okay, okay. We're going to win this."

"Fucking A."

"Okay, okay. Just need a minute, and I have to tell you some other things. I talked to the broker and a bunch of people after I got back last night."

"Is that what you were doing upstairs all that time?"

"I needed to make arrangements. All the money, Marco—"

"Come on, Breen."

"No, you come on. I've been thinking about it since I found out about it. A will—and it's just common sense. I mean I've hardly spent any of it, at least since I got here. And it makes more just sitting there. And now I have income from my advance on the next Bollocks book. I've been using that to pay you for all the work you do, but if I get lucky and sell the new book—"

"It's not luck."

"Whatever, that's more, and then the next Bollocks book, and anyway."

She had to stop, breathe, shove hands through her hair.

"I don't need all that money. I've been thinking about it, and after yesterday, I decided to get it going. A foundation sort of thing. I could put some of it into that, so I needed to talk to all the people who know how that works. I'm going to talk to Sally, too, because he's a smart, successful businessman.

"You're not saying anything."

"Because I'm listening."

"Great. So at first I thought a kind of grant or endowment or whatever the hell it's supposed to be for writers—people struggling like we were to make ends meet who are trying to write. Then I thought that's narrow and self-serving, really. What about somebody who wants to be a musician or an artist or an engineer or scientist or anything? Maybe they can't afford to go to college or they're working two jobs like you did. So I put some of the money into this foundation thing, and the people who know how to deal with that deal with it, and Sally, I hope, would help. It could change a life, like mine changed. And yours. Whatever happens, I want to do this."

She tried a smile. "I can still buy a new outfit in New York."

"Seems to me you need a website."

"Yeah, they said something about that, once it's all set up, and funded and we have a mission statement. And it started to make my head spin."

"Uh-huh. You gotta have a name for it."

"I thought . . . Finding You. I don't know if it works."

"It does. It all works. It's my Breen. You're my Breen, and all this you've had brewing? It's just another reason you'll be kicking ass."

"You're not upset about the will? It's just a practicality."

"Since you're not going to die, I don't care about that. It gives you peace of mind. Now put that on. I want to see it on you."

When she did, he studied it. "The stone got brighter."

"It did?" Frowning, she looked down. "I— It didn't before. It is brighter."

"Maybe that's because you didn't have me and this good dog here talking some sense into you. You're strong and you're going to stay strong. Now, since you're going to start giving money away, you ought to get in there and earn more. You only have a few hours left before we should head over."

She rose. "I wasn't going to tell you."

Shock just exploded over his face. "Say what?"

"I was wrong, and Keegan blasted me for even thinking about not telling you. Now I'm going to have to tell him, all over again, that I was wrong and he was right."

Marco stroked his goatee. "Is that gonna hurt some?"

"Oh yeah, but you know what? I'm strong enough to take it."

CHAPTER TWENTY-THREE

It would be one of those days, Breen thought. A bit cooler, off-and-on rain. And early training.

"We go from sword to archery," Keegan told her. "Morena, as you see"—he gestured toward the target where Morena stood with Marco—"will take Marco through the same, but in reverse."

Since Breen heard their laughter, she already felt cheated.

"They sound like they're having fun with it."

Keegan gave his usual shrug. "Morena's pleased I asked her to work with Marco, as Harken and Seamus are in the fields for shearing sheep."

Keegan put a hand on the hilt of his sword. "With me first, then with wraiths."

"Wait. Before we get started on my daily torture, I want to tell you you weren't just right about Marco, about me telling him."

Impatience shimmered, but she'd gotten used to it. "How was I wrong?"

"I mean you were right, but more, he didn't get upset, not the way I expected. He got pissed, said it was all bullshit and words to that effect. That I'd kick Odran's ass. And that he believed in me."

"People who expect less and to be treated as less often get less."

"That's one philosophy. And he told me to put the pendant on, and when I did, the stone went brighter. I felt it. I felt more from it."

"You don't wear it now."

"It's not something I'd wear for training."

"Wear it tomorrow, and we'll see. Now. Defend."

She held her own, for about five minutes. After the first time he killed her, she pulled out power. Her ears rang with the clash of steel, but twice she wounded him.

Before he killed her again.

"You forget your feet," he told her. "You forget the dance."

As he lowered his sword to lecture her, she spun, kicked up. Her foot nearly grazed his jaw as she followed through and impaled him.

Satisfying.

"You forgot your guard."

"Well done."

He conjured a wraith, stepped back to watch her form. The instant she defeated the first, he sent two. And when she fought them through a shower of rain, when fatigue had her form shaky and her sword arm ached, he sent three.

Lungs laboring, legs shaking, she felt the sting of a strike that grazed her arm. "Burn, you bastards."

They exploded into flame. Panting, she dropped to her knees. A demon dog whirled out of the air, charged.

And Bollocks leaped, sank teeth into its throat.

As it vanished, Keegan sent Bollocks a hard look. "That was for her to deal with."

Bollocks just wagged his tail and pranced over to lick Breen's face.

"We'll go again."

"You're past your rotation."

One arm hooked over the dog, Breen looked over to see Morena and Marco on a break. They sat on the paddock fence, nibbling biscuits as the shower moved off, as the sun brought a faint glow behind the layers of clouds.

"I could use a biscuit."

"The bow first." But Keegan reached down and pulled her to her feet. "You'll try your hand at wraiths there instead of targets. A moving target, we'll say, and one that can fight back."

Because she felt soggy, she dried herself off, then did the same for Bollocks.

"And no magicks for the first round."

"Why?" She had to bite back an actual whine.

"To test skill, timing, aim, strategy."

"Hey, girl. I gotta do it all that way." Marco jumped off the fence.

"Three bull's-eyes in the targets." Morena polished off the biscuit as she joined them. "And when we shifted to wraiths as Keegan wanted, my man Marco took two out of five."

"Show-off."

"I got skills, girl. Hey, Keegan, can I try a crossbow sometime? I could be like Daryl. You know, *Walking Dead* Daryl."

"Is this a story?" Morena wondered.

"Oh man, yeah. Totally wild. Breen won't watch it."

"I don't need to watch zombies chomping their way through humanity. But maybe I could try a crossbow. Buffy used one."

"To fight the vampires. She was the Chosen One." Morena stroked Breen's arm. "Like our Breen."

"Do as well as Marco, and we'll see about it. Enough talk, the day's wasting."

Breen rolled her eyes, started to follow him. It pricked at her skin, sharp, tiny needles. "Wait." She swayed with it, groping in the air for Keegan's arm. "Something's coming." Then as he turned back, took a step toward her, it struck her like a fist. "Something's here."

She might have gone to her knees, but Keegan caught her arms.

The contact brought it clear, and with the clearing, a knife to her heart. "The dragons! They're killing them. Do you see? Do you see?"

"I do now, through you. *Nead na Dragain!*" He shouted it. "Get Harken, get all the riders you can and any on wing. They're after the young."

"Lonrach." Terrified, she said the name, though she'd already called him in her head, her heart.

She saw Cróga first, a gold streak soaring from the west. The vise squeezing the breath from her throat didn't release until she saw Lonrach soar through the leaden sky.

Eyes fierce, Bollocks bounded onto his back. And knowing she couldn't hold him back, she mounted. She saw Amish streak by like a bullet, then she was rising up, flying east.

Defend, she thought, and prayed they'd be in time. She drew her sword with one hand, her wand with the other, and as they lost sight of Cróga in the clouds, put all her faith in Lonrach.

She could see nothing but gray.

Then, as she saw the first dragon fall out of the sky, her heart shattered.

Burned and bleeding, it dropped through the clouds. Lost, she knew, already lost. Beneath her, Lonrach sent out a scream of fury, one that echoed over and over as more dragons called.

Closing her eyes, she lifted both sword and wand.

"Part. Part and thin and sweep away to sea."

The clouds rolled away, stack by stack, layer by layer. But rather than the blue, they opened to streaks of red and black. Fire and smoke on the mountain where the dragons nested.

For one horrible moment, it seemed the entire mountain blazed. Then she saw it for what it was. The flaming arrows and spears hurling down, and the dark faeries who launched them, the pair of witches on the backs of winged demons who hurled down blasts of fire.

On Cróga's back, Keegan flew straight into them, while on the mountain, dragons answered with fire of their own as they fought to defend their young.

She saw another fall, struck by bolts of lightning as sharp as blades. She saw the red blood pour from open wounds, the black burns over the sapphire scales. And watched Keegan sever the head of a dark Sidhe as the attackers scattered.

Still too distant to use the sword, Breen imagined a bow, an arrow of power. She let it fly toward the witch and winged demon circling to strike at Keegan from behind.

Their screams joined the others, one short sound before they erupted into ash.

And with a bellow, Lonrach turned another attacker into a fireball.

More fell through the choking smoke, dragon and enemy.

She heard the roars, more dragon calls, from the east, from behind her in the west. With her eyes on Keegan, she would have missed the enemy flying up from below, and the flaming spear he prepared to launch at Lonrach's belly. But her dragon swept his tail, tearing wings and flesh, and sent Odran's Sidhe tumbling onto the mountain.

Banrion, Cróga's mate, crushed him underfoot, then trumpeted.

Lonrach soared up, and there Harken and Morena with him on

his dragon struck the second winged demon and sent it and the witch riding it onto the plateau. Dragons, young and fierce, leaped on them.

Cróga circled, and Keegan called out.

"Two fled—going east. You'll follow them, at a distance," he said to Harken. "See where they go and how they got past us to do this thing."

"Let me." Morena spread her wings. "They won't see me, and they'll expect a dragon to pursue." She lifted her arm, and Amish landed. "The murdering bastards won't see us."

"Aye, better. Go."

"Have a care." Harken reached up to touch her hand. "And come back to me."

"They won't see us," Morena reassured him, and flew east.

Breen looked down through the smoke, toward the cries of grief.

Blood, so much, and bodies. Some of the dragons barely bigger than the dog behind her. So many burned, bleeding, so still.

She took Lonrach down, jumped off. Already weeping, she knelt beside one of the young bodies, laid her hands on it.

A dragon, bleeding from wounds at the throat, burned near the back leg, limped out of the smoke. And growled.

"Let me help. Let me try to help. Please. I can feel his heartbeat, I can feel his pain. Let me try."

With the mother—she felt the mother's rage—watching her, Breen tried to heal. Arrow strikes—three. While he'd been playing with his nest mates. Burns from them scorching the scales, turning the green and blue scales black.

She called on all she had. If she could save one, even one, somehow.

Sharp pains, sharp and shocking. Hot breath over the skin, blowing down to bone. She let herself go, and swamped with grief, went deeper than was safe. But even one, and this one, even one. Light to light, heart to heart, power to power.

She felt him stir, felt him cry, not unlike a child might for his mother.

"Wait, wait, please wait." Even with her eyes closed, she felt the mother move closer. "I need more, a little more. I feel his heart, his strong heart now. His blood's on my hands, but inside him, it warms. I know it hurts, I know, I know, but it's almost done."

Her head fell back, and her breath came out on a long sigh.

"And I see you, I see you, Comrádaí, Finian's dragon, flying with him on your back. Flying over Talamh."

She opened her eyes and looked into his. "I know you, and I know your rider. But that's to come. Go to your mother."

He scrambled up, and his mother curled her tail around him. When her eyes met Breen's, Breen knew her heart.

Bolstered, Breen pushed up. If she could save one, she could save another. Then she saw Marg, cradling another of the young wounded. "Nan!"

"Some are lost, but not all. Keegan's sent for more healers, but I think it's for us. Any more to come will be too late. Do what you can, *mo stór*. Do all you can."

She healed three more young, working her way through the blood and ash until both covered her, until the taste of them coated her throat. She knew Keegan and Harken did what they could along with Marg, but the mewling of the young in pain, the cries of the adults in grief, tolled and clanged inside her.

She swiped at her face, then stilled when a dragon set a body, so small it had surely barely crawled out of the nest, at her feet.

She knew before she reached out its heart had stopped, and its light gone out. "I'm sorry." Weeping again, she gathered it into her arms and rocked. "I'm so sorry."

"Here now, here." Marg took the body from Breen, held it up. "Ah, Mother, I, too, have lost a child. I know your grief. It's my own."

As the mother carried her lost child away, Breen made herself stand.

"You can rest awhile," Marg told her.

"I hoped to save just one, but we've helped more. We can do more. The adults won't let me try to heal their wounds until we heal all the young that we can."

By the time other healers came, carrying potions and balms along with their power, they'd done all they could for the young. So she sat for a moment with Bollocks beside her, to gather herself to do more.

Morena walked to her with a skin. "Drink. It's from the Dragon's Pool and will revive you some."

Dazed, her mind as hazed as the air, Breen stared. "You're back."

"And so have been an hour. I left Amish watching while I came back to tell Keegan. He and Harken and other riders have gone to do what needs to be done."

"How did they get through, Morena? How could they have gotten so many through?"

"They have a camp in the high mountains, in the caves and well hidden, and well established. I'd say they've been there some months, and maybe longer. So not come through the guards, but already here and hiding out, with their witches conjuring shields and—what is it?—the camouflage. A good dozen of them from the looks of it, and the two that fled from here led me right to the camp.

"Drink now, Breen, and I'd say none of the dragons would object if you used their pool to wash."

She took the skin, drank deep. "That can wait. So many were hurt."

"We've more healers now, and I'm grieved to say no more of the littles left to help."

When Breen dropped her head on her shoulder, Morena wrapped an arm around her.

"Never have I seen such a horror as when I looked down at all this. May those evil bastards burn in eternal torment. Some were nestlings still."

"How many lost? Do we know?"

"I don't have the heart to count. But oh gods, Breen, Brian's Hero fell."

"No. No. No."

"Aisling's here, and she told me. Brian felt him fall, as a rider and dragon are bound. He felt him fall, one of the first, here as his mate's nesting. He fell fighting to protect the rest."

"What will he do? Oh, Morena." She pushed the skin back into Morena's hand and rose. "There's no punishment harsh enough for this."

Covered with blood and ash, she walked to the center of the plateau, then held up her hand. Waited, waited, then closed it around the pendant that came to her.

She draped it over her filthy shirt where it glowed like a bloodred sun.

"Odran the Damned, hear me!"

"*Mo stór.*"

She thrust out a hand as Marg moved to stop her.

"Hear me and know. Hear me and fear. Hear me as I stand on this ground bloodied and burned. On ground where magicks lived before you, and where they'll live long after. Hear my voice as it travels beyond this world and into yours."

And he did, she felt it, saw it. Saw him as he stood, his eyes black smoke, on the high cliff of his dark world. He reached for her, as if to draw her in, then jerked back as if burned.

"Feel my wrath and know I am your destroyer. For all your sins, time across time, I will exact payment. But for this, for this and this alone, I will make you burn. No dragon fire runs so hot as mine when it comes for you."

Around her, dragons stood, hovered, rose up, and watched.

"Hear me and know. Hear me and fear. Here me as I make this vow at this time and on this place: Even in death I will end you and all who stand with you. My light burns beyond this life, this body, and will see the black embers of yours turn to cold ash."

And she smiled as she saw the ground beneath him shake, saw the lightning—hers—crack like whips across his sky.

"See me and know. See me and fear. And in me you see your end. I swear it." She took the knife from her belt, drew the blade over her palm, then pressed her hands together. "And this I swear on dragon's blood and my own."

She lifted the bloodied blade high. Dragons rose up, a flood of color, of rage or grief.

And their cries boomed like thunder.

When she swiped the blade over her pants, sheathed it, Marg walked to her. Marg took her hands, healed the cut.

"You tempt him, Breen."

In that moment, her face glowed as fiercely as the pendant she wore.

"I *dare* him. Believe me, Nan."

"I do. Come now, we've done all we can. Others can finish. You should go back now."

"Not until every wound is healed that can be."

Dark had fallen before she walked with Bollocks through the woods toward the cottage. She'd had word, though not much of one, that Keegan had taken two survivors from the enemy camp to the Capital.

What would happen from there, she couldn't say. For now, she wanted a shower, as long and as hot as she could stand it.

"Go on, go take a swim." She bent down to hug Bollocks. "You're as filthy as I am. You were so good today, helping comfort the baby dragons. You have such a good heart. Take a swim."

She turned toward the cottage, and Marco opened the door.

"Breen."

Filthy or not, she rushed to him, gathered him close.

"I'm sorry. I'm so sorry. Is he here?"

"Upstairs." Marco's tears spilled onto her neck. "He won't eat. And I don't know if I found the right words. His heart's broken, Breen. I knew you were okay, because Morena flew back once to let us know what was happening. But Brian—"

"It's like losing a part of yourself, of your heart. I don't know how to explain. I felt such terrible fear when I saw the attack, before I felt Lonrach coming."

"Could you— Jesus, I can see you're so worn out, but could you . . ."

"You want me to talk to him. Another rider," she said with a nod. "Yes, of course I will. Bollocks is going to be hungry."

"I'll take care of him. He's hurting so deep, Breen."

"I know."

She went upstairs, not sure what she could or would say. But she tapped on the door, and opened it to see Brian sitting in the dark by the open window.

"It's Breen." She stepped in, closed the door. "I won't stay if you want me to go. I'm just so sorry." Taking a chance, she crossed to him to lay a hand on his shoulder.

He reached up, closed his around hers.

"I felt him fall, and part of me died. I felt him fly up, take arrows, flaming, using himself as a shield for the young. And falling, his great heart stopping."

Saying nothing, she laid her cheek on top of his head.

"So my heart stopped, for a moment. Just stopped like death. And I didn't want it to start again. But . . . it did, and I think it might not have beat again, but Marco's in it."

She came around the chair to kneel in front of him. "There are no words deep enough, Brian. I know that because my heart and Lonrach's are bound. You can be proud Hero died to save others, but that pride can't cut through the grief. Marco's heart and yours are bound, too, and still, a piece of yours broke today."

"Aye." He took her hand again. "He wants to comfort me, but that piece won't ever meld full. It's not meant to."

"No, it's not. But the rest of your heart, and all of his, will be strong again."

"How many are gone?"

"I don't know, but I know we healed many, saved many. One, so young, so badly hurt, I was afraid I couldn't help. But as he healed, I saw him. I've seen him before, in my head, and saw him as he healed. He'll be Finian's. Mahon's boy. And they'll ride, Brian."

"Truly?"

"Truly."

He nodded. "And the ones who did this evil thing?"

"Dead, all but two. Keegan took them to the Capital."

"They'll face Judgment. One day, I might feel that's enough. One day. But this day, nothing could be. Lonrach? I didn't ask."

"He's fine. He's all right. He's—"

"Is this their blood?" he murmured as he touched her face. "Dragon's blood?"

She nodded. "Healed," she began, but tears began with it. "Most, I think, most."

"What's this now?" He wiped at her tears, at the blood and soot.

"Sorry. I'm just tired. I should—"

But he gripped her hands again, and the tears wouldn't stop.

"So many. There were so many. We couldn't help them all. And I held one, so small, and gone, gone while his mother looked at me, hope dying out of her eyes. And when they cry, when they cry, Brian, it sounds like a thousand hearts breaking."

He slid down to sit on the floor with her, so they held each other, wept together.

In the Capital, Keegan stood with his mother, his brother, with Mahon, with the council as the sea thrashed below. He'd learned all he needed to learn from the two, a male and female Sidhe, he'd taken alive.

"You lived like vermin in the caves of a world you betrayed. Near to a year now, so you say, stealing from the farms, from the villages. You fought against and killed your own kind in the battle waged here, then slithered off again to your caves to plan and plan what was done this day. Twenty-six dragons, twenty of them not yet grown, slain."

"Odran commanded it, and Odran is god of all."

When Keegan flicked a glance at the female, she sneered. It burned in him she had the gall to wear a warrior's braid.

"He will burn you out as we burned the dragons this day. This glorious day! This is not your Judgment, Taoiseach, but Odran's. And even this is not the place you sit in your chair and pretend to have power over any."

"You have confessed your crimes. Though I'd call it bragging. But no, this is not Judgment, this is not the Judgment of the Fey. For there is an older law. The Dragon's Law."

The male's eyes went wide. "We are of the Sidhe, and we demand the Judgment of the Fey. We choose banishment."

"You are of Odran, and have rejected your tribe. You are no longer recognized as Fey, and your crimes, your sins are against the dragons. We stand by their law on this. We give them this respect."

He brought down the staff. "So it is done."

The male dropped to his knees, shouting pleas for mercy while the female spewed curses in a voice that shook with fear.

They'd chosen Hero's mate. Keegan recognized her as she arrowed down, as his mother reached for his hand.

Hers shook once, then steadied as the dragon shot her fire.

It was quick, and Keegan supposed that was a mercy. From flesh and blood to ash in seconds.

And the dragon let out a cry that still rang with grief before she circled over the sea and flew west.

For a long moment, no one spoke, then Tarryn stepped forward.

"The Dragon's Law, though not called on in my memory, is sacred. We have held to it. Let it be known Talamh will have a week of mourning, and the banner will fly at half-staff for a fortnight."

"They earned their fate." Flynn stared at the charred ash. "Though I hope never to see such a thing again."

"I'll take the ash to the Bitter Caves."

"No." Harken put a hand on Keegan's arm. "I'll do it. It's enough you've dealt with. And I want my own bed tonight. I'll see to this, then go home. You'll be needed here, and I'll see the valley knows what's been done."

"All right then. I've some arrangements to make. I'll be sending for any rider who lost their dragon. There must be acknowledgment, and comfort given, such as it is."

"Safe journey, darling." Tarryn kissed Harken's cheek. "Come now, Keegan, come now, the rest of you, come inside. We'll lift a cup to the lost."

But Keegan remained a moment longer, looking out at the lash of the night-dark sea.

CHAPTER TWENTY-FOUR

On the final day of mourning, all of Talamh stood in the fields, on the hills, on the mountaintops and villages. They gathered as families, as neighbors, as tribes united with one purpose.

To give tribute to the lost.

Dragons of every size, of every color and age, streamed across a sky that held its spring blue. A tribute of its own. They flew, those who had flown for centuries and hatchlings barely fledged, from north to south, south to north, west to east, east to west, their shadows touching every part of Talamh.

And they flew in silence.

And in silence, like all riders, Breen rode, circling the land below. In a gesture she hoped showed respect, she wore the pendant, the diadem given her by the Trolls, and the mermaid's bracelet.

She saw Keegan on Cróga, the dragon's heart on his staff gleaming. And Brian, mounted on Hero's mate for this last solemn journey.

Nothing spoke but the wind, and she knew the land and seas below held equally hushed.

This was reverence.

The young dragon she'd healed and would one day be Finian's flew beside his mother in formation with his nest mates who'd survived. Mothers and sires carried the bodies of their children, and others formed lines to bear the great bodies of their dead for this final flight.

Over the green, the sky filled with the golds, scarlets, sapphires, emeralds, ambers, and silvers. Marg rode, and beside her flew the dragon that had been her son's.

Breen felt Lonrach's heartbeat as her own, as he felt hers. And this, she knew, was comfort.

As the sun lowered in the west, they flew toward it, and finally out to sea.

They would fly, Marg had told her, farther than any boat traveled, to Eile Dragain, an island of stone. To this sacred place where no one walked, the dragons took their dead to put their remains to the fire. To let the wind carry their ashes across the sea and to their rest.

The sea rolled below, empty, it seemed, toward the far-distant horizon. Above that horizon, the sky went as brilliant as the dragons themselves, as the falling sun painted the blue in vivid reds, shimmering purples, striking golds.

Eile Dragain rose up from that rolling sea. What she'd first taken as a kind of mist became solid, gray and wide, with sharp juts of mountains like towers.

In the sea around it, beyond the thrash of waves against rock, Mers waited.

Lonrach circled with others as the bearers placed the dead on the island.

So many, she thought, and some so small. She saw the one she'd held in her arms, unable to save. And grieved again as she and other riders dropped a tribute of flowers onto the bodies and the stone.

When the last body was placed and the bearers rose up to join the circling dragons, the Mers sang.

It sounded like heartbreak and carried into the air, over the sea, across the island of stone where no one walked.

Voices soared, and on the sea, Mers spread more flowers that floated on the deepening blue water.

As those voices slowly faded, as the last arc of the sun slipped away, the dragons, as one, released a single, deafening roar. And the world quaked with it.

Fire followed.

Great billowing bellows of flame speared down so it seemed the whole of the island turned to fire, burning the stone red. The heat of it coated her, and the rise of smoke came pure white, another tower rising, like the flames that licked the air.

Ash spun up, embraced by the wind that carried it away.

When it cleared, the flame and smoke and ash, there was nothing below but the stone and its towering mountains.

The dragons circled once, twice, a third time, then flew toward Talamh as the first stars woke in the night sky.

The land held quiet, more reverence, when Lonrach came down on the road by the farm. For a moment, Breen lay on his back, stroking his scales. When she dismounted, she walked around to his great head, looked into his eyes.

"Call me when you're ready. We'll fly when and where you need."

He turned his head to look at Bollocks, who sat on the wall with Morena.

"Yes, of course. He'll come with us."

She stepped back, and Lonrach rose up. With a spread of ruby wings, he flew into the night, toward the Dragon's Nest.

"Never in my life have I seen such a thing, nor has anyone."

With a nod, Breen walked over to sit on the wall with Morena, and Bollocks between them.

"Nan told me this was a first in her memory. That when a dragon dies, it's taken in private."

"Aye, but this wasn't a death of great age or in battle. This was . . . well, it's beyond my words what it was. The tribute was beautiful."

"It was."

"They went bright. You could see the fire all this way, and I swear, not even the littles made a sound." She glanced behind her. "Harken needed a walk, and on his own—well, with his other wife, as that dog wouldn't leave him. His dragon lost a nest mate, and he feels it. I know I can't in the same way, so he needed a walk on his own."

Breen took Morena's hand, found comfort, gave comfort.

"It may not be in the same way, but everyone in Talamh feels it. They know that, the dragons. I think that's why they allowed us to be part of this."

"I think the same. And gods, Breen, though beautiful, I hope to never see such a thing again. I should tell you Marco's gone over with Brian. I saw Keegan fly east on Cróga. You're welcome to share the evening meal, such as it is, with us."

"I think Harken will need you when he gets back from his walk. I could use a walk myself. Bollocks and I will take our time going back to the cottage."

"I'll go in and wait for him. He waited for me, after all, and for more than the time to take a walk."

Scattering lights ahead, Breen took her own walk. "I know you'd have gone with us today," she said to Bollocks. "And I know Lonrach would have liked it. But it just wasn't allowed this time. Next time we go up, it'll be the three of us."

She'd never forget the sights and sounds and feelings of this day, she thought. All those hearts beating, and all the hearts that never would again.

When they came out of the woods, she walked down to the bay. While Bollocks swam, she sat on the shale, studied the stars and the thumbnail moon.

What comes next? she wondered, and wished she could see. But she'd looked in the fire, searched the labradorite globe, and nothing showed itself.

She'd seen the attack too late to save those who'd gone to their rest today. How could she have this power and duty, and still not see before it was too late?

When Bollocks came out, she dried him. Then he sat with her awhile longer, looking out over the water and up to the stars.

Inside, Marco waited alone.

"Brian?"

"He just went upstairs." Marco came over for a hug. "You know when we went to the Leaving at the castle? I thought I'd never see anything more beautiful and heartbreaking. Today I did."

On a sigh, he gave her a last squeeze. "You need to eat."

"I will. Go upstairs, be with him."

"I will. It was hard for him. For you. For everybody, but the riders especially. I get that. But I think he's better. I think today helped. He ate some, and he told me he felt Hero found peace. That he gave his life to protect others, and found peace. And . . ."

He slid his hands into his pockets. "I told him how I'd stay when you went to New York."

"We could put the trip off," Breen began, but Marco shook his head.

"He said no. And I mean he said no fucking way no. Got a little, you know, miffed with it. I was going with you, and stop being a git about it. He reminded me about Sally, and the birthday present."

Now Marco smiled. "So I know he's doing better, because he got miffed, and he's really damn proud of the present."

"He should be—proud, not necessarily miffed. Go on upstairs. Bollocks and I are going to have our dinner and call it an early night."

Since Marco wasn't there to scold her, she got her laptop and worked as she ate. She wanted to write down her impressions and thoughts on the day. Nothing she could use for the blog, she reminded herself. But maybe one day in a book. Or just something to remind her, if and when she needed it, what they fought for, what they fought against.

She tidied the kitchen, then worked a little longer, drafting out a blog for the next day. It would save time in the morning, so she could work more on Bollocks's next book.

"Fallen behind on that," she told him as he curled by the fire. "I guess I'm not going to have it finished by New York. And I shouldn't be thinking about the next fantasy novel when I haven't even sold the other. But it's starting to push some. I guess that's a good thing."

She put everything away, retrieved the globe from her desk. She liked setting it beside the photo of her father and his bandmates when she went up for the night.

"It's late, but I don't think I can sleep yet." As she closed the bedroom door, Bollocks went straight to his bed and his little stuffed lamb. "I guess you can."

She lit the fire for him, then put away the pendant and the rest. After she'd changed, she picked up the book she'd borrowed from her grandmother, one full of stories on Talamhish lore.

She needed to know more.

She hoped reading would tire out her mind to match her body. Instead, the stories engaged it, and had her turning page after page.

When Bollocks's head shot up with a soft woof, she was on her feet in a flash. One had reached for her sword, and the other lifted to grip power.

Keegan opened the door and stepped in. "Not sleeping then as you should be. It's very late, and you've training tomorrow."

She hadn't spoken to him in days, but couldn't find her annoyance with the greeting. Not when he looked exhausted.

"I didn't expect you."

"I needed to break away from the Capital." He didn't come to her, but walked to the windows, threw them open as if he needed air. "You rode well today, Daughter of dragons."

"I— What?"

"They call you that now. Daughter of the Fey, of man, of gods, and now of dragons. I wasn't there to see you call on Odran, to hear your vow, a blood vow at that, as you stood in carnage. They say the ground quaked even as he did."

He glanced back. "And did it? Did he?"

"Yes."

"So now they call you this."

"Who does? I—"

"Well, the dragons, of course. I told you I can call them, and so it seems, they can call me. So hearing this, I knew what should be done today."

He took off his sword, stood it beside hers.

"It was beautiful. It was right."

"As right as it could be. You taunted him." Now he reached out, touched his fingertips to her hair. "I've yet to decide if it was brave or foolish, so think both at once."

It rushed back into her, the sights, the smells, the feelings.

"Their blood was all over me, Keegan. I held a dead baby in my arms and watched the light in its mother's eyes go dim because I couldn't help. And I couldn't stand it."

"What about the prisoners? The two you captured?"

He turned away, and back to the window. "Dragon's Law."

"I don't know what that is."

"Quick, cruel, final. Could I have stopped it? I don't know, and never will. But had I tried? At what cost to the bond we have, at what price the dishonor to the dead? Suicide it was for them."

His voice snapped out now, full of anger and disgust. "In Odran's name, for no reason but to demoralize the Fey. A dozen or so, with their pair of sorcerers against dragon fire and claw? The dragons would have rooted out any who survived, as they'd have no way to break out of Talamh. They struck at the young, as that is the most pain for all."

"What's Dragon's Law?" she asked again, though the way her heart thudded in her throat, she thought she knew.

"Death. Death by dragon fire."

Shaken, she sat on the side of the bed. "Is it because I asked you to promise not to open the portal for banishment? If I—"

"It's not, no. This law is older than Talamh and ours. It's done."

More weight for him, she thought, and rose. "I held babies, burned, bloodied, and too many beyond what we could do to save. I held Brian when he wept for Hero. This, all of it, sits at Odran's feet, Keegan, not yours."

"I hold the staff," he said simply. "And it's done. I thought as I watched how it is they'd never understand that Odran doesn't think of them. Their deaths are nothing to him. He sent them to their death. I know this. They've hidden in the misery of those caves all this time, and for their trouble, he sent them to their deaths."

"He won't win."

"I hold to that." He sighed again, nearly smiled. "Daughter of dragons."

She went to him, and when she took his hands, he gripped hers tight. "You should eat. I can warm up—"

"No, no. I don't yet have the stomach for it. I felt them cry—this gift I sought—so I felt them cry, every one, as they laid their brothers, sisters, children, mates on that stone as the sun set. I won't forget the sound of it. I don't have the stomach for food, or even ale. I need to sleep, and I wanted you beside me."

"Then come to bed."

He nodded, then sat to take off his boots. "Your father's dragon flew beside Marg today. It's said since Eian fell, his dragon only flies at night, and spends his days on Eile Dragain, waiting for his own end. But today, he flew in the sun."

"I saw him, and knew him. I'd seen him, with my father riding him, in visions."

She looked at the photograph, her father, Keegan's.

Beside the photo, images began to swirl in the globe.

"Keegan, come and see."

"I've seen the photograph, and it's a fine memory."

"No, in the globe. Shadows are moving, clouds clearing. Do you see?"

He came to stand beside her and look. "I only see the globe."

"There's movement. There's dark and light. Voices—there are voices. Someone's screaming. Can you see?"

He took her hand, linked their fingers. Through her, through the globe, he saw as she did.

Fire roared in the hearth and shot light, broody red, over a bed fashioned with gold posts and silk bedding. Candles burned throughout the chamber with its windows facing the night.

The sea thrashed beyond, a violent, angry sound like the screams and curses of the woman who thrashed on the bed.

Shana beat her fists in the air, clawed at the silk. Her face twisted to wring out every ounce of beauty as she screamed.

"Get it out of me! Get this thing out of me!"

A woman, her hair knotted on top of her head, a collar around her throat, knelt between Shana's legs. Her face bore the raw scratches from where Shana had raked her nails.

"It's turned wrong yet."

Yseult, eyes cold, face set, stood watching. "It's too soon. The child must stay inside her."

"Her waters have broken. I can't stop what will come." Pain rippled over her face when the single stone on the collar pulsed. "Whatever you do to me, I can't stop what will come. I can only try to turn the child in her womb. It damages her. You can see!"

"Give her more poppy," Yseult ordered a young girl who stood near, trembling.

"Be careful with it," the midwife ordered. "You mustn't push now. You mustn't. It will hurt her," she told Yseult.

"Do what must be."

"I'll kill you!" In her rage, in her pain, Shana struck out at the young girl. The cup flew from her hands, and blood trickled down her cheek where Shana's ring sliced flesh. "I'll kill all of you, and Odran will crush your bones. Get it out of me!"

"Hold her down," the midwife ordered. "Yseult, if you would cut her pain with your great power, or give her a few moments of sleep—"

"Birthing is blood and pain. Do what you must."

The screams, the horrible screams turned inhuman as the midwife reached inside Shana to try to turn the child. She let out a cry of her own, drew back a hand gashed and dripping blood.

"It— There are claws. It rips her."

"You, you, hold her down, do you hear? You, go tell Odran his child comes. And you?" Yseult moved closer, closed a hand around the midwife's throat. "Birth this child or die."

Screams ripped and tore the air. Shana's hair, gray and matted from sweat, fell around a face tortured with pain.

It took four to hold her down as the midwife worked.

Still she cursed, used every breath to damn them all, to damn the thing fighting to be born.

"It's turned!" Dripping with sweat and blood, the midwife hunched over Shana. "Push now! Push."

Instead, Shana lay laughing. "Dead, dead, you're all dead. I bathe in your blood."

But it was Shana's blood staining the silk as the midwife reached in, fighting to help the child along. "Push now, push, lovey. Yseult, I beg you, help me. I can't do it alone, and she has no strength left."

Yseult moved to stand over Shana, looked down into mad, glazed eyes. "Push this child into the world." She held her hands over Shana's distended belly. "Bring it to life."

Baring her teeth, Shana lurched onto her elbows. Screaming again, screaming as she pushed.

"I have the head, hold now, please, Yseult, have her hold now."

The head, coated with blood, showed eyes slitted and swollen, a mouth in a grimace where fangs, short and sharp, snapped.

"Gods have mercy," the midwife murmured, then cried out as her collar shot pain into her.

"There is no god but Odran. Now bring his child forth."

It squirted into the midwife's bloody hands, small enough to cup in them, with a body twisted like rope. It let out a weak, mewling cry as its clawed hands scrabbled.

On the bed, pale as death, Shana let out a laugh, a low rumble that sounded like the madness in her eyes.

"He breathes," the midwife said, "but not, I fear, for long. I must cut the cord, deliver the afterbirth. She needs tending or she will die as well."

"Give me the child."

The midwife's hands shook when Odran spoke from behind her. And with those trembling hands, she cut the cord, and held the child up to Odran.

He stared down at it. "There is no power in this. Only sickness, deformity, and death. Can you change that?"

Yseult stepped to him, studied the child lying in his hand. "He won't live through the hour, and is beyond my powers."

"And what of her?"

"She will never conceive another child."

"Can she be healed enough to live?"

Yseult looked back at Shana and the midwife.

"She has lost much blood," the midwife said, "and the birthing caused much damage. I can do only so much alone. With help she may live, but . . . it will take time, my lord Odran. And much work."

"I wish her to live, for a time. See that she does."

As he stepped back, Yseult hurried to him. "My lord, my liege, my all, of what use can she be to you now, barren and mad?"

"She has uses in her madness. Make her strong in body, Yseult."

"I will do what you ask, but it may take weeks. She is very near death."

"Make her strong, and find a way, when she is, to send her back to Talamh."

"All that you wish, all my powers can give, but—"

He closed a hand over her throat as she had done with the midwife. Red glinted, just for an instant, in the gray of his eyes.

"Did you cause her to grow this thing I hold, to die birthing it?"

"My lord, I would never harm what is yours. I brought her to you.

I will do all in my power to do what you ask of me. I will always serve you, and only you."

"Then make her strong. She has entertained me these past months and been of use. So I will grant her fondest wish. A final wish."

"My lord."

"She will go back and kill the one who turned from her. The one who betrayed her. She will kill the taoiseach. And with his death, the child of my child will come to me."

He looked down at the small, twisted thing in his hand. "Its blood is dark, weak, and without power."

He cast it into the fire, and left while Shana lay giggling.

In the cottage, Breen took a step back, then another, another, until she found the side of the bed. She lowered herself slowly.

"Oh God. Oh God." When Bollocks planted his feet beside her, she buried her face in his fur. "He—he threw it into the fire like, like a brick of peat."

"Stay with her." He went out while she clutched the dog and trembled.

When he came back, he pushed a glass of wine in her hand.

"Whiskey would serve better, but you don't have a taste for it." Since he did, he drank from the glass of whiskey in his hand.

"You saw? You saw all of it?"

"Aye, and heard. I've managed to avoid witnessing any birthings, but I think if that was the way, there would be no second child for any."

"I've only seen one—Kelly's—and only part of it, but I can say, absolutely, that's not the way."

"You said before what was in Shana was wrong and dark and damaged."

"Yes."

"You had the right of that, and from what we saw, I think it wasn't the first of his to be so wrong."

Her body shook, and the heart inside it trembled.

"He only wanted it for the power. He had no feelings for it."

Keegan sat beside her. "Odran has no feelings for anyone or anything but power. You know this."

"I know it, but to see him—his own child." She drank a little wine, then a little more. "We have to end this, Keegan. The suffering, the cruelty. The midwife, one of the Wise, kept as a slave. Her hands, what it did to her. What they've done to her. It has to end."

"Shana. Will she live, do you think?"

"They seemed to think so. But I think there was too much blood loss, too much damage to heal her by means of light. I think Yseult will use dark magicks. Oh God, more sacrifices. To kill you. God, Keegan, to try to get her back here to kill you. We can't let her come back."

But he sat, coolly, and obviously considering. "It wouldn't be the easiest thing, on any part of it."

"She's crazy, and probably crazier after this, and after whatever they do to keep her alive. Make her strong, he said. You have to be careful. You have to have protection. I'll cancel the trip to Philadelphia and New York. We'll—"

"You'll do no such of a thing."

She rounded on him. "Do you think I'd leave when he's beefing up an insane assassin to kill you?"

"I think I'm well able to defend myself against such as Shana."

She fisted her hands in her own hair and had to resist the urge to tear it out.

"Did you hear him? Her fondest wish, and he's right. He's smart enough to know she wants you dead more than anything else."

"I'd say you rank high on her list as well."

He spoke easily, the leader of the Fey, gauging his ground, judging his enemy.

"So we'll all have a care, as she's mad enough to go against him and try for you again. Weeks, they said, in any case, and what I saw? I'm not altogether sure even with magicks dark and light they'll heal her body enough. And don't you think we saw what we saw so we'd be prepared for it if they do?"

"Yes, I do, which is why I'm staying."

"You're not. I'm taoiseach and a warrior and of the Wise. I know the enemy, Breen Siobhan, and very well. Mad she is, but no warrior. And if you think a mad elf could get the better of me, well, I'm insulted. Add to it, you'll be gone for a handful of days. What we'll do is tell those who need to know there's trickery expected at a portal. A pity we don't know which they'll use, but we'll keep an eye on all."

He gave her an absent kiss on the forehead. "Finish your wine and steady yourself."

"Damn it, I'm steady enough."

"You are. You don't flutter about as long or as much as you once did."

"I never fluttered about. And you're trying to annoy me so I won't argue with you."

"Arguing about it just wastes the time, and we need some sleep." He set his empty glass aside. "Trust me on this. I expect your trust."

"It's not not trusting."

He kissed her again, then rose to strip down. "You can worry a bit. But not too much. Too much goes back to being insulting."

"You're not invulnerable, Keegan."

"Witch, warrior, dragon rider, taoiseach against a mad elf who never fought in a single battle."

"She killed Loren."

"Because he loved her. I don't. Go on to your bed," he told Bollocks. "I've got her now."

He took the wine from her, a glass still half-full, set it aside. Then just plucked her up, laid her down.

"Do you know what Han Solo said to Luke Skywalker?"

"I like those stories." He pulled her over so her head rested on his shoulder. "Which thing? 'May the Force be with you'?"

"No, but you can have that one, too. He said, 'Don't get cocky.'"

He laughed and rolled on top of her. "Now you've challenged me and my cock, so sleep has to wait a bit more."

CHAPTER TWENTY-FIVE

Worry didn't help, but it simmered under the surface in the days that followed. And when it bubbled up, she tried, through the globe, through the fire, to see more.

But Odran's world stayed in the shadows even as April burst and bloomed.

She packed as carefully and lightly as possible, reminded herself they'd be gone only a handful of days. But those days held a party at Sally's, meetings in New York.

And her mother.

"I just can't take you," she said as Bollocks continued to sulk. "And you know you'll have a good time with Nan, with Brian, with Keegan. And you'll spend time at the farm with the kids and Mab and Darling."

When he just lowered his head, she sighed. "Honestly, it's only three days."

Keegan walked into the bedroom as she added just one more thing to her jammed suitcase.

Surprised, and guilty, she flipped down the lid. "I thought I'd see you on the other side."

"Marg gave me a look."

"A look?"

"A look that said I should come haul your bags over for you." Now he gave her suitcase, laptop case, and shoulder tote a look. "Three days, you said. Not three weeks or a month or half a year."

"I have . . . activities. Varied activities that require different clothes. You can bet Marco's got at least this much, so don't start."

"He can haul his own, or have Brian do it."

"I could just, you know." She waved a hand. "Send it."

"You could, but I'm here, as magicks don't always need to stand for muscle." He lifted the suitcase she'd zipped closed. "Which is needed. Do you pack stones to take back for souvenirs?"

When you had clothes you actually liked, she thought, it was hard to decide exactly what to pack. So rather than answer, she lifted the tote and her laptop.

A year or so before, she considered, she could have packed using the tote alone. Because her clothes had been beige and boring.

So the suitcase just demonstrated positive change.

"Since you're being helpful, you can carry Sally's present."

He put the colorfully wrapped package under his arm.

"It's a fine gift. He'll be pleased, I'm sure. Is this all of it then, or do you have another bag tucked away?"

"That's it, and if you're going to complain so much, I'll ask Marg to save her looks."

"I wouldn't mind that. They're rare but ferocious."

She decided to be amused as they started downstairs with the dog slowly trailing after.

Marco and Brian stood in the living room sunk in a kiss, with Marco's bags at their feet.

"He doesn't have so much as you," Keegan pointed out.

"Because I've got the gift, and . . . girl things."

"If I said *girl things* to you, I believe I'd get another ferocious look. Are you ready then, Marco?"

"Yeah." But he looked around the cottage. "Don't forget the casserole. All you've got to do is warm it up. And I froze some red sauce if you want pasta. You just boil the water and—"

"Ah now, don't fuss. We won't starve." Brian lifted Marco's suitcase. "Not that I won't miss your cooking, but it's you I'll miss more."

Marco shouldered his own laptop case, then took the gift from Keegan.

When they stepped out, Breen looked over at the garden they'd planted, the rows and the mounds, the new green rising.

"I grew up on a farm. I think I can tend a little patch such as that for a handful of days." With a shake of his head, Keegan carted the suitcase toward the woods.

She'd hung wind chimes, made in her grandmother's workshop, on the branches. For beauty and song, and another layer of protection. They swayed, tinkling, in the light breeze, their jewel colors catching both sun and shadow.

And the pixies would come at night, she thought, so he'd have them as warning if he stayed at the cottage. He'd have Harken and Morena at the farm, and a score of warriors if he went to the Capital.

If she could only see whether Shana had recovered. If she could see whether they'd found a way, some way, to get her through.

I need you to look after him, she told Bollocks, and his drooping head lifted. *I really do. Stay close when you can, okay? Do that for me.*

His pace picked up; his tail swayed. He wasn't being left behind but given a task. Protect.

"You'll take pictures to show when you get back," Brian was saying. "Of the party, and of the great city. And, Breen, you'll write of it so we can read on Marco's machine when you come home again."

Home again, she thought as they approached the tree. She wasn't going home, but taking a short trip. And in a few days, they'd come home again.

When they stepped through and into a thin April shower, she saw a welcoming—or a bon voyage—party. Nan, Sedric, Morena, Harken, Aisling, and her boys—with Mahon off on patrol.

The pup, already twice the size she'd been at Christmas, leaped joyfully at Bollocks.

"And here they are, the travelers." Agile, Morena danced back from the wrestling dogs.

Kavan lifted his arms to Breen, so she set down her bag to pick him up.

"He's ready to go off with you," Aisling told her.

"Wouldn't that be fun?" She gave him a nuzzle. "One day we'll go."

With him on her hip, she hugged Marg. "We'll be back, right here, in three days."

"You enjoy your time, and wish Sally a happy birthday from all of us."

"I will. We will." She kissed Sedric's cheek. "See you soon."

She set Kavan down, started to pick up her bags. Keegan swept her into a kiss that had Finian laughing and Kavan hooting. "You'll miss me, won't you now?"

"Maybe. Yes."

"Good. As I'll miss you. So much baggage here." He looked toward Sedric, who smiled.

"It's no problem at all. Take hands now, as it'll be easier."

"We could still fly—I mean in a plane." But Marco took her hand. "You're sure we'll end up back in the old apartment?"

"That's where I opened it," Keegan reminded him. "Meabh won't be there, as she knows you're coming. And you know the place of the portal in New York."

"Yes." Nerves began to spark along Breen's skin. "It's all written down."

"All right then." Keegan walked over to stand with Marg and Sedric. "I expect you can do it on your own," he said to Sedric, "but I'll give you a hand with it."

"I'll take it, and thanks."

They both lifted their hands, palms out.

"What was opened was closed again. What was closed will open for the travelers into the world beyond. Hold them safe as they pass."

Light swirled on the road, spread above it, circling, widening.

Kavan let out a squeal of delight, but at their mother's feet, Finian stared, and his eyes deepened.

Throwing his power in, Breen realized. Sweet, magickal boy.

Breen drew in a breath. "Here we go."

Marco said, "Oh shit," but gripped her hand, and stepped in as she did.

She heard Kavan's voice. "Bye! Bye! Bye!"

Then it was all light and wind and Marco's hand. The breath she'd drawn in was lost in it. Her heart took one hard leap.

In little more than a flash, she stood in their old apartment, and Marco went down on his hands and knees.

"Are you okay? You're okay. I'm right here."

"Little dizzy, out of breath. Hold on."

"I'm right here. I have some potion in my bag."

"Just catch my breath. It— Jumping Jesus, what a rush. Not as bad as the other time, but whoa!"

Still gasping, he sat on the floor. His eyes, a little wild, ticktocked everywhere. "We're really here."

"We really are." She dug into her bag for the potion. "Two sips, and if your head doesn't stop spinning, one more."

"Not my head so much as the whole damn room." He sipped, sipped again. "Okay, yeah, better. Fast trip, huh?" He managed a smile, and since his color had come back, she smiled with him.

"We've beamed up, Scotty."

She sat with him, looked around. Meabh had added a few things, shifted some of the furniture, but it was much the same.

Nostalgia, she realized. She felt nostalgic for all the good memories she'd made there with Marco. But she didn't pine for it.

Not home, not anymore or ever again.

"Place looks good."

"Do you miss it?" she asked him.

"I wondered if I would, but I don't. It's good to see it again. It's like—you know how you walk through your old high school, and you remember stuff, or feel stuff? It's good, or it's bad. But either way, you don't want to go back."

"Do you think you want to take anything back with us?"

"No, I got—or Sedric got for me—everything I wanted. You?"

"I want to take the table, our dragon table. The one you had painted for me for my birthday. Not this trip, but after."

"We had us some good times at that table."

"We did." She rose, reached down for his hand. "Steady and ready?"

"You bet."

"Then we'll go check into our hotel."

"Feel funny and, well, bougie, to be staying at a hotel in Philly."

"We're going to have a bougie three days. We'll check in, then I'm going to see my mother."

With a quick trip to see Marco's first.

"I ought to go with you, girl. Let me—"

"I need to do it, and get it done. Then we'll dress ourselves up and go surprise Sally. Once I get this done, Marco, everything else is positive, happy, and fun."

"You're not taking the damn bus."

"Deal. Let's go check into our hotel like a couple of tourists."

More memories flooded when Breen knocked on the Olsens' door. Cookouts in the tiny backyard, watching Mrs. Olsen bake a cake in the homey, spotless kitchen, hearing the wonder of gospel music.

Plenty of good memories, she reminded herself. She only had to block out those of Marco's tears shed against her shoulder when his family condemned him for being who he was.

Annie Olsen opened the door, offered a polite smile. Then blinked—her eyes so like Marco's—and clapped her hands together.

"Breen! Oh my goodness, it's Breen Kelly. I swear I didn't recognize you for a full hot minute. Just look at you!"

"It's good to see you, Mrs. Olsen."

"Girl!" She threw her arms around Breen, a short, hefty woman with a cap of rigorously straightened hair. "You come right on in here. I didn't know you were back!"

"Only for a day."

The house, just as she remembered, shined. Mrs. Olsen took the cleanliness and godliness trope very seriously.

"Marco and I came for Sally's birthday, then we have meetings in New York before we go back to Ireland."

The smile wobbled a bit, but Mrs. Olsen nodded. "Jet-setters. You sit down, and I'll fix us some coffee."

"Maybe I could come back with you like I used to. I always liked watching you cook. Marco sure got his skill in the kitchen from you."

"Come right on back. I got some of the angel food cake I made yesterday, so we'll have some with the coffee. You could use some fattening up."

She won't even say his name, Breen thought, and felt her heart thud in the base of her throat.

"How have you been, Mrs. Olsen?"

"Fit as a fiddle. Sit right there at the counter like the old days. Meetings in New York, you say?"

"Yes, with my publisher and my agent. And Marco's meeting the publicity people he's been working with. Plus, my agency's very interested in the idea of him writing a cookbook. In fact, he'll sign with them when we're in New York."

Mrs. Olsen put the coffee on, then took the glass dome off the cake.

"We're just so proud you're going to have that book published. It's sweet, writing books for children. And my goodness, Breen, you look so pretty and grown-up. How's your mama?"

"I'm going to see her today. Mrs. Olsen, I really stopped by to see you to talk to you about Marco."

"He's in my prayers, as you are." She put a slice of cake in front of Breen.

"Marco's getting married this fall." She said it fast, because she already knew the response. "Brian Kelly, he's actually a cousin of mine, and—"

"Breen, God doesn't recognize such aberrations, but condemns them. It breaks my heart that boy's rejected God's word, God's law, and I pray every night for his soul. He's made his choice, and I pray he'll repent it and find his way back again."

She gave Breen's hand a light pat. "Have some cake now. You need some meat on those bones."

"I need to tell you he's happy. I need you to know he's happy and with a good person who loves him. I need you to know a part of him will always miss you, but he's making a good life."

And all Breen saw in Annie Olsen's eyes was sorrow.

"There's no true happiness in sin, Breen, and I grieve for how he'll suffer when judgment comes." Tears glinted but didn't fall. "I carried that boy in my womb and in my heart. I raised him to know God's

word and live by it. But he took the wrong path. I'll pray hard tonight."

"I'm sorry. I'm only upsetting you, and I should go." She rose. "You
were always kind to me, and I'll never forget it. Marco has the bright-
est heart, the kindest spirit of anyone I know. I think that matters, so
much, in this life and whatever comes after."

She let herself out, and though it would be a long walk to her
mother's duplex, Breen thought it might settle her.

She'd hoped, and could admit now that hope had been foolish.

Marco had family, she reminded herself. He had her. He had Sally
and Derrick, he had everyone in Talamh. And now he had Brian.

And every one of his true family loved and accepted him, not despite who he was but because of it.

She warned herself to remember that, because the same applied to
herself.

She knew her mother was home. She'd looked. The globe might
not show her Shana or Odran's world, but it showed Jennifer at home
in her polished town house, going about her Saturday routine.

The gym with her personal trainer first thing, followed by house-
hold shopping.

Every fourth Saturday was a salon day. Hair, nails, a facial. But
that wasn't today—something checked before she'd booked the ho-
tels and made the appointments in New York.

Still too early in April to risk the outdoor plants and pots, but Jennifer would have opened the windows for at least an hour. She'd do
whatever laundry she didn't send out, deal with any bills or banking
online.

Though she had a cleaning service, she'd go through the house,
fluffing pillows, arranging the flowers she'd bought that morning,
and so on.

Some would call it puttering, Breen supposed as she stood outside
the duplex. But for Jennifer Wilcox, it was a mission. Hell, a religion
every bit as inflexible as Annie Olsen's.

Perfection in all things—except her only child, who'd fallen well
below the mark.

Drinks later, maybe, with a friend or, more likely, working on an account. Her rise up to media director of a successful ad agency had involved plenty of work at home.

Perfection in all things.

She walked to the door, knocked. Then stepped back to stand on the walkway.

There'd be no offer of coffee and cake here. But under that polite, homey veneer, it was the same, wasn't it? she realized.

I birthed you, I raised you, but I won't accept who and what you are. Who and what you are will never be welcome here unless and until you reject it all and fall in line.

Become what I can accept, or I won't even speak your name.

She'd kept the highlights and the chin-length swing, Breen noted when her mother opened the door. She'd dressed for Saturday, trim black pants, light blue sweater, ballet flats, careful and casual makeup. Gold studs, a thin gold chain with a row of small gold beads, a fancy tracker watch—that was new.

She noticed every detail, including the sharp surprise on her mother's face.

"Breen. I didn't know you were in Philadelphia."

"Briefly. For Sally's birthday."

"I see. Well, come in."

"No, I'm not welcome. What I am, who I am, isn't welcome."

"We'll discuss it."

"There's no point in discussing something you can't accept and I won't turn away from." She tilted her head when she saw her mother glance over to the connecting house.

"Worried what the neighbors think?"

"They're away for the weekend, but I'm not going to have this conversation standing out here." She started to step back, and Breen flicked out power, shut the door.

"You will, but it won't take long."

"I won't have this, Breen. I made that clear."

Her voice shook, Breen thought, and that was temper as much as fear.

"You did, and perfectly clear. You won't have this—who I am. You'll only have that—who I'm not, who you worked so hard to make me become. I've become something else, and I'm happy. I wanted to tell you, I'm happy. My life isn't perfect. It's never going to be, but it's mine."

"It's not! It's what they've put into you, and into your head. I'm the one who raised you, the one who gave you a home, and stability, and a direction, a purpose."

"All of that was yours, your home, your version of stability, your direction, and the purpose you chose. Now I've chosen. My book comes out soon. I'm going to New York tomorrow, and I may sell another. Writing makes me happy. It's work, and it can be hard, but it makes me happy. My gifts make me happy. They're work, and can be hard, but they give me joy. I have my own direction, my own purpose."

"It's a fantasy, and a dangerous one."

"You're not altogether wrong, but it's still mine. But I know you worked hard to give me a life, a home. I've thought a lot of things about you, and us, over this past year. I realize you did your best, and that has to be enough."

"Open this damn door and come in the house. I won't air out this nonsense in public."

"I'll open the door for you in a minute, but I won't come in." Now, Breen thought, or ever again.

"You lied to me, all those years, and with the lies took something so precious from me. You made me feel, constantly, lacking and less and inadequate. And so unhappy. You had to know how unhappy, Mom."

"You were safe, healthy, with a good education and a perfectly good career."

"And miserable struggling to push myself into the mold you made for me out of your own prejudices and fears. I never fit. I broke that mold. It wasn't easy, but I did. And now I fit. I can't make you fit into the mold I might wish for, and I won't try. You did your best, I accept that, and I'm grateful. You lied, and you were wrong to lie to me, wrong to dismiss my happiness until I believed I just wasn't entitled to it.

"I won't come back again, but I needed to tell you that. You were wrong, and you hurt me. And I forgive you."

"You— I've done nothing but—"

"I forgive you," Breen repeated. "And hope, sincerely, you have the life you really want." She turned and walked away. "Door's open."

It had been a weight, so heavy, and now it simply spilled off her shoulders. Lighter, so much lighter, she walked and walked on a cool April afternoon.

She walked, light and somehow free, passed the tattoo parlor, glanced down at her wrist.

And, again on impulse, went in. She had it done in the same script as the first, just below the shoulder of her sword arm.

When she stepped out, Sedric waited.

"I should've known you'd check on me."

"You needed the walk, then in you went. I thought to wait, and now I see no sad in your eyes."

"No." She stepped to him and into his arms. "I went to Marco's mother, and I did what I needed to do. I said what I needed to say. And realized, when I faced my own mother, how alike they are in this way. This immovable way.

"So I did what I needed to do, said what I needed to say to my mother. Then I forgave her."

"Ah." Smiling, he brushed a hand over her hair. "And so the burden's gone."

"I did it for me, not for her."

"Forgiveness is forgiveness." He cupped her face, gently kissed her cheeks. "Now your heart holds more light. Your nan will be pleased, and proud as well. Now, what did you have put on yourself this time?"

"Here." She tapped her shoulder. "A little sore yet. *Iníon na Fae.*"

His eyes smiled first. "Daughter of the Fey."

"Because I am, and it felt like forgiving my mother and saying goodbye to her—I guess doing the same with Marco's mother— made it only more true."

"It's always been true."

"I have to call for a car and get back. Why don't you come with us to the party?"

"And good craic it will be, no doubt. But Marg is waiting. She worried you'd be unhappy. Sure I can tell her not to worry a'tall. But

I'll stay with you while you wait for the car, then I think I'll find one of those pretzels before going back. They're more than fine."

She dashed into her hotel room to find the adjoining door open and Marco pacing between. He'd laid out her party dress, and being Marco, the appropriate underwear.

"I know you texted you were fine, and just delayed, but—"

"I am fine! Just later than I figured. You're already dressed!"

"We said we wanted to get there early to—"

"I know, I know. I'll be quick."

"You gotta tell me about seeing your mom. Come on, girl!"

"It's all good, it's done."

And she'd never tell him about going to his mother's.

No point.

She grabbed the clothes from the bed, dashed into the bath.

"I said everything I needed to say—nothing changed with or in her, and nothing will. I accept that. I told her I knew she'd done her best."

Over the drum of the shower, Breen lifted her voice.

"I told her she lied to me, hurt me, blah blah, and that I forgive her."

"Oh. Ouch!"

That brought a laugh. "I guess it might've stung. But I meant it, Marco. I forgive her, and I'm not carrying that resentment anymore. It's liberating."

She jumped back out of the shower. She'd wear the green dress again, the gift from Sally and Derrick. And had no doubt the choice had prompted Marco to wear an emerald-green shirt with the long leather vest Nan had given him.

To save time she did a glamour, a serious one, as Marco would give her grief otherwise.

She added her Troll earrings, the mermaid bracelet, then dashed back out.

"Breen. I'm proud of you."

"Because I showered and dressed in under ten minutes?"

"You know why. It took me a long time to forgive my parents, my brother, so I know it takes a lot. You did it inside a year. So I'm—What the actual fuck! You got another tat! Without me!"

"I'm sorry, I'm sorry."

She sat to put on her shoes.

"It was a moment. I was walking, feeling liberated, and there was the place, and I just had to do it."

"Crap, do I have to get another one now?"

"No."

"What's it say? I can't read that stuff."

"Daughter of the Fey."

He blew out a breath. "Well, hell, I get why. How come it's not all pink yet?"

"It's still sore, but with party time I didn't want it to look funny, so I—" She wiggled her fingers.

"Good thinking. We do look total, you and me."

She picked up the gifts. "Let's go see our mom."

It felt good to walk into Sally's, see the club crazily decorated for his birthday. Derrick's doing, Breen thought. They'd come early, so only a scatter of tables had customers, and another scatter on barstools where a woman with short raven hair and huge, brilliant blue eyes held a conversation with one of the stool sitters.

She even looked like a faerie, Breen thought, with her big almond-shaped eyes, sharp cheekbones. Those brilliant blue eyes looked up and beamed welcome.

Marco didn't hesitate but went straight over. "Hey, Joey."

The bar sitter popped up. "Marco! Haven't seen you in forever. Everybody said you'd— Breen!" He grabbed them both in one-armed hugs. "It's reunion time, and I'm buying. Hey, this is Meabh. She's from over where you guys are hanging out."

"My replacement."

She sparkled at Marco. "Ah now, sure and no one could replace the amazing Marco. I'm so pleased to meet you both at last."

"She makes a Cosmo," Joey claimed, "that's magic."

"I bet she does." Breen held out a hand. "Greetings from home.

Thank you," she said softly as Marco and Joey caught up. "For all you're doing."

"No need for it. I like the apartment very much, and here, well, it's another home. They treat me like family and make me feel it. That's a gift."

Studying her, Breen understood. "You're going to stay."

"For a time, at least." She touched a fingertip just below Breen's new tattoo. "As will you, each our found places."

"We'll catch a drink later," Marco told Joey. "We want to see Sally before the party gets going."

"In his dressing room," Meabh told them. "Making himself gorgeous."

"I'm coming back." Marco pointed at her. "We're going to have us a Cosmo mix-off."

"I'll take that challenge, brother."

As they started back, Derrick came out. Both hands went to his lips, and above them his eyes teared up.

"I don't believe it. I can't believe it. Oh man, man. Let me look at you. Both of you."

After hugs, hard and long, he touched Breen's hair, rubbed Marco's goatee. "You're really here. You don't know how happy this is going to make him. How long are you staying?"

"Just tonight. We're taking the train to New York tomorrow, having some meetings, and heading back from there."

"Listen to you." He teared up again. "Going to New York for meetings. I don't know what that is"—he pointed to the bigger package—"but it's not nearly as big a gift as having the two of you here, even for just tonight."

"We couldn't miss Sally's birthday. But"—Marco patted the package—"I think this is going to be a hit."

"Let's go find out. Well, Jesus, you've got to tell us everything. Where's that handsome fiancé of yours, my boy?"

"He couldn't make it this time. Quick trip, but I'm going to get his fine ass over here to meet you before the wedding."

"Don't get Sally started on the wedding." He paused outside the dressing room. "He won't stop." He gave the door a tap. "Hey, babe, you decent?"

"I should hope not!"

Derrick poked his head in. "Got something for you."

Sally sat at the lighted dressing room mirror, his hair covered with a skullcap as he applied, with precision, false lashes.

His hand stilled as his eyes met Breen's in the mirror.

"Well, damn it all, there goes my makeup."

CHAPTER TWENTY-SIX

Hugs, tears, and more hugs.

And home, Breen thought, wasn't always a place. Sometimes it was a person.

"I'm getting champagne. Don't you open those presents until I get back," Derrick warned.

"That man knows me." Sally sat again, dabbing at his eyes. "Seeing you, both of you, right here, it's the best birthday present in the history of them. God, look at my beautiful kids."

When he teared up again, Breen sat at his feet, laid her head on his knee as Bollocks often did with her. "Missed you."

"Missed you more. And you, engaged. Is he out there?"

"Not this time. We're in and out, but I promise you'll meet him for real soon. He's wonderful, Sally. I love him so much."

"Don't get me started again. We're going to throw you the mother of all weddings. I've got ideas. Tails, white tie and tails. And Breen in a gold dress because I see black and gold, splashes of white. White flowers, everywhere, and—"

"You got him started, didn't you?" Derrick carried in a tray holding the champagne, already open in a bucket of ice, and the flutes.

"First, I was thinking rainbows, then it came to me. The elegance of black and gold." Sally circled his hands in the air. "And the white flowers. He better be worthy of you."

"I can attest." Breen took a flute from Derrick. "Happy birthday, Sally."

"I can attest. Now, I've got to see what's in here. What you brought me all the way from Ireland."

"Open this first." Breen held out the smaller, narrow box. "It's from Nan."

"You— Your grandmother sent me a birthday present?"

Almost reverently, Sally opened the card.

Dearest Sally,

You've given so much to Breen when I couldn't, and no gift can shine so bright as the gift of family. You're hers—and Marco's as well—and so you're mine. This small gift comes with wishes for the happiest of birthdays to the mother of Breen's heart.

Lá breithe shona duit, Marg

"I'm going to need a crate of tissues before I'm done."

Blinking at tears, Sally opened the box. "Oh, this is gorgeous!"

He drew out the trio of stars dangling from a silver chain. They caught the dressing table lights and exploded with color.

"She made it for you."

"*Made* it?"

"Nan is . . . ha—crafty."

"I'll say. It's just beautiful."

"She said you're a star, so should have stars."

Overcome, Sally wiped at his eyes again. "Okay, now I'm in love with your grandmother."

"That makes two of us." Derrick took the suncatcher, turned it this way and that. "Bedroom window, babe, so we can wake up to stars."

"Perfect. I'm going to write Marg a thank-you note, but tell her how much this means to me."

He set his flute aside again and got to work on the wrappings.

"This'll take awhile," Derrick warned them. "They're off to New York tomorrow for meetings."

"The professionals. Makes me proud. Look, it's wrapped twice." He revealed the brown paper. "Not my fault it's taking awhile."

"You can rip that paper, Sal. Come on now."

"All right, all right. He can't stand suspense." So he ripped, then his hands stilled as he caught his first glimpse of the painting beneath. "Well, God, what is this?"

"Rip, rip, rip!" Breen bounced. "I can't stand the suspense either."

"Oh, babe, it's you. It's you in your unmatched Cher. You're gorgeous."

"I am." Sally swallowed hard. "It— Did your Brian do this?"

"Yeah. It's wonderful, right? He's so good. It was Breen's idea, and we got the photo from the website. Brian fiddled with it. I helped make the frame—I want credit."

"The same craftsman who did the box made the frame, with Marco. We both wanted to have a part in making it."

Sally stood in the spotlight of the stage, the long black hair raining down the back of a slinky, spangled red dress. He held a mic in one hand, with the other on his hip. Roses littered the stage all around his red stilettos.

"I don't have words—and that never happens. I think he may be worthy of you, Marco. He's sure as hell talented. This—I'm so touched that you'd think of this, that you'd do this for me. That you'd come all this way to give it to me and have this time with us. I love you both more than . . . than my collection of Louboutins."

"Holy shit." Grinning, Marco wiggled his eyebrows at Breen. "We beat out the Louboutins."

"This is a gift for me, too. We're going to hang it in the living room. I want to take it out tonight, put it up on the wall, but after tonight, it goes home with us."

Sally nodded.

"I'll take it out. You need to get your face on." Leaning down, Derrick kissed it. "You have to make your entrance."

"I'm going to go out with him. I got a Cosmo mix-off with the new girl."

"She's a wonder. You'll like her."

"Already do." Bending down, Marco kissed Sally's cheek. "I like the black and gold and the white."

"Can I talk to you while you do your makeup?" Breen asked.

"You know you can. Now." When the door shut, he swiveled around to start. "Have you got something on your mind other than catching up?"

"A few things."

She told him about seeing Marco's mother, then her own, and when she'd finished, he nodded, set down his eyeliner.

"Good, on both counts, because I know you've carried some hurt and resentment for Marco's family, and you can toss that now. They are who they are."

"I needed to try. I'm not going to tell him."

"He's moved on. He's let it go, so telling him would only stir up what's settled. As for your mom?"

Sally paused, sipped some champagne.

"You know a good mad can be healthy, baby. But getting to the point you can toss the mad out? It'll keep the insides cleaner. I'm sorry for her, that's the down-to-the-balls truth. Sorry for both of those women. And I'm grateful to them because I have you, I have Marco."

"You sound like Nan."

"Then I must sound smart as all hell, because I figure she is. Now, what's this?"

She rubbed gently on the tat when he gestured to it. "It means Daughter of the Fey. The Fey are—"

"Honey, I know what fey means. Magic people, like fairy folk. Makes sense, since you've made your home in Ireland. And it suits you. Ireland. Now, what else?"

"It's about the money. First, my agent thinks she can sell the novel—it's finished, and she read it—"

"Well, good God, girl! Pour more champagne."

"I will, but don't— I don't want to talk too much about that and jinx it."

"Fey." Sally rolled his heavily lined eyes. "Superstitious."

"Anyway, about the money."

She told him about starting a foundation with what she thought of as part of her inheritance.

"I know the financial people understand how to set it all up, even run it. But I wondered if you and Derrick— You know money stuff, and business. I wondered if you could help. They said we need, like, a board, and we'd have to have meetings—we could Zoom them. Marco and me, and if you and Derrick—"

"Breen." Sally reached for her hand, gave it a squeeze. "We'd be honored. I didn't know your dad, and I'm sorry I never met him. But I'm betting he'd be proud of what you're doing."

"It changed my life, what he did for me. Thanks, seriously thanks. It felt kind of overwhelming. No, not kind of," she corrected. "Completely overwhelming. Knowing you and Derrick can help makes it feel doable."

"Done." He lined his lips. "How about that hot Irishman?"

"How about him?" She laughed. "I guess we're sort of halfway living together."

In the mirror, Sally's eyes narrowed. "What the hell does that mean?"

"Just that. It's working, and it's fine for now."

"Do you love him?"

No one had asked, so the question caught her off guard. She answered without thinking. "Yes. Oh God!" She pressed a hand to her stomach. "I love him. I knew it. I'm not stupid, but I never said it out loud."

"Does he love you?"

"Not as sure of that. He cares, and neither of us has been with anyone else since . . . since we started. He's honest with me, and that really matters. He treats Marco like a brother—because he considers Marco like a brother. And that really matters."

"You're happy."

"I am."

"That really matters."

Later, as she watched Sally onstage, belting out as the crowd-favorite Cher, as she helped judge the Cosmo mix-off (a solid tie), as she danced with Derrick, she came to a decision.

On the train the next morning, with Marco glued to the window for the first glimpse of New York, she shared it.

"I decided something last night and want your input."

"Sure. Some night, huh? And more to come. After we dump our bags, we're heading out, girl. I checked the weather. Mostly sunny and sixty, so not bad."

"I'm going to tell Sally and Derrick."

"About the weather?"

"Marco, latch on."

"Sorry. What?" With obvious effort, he pulled himself away from the view.

"I want to ask them to come over, after. It has to be after, but I want them to come." If I live through it, she thought, but didn't say. "Maybe in the fall, maybe even for your wedding. Your first wedding."

"That's in Talamh, at Brian's—" He latched on, then grabbed both her hands. "You mean it?"

"I can't stand not telling them. It's like lying. It *is* lying. And they're family. I think I decided when I walked away from my mother. But I absolutely decided last night. If you think it's the wrong thing, tell me."

Eyes closed, Marco let out a long breath. "I've been carrying it this whole time. Every time we talk to them, when I had Brian first sit in so they could meet him that way. I want them to really know him, and meet his family, and Nan, and everybody. But I know it's yours to tell."

"Not just mine. I have to ask Keegan. He's not just the guy I'm sleeping with, he's taoiseach. It may be too much, and I—we'll—have to accept that. But I'm going to put up a good, solid argument."

"I've got your back on it. This lightens my load, Breen. But maybe when you tell them, show them, you could do it with less—"

He tossed his hands up on the sides of his face, made a bomb sound.

"That's a definite."

"This is great. Hey, do I still get two weddings?"

"That's another definite. I want that gold dress even more than I want to see you in white tie and tails. And there's New York."

Just as thrilling as the first time, Breen thought, and only more so, as she had Marco and his unbridled excitement with her. She'd booked the same hotel she'd used on her first and only trip, but splurged this round.

Marco gawked at the small but lovely two-bedroom suite as much as the view out the window.

"Girl, you went swank!"

"We get two nights, and we deserve the pretty little parlor so we can hang out when we're not out on the town."

The parlor offered a sofa plumped with pillows, a pair of streamlined chairs. The long, low coffee table held a bowl of fruit, a complimentary bottle of red wine, and a pair of glasses.

And the big windows opened their world to downtown New York.

Because she'd gone over the amenities, she picked up the TV remote. "Check this," she told him, and pointed it at the big mirror facing the sofa.

The mirror shifted to TV mode, and the hotel screen.

"Now we're talking!" In triumph, he lifted his face and his arms to the ceiling. "Technology, I'm back! I gotta have me one of these. When we do the cottage, I gotta have one of these sweet things."

He spun around. "I gotta take a picture for Brian. Pictures of everything. We'll do a video. I want to sit on the sofa, and those chairs, and the one in my room, flop on the bed, dance in the shower. Same in your room. But we gotta get out there."

"I'm going to unpack." She shot a finger at him. "We've got all day, as long as we're back here and dressed by five thirty."

"Unpack fast, 'cause we need to hit this city, and hard. What's five thirty?"

"That's when we need to leave for our pre-theater fancy dinner reservations."

"What! Fancy dinner? Theater? We're going to a show?"

"Oh, Marco, not just any show." She reached in her bag, took out an envelope. "What I have here are two tickets, orchestra, third row center, for . . . wait for it. A revival of . . . drum roll. *La Cage aux Folles.*"

He dropped down on one of the streamlined chairs. "Don't you toy with me, girl."

"Carlee helped me score them. How could I come to New York with my gay best friend and not get tickets for *La Cage*?"

He sprang up, danced around the room, grabbed her, danced her around the room.

"It just gets better and better. Thank you. I love you! Oh, holy shit, we're going to see *La Cage* on fucking Broadway."

He kissed her hard while she laughed. "Get yourself unpacked because I'm paying you back. Your gay best friend's going to help you find the perfect outfits for tomorrow."

"Ten minutes," she promised, and turned toward her room. "'Outfits'? That's plural."

"You got a business-type lunch and a business-type dinner. That's two."

"But I brought—"

He shot up a hand, made an *Eh!* sound. "Don't make me pull out my serious-as-fuck face." And singing "Downtown," he walked to his room.

Marco was a force, and one that could not, would not be stopped. Or even slowed, Breen discovered. He whirled her into shops where he chatted up the clerks until they fell under his spell.

He took countless pictures and videos on the streets, talked to sidewalk vendors and cart operators like old friends. He insisted they take the subway to Midtown because he was going to, by God, walk on Fifth Avenue with her just like Fred Astaire and Judy Garland.

He dragged her into souvenir shops and boutiques with equal fervor, taking a break only to sit down to a New York pizza—a must on his very long list—which he graded exceptional.

Because she, too, fell under his spell, she bought too much and had one of the best days of her life.

She turned it around to give him the night.

Dinner for two, candlelight, a good bottle of wine, and food presented with a quietly elegant flourish.

Yet another world for both of them, she thought. One neither of them would spend much time in, but so perfect for this one day, one night.

When he snagged the check, she slapped a hand over his.

"No, Marco. This is my treat."

"Nope. You gave me New York. You gave me Ireland and Talamh, and that gave me Brian. I'm writing a cookbook and signing with an agent because of you. You're giving me Broadway, so don't make me pull out my SAF face in this fancy-ass place, Breen. I'm buying my best friend and first love of my life dinner in New York."

She drew her hand back. "Thank you, Marco."

He grinned as he took out his credit card. "Good thing you pay me the decent bucks while I'm living rent-free. I never in my life expected to be able to do something like this. Feels so damn good. It's not our life, all this, so that makes it special."

"And our life, the one we'll go back to, that's what you want?"

"I'm going to bring Brian here one day, and I want to see other places, too—like we always talked about. And I want one of those awesome TV mirrors. But I got you, and I've got somebody who loves me and wants to make a home with me. There's nothing I've ever wanted more than that."

The show was everything. She lost count of the times he looked over at her with wonder in his eyes. There were all kinds of magicks, she thought, in all kinds of worlds.

And in this one it soared with color and joy and voices and movement. She'd come back again, if she could, and bear witness to magic.

And when she tumbled into bed, very late, as they'd shared some wine and talked and talked about the day, the evening, the show, she took the magic with her.

When Marco surfaced in the morning, he walked into the parlor to see Breen sitting at a room service table.

"Coffee!" He lunged for it. "You ordered us breakfast? I figured we'd go out, try a deli or something."

"Just bagels. We've got lunch at one thirty, and it's after ten."

"Don't tell me you got up at dawn and worked out."

"Habit. I need to talk to you."

"Sure. We can walk, you said, to the agency place. I meet Carlee face-to-face, then—gulp—talk to Yvonne about the cookbook. I'm trying not to think about it. Then I head over to the publishing place and get my tour before we all meet up for lunch. Can't wait to meet the publicity gang, and Melissa in Marketing. Hey, really good coffee!"

"Marco, Carlee called this morning, about an hour ago."

"Yeah?" He took the warming lid off his bagel. "Berries, too? Nice." Then he looked up. "Ah hell, does she have to cancel?"

"No. Marco—"

"How come you're wearing that face? That's your twisted-up-inside face."

"It's not, exactly. She said she'd just gotten off the phone with Adrian."

"Editor girl."

"Yeah, and they . . . Marco, they made an offer on the book."

"Jesus jumping Christ!" And he jumped up with it. "Mimosas! Now!"

"No, Marco, no. Wait."

When she squeezed her eyes shut, he dropped down in front of her.

"A crap offer? Okay, so a crap offer's still an offer, right?"

"No, not crap. Carlee said it was pretty solid, but— Okay, give me a minute. She said she feels it's on the low side, and laid out three choices."

"Let's hear 'em."

"The presales of Bollocks's book are pretty good. Better-than-expected good. That's all the work you've done, his social media. She said that."

"All right, I'll grab onto some credit."

"Because they are, she thinks we can counter, that she wants them to have more invested. So first choice would be just take the offer. You know, bird in the hand, and it's a hell of a bird, Marco. They'd publish my book, and that's—I can hardly breathe thinking of it."

"You're doing fine. I'm thinking second choice is to let your agent do her agent thing and say how about some more?"

"Yeah, basically. And there's stuff about subrights and percentages. Anyway, that's door number two. The third is to let her send it out, other publishers. She thinks she can drum up some interest shopping it around and get more than the more."

"Now tell me what my Breen wants."

"To get it published."

"Goes without saying, and it will be. What do you want to do?"

"I could just grab it, and it's done. And it's more money than I ever thought—you haven't even asked what they offered."

"We'll get to it. It's not the important thing first off."

She closed her eyes again because he understood. Of course he did. "If she shops it around, there's a possibility of a lot more, a bigger house, all of that. But—"

"Door number two, because you trust her to do her job, and you know your editor, you know the people at McNeal Day. You've got a relationship."

"It would be like putting the eggs in one basket."

"What's wrong with that when you feel like the one holding the basket's going to take good care of them?"

"That's how I feel. She told me to think about it—not to feel I had to jump because we're having these meetings today. That's why Adrian called first thing with the offer, but I shouldn't feel pressured to decide. I've spent the last hour trying to think, to think smart and beyond the holy shit, somebody wants to publish my book."

"It's a damn good book. Now I'm going to sit down, eat my bagel, drink my coffee, because I know you and what you're going to do. You're going to let Carlee do her agent thing with this offer. And maybe they come up some."

"I guess I am. Yes. Yes, I am. And if they don't come up some, I'm just taking the offer. I want my eggs in this basket."

He tapped the phone beside her plate. "Go on, call her back. You won't eat that bagel until you do."

"Okay, you're right. We might not get the yes or no or whatever to-day, so let's not feel all weird when we have lunch later. Or the whole dinner deal tonight."

"What's to feel weird?" He lifted his shoulders. "It's just business, girl."

Just business, she thought as she dressed in Marco's Choice.

Still in a kind of daze, she put on the dark gray pencil skirt that hit just above the knee, pulled on the oversize turtleneck, like a pale gray cloud. She added the earrings Marco helped make for her for Christmas. A dangle of tiny stones, all chosen for a writer. Then the ankle booties with their thin short heels—red because Marco decreed everyone needed red shoes.

Because she couldn't decide what to do with her hair, she left it alone, then spent more time than usual on makeup because her hand tended to tremble.

He tapped on her open door. "Look at you! I knew it! Not a suit. You got the New York chic going on, girl. You got it *down*."

"And look at you."

He wore a bright pink shirt with a black tie sporting pink flamingos, black pants, leather bomber jacket, and bright pink high-tops.

He looked absolutely amazing.

"Marco." She walked over to take his face in her hands. "We're really doing this. You and me. Whatever happens today, or tomorrow or the days after, we're really doing this right now. You and me."

"There's always a me with you, and a you with me. Let's go kick some publishing ass."

"You're not nervous?" she asked as they walked to the elevator.

"Do you see my outfit? Are you seeing how I *own* this outfit? Nobody who looks this fine's got nerves."

This time he stopped to buy flowers—two bouquets—on the short walk to the agency. She loved him for it, and loved him more when they stood in Carlee's office and he held a bouquet out.

"I'm going to get spoiled. Thank you, Marco, and it's wonderful to meet you in person, finally."

"I wanted to give flowers to the person who's taking care of my best girl."

"She makes it easy."

"And for helping her get those tickets. It was amazing, just amazing."

"I'm so glad—I need to see it myself. Lee gets most of the credit for the tickets."

"Oh, well then."

When he made to take the flowers back, Carlee laughed. "We'll share them. Lee will put these in water, and come back to take you to meet Yvonne, Marco, but let's all sit down for a few minutes first. Give us ten, will you, Lee?"

"Absolutely." The assistant took the flowers and made a discreet exit.

Carlee sat at her cluttered desk, her slim black pants, crisp white shirt, and streaky blond pixie cut reminding Breen of the first time she'd sat here.

So much the same, so much different.

"How are you enjoying New York?"

"I'm loving it. Walked Breen's feet off yesterday."

"Some change from your cottage in Ireland. There are days I envy you that quiet nook. It obviously works for both of you, and I hear, Marco, you're engaged. So congratulations, best wishes, and all the rest."

"Want to see a picture?"

Carlee gave a quick laugh. "Well, yeah."

He pulled out his phone, scrolled through for a selfie he'd taken of himself and Brian with the Irish bay behind them.

"Good God, that much handsome could stop a heart. He's nearly as gorgeous as you are. I hope he'll come with you on another trip."

"We're planning on it."

He put the phone away, sat again, and Carlee shifted her attention to Breen. "So, I contacted Adrian with our counter, and she took it up the chain. I just heard back from her—you'd have been walking over from your hotel. They accepted. So, we have a deal."

"I'm sorry, what?"

"They met the terms we discussed, and from the turnaround, I'd say they expected the counter. We have a deal if you want it."

Breen just lowered her head between her knees.

Carlee started to jump up, but Marco waved her back. "She's okay." He patted Breen's back.

"I'll get some water."

"She's okay, just needs a second. Don't you cry now. You did a real good job on your eyes this morning, so don't go ruining it. She's going to say yes, and thanks, in a minute."

"Not the reaction I expected," Carlee admitted.

"Sorry." Slowly, Breen straightened. "Sorry."

"Don't be. Not the reaction I expected, but it may be the best. It definitely ranks in the top three. Do you want some water?"

"No, I'm fine. I'm good. And yes, thank you to taking the deal. *Thank you*'s not enough. You made a dream come true."

"I didn't write the book."

"You believed in it, and in me." She looked at Marco. "Having someone believe in you, that's everything."

Now she took his hands. "Like I believe in you. Go talk cookbook with your agent."

"Got me an agent." He grinned at Carlee as he rose. "Well, I have to sign on the dotted line and all, but I got me an agent."

"And we're thrilled to have you."

Breen would have floated through the day, but there was such energy all around. And the toasts at lunch, to her, to Marco, to Bollocks. The publishing talk swirled around her head like another dream.

Then the celebration dinner, with her editor's enthusiasm for the new book, the careful suggestions for a handful of changes, and the question she hadn't expected.

Would she consider a follow-up?

"Actually, I have an idea."

Adrian leaned across the table. "Tell me it involves Finn. He wasn't the one for Mila, you made the right choice there. But I really fell for him."

"As a matter of fact. It's just an idea that I thought I'd try to work with when I finish the current Bollocks book."

"Can you give us a little?"

"A follow-up, so a lot of the same characters, and some new ones. At the center there's a very, very old witch who lives in a cottage in the deep woods with her cats."

"Is she a good witch or a bad witch?"

"That's the question, and one Finn needs to find the answer to."

And she could do it, Breen thought as she walked back to the hotel with Marco on an April night full of sound and movement. She could write it. All she needed was the courage to start. And time.

And her best pal was, by God, going to write a cookbook.

"I have something to ask you."

"Tonight?" Breen lifted her face to the sky. "I'd say yes to anything. That's how good I feel."

"Great because Yvonne—you know, my agent?"

Breen laughed as he wagged his shoulders. "Yes, I do. I believe we met today."

"My agent, who's got ideas, girl, and lots of them, suggested how maybe it would be an idea if you wrote like a foreward to the cook-book."

She stopped in the middle of the sidewalk. "A foreward, to your cookbook?" She bounced on her toes. "Oh boy, oh boy, now I'm go-ing to find the fun! Yes, yes, yes! Oh, Marco, I have to say it again. Look at us!"

"We're something to see, my Breen."

And for the fun of it, he danced her half a block.

They checked out before dawn and rode the subway to Central Park. She'd written down the directions, but had them etched in her brain. She followed them as they rolled their suitcases, juggled shopping bags.

"Airplanes work, you know."

"Maybe next time," she muttered, admittedly a little spooked to walk the paths in the dark.

Then she saw it, the castle, the rocks at its base that would open and take them back to Talamh.

Sedric stepped out of the shadows.

"Dude! Shit! Heart attack time."

"Ah now, you're too strong for such things. There's no one about just now, but we'll be quick and quiet."

"Like a cat." Breen smiled, but it came off sheepish. "Sorry about all the bags."

"Not a problem a'tall. Here, pass some to me, and join hands."

He brought the light, a spark that spread and widened below the fancy of the castle.

"Quick and quiet now," he repeated.

With Marco's hand tight over hers, they stepped through together. And into the sun and balmy air of Talamh.

"Marco," she said instantly.

"Okay, not too bad. Just a little wheeee! Gonna sit right on the wall there." He did, his back to the farmhouse. "Hey, Sedric, got you a souvenir."

"Did you now?"

"Souvies all around. Still got some wheee going."

Breen kept a hand on his shoulder as she looked around.

Harken and Morena in the fields. Boy grazing with other horses in another. A dragon and rider gliding overhead.

And racing up the road, joyful barks sounding, came Bollocks.

Breen ran to meet him, crouched down with her arms wide, and laughed when he just bowled her over.

CHAPTER TWENTY-SEVEN

She'd gone through portals, or the useless witch Yseult had pulled her through. One, two, three of them. And each made her sicker than the last.

Shana despised the worlds they traveled through, however briefly. One of thick red vines and stinking ooze, the next of light so bright it seared the eyes. And into wild wind and stony mountaintops in the world of man.

And there, Yseult left her, the ugly bitch, with some hard-faced spy who took her in the way of man in a car that bumped and whined, then a boat through fog, and again a car on roads that wound and wound.

He took her as far as a village with more cars that stank and people who deserved to be burned to cinders and tossed to the winds.

When they were, she'd laugh and laugh.

From there, she'd been told to use her feet. And oh, one day she would slit Yseult's throat and pour out her blood for the dogs to lap. Though she no longer felt sick, and indeed felt stronger than ever she had in her life, she resented every step of the journey.

One with true power would simply have whisked her where she needed to go. Instead, she'd traveled four days and three nights, faced the bitterness of cold, the brutality of heat, the endless boredom of roads.

She never questioned why Odran didn't do the whisking, this god of all she worshipped, but laid it all at Yseult's feet.

She never thought of the child at all, but remembered every moment of pain.

And this, Odran had whispered in her ear as he'd given her sparkling wine to drink and fine meats to eat, came from Keegan O'Broin.

The taoiseach had reached through and given her all the terrible pain, had destroyed the son she'd made for Odran out of spite and jealousy.

No blame to her, Odran said, none at all.

Keegan O'Broin, her betrayer, her tormentor, who chose a mongrel bitch from the other side over her, all the blame was his.

So Odran gave her a knife conjured from poison. Even a scratch, the barest nick from it would kill any living thing. For fun, she tried it on Beryl, her personal slave, and had watched the girl die choking on her own blood.

And laughed and laughed.

She saw this weapon as gleaming gold with jewels shining from the hilt.

But this was her madness, as the blade was black and twisted, like her mind. Like her heart.

She would kill the taoiseach, and throw Talamh into chaos. Through the chaos, the tears of mourning, the cries of despair, Odran would ride his winged horse. Before he took her up on it, he'd place a crown of gold and sparkling jewels on her head. Then together, they would burn all.

She would take the redheaded bitch as her slave and sit on a golden throne to rule beside the god as a god.

She wanted the golden crown sparkling with jewels, wanted the golden throne, wanted the redheaded bitch who'd burned her hand as a slave. She wanted to plunge the knife into Keegan and watch him die at her feet like the slave who'd served her.

So she walked this last part of her journey wearing a smile frozen with her hate. Those she passed stepped away, and felt the chill shake through them.

No one spoke to her, and parents lifted their children into their arms and moved quickly away.

Do this for me, my beauty, and all you want is yours. His voice rang in her broken mind as it had when he'd given her the sparkling wine. The wine that was his own blood. The blood she'd sipped like wine, to make her strong again.

The blood she'd drank that was never wine, and corrupted the last light left in her.

She muttered as she walked, and sometimes laughed as she imagined herself gliding along in one of her beautiful gowns, dripping with shining jewels there to sit on a golden throne.

Her hair had lost its luster and lay tangled and dull down her back. Her eyes sat sunken and dull in a face where beauty had fled.

In her broken mind, and in any mirror in Odran's world, she saw only beauty, even more than she'd had.

She walked into the woods and felt featherlight and strong as any plow horse. To amuse herself, she dashed from tree to tree, merging with them. Or so she saw herself. But the body she believed lithe and agile sagged yet at the belly and breasts from the carrying and birthing of the child she gave no thought to.

She moved quickly, but not with a blur of speed as she once had.

She saw the cottage through the trees and sparkling wind chimes. Teeth bared, murder hot in her blood, she started to walk through. But sharp shocks repelled her, threw her back so she fell. And there beat angry fists on the ground.

She saw the garden and promised herself she would stomp the young plants into the ground. Rip up flowers by the roots. She would set fire to the thatched roof and dance while the cottage Marg made for the mongrel burned.

And kill them all with her golden knife.

She heard someone coming; her Elfin ears still served her. And crawled to a rock, rolled into it.

And watched, and waited.

He had to make time for it, Keegan thought as he stepped into the Irish woods. She'd be back before much longer, and it hadn't rained a drop on this side since she'd left.

He needed to water her damn gardens and the pots, which he

hadn't had the time—all right, bugger it, he hadn't taken the time—
to do the past three days.

He could have asked Seamus, who'd have seen to it all happily
enough. But hadn't he made a point of telling the woman he'd see to
it himself? So it was his own bloody fault, wasn't it then?

He slept the first night at the cottage, the next at the Capital, and
the last at the farm. And all of the nights restless, as she didn't share
the bed with him.

Which was a ridiculous matter, as he spent night after night at
the Capital when needed. The difference lay—and he admitted, to
himself at least, the idiocy of it—in that before, he'd been the one
away.

Since she'd be home soon enough, the sensible thing to do was
push all that aside and not think about it.

He preferred being a sensible sort.

Other than the restless nights and some wondering what she was
up to in the American cities, things had been quiet and productive.
He found working at the farm satisfying, and nearly as challenging
as a good training session for keeping in tune.

The trip east with stops all along showed him spring across Talamh.
All the young foals and lambs and calves, the fertile fields, the wash
hanging on lines to dry, and all the blooming things spoke of a promise kept.

And quiet, he thought again. He had such a yearning for the quiet.

He sensed her before she leaped out of the rock. It didn't surprise
him, as he'd anticipated they'd find a way to send her.

And still the sight of her sent shocks through him. The look of
her, all her beauty leached away and withered like a flower gone
too long without water. The hair she'd had such pride in lay in
limp, tangled strings, and her body, the high, generous breasts, the
narrow waist, long, slender legs, now sagged inside the old trousers
and dirty shirt that would never have touched her pampered skin
in the past.

The past was gone, and so was she. And he thought that with pity
overcoming the shock.

She held a twisted black blade in her hand, and madness lived in her eyes.

She laughed, a terrible sound, as she jabbed the blade toward him.

"What, no welcoming kiss for me? And here I've traveled such a long way to see you again."

"Put that aside, Shana, and let me do what I can for you."

"What you can, for me?" She laughed again, but now the bitter came through with the mad. "You've done all that already, haven't you now? Taoiseach. Used me and used me only to toss me aside for the whore who lives just over there. Is she waiting for you inside her cottage? I thought to pay her a visit, but she's barred the way well. Once I've killed you, I'll claw my way through, you can be sure of that. Odran will make sure of it."

"He won't." And the pity came through. "He sent you here to die."

"He sent me here to rid the worlds of the likes of you. I'd have ruled beside you."

"I don't rule."

"That's your mistake, isn't it? Always was."

She danced in a circle, and though he laid a hand on the hilt of his sword, he didn't draw it. Simply couldn't.

"I'd have changed that, oh aye, changed that I would. But you betrayed me for the whore who belongs nowhere. I'm not to kill her. Odran wants her alive and well, to suck and suck and suck her dry. But there could be an accident. Oops!"

She tossed back her head, laughed and laughed.

"But I might let her live, as Odran's promised her to me as a slave when I sit on my golden throne. Oh, it's beautiful there. All the jewels and the shine, and all the blood and the screaming! Oh, and when he fucks me, there's ice and fire, fire and ice, and fear and sweet, sweet pain, and pleasure so dark it's like blindness.

"You never gave me that." She jabbed playfully at the air. "And still, haven't I come to see you? Days it took, days and nights, through the red vines, through the boiling sun, into the cold wind of man, in the machines that bump and zoom on the black roads and smell, in boats through the fog. And still, after I've come so far, you only stand there."

She grinned at him. "Give us a kiss, won't you?"

And lunged.

Morena flew straight over. "Welcome home, the both of you. And would you look at all this!"

Breen could only wince at the shopping bags. But Marco simply beamed. "There's something for you and Harken in there."

"Is there now? Well, give it over then."

"We're not digging through all this now." If she didn't put her foot down, Breen knew, madness would ensue. So she settled it by sending the bags, the suitcases, laptops, to the cottage.

"We'll sort through and bring the souvenirs back tomorrow."

"She's gone strict on us, Marco." Morena cocked her elbow on his shoulder. "But it's just as well, as I'm grubby from the fields. Marg's up with my nan." She gestured up the road toward Finola's cottage. "Brian's at the waterfall, and as it happens, Keegan's gone over to your cottage just moments ago."

"Since I don't get to give out presents, and don't have to carry everything over, maybe I'll take a ride, see Brian. I can barter for some fish on the way back. Got some fun stuff in those disappearing bags for bartering, but the Mers will give me credit. Fish and chips tonight, Breen."

"Sounds perfect. You do that. I'm going to go unpack, maybe do some yoga. Or take a nap."

"We kept her busy. Shopping and Broadwaying and—I'm beating you to it, Breen—drinking toasts because she sold her book."

"Oh, that's the best of news!" Morena jumped from Marco to wrap around Breen, wings spreading as she circled with her two inches off the ground. "Such happy news. I need to tell Harken."

Dropping Breen, she winged off.

"I'm so proud of you, and happy for you." Sedric leaned down to kiss her cheeks. "Will I tell Marg, or do you want me to hold it back so you can do the telling?"

"No, you go ahead, and tell her Marco's writing that cookbook. I'll see her, and you, tomorrow. We have lots of stories packed into three days."

"And we want to hear every one. Do you want company on your ride, Marco? I wouldn't mind trading for some fish myself, and I want to hear all about your cookery book."

"Got me a New York agent." Poking a thumb into his own chest, Marco laughed. "Life sure has taken some turns. Let's saddle up and put on our bargaining hats. Flip side, Breen."

"Let's go, Bollocks. We'll check our gardens, see what Keegan's up to over there. Get unpacked, right?" she added as they walked up the stone steps.

"I don't know what he's going to think of that silly glass dragon Marco talked me into getting him, but it's got to be better than the King Kong on the Empire State Building sweatshirt Marco tried to convince me Keegan had to have."

They crossed from Talamh into Ireland.

"Out of one world, into another, now back again—sort of—in, what, twenty minutes tops?" Breathing it all in, she hugged herself. "Marco's right. Life's taken some turns, and it's a strange and wonderful one we live, Bollocks. Strange and wonderful."

He looked up at her as if he agreed completely, started to dash toward the stream where wild columbine sprouted on the banks waiting to bloom.

Then he stopped. His eyes changed; his teeth bared. He growled low.

He charged ahead before she could tell him to stop. Instinctively, she reached for the sword that wasn't there. Of course it wasn't there, she thought as she ran. But if something waited ahead, she had power with her, always.

He dodged the knife easily. She was clumsy, Keegan thought, and slower than she'd once been.

"Shana."

Her mind was gone, her heart pitch-dark, and he knew there

would be no retrieving either. But he had to try, one last time. "Odran doesn't care a whit which of us falls here. He's only for the blood and the death."

"You'll die, and Talamh burn. He'll give me your bitch of a mother to kill with my golden blade, and your whore, emptied of power, as a slave."

She did a spin, wobbled, spun again. "Oh, I'll pay you back for the pain, pay you back double. It might be I'll take your brother to my bed before I gut him like a fish. He has the look of you, after all, and I'll snip the sneering Sidhe's wings from her back while he watches.

"I am a god now, you see?" Those mad eyes gleamed as she spread her arms wide. "Your powers don't touch me. I am Odran's chosen. Come now, I can make it quick, or it's a scratch here, a cut there. It only takes the one, but a good clean blow will end it quicker."

They heard it together, her elf ears, and the elf in him he'd explored. Coming fast down the path.

"Company!" She spun, and vanished.

Did she think he couldn't see? Keegan thought. Did she think she'd blurred so he wouldn't know she'd slid into the tree, her knife lifted, ready to strike?

Making his choice, he drew his sword.

Even as the dog charged down the path with Breen racing behind, he saw Shana, the shadow of her on the bark of the wide trunk. And he saw the dark hate come into her eyes, and the thirst for murder in them.

As she started to lunge again, now toward Breen, he plunged the sword into her.

She made no sound, not even a gasp, but for a moment, endless to him, her eyes met his. And in them he saw confusion and nothing more.

She fell out of the tree at his feet, with the knife thudding on the path.

"Don't touch it. Stop," he snapped at Bollocks. "It's made of poison. Back now, well back."

He shot fire at the blade, held it while the knife bubbled and smoked. Over Shana's body, he looked at Breen.

"I couldn't reach her. There was nothing in her to reach."

"I'm sorry."

"He sent her for this. In hopes to kill me, but knowing she'd never live long enough to get back to the damned and bloody world she'd chosen. Is he so hell-bent, Breen, that he couldn't see she wanted your death more than she ever wanted mine?"

He sheathed his sword.

"I'll need salt, and I carry none with me. Salt for the stain the poison's left on the ground. And more, if you'd get some for me, for her. I'll take her to the Bitter Caves."

"I'll get the salt, and I'll go with you. I'll go with you," she repeated when he shook his head. "You don't do this alone. We'll go with you," she said, and laid a hand on Bollocks.

"Cróga will carry us, and her. When it's done, we'll bring you back. I'll go to the midlands and tell her parents."

"Don't." She went around the body, went to him. "Don't do that, Keegan."

"Don't tell her family she's dead at my hand?"

"They've already lost her, already grieved."

"I took her life."

"She ended it when she chose Odran. You finished what she began, and what good would it do to tell them this, what happened here? They'd lose her a second time and have fresh grief over the old. And more, every memory of her they hold would be scarred by it. How could they ever heal from that?"

"Aye, aye, you've the right of it."

He called for his dragon and waited while Breen got the salt. And waiting, bent to stroke the dog, who stayed at his side.

"You'd have protected me as you do her. You're a fine one, you are, Bollocks the Brave, Bollocks the True."

When Breen came back, he cleansed the stain, from the poison, from the blood, then with Breen and the dog, mounted Cróga. With the body in Cróga's claws, they flew up, flew high into Talamh, and high over it. Beyond the Troll camps and mines, and higher still to a stone-gray mountain rising from the edge of the sea.

She learned the Bitter Caves had earned their name because the air in them held as cold as winter and somehow hard so it seemed it would break at a blow like brittle glass.

In them, the high roof of the cave dripped with stalactites, their points as sharp as swords. The light Keegan brought ran red so it seemed blood washed across his face as he split the stone ground into a grave.

He placed Shana in himself. Then stood, searching, floundering.

"I can think of no words to say over her."

"We'll wish her the peace she couldn't find in this life."

"That's kind of you. Aye, we'll wish her that."

Then he stepped back, gave Cróga the order. The flames shot out and took her to ashes.

Keegan took the salt, spreading it over them as he spoke.

"And here, what remains never to rise again, never to cause harm, never to spill blood. What was is gone, what's left, ashes of the shell, stays here for all time."

He closed the stone over the ashes and salt.

"Come, we'll leave this place."

But when they left the caves, he stood on the high ground. The mountain was stone and stark, but the world beneath it simply glorious.

"I could have stopped her another way. She was mad, laughing, dancing, and, oh gods, broken in all ways already. She told me enough so I know how they got her as far as they did. I could've stopped her, but she said things we need to know. And she said he didn't want you dead, but, well . . ."

He shrugged with that. "But he'd promised her she'd have you as a slave once he was done with you. And she'd slit my mother's throat— such a hate there for a woman who was never less than kind to her. I never saw it in her. And wouldn't she bed my brother before she killed him. She'd cut off Morena's wings.

"She meant it all, you see. She wanted it, the blood and killing, the burning, the fucking golden throne he promised her. She wanted all of that with all she'd become, and gods help me, with any left of what she'd been.

"But I could have stopped her another way."

"You're wrong, Keegan. I saw her. She didn't have enough left of what she'd been to become one with the tree, so I saw her. If we'd come down the path and you hadn't been there, she'd have died by my hand. I'd have made the choice, the only choice, Keegan, because of the ones she'd made."

Though they'd yet to touch each other, not once, she turned to face him. "Banishment? You're thinking you could have stopped her, bound her with power, and banished her. But she'd never have stopped. She couldn't. And if Odran felt she was in any way useful, he'd have found a way to use her still."

"The banishment, the Dark World, would have destroyed her in any case. She was so broken, and I saw that, knew that. It seemed too cruel, and the sword somehow kinder."

"You're right, and I'm sorry it had to be this way."

"I'll tell the council, here and in the Capital, the whole of it. It will go no further. You were right about her parents. Telling them would lift some weight from my shoulders only to lay it on theirs."

He stepped back from her. "I don't want to touch you here, not near the caves where so much dark is under the rock. This isn't how I'd have welcomed you back home."

"Then let's leave the dark to the dark and go home."

As they mounted Cróga with the dog between them, he turned and glanced at her. "The gardens need watering."

"Really?"

He shrugged. "I'll see to it."

She waited until they flew, flew over the green and the brown and the blooms, then with the dog between them, leaned forward, to put her arms around him.

When they stood at the cottage, Cróga soaring back to Talamh, Bollocks rushing toward the bay, Keegan put his around her.

And took her mouth with his in the sunlight, in the spring air that smelled of grass and earth and brave blossoms.

The cold, hard air of the Bitter Caves and all they held blew away in the warmth.

"I missed you more than I wanted." He cupped her face. "This face of yours, I missed seeing it."

"Good." She cupped his in turn, pleased to see the green of his eyes clear of grief and guilt.

"And while you're so happy to see me, I have something to ask you."

"Well, you can ask as you please, but the answer might not be as you please."

"I'm aware. First, I saw Marco's mother. I couldn't get through, couldn't make her understand or accept. And I'm not going to tell him."

"Because it would bring back grief, and lay weight on him."

"Exactly. I stopped trying because all I was doing was hurting her. After, I went to see my mother, and unburdened myself."

"All right. How is that done?"

"By forgiving her."

"That's wise of you." He turned and brought a gentle shower of rain down on the young vegetable garden.

"Taking the easy way."

"This time, so I can hear you out. I'm saying that was wise, and I'm thinking I couldn't find that much wise in myself."

"It's taken the weight away, so in some ways I did it for myself. Then I got this." She pulled the sweater she wore down her shoulder.

He shook his head, but his lips curved as he trailed a finger over the words. "You will decorate yourself, won't you? But that's a good way to do it, *Iníon*."

"I thought so. Then we went to Sally's."

"Are these stories you're telling me or an asking?"

"I'm getting to the asking. It's all connected—I realized that when I saw Sally and Derrick. They're already planning Marco's wedding there. Or mostly Sally is."

She tipped her head. "You should look excellent in tails."

"I'd look good with a tail?"

"No, tails—it's a form of men's dress. Very formal dress. Anyway, I want them to have that, all of them, where Marco's sister can come, and all our friends from there. Oh, Meabh is wonderful, by the way. I want them to have all that," she continued. "But I want, very much, for Sally and Derrick to come to Marco's wedding here. I want them to know, I want to stop lying to them, and to show them Talamh and what I am."

"Well, all right then."

Now she stepped back. "Just like that?"

"They can't pass through the Welcoming Tree if they mean harm, and all I saw in your Sally when we met was love for you, and Marco as well. And a clever, interesting sort of person beyond that.

"Forgave your mother, did you? It's more than that. By forgiving her, you've accepted she bore you, raised you, but she's not mother to you. You want the one who is to be part of your life. And Marco's. And this is your life, and his."

"There's that nutshell again. Yes, exactly that. When it's safe, I want them to come here, see the cottage. I want to explain everything to them and bring them over to Talamh and show them. I want them to meet Nan and everyone."

"All right then," he repeated.

"All right." She thought of all the strong arguments she'd prepared. Then just smiled. "I'm going to unpack. Don't forget the flowers, and the pots."

"I'll get to them. You haven't said any of the New York business, and the meetings and all of it."

"It was great, it was good. Lots of stories, like Marco signing with an agent to represent the in-progress and tentatively titled *The Fun of Cooking* cookbook."

"That's grand. We'll give him all the help we can by sampling any dish he thinks of putting in it."

"Selfless. And they bought my book."

"As I told you they would. You don't sob with it this time, I see."

"I got light-headed for a minute, but I didn't cry. My editor's going to send an email with a few changes."

"I didn't read anything that needed changing."

"They're actually really good changes. A few days' work, and it'll be better and stronger." She covered her mouth with her hands and laughed. "I sold my book."

And launched herself at him. Wanting in on the fun, Bollocks ran out of the bay, shook water all over as he raced circles around them.

"*Magicks Dark and Light* by Breen Siobhan Kelly, coming to a bookstore near you whenever they figure that part out."

"I like this better than the weeping."

"Me, too."

"But I remember very well what came after the weeping, and I think that bears repeating."

With her arms and legs wrapped around him, he walked toward the house.

"You can unpack later."

"I can unpack later," she agreed, and since he'd forgotten, sent the gentle shower over her flowers and pots as he carried her into the cottage.

CHAPTER TWENTY-EIGHT

Breen sat in on council meetings in the valley, and worked with Marg, Finola, and others on plans for the festival. She worked in her gardens and finished her revisions (with fingers crossed they worked). And focused her writing time on Bollocks's next adventure.

If the ideas for the new book sounded too loud and long in her head, she shifted over—no more than an hour allowed—and let them play out on the page.

She trained, as hard as she knew how, and practiced her craft with Marg.

With the days full and growing longer, she barely had a moment that wasn't designated for specific tasks.

And April bled into May.

The cracks in the portals, every one, widened. Almost imperceptibly, Keegan told her, but they widened.

Would Odran wait for the solstice? she wondered. Or would he come sooner? Or wait longer yet?

Though she treasured every day, the spring rains, the spring sun, the way the sky stayed light later and later in Talamh and in Ireland, she wanted it over. One way or the other, over and finished.

She watched Fey start the work on Marco and Brian's cottage, with so many giving their time and skills—and their opinions.

"We could have it done sooner," Marg told her, "as we did with yours. But there's time enough, as both of them say they'll stay with you until we're finished with Odran."

"However fast or slow, it's going to be so right. I love the opening

Seamus made, and the arbor. It makes it like walking from one fairy-
land to another."

"He's got a way, Seamus does." As pleased as Breen, Marg looked
back at it, the tall arch where fuchsia and white roses twined together.
"And the scent of the roses carries from one to the other. Your gardens
do well indeed, *mo stór*. You've a way of your own."

"I love growing things. That comes from you and my father."

"The love of it, but your strong connection, that's yours. I have a
touch, as did Eian, but not so deep as yours. Ah, look at that dog,
would you? Running about, nosing into everything."

"He loves having everyone around. It's a party every day for
Bollocks. And when Morena or Harken brings Darling over, it's a
lovefest. He'll be thrilled when he can run from one cottage to the
other."

"And yours, *mo stór*, is there anything you'd want to change? It can
be done easy enough."

"I love it, Nan. From the first moment I saw it, I loved it. I didn't
know then it was my homeplace, but it was, and it is."

"Aye, but . . ." She took Breen's hand, strolled back through the
archway. "I wonder if you might want a true writing place, or a room
tucked up for the books and the reading."

She led the way in, left the door open in welcome as Marg did.
She'd make tea, she thought, and plate some of Marco's cookies. They
could enjoy it on the patio in the warm air with the buzz of activity
through the hedgerow.

"Well, if you do, it's easy enough. It might be you'll find the need
for another bedroom or two."

"I'll have Marco's when he and Brian are settled in their own place."

"That's true enough, but it might be you'd want more than one. If
children come along. I don't think I'm wrong that you'd want children."

"You're not." And she hoped, oh she hoped, children and a life
raising them, loving them, would be part of her destiny. "But I can't
even think about that, Nan, as long as Odran exists. Until he's gone,
any child of mine would be at risk.

"If I survive this—"

"Ah, Breen."

"That's part of it, so if I survive and he doesn't, I'd like to think of a future with children."

"Now, you'll forgive a nan for poking in her nose. Have you and Keegan talked of that future?"

"No." Breen got out a tray, began to arrange things on it. "I don't know what he wants, after."

The young, Marg thought with an inner sigh, so often moved slow. "So you don't ask or tell what you want?"

"I need to know I've got a future, then I guess I might ask, or tell. I'm happy as things are, and that counts for a lot."

"It does, of course. Ah, but he looks at you, my darling girl. How he looks at you."

"He does?"

She laughed at that and tapped a finger to Breen's cheek.

"I know a man besotted when I see one, whether or not he knows it himself. So I'll please myself, thinking of bedrooms for children, and that true writing space for my lovely scribe of a granddaughter." She wandered into the dining room. "Oh, and a little glass solarium sort of thing, so she can putter about with plants in the warm during the winter chills."

"Oh, that sounds—" Catching herself, Breen lifted the tray. "Seductive, as you meant it to. We'll just wait. We've got a multiday festival to plan."

"That we do, and look here, there's Finola and Morena come along early to help do just that."

Breen set the tray back down. "I'll get more cups."

Bollocks dashed through the arbor, visibly beside himself with excitement over yet more company. He got his greeting, and since Finola offered him something out of the basket she carried, a treat to go with it.

"What a lovely day! Oh, and look at the gardens!" Nearly as thrilled as Bollocks, Finola beamed everywhere. "Breen, sure you've a Sidhe's hand with the planting," she said as Breen brought out the tray.

Finola looked like a flower herself in leggings of rosy pink with a long white shirt covered with rosebuds over them.

"Seamus is a patient and wonderful teacher. Is it too noisy out here with all the work going on? We can take this inside."

"Not on such a day. Now, in here I've got some very nice cheese from the farm and some bread baked this morning." Out of the basket they came. "And some of the agenda, we'll say, for the festival. We'll fuss that out among the four of us, won't we, before we pass it along to the rest."

"Having it mostly settled, Nan says, will save time and, more than time, the trouble of arguing." Morena snagged a biscuit. "Mostly she just doesn't want Jack and his sister Nelly wading in until the whole business is sunk in more plans than doing."

"That's the truth of it. So we'll spend this part of a lovely day working it all out, then Marg will take what we've laid out to them, Michael Maguire, and Dek of the Trolls."

"Oh now, Fi, you, my friend all these years, would set me to such a task!"

"There's not a one of them who'd go against Mairghread O'Ceallaigh, and not a one of them who wouldn't argue to death such as me."

"Especially Nelly," Morena added. "She'd be Mina's great-grandmother, Breen, the young elf who runs the fields and woods with her friends."

Laying some cheese on a bit of bread, Finola wagged them in the air. "Three years past at a valley fair, my peach pie won the prize, and never will she forget I nudged her out of it."

"And your plum jam beat hers as well," Marg recalled.

"True enough, though I'm not one to brag." Laughing, Finola brushed a hand at her sassily cut chestnut hair. "We'll have the baking contests for the festival for certain, and for certain as well, I fear we'll all fall before our Marco. Is he over there then? The handsome Marco?"

"He is, learning how not to bang his finger instead of a nail with a hammer."

Finola dimpled at Breen. "I'll just go over, say a hello, see what's what. And please my eyes with a look at all the men with hammers."

"Not that she won't please her eyes," Morena began when Finola strolled away, "but she's wanting to give us the time to talk of what we can't in front of her. It's safe to do so here if we need, you said, Marg."

"Odran can neither see nor hear anything that's done or said in Fey Cottage or its land. We've seen to it, layers of seeing to it."

"We're careful what we say at the farm, but for when we have the council meetings and close him off there. I don't know if it's that I can all but feel him watching or my mind playing the trick on me."

"He has to know Shana failed." Breen glanced toward the woods. "And I'm actually not sure he ever expected her to succeed, but it's been weeks, so he knows. And the cracks are widening, just a little more every day."

"With Yseult's dark magicks tied with his own, he'll look through the cracks, through the glass, through the fire and the fog. But what will he see?" Marg asked.

"Talamh," Breen answered. "Preparing for festivals to celebrate the solstice, and the Daughter's return. More concerned, for those three days, it seems, with fun than any threat. Warriors competing in feats of skill and strength rather than training."

"The Fey," Morena finished, "dancing and feasting and ripe for the burning."

"He doesn't know us." Marg listened to the laughter, the banging and buzzing behind the hedgerow. "In all his years he's never learned, and never will, who we are and what we'll do to hold this world. He sent that wicked girl to strike down our taoiseach, believing if she put that poisoned blade in Keegan, the whole of Talamh would fall into chaos and fear and despair. I'm grateful every day she failed, and can't find any sorrow in me for her death.

"Her parents have mourned already." Marg laid a hand over Breen's. "Convincing Keegan to let that be was a kindness to them. But had Keegan fallen that day, on the path between the worlds, Odran wouldn't have found chaos and fear and despair."

"Rage and strength." Morena nodded. "We find it and grow it tall even in our grieving. And what she told Keegan in her mad bragging? The red vines? We know that world and have it mapped, as we do the ice one with its searing light and its portal that connects it to this. The heat and the cold, and the portal that steams from the clash between them."

"Sedric's gone back this day to hunt yet again for the portal that must link Odran's world to the red vines."

Breen turned her hand under Marg's to grip it. "You didn't say he'd gone again."

"Not alone. He has three with him."

"But you worry."

"Love is worry. It's a small world, he tells me, brutal with the wet heat, the thick vines, and the bogs. A red sun and a single small, hazy moon. He swears they'll find it on this trip, as they've covered most of it on the others."

"Will they seal the portal?" Morena asked.

"Keegan says no. They'll lay a trap instead." As she spoke, Breen glanced over toward the arbor, knowing this wasn't for Finola's ears. "It's the connecting portal they'll seal once they're sure this is the way Shana came."

"Ah, I see, I see." Morena sampled the cheese. "And so they'll have no way through."

"More. The traps spring. When they come, when we know, we'll seal the way back. I've been working on the spell for it," Marg told them. "And with Sedric's gift, we can do this. There'll be no way back and no way forward for any he sends in that way."

"It would take them days to get here that way, Nan. You protect this side, as those he'd send through would attack here. Keegan and his scholars believe she came into Scotland from the Ice World, and from there to Ireland and the woods right there."

"The Fey pledge to protect all, and so we will. Do I worry? Of course. Sedric doesn't just share my bed but my entire world. In truth he brought my heart back to life. But he's as clever as the cat he is, so I trust he'll come home to me, and stand with me when we celebrate the end of Odran.

"Now, Morena darling, go fetch your nan. We'll talk of the festival and the fun—and gods, the headaches of seeing to the fun. And we'll talk of the defenses we'll have in secret that all in Talamh must know."

When they planned the festival and the fun, Breen wished the complex logistics of that could be all of it. But every contest and game for the young, and the not so young, held under it a defense or an offense, or both at once.

Every prettily aproned table holding food for feasting or goods for judging would have weapons stacked beneath the colorful cloths. Everyone competing in contests of skill and strength would prepare to use the bow or ax or club, the power and might to fight what came, whenever it came.

Any who danced to the pipes under sunlight, under moonslight across the whole of Talamh would launch into battle at the first sound of the horn.

The layers blinded Odran to those plots and plans, but those layers meant Breen couldn't see Odran's world from the cottage, not even in dreams.

But she felt him pushing, doing what he could to burn those layers away.

"Aye, he pushes," Keegan agreed as they walked back through the woods after a marathon training session that left her feeling battered. "That's what you'd call his ego, isn't it? Ah, they'll hide nothing from me."

"But isn't he bound to wonder why? Why he's blocked from here?"

Since Bollocks brought him a stick, Keegan obliged and threw it for him. "And as I've said before, it's why we had Marg do the covering spell. Your nan who frets for you, all the more since Shana made her way through, and all but to your doorstep. And if he wonders of you, you still come to Talamh every day for all the festival planning."

He paused, took the stick Bollocks brought back, tossed it farther—but this time into the stream to distract the dog.

"All the fuss about what colors for the banners and the buntings, is there to be a horse race here or there, how many lollies are needed for the littles. If there's a golden arrow as prize for the archery, should there be a gold spear for the spear chucking, and on and on. And I have to hear all this and more, not just in the valley but everywhere I go."

"These things matter, and in their way, almost as much as the arms you'll have stockpiled, and the way you've stationed your warriors, the trap you laid between the worlds Shana passed through."

"Ah, sure that was Sedric's thinking. A fine, sly mind he has."

"And a broad worldview. Or worldsview," she corrected. "What damage would Odran have done to this side with even a handful or two of his faithful attacking here while the others attack Talamh?"

"Now they'll live out their days, and considerably shortened at that, with the vines and the bogs and drenching heat."

"They'll turn on each other," she added. "That's the nature of the dark."

When they came out of the woods, he turned to her. "I find this a reversal of things."

"What reversal?"

"That your thoughts should lean to the dark. That's the usual place for mine. But you've shifted our places."

"What are your thoughts?"

He strolled down toward the bay as Bollocks arrowed to it, so she walked with him.

"That the time's come to end it, and we've a plan to do just that. Weapons, and the keenest in you, to end it. My father died, as did yours, in the trying, as did countless others since the first song or story of Odran came to Talamh. Never have we ended it, and not for lack of courage or power or unity. With that, all that, we beat him back.

"We had times of quiet and peace, but we never stuck a blade in his black heart and ended him. So he grew strong and turned the ruins of his black castle into its shine again. Stealing our children and murdering them on his altar. Dragging us to his world as slaves."

"Those are very dark thoughts."

Keegan shook his head as Bollocks swam and splashed.

"That's what's been. We keep our world in peace with our laws, our ways." He glanced over. "The ways of magicks, Breen Siobhan Kelly."

"I know."

"He wants to destroy that because he sees only the power here."

"He sees power like a pie, like some people see love."

Curious, he turned to her. "A pie, is it?"

"Yeah, a pie, where there are only so many pieces of it, and if one person has a piece, there's less for you. Since he doesn't believe or understand that power—like love—is infinite, that it only grows when shared, he covets."

"A pie," Keegan repeated. "Ha, that's a fine way to say it all. It's now we'll end it, and him, so he won't have what he sees as any piece of it. Not in this world or any. We end him, *mo bandia*, this time, for all time. I feel that in a way I've never felt before. So my thoughts aren't so dark. There's light coming."

"The longest day."

"We'll know soon enough. The dog has a fine idea there with a swim in the bay. A good way to end a day in May after an easy training session."

"You call that easy?"

"I do, aye, so it was. Taking it easier on you so if Odran looks, he sees that, and how quick you tire and fall so he thinks you've little skill."

"Bollocks, and I don't mean the dog. And I'm ending my day with a long, hot shower and a glass of wine."

"Sure you won't need the shower after a swim."

He plucked her up, tossed her as easily as he had the stick. She managed one stunned curse before she hit the water.

Drenched, she pushed up to stand in water nearly to her waist while Bollocks swam happy circles around her and Keegan stood on the shore grinning.

"Jesus! Men are such *boys*!" She shoved at her dripping hair.

"So you may think, but I'm looking at a wet woman with her clothes all clinging to her body—clothes I'll remind you I didn't strip away without permission. And I'm not thinking like a boy, not a'tall."

"So you throw me into the water fully dressed. And it's cold!"

"Bracing." He stripped down to the skin with a flick of his hands, then walked in. "That's what it is, bracing."

"My ass."

"I've a great fondness for it."

"Then you can watch it walking away. I'm going inside."

"Ah now, *mo bandia*, swim with me awhile, on a bright spring evening."

He circled her waist and towed her out until she was over her head. "Why don't we get those clothes off, and on the shore with mine. With your permission, of course."

"I'm not skinny-dipping in the bay. Marco and Brian are in the cottage. They left before we did. And the water's cold!"

"Swimming will warm you quick enough." He twirled a finger in the air, calling a mist. "And there, you see, like a curtain. We'll have those wet clothes and the sodden boots off you, and dry on the shore."

He kissed her as he said it, and as he held her now skin to skin.

"Your body doesn't spark in the blood of those in the cottage as it does in mine. But they're men and lovers and will likely suspect what's going on inside the mist."

"Swimming."

"Aye, but after, if you will. Let me push those dark thoughts away for you."

"We might drown."

"There's Mer in me, and I've been practicing. Let me show you." He kissed her brow, her jaw, her lips.

He slid inside her.

"Give over to me, will you, Breen Siobhan? In the waters and the mists, give yourself to me."

He rocked her in the waters and the mists, slowly, so she floated on them. So she gave herself to him.

And when he took her under, she felt no panic, only pleasure as his hands streamed over her. As his mouth, joined with hers, breathed air into her.

Under the water with the sun sparkling its surface, with the mists rising, he took her and took all he wanted. When she came, she had no thoughts at all, only the sensations rippling over her skin and under it, only the heat that burst into her.

He took them up, still joined, still clinging.

She felt the rush of air, the spin of the mist, the sway of the water. And him. And him.

When she peaked again, he went with her. So they floated down together.

She couldn't claim to be cold now.

"You've been practicing that?"

He laughed against her throat. "Not all of that, no, but I imagined it well enough. I've been seeing how long I can stay under, and it's longer each time. Longer by far now than even the day I took the sword, and on that day the water's charmed for it. Not as fast as a Mer in the water, or an elf on the land, but faster on both than I was before I reached for it.

"Good training," he said. "But this is a different matter, this with you, and a different gift."

He cleared the mists enough she saw Bollocks onshore, and just how far out they were from it as he jumped in again.

"We're really far out." This time, she felt a lick of panic. "It's too far for him to swim."

"Sea dog he is, but we'll meet him. I'm here if you tire, but I know from the river by the falls, you're a strong swimmer. I'd say I'd race you, but it doesn't seem fair."

"Then give me a head start."

She aimed toward shore, and thought she cut through the water cleanly enough. By the time she reached the dog, she saw Keegan streak by them, as fast as a fish.

"You might have to haul me in," she told Bollocks, "since he's busy showing off."

Then she realized her feet touched the bottom. Treading water, she called out to Keegan, now standing back onshore.

"I'd appreciate that mist again before I get out."

"The child of man in you worries too much about naked."

He didn't, she mused, as he stood naked, warrior's body slicked with wet and gleaming in the evening sun.

She brought the mist herself before she walked out of the water.

She ran her hands through her hair to dry it as Keegan rubbed the wet from Bollocks. As they dressed, she studied him.

"You believe what you said before, that this is the time it ends, for all time."

"I do. As I believe you won't be asked to sacrifice your life to end it."

"Why do you believe that?"

He shrugged. "Because that's not how it ends."

"How does it end?"

"With Odran destroyed, with Talamh at peace, with you living content in your cottage and writing your stories with the dog napping by the fire, with Brian and Marco just over there. With you coming through the portal into Talamh as you please."

Her cottage—that struck hard. Hers, not theirs.

"A happy ending."

"Not for Odran. For the rest of us, why shouldn't it be? You're the key, and when you open the lock, it's done. We'll fight so that you can, and some will fall. It's enough. It's bloody well enough, Breen, and that's what I believe. And believing's what makes magicks strong. So believe."

"I'll work on that."

She wanted to tell him she loved him, but held back. Not from fear, she realized, but for much the same reason she'd had to stop him from telling Shana's parents of her death.

What good would it do if belief wasn't enough in the end? If she was the one who fell, how much harder for him to accept if he knew all she felt, all she wanted, all she hoped for?

"I'll work on that," she repeated, and reached for his hand.

CHAPTER TWENTY-NINE

Spring rushed by. Breen remembered that in her old life May had dragged its pretty feet so the last weeks before the summer break seemed endless. Now it raced like an elf. No matter how she tried to hold each day, one simply slid into the next.

June brought constant inner conflict. As much as she wanted it all over, wanted the chance to live a life without fear and threat, she dreaded what would come.

What had to come.

She reminded herself she'd been given a year of wonder, of love and discovery, of dreams coming to fruition. If she could have no more than that year, it had to be enough.

And still she looked, she searched, in the fire and the smoke, in the flicker of a candle flame, in the globe, in her dreams.

But visions remained shadows, silent and secret.

She worked the garden, found real joy in watching the flowers bloom, in hoeing rows, mounding potato plants, learning how to stake tomatoes.

She wrote, and the writing became a kind of escape. She completed the next Bollocks book, then ordered herself to hit send and zip it off to New York.

Because she desperately wanted that escape, she barely took a breath before she began the next. And beginning the next gave her hope she'd live to finish it.

Live her wonder of a life in two worlds.

She trained, though her aches and bruises belied Keegan's scale of light and easy. She practiced, with Marg and on her own. Every skill learned, every skill honed, made her stronger.

She helped with plans and preparation for the festival.

Then, so fast, the time of planning and preparation ended.

She rejected Marco's wish for her to wear one of the summer dresses he'd talked her into buying in New York. If she had to fight to the death, it wouldn't be in a sundress.

Besides, and he agreed, the sword at her side ruined the look.

"I hope the sun's shining over there." Though he'd already delivered contributions of a honey-glazed ham, had Brian haul over boxes of baked goods, Marco carried more.

"It is."

"What is what?"

"The sun. It's a bright day in Talamh."

"How do you know? Wait. You can tell from over here?" Eyes rolling, he gave her an elbow bump. "Why the hell haven't you said so before?"

"Once I figured out I could look and see, I realized I kind of liked the surprise of it, so didn't. But I did today."

"Girl, get my sunglasses out of my pocket and put them on my good-looking face."

Since she carried less than he did, she obliged.

He'd tied back his braids with a red leather band that matched his T-shirt and high-tops. The high-tops sported silver laces that matched his belt and the stud in his ear.

He put rainbow ribbons in Bollocks's topknot. And the dog seemed very pleased with them.

He'd entered contests—today's entries included cherry pie and strawberry shortcake—and he'd man a stand bartering sweets when he wasn't serving as one of the judges on fruit jam or putting in time as a coordinator of two of the races for littles.

He and Breen would also, as he wouldn't take no, help provide musical entertainment.

Marco, Breen thought, had fully embraced life in Talamh, and the community of the valley.

"Brian'll be off portal duty in a couple hours. He's in the first round of the archery competition, and I gotta be there to cheer him on. You know I had to give him a lot of nudges to enter."

"I know, and you did right. Busy helps dull grief. I know it'll be hard for him to see the dragon riders doing their flying tricks."

"I was thinking we could plant something over at our cottage for Hero. A pretty tree or something like that, but I don't know if that'll just be an always reminder."

"I think it's the perfect thing, Marco, and in time the reminder will be a comfort."

She didn't need to see his eyes behind the shades to see the worry in them. "Do you think?"

"I really do. A pretty tree, and a bench under it. One of the stone-masons could do a dragon motif."

"A dragon motif," he murmured. "Yeah, yeah. That's good, Breen, thanks." At the tree, he shifted his boxes. "Ready to get your festival on?"

"Not as much as you are, but I'm ready."

They stepped through into the promised sunlight. And color.

So much color, Breen thought. She'd helped with some of the banners, the bunting, the stalls, the brightly flagged ropes dividing fields into contest areas, and still it dazzled.

Fires smoked, and the smoke carried the scent of roasting meat. Stands with their pretty awnings held displays of baked goods, fruits, vegetables, crafts.

A juggler danced up the road, then spread blue wings and took his performance to the air. Kids swarmed, already holding lollies or munching biscuits or spinning hoops on sticks.

But she saw, as planned, at least three adults move along with the groups of children. Warriors might have moved casually along with farmers, craftspeople, cottagers, but every one, she knew, held prepared should this be the day.

"Man, it's really beautiful. It's like a movie set. Listen to that piper, Breen. That girl's got it going on!"

Some of the women wore dresses as bright as the flags, others opted for trousers, and others, like Breen, for leggings. Better movement in case of battle, she'd decided when she'd dressed. Even if now she felt a purely feminine longing for the breeziness of that summer dress.

She started down with Marco and gave Bollocks the go-ahead. He leaped over the wall to meet Darling—adorned with ribbons and tiny bells.

Finola rushed over. "There you are! And with more treats. Marco, we put out the biscuits you sent early with Brian, and every crumb gone."

"Yeah? I got more."

"I did the bartering for you, so I hope you're pleased. We'll want to get your pie and cake right over to the contest area, as they'll start the judging in an hour or so."

She bustled them along, weaving through the crowds. "You've missed the first round of the first feat of strength. Loga won it, as expected, but wouldn't you know young Ban gave him some stiff competition, so he along with three others move along to the next round."

"Is Sul here?" Breen wondered.

"Oh aye, and cheering on her mate with the new babe in a pallet on her back. Barely a month old and young Breen of the Trolls looks strong enough to compete herself."

She stopped, linked her hands together. "And here's where we've put you, Marco—a popular spot, as I said. And you can watch the archers from here when that starts up. I like we did all the awnings in red and white. It makes a nice picture."

"So do you," Marco said, and got the flirt-eye in response.

"I felt in the pink, so I dressed in it." She did a quick turn in her palest-of-pale-pink dress so it swirled around her knees. "What a fine day it's been already. We miss Keegan, of course, but as taoiseach he's obliged to open the festival in the Capital. Still, you won't lack for dancing partners tonight, Breen."

Breen just smiled, moved behind the stand. "Get your goodies to the contest tent, Marco. I'll set out what you have to restock the stand, if you trust me to handle the bartering."

"You don't mind?"

"Not a bit. It's a great view from here."

"Prime real estate, we'll say." Finola winked. "And here's Morena now to lend a hand."

She wouldn't be left alone, Breen knew. Another part of the planning meant she'd have someone with her or shadowing her until she crossed over again.

Morena had a trio of braids tied up high to bounce with bells at her back, and leggings like Breen, but hers with a shirt whirled with shades of purple. She'd gone with a short sword, and Breen knew she had a dagger in her boot.

"Thank the gods you've brought more. The Trolls all but cleaned you out, Marco, before any of the rest of us had a chance. Breen and I will take over here while you take the rest for the judging."

"Appreciate it. I'll be back!"

Morena came around, glanced down. Below the table, swords, bows, quivers were stacked.

"We've gotten off to a fine start," she said. "The littles are half-mad with it all. Aisling has her hands full organizing them into groups for games, but she's plenty of help with it. Harken's just down there, do you see? Between helping with the pony rides and organizing today's horse race—the starting line's near Marg's cottage—he has his own hands full."

She unboxed biscuits as she spoke. "Marg, she's up closer to Nan's cottage, helping with the wool and sweaters, caps, scarves, and such. I've sheared more sheep this spring than I ever hope to again."

Letting me know where everyone is, Breen realized.

"I'll have to take a look—not at the wool, since my knitting's hopeless, but at the sweaters and such. Is Sedric with her?"

"Close by with his own baked goods stand. The competition in the judging tents will be fierce for certain."

They talked like two friends without a care in the world, and before long had customers. Since Morena proved a better barterer, Breen let her run that show and wrapped the goods.

"I'm told Tarryn will come in with some dragon riders tomorrow," Morena continued. "She'll have time with the family. Keegan visits the festivals in the midlands today after the morning in the Capital, then to the North, the South, the Far West, before he comes to the valley for the solstice."

She knew all this, of course, but it comforted her to hear it.

"I'm sorry your family won't be able to visit and see how beautiful it all looks in the valley."

"They've more than enough to keep them busy at the Capital."

And the Capital required warriors at the ready, and others to keep the young safe.

Yet she felt no threat here, not here, Breen thought. Here it was all excitement and color, a cheerful kind of carnival, where fathers carried children on their shoulders, people cheered and applauded at the contests. Couples strolled hand in hand and the flags and bunting swayed in the warm breeze.

Well into the afternoon, Marco strutted around, his belled ribbon on his sleeve.

"Sedric nipped me on the pie, but nobody tops my strawberry shortcake. And that one's going in the book for sure." He draped an arm over Breen's shoulders as they walked to watch the first rounds of archery. "How you doing, my Breen?"

"Absolutely fine, even knowing I've got another long stint of cleanup coming, since there's not one of your cookies or tarts left."

"I'm doing some soda bread for tomorrow's contest. No way to beat Finola there, but a man's gotta try."

They watched Brian and Morena advance to the next round. She laughed until her ribs ached at the kids in their sack races. She cheered along with the others gathered when Harken signaled the start of the horse race that sent the mounts and their riders thundering down the road.

With Marg, she wandered the stalls, and bartered.

She sang with Marco as afternoon blurred toward evening, and danced with Sedric, with Brian, with a sleepy Kavan, who rested his head on her shoulder.

And as the sun set on the long day, the fire lit.

Finian slipped his hand into hers. "Ma says we can stay only a few more minutes."

She glanced over, saw Kavan asleep in Mahon's arms, and Kelly in the sling Aisling wore.

"There'll be more fun and games tomorrow."

"The dragons ride tomorrow. I dreamed of my dragon again, the one you said I'd ride one day."

"Did you?" Because he looked so sleepy, she picked him up so he could rest against her.

"Do you think it'll be soon? I can ride my horse very well indeed, though Da says no racing as yet."

"I think it'll be sooner than you think, but not as soon as you want. He still needs his mother."

"You healed him that day. I felt it," he said, eyes half-closed as she looked at him. "They hurt him, the dark ones, and his light near to went out. But you found it and made it strong again."

"Did you feel it or see it?"

"Both. Do you think I could ride with you and Bollocks on your dragon sometime?"

"If your mother says you can."

She started to carry him to Aisling, then saw it. Saw in the fire and smoke.

Saw Odran's world, saw herself in it. The terrible sky, the raging sea, the black castle, the jagged cliffs.

Where she stood with Odran, her sword stained with blood, and he, his golden hair streaming in the wild wind he called.

And she saw, in the fire, the choice she made. And the end that came with it.

"I saw you," Finian murmured, and yawned as he snuggled against her. "I saw you there. Where were you? I don't know that place. It wasn't good, though. I could tell even though it wasn't clear. You should stay here with us, in the valley where it's good."

He'd seen because she had, and because his powers continued to rise. And he was a child, not yet four, who shouldn't see dark places.

"I'll be back in the valley tomorrow." She turned her head to brush her lips over his hair and send sweet dreams into his mind.

He slept in the way of young children, so trusting and deep. She took him back to his parents and watched them carry their three boys home to bed.

"Don't even tell me you're ready to call it a night."

She turned to Marco. "Who said I was?"

"You, usually."

"I'm wondering why you aren't dancing with me."

"Yeah?" He grabbed her hand, spun her away from the fire, from visions, and into the dance.

She didn't dream that night, and pushed away the dreams that wanted to creep in during that fragile hour before dawn.

Instead, she rose and let Bollocks out for an early swim. She brought light to join the pixies and wandered over to look at her garden. She walked through the arbor to admire the progress on Marco's cottage.

Daffodil-yellow walls, he'd decided. Because they'd be cheerful even on the cloudiest day. She imagined him there, working in the kitchen, or in the room he'd have for his music.

So much change in one year. So many wondrous changes.

She went in, wrote a blog about the gardens, Marco's cottage, about all the gifts given in a single year of her life.

When he, too, rose early, Marco baked. Brian kissed him goodbye, and Breen tackled the dishes and pans.

Once again, they carried boxes into Talamh.

She ran the stand with him, while watching Morena give hawking lessons. She watched the dragons and riders fly in from the east, then gave a young boy his wish and flew him up on hers to join them.

"Did you see me, Nan, did you see me?"

When they landed again, he ran to Tarryn.

"Sure I did, flying like the wind. And did you thank Breen for taking you up?"

"I did, I did, but thank you again. Come watch me win a prize tossing the ball!"

"I'll be right along." Tarryn held out her hands to Breen as Finian raced away. "You put a light in his eyes."

"I think that was Lonrach."

"One and the same. Oh, I'm glad to be in the valley. The festival in the Capital is glorious, I can't say different, but I so looked forward to having this time here. Are you enjoying it all?"

"Every minute. Minga didn't come?"

"Not this time. She's needed where she is. As is Keegan, I'm afraid. But you'll see him here tomorrow."

Tomorrow, she thought, and watched Finian win his prize, saw Morena and Brian advance to the next round. She sat with Marg on a wall and ate hand pies full of meat and spices.

Marco's soda bread fell to Finola's, but his lemon meringue pie triumphed.

"And look at you, two ribbons, is it?" Marg heaved a mock sigh. "You put us to shame, Marco."

"Wait until tomorrow, and my pound cake." He dropped down with them, with his happy excitement flowing. "And speaking of tomorrow. I have to root for Brian, because true love. You, Breen, you've got to root for Morena. We want one of them to score that golden arrow. Good thing Keegan's not here and can't compete any-way. Downside of the taoiseaching. Brian says nobody beats him with a bow—plus, you'd have to root for him, because true love. And don't bother saying different."

She shrugged before she realized that was Keegan's move. "Girl solidarity."

Eyebrows wiggling, Marco elbowed Marg. "But she didn't say different."

She enjoyed it, every minute, even as another day slipped away, as the moons rose too soon.

And when dawn broke on the longest day, she stood in Talamh watching the light come, hearing the stones sing.

Feeling the magicks rise.

She could have asked for nothing more beautiful, or a stronger sign that she would make the right choice. That when the longest day came again, the light would come and the stones sing.

Being Marco, he took over the farm kitchen for a big solstice breakfast. She sat at the table with so many she loved, listening to the voices, seeing the faces.

No, she could have asked for nothing more.

"This is the big one," Marco said as they walked the path back to Talamh after a trip to the cottage to get the last mountain of his baked goods. "And you know, maybe it'll be just what it's supposed to be. Just a celebration. Nobody's seen any sign the last couple, right?"

"Please don't count on that, Marco. You need to stay prepared."

"I'm prepared. I'm prepared to win my third ribbon, because nobody nowhere's tasted the likes of my kick-ass pound cake."

"I can't argue with that, because I've had your pound cake."

"Damn straight. And I'm prepared to fight that psycho if he tries to spoil everything. We've got you, Breen, today and always."

They crossed over.

"Glad we got here earlier today," he said. "I want to see if Loga holds his championship. Man, look at those jugglers today! Tossing flaming torches back and forth up there. Cirque du Soleil's got nothing on the valley."

She walked with him to his stand. "It's home for you now, like your cottage will be. We both ended up living in two worlds, Marco, when for most of our lives we never really fit in one."

"Except at Sally's."

"Except at Sally's."

"I see worry coming in, right here." He tapped a finger between her eyebrows. "You just . . ." He trailed off, smiled. Then he turned her around, pointed up. "Look up there."

She looked, and saw Keegan soaring in on Cróga, flanked by two riders.

The cheers rose up, and she imagined they rolled from one end of the valley to the other. The taoiseach was home.

She stayed where she was. It would take time, she knew, for him to make his way to her. Duties, responsibilities, traditions.

She understood all of that.

When he did, people parted ways for him to approach. He studied the baked goods, pointed at a peach tart. "I'll have that, and what will you have for it?"

"I think for the taoiseach, there doesn't need to be a trade."

"That's not the way, no. Effort and skill went into it, and a trade's a trade. Did you have part in the making of it?"

"If peeling peaches and cleaning up after's a part."

"It is, of course. Well then, I'll trade these."

In his palm he showed her a pair of sapphire earrings, delicate drops that fell from silver wires into slim points.

"They're beautiful, and too much for a tart."

"Take the trade, woman. Ninia in the Capital said they were meant for you, so take them and put them on." He took her hand, dropped them in, then snagged a tart.

"Liam, come mind this stall, would you? Put them on," he demanded, then grabbed her hand before she could and pulled her away. "I want a walk, and away from most of the bustle for five fecking minutes."

He lifted her over the wall, then pulled her up the steps and over to the other side.

"What are you doing? What are you doing? They're all going to think you yanked me over here so you could just bang me against some tree."

"Why would I bang— Ah, I have it." He actually laughed as he shoved at his hair in a way that told her he was exhausted. "Would there was time for it. But let them think it, and let Odran think the same, as I have no doubt he's got us in his sights by now, for it's today. I know that as sure as I know my own name."

She looked into his eyes, so green, so intense. And right now, so full of life and light. "It's today."

"You've seen it."

"I feel it."

"As do I." He paced away. "The summer solstice, it's important to us, and he knows that. He thinks its importance to us means we're unprepared for him. He's wrong. I wanted to speak to you where he can't see or hear, and I was delayed some, as Harken tells me Eryn, the mare who mated with Merlin, is at her time."

"She's going to foal? Does he need help? I've never—but I could try."

"He'll deal with it, and sees no problems with the birthing."

He stopped pacing to scowl at her. "Why aren't you putting them on? You don't want them? They don't suit you?"

"No, of course they suit me. They're beautiful, but—"

"Then put them on, and get that much off my head, would you?"

"Okay, all right. What did you need to say to me here?"

"That it's today, which you already knew yourself, and to remind you not to wander. Stay close. I have to mix about, as it's expected. So stay close with others, and no wandering about on your own."

He took her shoulders. "Be ready. We'll fight, and we'll draw him through as we planned. We draw him through, as he'll be weaker in Talamh than in his own world. We've taken the battle to him time and again, and stopped him, but never ended him."

"I understand that."

"Don't be afraid. You have all of Talamh with you."

"I won't be afraid."

He touched a finger to one of the earrings, sent it swaying. "They suit you well enough, I think. And while I'd enjoy banging you against a handy tree, and I'd make certain you enjoyed it as well, we'll settle, for now."

He drew her in, took her mouth as she took his.

She wanted the taste, the feel, the scent of him, so drew it all in. And held on a moment longer.

"I'll need you to go with me to the Capital." He drew back, held her shoulders again to look into her eyes. "To fly over all of Talamh, and to stand with me where all can see so they know the dark is done."

"It's not done yet." She reached up to touch his face. "But I'll be with you, and all of Talamh will know it's done."

"We'll have a quiet time after all that. A quiet time is what I want with you."

He kissed her hand, a rare move, but in an absent way that told her his mind was already elsewhere.

On Talamh, the battle, the end.

"Don't wander," he said a last time before he led her back from one world to the other.

She stepped into the color and music and movement. Into the magicks that had changed her life. That had, she thought, made her life.

So she turned to him, in Talamh, took his face in her hands, and lifted up to kiss him where any who wished to could see.

Then smiled at him. "I'll be with you, and I'm ready."

She saw faces she knew grinning back as she walked to the stand.

"I've got this, Liam, thanks."

She watched Keegan cross the road while dragons flew overhead. While crops grew in fertile fields and livestock grazed.

In the stables, a life was coming, and opening herself to it, she saw it would be a colt with Merlin's markings.

She laid a hand on Bollocks's head, and watched her world, their world. And knew the wonder of peace.

For a moment, one crystalline moment, absolute peace.

When the horn sounded and the alarm carried across the valley, she stood ready.

She'd made her choice.

"Protect the children," she said to Bollocks, and drew her sword.

CHAPTER THIRTY

Faeries spread wings to fly children to safety; elves blurred away with littles on their backs or in their arms.

Many whisked through the portal, where they'd stay on the other side until it was safe to return to Talamh.

Safe, Breen thought, if—no, *when*—they won this last battle.

Warriors, and any who could fight, took up sword, bow, club, spear from the hidden stockpiles. She took up a bow, slung it and a quiver on her back.

Several of the Wise would bespell the tasting tents into fortified healing stations for the wounded. On the fields where children had raced, the Fey formed lines of defense. So it would be across Talamh.

This ambush would meet a well-armed and well-prepared army.

Odran would not take the valley. He would not take Talamh.

She reached down under the stall where she'd kept them, put on the pendant, put on the diadem.

She'd wear both into battle.

As she called her dragon, horses and riders thundered down the road. Dragons and riders swept through the sky, all to form other lines, to move in as reinforcements at the waterfall.

And scouts headed east to sound a call if the enemy broke through the line at the next portal.

Had Sedric sealed the crossing in the world of the red vines, she wondered, trapping the enemy inside?

She trusted he had.

When Lonrach landed, she ran behind Bollocks to mount.

"Wait! Breen!"

Marco came running. He carried a crossbow, a sword.

"I'm going with you."

"Marco."

"I can handle it! Brian's at the waterfall. He's at the damn front, I'm going with you."

She didn't argue. "We won't let you fall."

"Just get there."

She felt him tremble once as Lonrach rose.

Even as they flew toward the fight, Harken and Morena, on dragon-back, fell in beside her.

"We're with you," Morena called out. "Keegan and Mahon and a dozen more are well ahead of us. Aisling has children safe on your side, and my nan has more in the next shelter."

"My nan, Sedric?"

"Springing the trap as planned," Harken told her. "They'll not get through that way."

She saw riders and winged warriors flying in from the Far West. The Mers would hold the sea line, she knew, and fight from the bay as well. She could hear the wild war cries of the Trolls charging to battle with their clubs and spears, and thought of Sul and the daughter she'd birthed on a pretty day in May.

She felt her heart drumming, pounding, thudding inside her chest, in her throat. It wasn't like the battle at the Tree of Snakes. That had happened so fast, and this, this was planned, coordinated, expected.

Here, she didn't fly to warn, but to fight. To kill. To end.

Though she'd told Keegan she wouldn't be, she was afraid. Afraid she wouldn't be enough, and she had to be.

For a moment, she closed her eyes, let the power rise up, let the whole of herself embrace it.

She would be enough.

Then they winged through the woods toward the thunder of the waterfall, the cries and clashes of battle, the stench of smoke and death.

Bollocks let out a rumbling snarl and leaped off to sink his teeth into the throat of a dark Were in wolf form. Breen shifted, gripped her friend's hand, met his eyes.

"Stay alive, Marco."

And jumped after the dog.

Don't think, she remembered. Act.

She hurled power at an elf, caught him as he blurred to attack. She blocked the sword of one swinging toward her, one that hesitated when the dark faerie wielding it recognized her.

So she followed through and plunged her own into the heart.

Capture, she realized, not kill. Of course.

That gave her an advantage.

She used it, fighting with sword, with power, with feet and fists as every hour of Keegan's unrelenting training had taught her. Using all she had to keep the enemy from breaking through.

But they came and they came, so many.

She beheaded a demon dog, and everything in her shook at the horror of it, at the wash of blood on her hands, at the taste of it in her throat.

She whirled to meet power with power, watched the witch with the dark face, dark heart move steadily forward as she tossed tiny fireballs, small, keen bolts. Breen felt the sting when one slipped through to graze her side.

"Only a little blood," the witch said, smiling. "Odran wants the rest."

"He won't get it." Breen crossed her arms, pressed a hand to the wound. And when she flung her arms apart, hurled power and blood.

Burning, the witch screamed as she ran, shrieked as she fell, smothered by flame and smoke.

A gargoyle leaped out of a tree, onto her back with claws digging. Too crazed with battle and blood to stop, he bared his fangs to bite.

Before Breen could defend, he fell to the ground, an arrow in his back.

"I'm with you," Morena said, and nocked another, then another, letting them fly at the gargoyles poised to leap from the same tree.

Bollocks charged through the smoke to finish one that crawled, fangs snapping.

"Marco?"

"Fighting like a mad thing. He got through to Brian. Mind your right."

Breen spun and slashed what came.

"Brian's wounded, not badly." Out of arrows, Morena shifted to her sword. "Harken closed the gash. You've one of your own."

"It's nothing. There's too many of them, Morena."

"Aye. We'll need to fall back, let them give chase and come against the second line. Keegan— Ah, he's already thought the same."

Breen looked up as Keegan, on Cróga again, swooped low. Leaning over, he grabbed Breen's arm to haul her up. "Now, Morena, fall back now."

She spread her wings as the horns sounded retreat.

"You're bleeding," he said to Breen.

"I'll fix it."

"Then fix it. We've cut their numbers, and deep." He spun Cróga, laid a line of fire to slow the enemy advance. "The second line will meet them and cut it deeper yet. You'll stay behind the line now, as once they hit that line, they'll know we laid a trap."

"I can fight."

"And fight you will, but behind the line. Some will get through, so we have a third."

He soared over formations of archers, of those with swords, those with spears. On horseback, on wing, on feet fleeter than both.

"Hold!" he shouted. "Hold until they're clear of the trees. Once they are, take the rescue in to bring out our wounded. Riders!" He whirled again toward the dragons and riders hovering in the air. "No flame until I give the order."

He dived down. "Off you go. Behind the line, Breen. Stand strong, but behind the line."

She dropped to the ground. The waiting was worse, she found, so much worse than the fighting. It kicked the heart into a gallop, rang like bells in the ears.

The energy simply waved from the warriors, hot, so hot and still. For a long moment, the world seemed the same. Hot, so hot and still. Without a breath stirring under the bold, bright sun of the longest day.

Morena, quiver full again, dropped down beside her.

"There, the first of us. They'll think we're running, that they broke our line."

Harken flew out, and she nearly wept to see Bollocks riding with him. The shouts and cries came with them, tribal and fierce. And on the second line, the drums began their beat.

Brian flew out, one arm around Marco.

"I'll just give him a hand with our friend there."

Morena zipped over, wrapped an arm around Marco to take some of the weight.

They dropped him beside Breen, stayed hovering above, Morena with an arrow nocked, Brian with sword drawn.

"Brian got hurt, but he's okay. He's okay."

She gripped his hand, grateful to look and find none of the blood and gore on his face, staining his shirt, was his.

"Jesus, Breen, here they come."

"Archers," Keegan called from above. "Hold! Hold!"

They charged out of the trees. On the ground, in the air, a flood of them, screaming in triumph at the retreat.

"Now!"

And the flood was met with a storm of arrows that turned screams of triumph into screams of pain.

"Riders! *Lasair*!"

Fire spewed, a terrible roar, a terrible heat of gold and red and molten blue. Screams became shrieks. The enemy became burning, writhing columns. Smoke rolled, thick and black and fetid, choking clouds of stink and death.

And still they came, those who escaped the arrows and flame.

At Keegan's order, the Fey charged to meet them.

"Get ready," Breen whispered.

She fought again, any she could meet who got through the line. Winged or clawed, swirling power or snapping jaws, she fought as more cut through the line.

But they'd broken the enemy advance, she could sense it. However many got through, there would be others to meet them, drive them back or down.

And still, the victory wouldn't be the end.

Would he come? Her vision hadn't shown her. If he did, if he came for her into Talamh, what cost to the Fey? Even weakened, he was a god.

She wiped at her stinging eyes, so tired, so tired of the blood. And heard Marco cry out.

She stopped thinking, spun, and saw her friend fall. She saw his face go ashen, and the blood bloom on his shirt. She saw the snarling elf prepare to strike the killing blow.

What erupted inside her, what she hurled was as much rage as power. When it struck, it turned the enemy to dust. She dropped to her knees, tears filling her smoke-stung eyes, and pressed a hand on the wound in his side.

Oh, deep, long and deep.

"I'll fix it, I'll fix it." She said it between chattering teeth as fear overcame fury.

All around, the battle raged while Marco's eyes locked with hers. His were glassy with shock.

"It doesn't really hurt."

"It's going to. I'm sorry. I'm going to fix it."

She went deep, long and deep, numb to the pain she took from him into herself, blind to the blood that coated her hands, deaf to the sounds of steel striking steel all around her.

Here there was only Marco. Marco, her friend, her brother. Marco, who'd never failed her. Marco, who'd opened her to dreams. Marco, who'd leaped into another world with her, for her.

Sweat rolled down her face, mixed with tears, with blood as she pushed deep.

Even with the pain she took, his body arched with it.

"Sleep, sleep now." It would be easier for both of them if he slept. "Sleep." When he went lax, she made herself slow down.

She heard something cry out and thud behind her, but didn't stop. Couldn't.

"Ah gods." Keegan stood beside her now. "Gods damn it all to hell and back again. How bad is it?"

"Bad, but, but better." Her words came in pants. "I think better. I need more time."

"You don't have it here, and the both of you nearly were cut down. Call your dragon, take him to the first healing tent."

"If I move him—"

"If you don't, he dies here when one that's gotten through finishes him and takes you. Get him safe away. Fuck it all." He threw power, and something else screamed. "He's not safe here, Breen."

"Yes, you're right."

Lonrach landed.

"Hold any off us now while I get him up. Be ready and defend."

She'd more than defend, she thought. She'd annihilate. She raised her sword to impale a charging demon dog, and before she could, Bollocks streaked out of the smoke, tore its throat. Without pause he leaped onto Lonrach, laid his paws over Marco.

And howled.

"Get him safe," Keegan told her. "We won't lose him this day."

"No, we won't lose him."

She flew, her hands on Marco again, to keep him asleep, to continue healing. As she neared the healing station, she saw her grandmother, Sedric, a few others battling more who'd gotten through.

Not many, she thought as she took Lonrach down. But too many. Evil always found more.

"We've got him. We've got him, Daughter." One of the healers lifted Marco from Lonrach's back. An Old Father, she thought, stronger than he looked. "You've given him sleep and begun the healing. That's good, that's fine. We've got you, Marco."

Inside there lay more wounded, some recovering, others in deep sleep as a healer worked.

"Let's see what we have here, let's take a good look."

With his eyes closed, the old man laid his thin hands on Marco.

"The sword went deep. I see the shadow of it, the slice through the liver as well. But you've made that whole again, and begun to knit and close."

"Can you— Will he live?"

The old healer opened his eyes as his hands began to float, delicate as butterfly wings, over the gash. With Marco's hand in hers, she felt that power, the spreading warmth of it.

"Now, of course he will. Young and strong, isn't he, our Marco, and the Daughter herself began the mending. Leave it to me now, leave it to me. Con, I'll need a potion here for the loss of blood and the shock of it."

"Thank you. I need to go help. Some are too close to the station. Bollocks, stay with Marco. Stay. Protect."

"Daughter, you should sit a moment, regain your strength after the healing you've done."

"I can't. My grandmother."

When she ran out, she opted for her wand rather than the sword, because the old man wasn't wrong. Her physical strength had waned.

She ran down the road, one she'd walked so many times over the last year, and saw her help wasn't needed.

Marg and Sedric stood alone now with the others fanning out to the fields after retreating enemy. And the enemy dead lay in the road.

She started to call out to ask her grandmother if she'd come help the old healer with Marco.

It happened so fast. In the blink of an eye, in the flash of an instant.

Marg turned, had a moment to look at Breen with relief, to lay a hand over her heart to show it.

The fog swirled at her back, and Yseult stepped out of it to hurl a stream of power, red, vicious, sharp, at Marg's back. Cat quick, Sedric spun between, and with his arms wrapped tight around her, shielded Marg with his body.

He took the killing blow.

Even as Breen cried out, struck back, the fog swirled. Yseult was gone, and Sedric lay on the road, Marg dropping down to cradle him.

"No, no, no. My love. My life."

"We'll fix it." Though she knew no power could, Breen threw herself down beside them. "Together, Nan."

Marg only shook her head, tears raining down, and lifted Sedric's hand to her cheek when he couldn't lift it.

He said, "Marg."

"I'm here, *mo chroí*. I'm here."

The fingers lay limp in Breen's hand when she took it, but tried to curl with hers. "My beauties. Marg," he said again, and died in her arms on the road near the cottage where they'd made their life.

Marg's keening wail rose into the air, seemed to shake the sky. Beneath her and her dead love, the ground quaked.

"How much, how much will she take? She will not live out this day, I swear it. I swear to the gods, dark and light, she will not live out this day."

"I'm sorry, so sorry." Shaking with her own sobs, Breen wrapped her arms around Marg.

"He died for me, and for Talamh." Rocking him, rocking him, Marg pressed her lips to his silver hair. "For so long we lived for each other, and Talamh. She took him from me, as they took my son. And I will have justice."

She lowered to lay her lips on Sedric's, then just wept with him in her arms.

"You can't stay here. I'm going to get help, to take him away from the road. I'll get help, Nan."

She'd barely run three feet when the fog surrounded her. Dimly, she heard Marg cry out.

So this is how it would be, she thought, cold and calm. She'd meant to kill Marg, out of petty rivalry, and to distract, and had killed instead the one who'd been a father to her father, a grandfather to her.

Yes, she thought, there would be justice.

"Show yourself, Yseult."

"We have a journey to take first." The voice came from all around, part of the fog. "It's time you came home."

"Odran's world will never be home, and my true grandfather lies dead by your hand." She knew they moved, sliding like that fog, but let Yseult believe otherwise. "I won't go with you."

"Child, child, foolish child, you were made for this single purpose, your destiny waits. This was all designed long before you took breath."

"You foresaw this? All that's happened from my first breath to now?"

"Of course."

Liar. Weak, lying coward. "If you foresaw, why did you let me cut your skin to ribbons?"

"Your power exceeded even my expectations. My small sacrifice will only reap more rewards when Odran takes that power and makes it his own."

"His forces lay dead, burned, bloody across Talamh."

"Aye, such a child," Yseult said with a laugh. "What need has he of such as them when he'll have you? The key that opens the lock, at long last."

Near the woods now, Breen sensed. The fighting continued in patches. She could hear the drums, the clash, the screams. But nearly done.

All of it, nearly done.

"Are you afraid to show yourself?"

"You'll see all you need to see soon enough."

"You sent Shana to kill Keegan."

"A foolish girl with a weak and broken mind. A pity she failed, but not unexpected."

"You've failed, time and again. So now you're afraid to pit your power against mine. You know I have more than you."

"Do you? Yet you're not able to clear the fog, are you now? You weren't able to stop my power from striking, and now Marg weeps and wails. Ah, like music that is."

By the river now, the green water, the green light. The battle here done.

She felt the stone at her heart pulsing there as they followed the river to the falls.

For Talamh, she thought, and the Fey. And closed in the fog, she crossed into Odran's world.

Children played on the grass of the cottage, on the shore of the bay, as children should. Aisling watched, praying with all she had they'd return soon, that their world would welcome them.

That her husband stayed safe. And her brothers, her mother, her friends. Safe.

Then Finian stepped up to her. "She's gone to the dark place, Ma, the one I don't know."

"What's this now?"

"Breen. Breen Siobhan, she's there now, like we saw the first night of the festival. In the fire."

Alarmed, she crouched down. "What did you see, Fin?"

"I was sleepy, and it was blurry, but I saw her in a bad place, and she saw it as well."

"Take my hands now, and go back in your mind, bring what you saw back so I can see with you."

"It was bad," he repeated, and put his hands in hers.

His eyes went deep and dark; power sprouted strong, Aisling thought, in such a little one. And with him, through him, she saw.

She pushed up quickly. "Liam, Liam, you'll watch the children."

Though he'd chafed at being assigned to the duty here, he rushed over.

"What is it?"

"I need to go over, and now. I need to tell Keegan."

"You're not to go over until they come to say it's safe again."

She took the knife from her belt in one hand, her wand in the other. "Do you think I can't do what needs doing? Watch the children."

Morena flew to Marg. "They said Marco— Ah gods, Sedric. Marg—"

"Yseult. She has Breen."

"But no, she's with Marco. Keegan said—"

"Yseult has her. Yseult did this. I don't know for certain how long it's been, for the trail of her cursed fog stunned me. Don't leave him like this, Morena. Get him to shelter."

"Let me get Keegan."

"I don't know how long," she repeated as her dragon landed on the road. "This part began with me, and I won't let them take her. I won't."

She mounted and streaked off as Aisling ran down the road.

"Fetch her back, Morena! Breen's crossed over into Odran's world. Fetch her back! Oh, no, no, Sedric."

"Bloody, buggering hell. Marg has gone after Yseult, who did this and took Breen. I need to get to Keegan, and so we go take the fight to Odran after all. Please, Aisling, don't leave Sedric here. The healing station's just there, as you see. Marco's in there."

"He's hurt?"

"Aye. Please, I need to—"

"Go, go. I'll see to Sedric, and to Marco. Go!"

The air changed here. Even through the fog, Breen could sense it. It held thicker, colder. And she knew, as she used the fog as cover as much as Yseult did, that some of Odran's forces had fled back to this world.

She knew in his rage, he'd slain many of them himself.

She heard the angry beat of the sea, the churning spin of the sky.

Because she willed it, she saw herself, draped in the fog, crossing to the cliffs beyond the walls and the sacrificial pool on this side, even now running with blood. She saw the cliffs, jagged and high, and the bodies strewn on them.

She climbed by Toric's body, dead on the rocks as she'd told him he'd end. So as Keegan expected, Odran had freed the banished.

Only to lead them to their death.

So she climbed, as if unable to resist the pull.

Until she stood, in the thinning fog, on the highmost cliff, facing Odran.

She had blood on her hands, her face. Some of it Marco's, some Sedric's. And he who'd caused all the blood stood pristine, clad in black, his mane of hair shining gold.

"There you are, Granddaughter."

"My grandfather is dead, a hero of Talamh. And you are a murderer of children, with your followers defeated."

"There are always more. Yseult, you've pleased me well. Go now, seal the portal so I have this time, uninterrupted, with my granddaughter."

"As you wish, my king, my liege, my all."

Do that, Breen thought. Because it all ends here.

"My grandmother brings her death. No seal will stop Mairghread O'Ceallaigh."

"Perhaps not." Smiling, he flicked a careless hand. "But as I said, there are always more. Such creatures as Yseult serve us, and when they're of no more use, we discard them. I offered you worlds, powers, the worlds and powers of gods."

"You lied."

He laughed and shook back his gilded mane. "Lies serve us as well. Come inside now, into my castle, and we'll begin."

"I think I'll stay here, and we'll end."

Yanking the sword free, she plunged it into him.

It took him a step back, but that, she realized, came from surprise, as he only sighed, a sound of disappointment, and drew the sword free.

He didn't bleed. Her mistake, she admitted, but not unexpected. Just one last hope.

"A sword? Are you so foolish to think a blade, a common blade, can kill me, can so much as mark me? Here, I am all!"

He raised his arms and shot lightning across the sky, turned his wrist to spear it down and strike a winged demon to send it burning into the lashing sea.

Now, with eyes dark as onyx, he faced her. "I'll drain your powers, but slowly, so you learn, and you feel the loss of them, until you beg to worship me. And when your light flickers dim, I'll keep you as a pet. For a time."

He could, she knew, and would if she allowed it. If she allowed it, Talamh would burn, and the worlds beyond it fall.

"That's not my destiny. I've seen my destiny. I've seen it in the smoke and fire. I see it now. I am Breen Siobhan O'Ceallaigh. I am the key, but not to open. To close, for all time. And with me ends the line."

She threw out power, what she had to stop him. And stepped off the cliff.

One life for all life, she thought as she fell. One light for all light. For Talamh and all the worlds. This is my choice.

She heard Odran's scream of rage, and closed her eyes.

Keegan swooped her out of midair, feet from the killing rock.

"What the bloody hell are you about?"

The world spun. "I didn't see this coming." Her head lolled on his shoulder, and she might have laughed to see Bollocks behind him on the dragon but was too dizzy.

"I had to . . . keep the vow. I—"

Then she saw Marg leap from her own dragon to face Yseult.

"Oh God, Nan."

"She needs her justice, and you need to be on the other side of this hell."

"No, no, wait." Think, she ordered. This time think, don't act. Think. "The sword, it can't hurt him, not here. It's why, it's always been why it didn't end."

She gripped his bloodied shirt. She'd offered her life, willingly, but that hadn't been her destiny. So she remained the key.

"It's the staff, Keegan, not the sword. It's the staff, it's justice. You have to bring it here. Call it. Bring it here. It's your staff."

"Best be right on it." Eyes on hers, he held out a hand.

And below, Marg slid off her dragon.

"You've tried for me before," Yseult reminded her, "and failed. I have more now, such deep and dark powers now, and the god of all with me."

Marg's face was stone, her eyes blue ice.

"You've tried for me before, and failed. I have more now, such as you never held. And my love's blood with me. I gave up the sword and staff, and still you took my child."

She circled as she spoke, as more flew through the portal to destroy the last of Odran's forces.

"In seeking to destroy the child of my child, to take all she is for the god you betray all for, you took my love, my heart."

"I sought to destroy you." Yseult flicked out a hand, and flame with it. Marg merely slapped it aside. The wind kicked up, whirling. "He simply got in the way."

"So as you'd see it."

Yseult flicked flame again, like a tease. "I see your weaknesses,

Mairghread. I see your weakened power and dimming light. I see tears still drying on your cheeks. I'll burn them away for you."

"Try," Marg invited, swirling a hand that stirred the wind to gutter out the flicks of flame. "You think to toy with me to gain time? Be bold. Show me how dark and deep you run now, Yseult. Show me all you have, this last time."

"And so I will." She, too, circled, and as her hands turned, turned, as her eyes darkened to midnight, as the air blackened between them, Marg waited.

When it hurled toward her like pitch, black, thick, burning hot, she waited. She met Yseult's gleaming eyes, heard the laugh as the black inferno rushed toward her.

And throwing up her arms, Marg let her grief rip free, let it tear from her heart, her belly, her bones. She brought it to form in light, blinding white and clear as glass. It shook the air; it tossed the churning sea up into walls of wild water.

When the dark struck the light, a sound like a thousand cannons firing, Marg stood, unflinching.

"So damned to you, Yseult. What you send returns to you three-fold."

And shot it back.

The thick, burning black covered Odran's witch so her own evil smothered her. For an instant, she stood like a pillar of smoking tar. Only her eyes showed through, then even they vanished in the dark.

When all that was left was a pool of simmering ooze, Marg looked down.

"I have my justice."

"Nan," Breen murmured. "She—"

"Did what she needed to do."

"Hurry, please hurry. I don't want any more death today."

"It has to come through one world to the next. It's not like fetching a cup from another room."

Then, with a slap of wood to flesh, the staff was in Keegan's hand.

"Down with Marg now."

"No, don't you see? It has to be me—it's always had to be me. A god against a god, blood against blood. Justice against evil. You have to give it to me, Keegan. Entrust it to me. I made the choice, to give my life. You saved it. Now trust me."

"I will." He put the staff in her hand. "But I'll not lose you this day, or any other."

"Take me back. Let me do to him what my grandmother did to Yseult. Let me turn the key. Lock the lock. Let me end it."

He flew toward the black castle where Odran stood on the cliff, hurling fire and lightning.

When he threw it at Cróga, Keegan swatted it aside. But the power sang up his arm.

"He's stronger here, *mo bandia*."

"So am I now. There are innocents inside. The child in the cage, slaves. You have to get them out."

"The chains are off the slaves and the bespelled with Yseult's death. They'll all get out and away."

Trusting him as he trusted her, she leaped off, and Bollocks jumped after her. With a last curse, Keegan did the same.

"Ah, the taoiseach and the faithful hound. You've brought me gifts."

"You've no business with them. Your witch is a puddle of ooze."

"So I see. I chose Mairghread for a reason. The power, the light, so delicious when turned. I will make her my slave, one more powerful than Yseult or any supplicant. And one willing if I promise to spare your life."

"You'll never touch her again. Or anyone I love."

"No?" Amused, he pointed a finger at the dog.

Breen held out a hand, pushed against the power until it shattered.

"No." It rose and spread, around her, through her. And what she pushed at him held him in place as the pendant around her neck burned like a red sun.

And the heart of it beat strong against hers. The key found the lock, she thought, at last.

"I am Odran." He roared it. "God of all. You will bow to me or all burns, all dies, all curse your name."

"No," she repeated, and took a step toward him.

"I am Breen Siobhan O'Ceallaigh." As she called out, her eyes went dark, dark and deep.

"I am the Daughter of the Fey, Daughter of man, of gods, Child of demon. I call to her, this innocent."

"She's mine."

He broke the hold, pushed forward. She shoved him back, and glowed.

"She is not yours. Only what you corrupted is yours. Her mark is on you, Odran the Damned. Not the mark of the gods who cast you out, but the mark of the demon, of her light, her innocence. I call to her on this longest day, on this day of light. I am the key, I open your lock, bright demon, I release your chains, and bring an end."

"I will devour you, burn all you love." When Odran bared his teeth, fangs formed. He slapped at the air, the power between them, so dark and light crashed. And that air flamed with it until the castle walls shimmered red.

Hold, Keegan had ordered on the battlefield, and she held now until he was nearly on her.

"No," she said a third time.

The heat and the dark, the cries of the demon, the innocent and the corrupted, all of it surrounded her, rose inside her.

In that moment, all inside her awakened. She became more. And made the final choice.

"I am the granddaughter of the taoiseach, the daughter of the taoiseach, the lover of the taoiseach. And with their staff, with their justice, I end you for all time."

She jammed the dragon's heart against his chest, against the mark he bore.

She swore she heard it snap, like a key in a lock.

And as his eyes widened in shock, she turned it.

His cry was a thousand and a thousand cries, the screams of all he'd consumed.

He didn't bleed, but opened like a broken, empty vessel where the dragon's heart struck.

The golden hair went black as it fell away from a charred skull.

His skin cracked like bits of glass, and through the cracks, something dark crawled. A roar rolled and rolled, overhead, under the ground and rock that quaked.

What flew out of him she couldn't say, but as it emptied him, it burned in the air like sulfur. Whirlwinds of flame, of smoke burned over the sea. Then so did he burn, Odran the god, with a gale that blew against her, through her, had Keegan grip her to hold her steady.

"Finish it, *mo bandia*. End it."

Alit without and within, she lifted her voice over the wind and thunder.

"You are Odran the Damned, and by blood of your blood, I fulfill my destiny. I am the Daughter, here I stand, and by blood of your blood the worlds are free. Demon long trapped, come into the light, and help me end his long, dark night."

She saw it come, a glimmer, a shadow, a spark.

"Sister, the light awaits, the door is open. The dark abates as these words are spoken. Ended here your long captivity. As I will, so mote it be."

The spark burned bright, and brighter. It shot toward the sky, a single spark becoming a thousand, erupting, fountaining against the sky.

What was Odran went to bones. What were bones blackened into ash. And even what was ash vanished from all worlds, for all time.

Breen stepped back, handed the staff to Keegan.

He slammed it against the rock so the sound carried.

"So it is done."

He took her hand, gripped it hard. "I won't kiss you in this place."

Still flooded with powers, she gave a breathless laugh. "I've heard that before, so I'll repeat. Let's go home. Oh my God, Keegan, let's go home."

He lifted her onto Cróga, waited for Bollocks to jump up. He flew, then swung around.

"Those held inside are freed. We raze this evil place, you and I, here and now. Children of the Fey," he shouted. "You fought, you bled, you stood in the light and for it. You've seen Odran's end, now witness his walls crumble and burn. This world will be purified, and the portals to it sealed. No life will come here, light or dark."

He held out his arms. "Your hands with mine, Breen Siobhan. Your power with mine."

She joined with him, and watched the black castle fall.

EPILOGUE

The longest day rang. Bells sounded across Talamh, from the Capital to the Far West. She heard them even as Keegan flew through the portal.

Word had traveled.

Keegan set her down in the green wood. "I would be with you, but—"

"Duties yet. In there."

"It must be purified and sealed. Once done, I'll find you. I have much to say to you."

"Good, I've got a lot to say, too. Let me say here, before you go back, thanks for the catch."

"It stopped my heart when you fell. Just stepped off the cliff as if . . . I thought I wouldn't get to you in time." He shook his head. "Well, that's done. It's done, and I'll find you. Call your dragon now. He fought as brave as any. And here's Marco coming through now, and the same can be said."

"Marco." Struck with relief, with gratitude, she nearly went to her knees, then all but flew toward him.

Jumping off the horse, he met her, yanked her up, spun and spun.

"So scared, so freaking awed. You were lit up like, hell, the solstice." He pulled her back. "You put me out!"

"I had to, I thought—" She laid a hand on his side. "Let me see."

"Nothing to see, not even a little scar. Dagmare said it'll be sore off and on for a while. He said it was bad, and you saved my life."

"I had to. You're my life."

She wrapped around him. "Sedric."

"I know. I know." On one muffled sob, Marco dropped his head on her shoulder. "They brought him in when I was coming around. I don't have the words for it. They're all twisted up in me. I loved him. I really loved him."

"We lost our grandfather, Marco. But we'll be there for Nan. We'll be there for her."

"Damn right we will." Swiping at his eyes, he looked back at the waterfall. "It's really over."

"It's really over. Couldn't you feel it?"

"I saw what you did, and all that stuff that came out of him. Ugly stuff, girl."

"Evil's ugly, whatever form it takes."

"You got that. Then that kind of sparking thing that turned into like fireworks before it just poofed away. Then Odran just, he just broke apart and died. Brian said he'd help them clean up, you know. He's doing okay. Wasn't hurt that bad. Keegan took some hits," he continued as they walked.

"He did? Some of the blood on him was his?"

"Took some hits, went right on. Listen to those bells ring. Perfect music. How about we go clean up, then come back over and find ourselves some wine. I mean a whole bunch of a lot of wine."

"Oh yes, please."

"Want a lift? My faithful steed can handle both of us, and Bollocks, too. Warrior dog."

"I'm calling Lonrach. Another warrior."

"I'll just ride along under you. Twice up on a dragon? That's enough for this man's lifetime."

It took time to get to the cleanup. So many to speak with, to embrace, to comfort.

And Marg.

She held her grandmother close. "Do you want to come to the cottage with us? You could stay for a few days, or as long as you want. You don't have to go back to your cottage alone."

"Oh, *mo stór*, I won't be alone. Sedric will be with me, the heart of him. And that's a comfort."

"She came so fast, Nan, so fast."

Fury sparked, burning with the grief. "At my back, like a coward."

"I saw what you did, how you ended her. I didn't know you could bring something like that."

"At my back, like a coward," Marg repeated. "And she took the love of my life, for he was and always will be that. I turned what she was, what she'd chosen to be, back on her. Nothing more, nothing less. You go on now. I'm going to sit awhile with Finola, watch the children. Watch them play in the sunlight, and with no more fears.

"This you did, for your da, for me and Sedric, for the Fey, and for yourself. Never forget that."

"Can we bury Sedric's ashes beside Da's?"

Marg simply pressed her cheek to Breen's. "He'd be so pleased you'd ask. Aye, we will, for they had a father and son love between them. Go now, and come back so we'll do what they'd both want."

"What's that?"

"Dance in the sun until the longest day ends. Then dance more."

She waited while Marco took his horse back to the farm, and wrapped around Morena.

"I only saw the end of it, only saw when you ended him, and that was enough. Are you hurt at all?"

"Some cuts and bruises, I think. You?"

"The same. We'll heal. I'm sick about Sedric, and I can't really work it into my mind he's left us. He was family to me."

"I know. Harken?"

"Barely a scratch. I swear to all the gods and goddesses, for a farmer he fights like a wild man. I lost sight of him so many times, and the fear—we won't feel that fear again. We'll live as we've chosen. I think I'll have a half dozen babies. At least that's what I'm thinking at the moment."

She glanced back. "He's in the stables now, seeing to the new mother and the colt he's named Solas, in honor of the day. It means light."

"A very good name. I'm going to go clean up, but I'm coming back."

"I could use a wash myself. Now I'm thinking I'll go pull my husband along to take that wash with me. We've got to start on those babies sometime."

She walked over with Marco, and while Bollocks took his swim, indulged in a very long shower. She discovered more cuts and bruises than she'd felt during the heat of it all, and spent time to heal them.

Then she changed into a pretty summer dress.

She studied herself in the mirror, the pretty dress of summer blue, the earrings Keegan had inexplicably given her, the cute—and impractical—summer sandals.

"You don't look like a warrior. Don't feel like one either, and hope never to be or feel like one ever again."

She came down to find Keegan sitting at the table on her patio with a bottle of wine. One glass in his hand, and the other waiting for her.

Bollocks slept at his feet.

He kept staring out at the bay when she stepped out.

"Marco went back over, all dressed in his finery."

He hadn't changed, she noted, but still wore his battle gear and blood.

"I thought you wouldn't mind the wine and a few minutes of the quiet before we go back. I could use a time away from the crowd."

"Suits me."

When she came around the table, he looked at her and got to his feet.

"You look very fine."

"Thanks. I wanted a major change from before. I may burn what I took off."

"I should've thought to wash and change."

"You've been busy." Her brows lifted when he held her chair out. "Thanks. And this is just perfect."

"Bollocks the Brave and True fought brave and true today. He's tired out now."

"I know the feeling."

"Every loss is a loss, but Sedric . . . It cuts deep."

"For all of us."

"Sure I'm sorry to ask you to go back, but it's important. My mother's seeing to things now, but . . . it's important."

"Oh no, I want to go back—but sitting here for a little while first is just what I need. I want to go back, be part of it. Be there if Nan needs me, see the new colt."

"He's a beauty."

"I saw him in my head. He takes after his father."

"Sire that would be, and he does."

"I want to see everyone. I want to hear the music and help make it. I want to see what happens next."

She drank some wine. "What happens next. That's a thing."

"Celebrations across Talamh. I'll need you to come with me to the Capital within a week. They'll want to see you. Fete you some."

"Fete."

He actually reached over to take her hand. "I know you're no fonder of that than I, but it matters, Breen, to everyone. The songs and stories they'll write, of this, of you. Of the end of Odran. We have the chance and choice to live in peace now."

He rose, walked a few feet, walked back, and sat again.

"You stepped off the cliff."

"It was a choice, the right choice. The only choice."

"Aisling says you knew, you saw on the first night of the festival. Finian saw it, or some of it, with you. But you said nothing."

"What could I say, Keegan? To Marco, Nan, you, anyone. I understood, deep in me, it was always going to come to that. No matter what anyone did or tried to do, it would come down to that moment, and that choice."

"We might have lured him in."

"No. And if I'd made a different choice, I'd never really have a life anyway. No future without the fear of him, no courage." She rubbed her wrist. "I'd never have risked having a child that he might come for, or try for."

"You did what needed doing, but for me you're after why I don't explain before I do what needs doing."

She drank again. "You have a point. Can I say, and can you trust, I honestly and simply knew I had to do it this way?"

He sat in silence a moment. "Aye, that's fair enough."

"And I think because I did, you were there to catch me."

"I like that part of it. So it's settled between us."

"I suppose it is, except . . . What comes next, Keegan? I need to know what you want, expect. If we just go on as we are, which is fine if— No, you know, it's just not. I want more."

"More what? More than what?"

"More than just going along. I want promises and plans and pledges and what goes with them."

He stared at her. "Didn't I give you the ear things, and in front of everyone with eyes? Didn't you take them?"

"Yes, and thanks again, but—"

"Thanks be damned, you took them, you're wearing them, so it's settled."

"What's settled?"

"You don't give such a thing—the sapphire, for certain—to wear that way to someone you're . . . romancing or bedding or whatever you'd call it, not with eyes witnessing, unless it's a pledge between the two."

"I'm sorry, what?"

"I brought them back for you—the pledging stones—and gave them in that way because I thought: No, I'll not wait until after, as she keeps talking about the after." He rapped a fist on the table hard enough to make the glasses shudder. "We'll pledge in the sunlight and before, as that's faith. It's fecking faith that we'd sit just as we are now, together. In the after."

She picked up her wine again, drank slowly. Then set the glass carefully down again.

"Are you telling me that these are like an engagement ring?"

The impatience rolled back, just covered every inch of him.

"They call them rings, don't they? And in Talamh it's the wedding where there are rings for the hands. But you're part of this world, too, so, rings. Which I gave and you took, witnessed. Done."

"I call bullshit." She shoved up. "I call bullshit."

Bollocks opened his eyes but decided to stay quiet under the table.

"Ah, gods, you want something else then? Fine, keep those and I'll get the something else you're wanting."

"You didn't ask me." When he pointed at her ears, she actually snarled. "Bullshit again. You never asked me, you've never said you loved me or wanted a future with me."

"Why would I give you the sapphires, the earbobs, well witnessed, and so pledge to you if I didn't love?"

"I want the damn words. I'm entitled to words, and if you can't bring yourself to say them to me—" She started to reach up for the earrings.

"Don't take them off like this. I'm asking you. It'll rip my heart, and my heart had enough tearing this day." He got up, took her hands, brought them down.

"And look at you now, after all you've done this day, in that lovely dress and those things on your feet no one with sense would ever call shoes. With hot tears in your eyes you're too angry to let spill."

He brought her hands to his lips. "You love me. I see it, and I feel it, and I know it. You haven't given me the words, Breen Siobhan."

"I—"

"Because you want them first. Need them first, and that's fair enough. I want no one but you. I think I never could, not through my heart, because I always knew you'd come. I love all you are, and that was a hard road for me to travel, as I knew it might come to what it did today, and I wouldn't be there to catch you. I wouldn't be meant to, do you see?"

He brought her hands to his lips again, searched her eyes with his over them. "To love you and not be able to have a life with you? I had love and duty pulling at me. I'm sworn."

"I know that." Anger dissolved like mists in the sun.

This was who she loved, the one who'd have love and duty pulling, the one who'd never, never forget he'd taken an oath. Not to Talamh. Not to the Fey.

And not to her.

"And the children, as you said." He lowered his forehead to hers. "How could we make them and put them in his path?"

She closed her eyes, grateful he'd felt that, too.

"Yet today, I wanted you to know, and all to know. This is my choice. I choose you because you have my heart, and only want you to choose me and give yours in turn. I swear I thought you had when I badgered you into putting the sapphires on."

She had love, she thought in wonder, right here. She had love, a chance, a choice.

"I chose you the night we lay in your bed, in the bed of the taoiseach, with the mural of Talamh overhead. I chose Keegan Byrne. I chose the taoiseach. I chose everything you are. But I loved you longer."

"We love. You love, and I love." He kissed her hands again. "But we'll be sure this time. I'm asking and you're saying you'll pledge to me."

"Yes, you can be sure."

He started to pull her in, then pushed her back.

"What now?"

"I'm covered with blood and innards and gods know."

"It doesn't matter."

"It does, of course. Hell with it." He flicked, and wore what she supposed he'd call finery. A clean shirt and trousers, a vest that fancied it up in his way. "That's better now, isn't it then?"

He yanked her back into a strong hold, a strong kiss.

"I like what happens next, Keegan."

"We'll have more of it, a lot more of it." Tender now, he touched his lips to her brow. "A lifetime of the next. A cottage here for your work and our fine neighbors, Talamh for family and duty and magicks. And peace. I'll love you long and hard in both worlds, Breen Siobhan."

He spun her around until Bollocks came out from under the table, rose up on his hind feet to dance.

And at the end of the longest day, with the battle won and the moons shedding their light, she stood with him, in Talamh, a child of two worlds.

Ready for what happened next.